AMERICAN BASTARDS

For Occupying Portland.

Thanks,

P.S. Find me at
www.americanbastards.com
and tell me if you have a
cool story.

TREVOR RICHARDSON

U S
HWY
O

AMERICAN
BASTARDS
a novel

INKWATER
PRESS

PORTLAND•OREGON
INKWATERPRESS.COM

For my family, who showed me the road
and encouraged me to keep following it.

CONTENTS

ACKNOWLEDGMENTS

Dedications are just a play on words. Acknowledgments, for me, are owed to people all over this country without whom I never would have made it.

Jeff and Lisa Richardson, my parents, who told me to question reality, challenge authority, make your own way, doubt the assumptions of American life, and, above all, for encouraging my fantasies instead of telling me not to quit my day job. Woodland, Washington.

Kevin Richardson, brother and oldest friend, who stood by me when I was a fool and always knew why I did what I did. Portland, Oregon.

Rebekah Richardson, sister and fellow dreamer, the one who, for my entire life, made me feel flawed and invincible at the same time. Portland, Oregon.

Thanks also to Umpy Barb and Uncle Dave who put me up when I wasn't sure where to go next and let me write in peace. Pittsburg, California.

To the rest of my family, Uncle Ken and his clan, who, in spite of likely being embarrassed by the content of this book, have made it through, stuck it out with all of us, and shouldered the weight of losses.

To Amy Ervin, my cousin, for her unflappable spirit and gentle heart wrapped safely in a bold mouth. Pittsburg, California.

Dusty and David LaDieu, cousins who unwittingly gave me an amazing childhood and have shaped themselves into brave men with warm souls. Pittsburg and San Diego, California.

Charles Ben Russell, old friend and inspiration, for being a true seeker, sharing with me the qualms of bad love and insomnia, and always being ready to pick up where we leave off. Austin, Texas.

Micah Newsom, the first person to talk to me at my new school in Texas and always having an open door. Denton, Texas.

Dylan Manley, a reliable friend in the mood swings of my life. Texarkana, Texas.

Jesi Cason, for trusting me when I was not so trustworthy, making me feel safe when I felt unwelcome, and wearing her flaws like jewelry. Tyler, Texas.

Thomas Johnson, for porch talk, coffee shop confessionals, and making me feel like a saint in tarnished robes. Orlando, Florida.

Erin Deale, who shares a world with me and helps me create it, finishes my sentences before I'm even sure how they're going to end, and gives me inside jokes. Remember the Alamo, Navajo blankets, road trips and IHOP. Portland, Oregon.

Thanks also to my rotating roster of roommates in New York City, to Jay Calhoun for a solid friendship in a shaky time, and Mitch Hedburg for that line about frilly toothpicks. To everyone who ever put me up when I needed a couch to sleep on, the revolving door of friends that have all given me something that shaped my outlook, and Hunter S. Thompson for saying it all better than I ever could. Also, a special thank you to the memory of every individual that inspired a character in this book, to Freakazoid (remember that show?) which taught me to be funny, Jimmy Holland for talking to me about music, and Samuel Beckett for saying that line about "failing better."

Finally, to everyone that will be mad at me for using so many bad words in this novel and to Bob Dylan because he hasn't already been thanked by every other wannabe beatnik.

AMERICAN BASTARDS

Field Notes from Bastard Land
1: Highway Zero

T he Tomato is burning. Everything it knew will soon be gone.
Right now I'm standing on Fry Street in Denton, Texas. It's
night and the flames are lighting up the walls a dirt orange, casting
a brown halo over the beat corners and sidewalk gatherings of the
young and the done for. We're watching the blaze in this old party
town's central hub, still haunted by the ghosts of students and
alumni. The Tomato is, was, this neighborhood's pizza supplier.
The split-level antique wood diner, well-coated in the welcome
tar remnants of its smoking patrons, has been as much a part of
Denton's Fry Street Village as marinara is a part of thin-crust discount pizza. Stories have passed through this corner of town that
could equal the weight of the building's wreckage in pepperoni
Sicilian combos.

"Oh, yeah, that reminds me," Brother Red says, "I quit smoking
today."

"Yeah?" I reply, "That's great, I usually quit smoking about
once a week."

"Me too," says Dennis Orbell, "I quit smoking three times yesterday."

"Do you think we're in danger here?" asks Jiggs.

"Probably," I reply, flicking a cigarette toward the fire.

The Head says, "It's just like *Of Mice and Men*. You know, how old Candy wished he'd been the one to shoot his decrepit dog."

Dennis replies, "Yeah, it's only right that something as beautiful as The Tomato gets destroyed by the people who loved it."

"You know," Red says, "even just six months ago I would have tried to light my cigarette off of those flames."

"Yeah, but now you quit," I smirk.

The arsonist's stage performance shatters the glass out of the restaurant windows and the crowd grows thicker to watch the demise of their favorite hangout. I light up a cigarette as the upper wood deck of the building collapses into the fire. Someone in the crowd mutters, "I know they were going to knock it down, but this is wrong, it shouldn't have happened like this."

"Bullshit," says Jiggs, "she went out on our terms. The people took her back from the Man. She was ours."

The Tomato is burning and with it the old days will burn, the old habits, old affairs, forgotten sex, cigarettes, drug binges, flings, sorrow, issues and baggage. All of our laughs, parties, songs, memories, traditions, movements, revolutions and art will burn to make way for the corporate chains coming to our side of town. The Tomato is burning because someone bought up Fry Street Village and decided to knock down the longstanding fixtures in the neighborhood around the University of North Texas. The bureaucrats decided to put up a Starbucks or a CVS Pharmacy or some shit in its place.

Everyone, this whole crowd, stands silent and watches our place, and an entire age, melt into the earth with wails of oxidized Formica and termite knot-holed wood whistling in the night. I see a thousand sets of eyes flashing yellow and orange in the city streets, every hand with a cigarette or a drink. Some cheer. Some cry. Everyone knows that this is important. This is history in the making with history fueling the furnace.

Jiggs says, "Did you guys know Allen Ginsberg used to hang out in there?"

"Yeah," Red replies, "over there next to the melting doorframes you could have found his name etched in the wood. Ginsberg hung out here in the days when Kerouac came through Texas to visit Old Bull Lee, AKA William S. Burroughs. They probably ate here when *On the Road* was still being written. That place had more history than any of us put together."

"And now it's burning," I say, "and the whole philosophy of the Beat Generation is going with it."

It didn't matter if it was true or not, we all know it is, even if it wasn't The Tomato back then. Even if it was a furniture warehouse or a hardware store or a place where they put those metal rivets on the corners of denim pants, it was and always has been The Tomato. But now it's going to be a Starbucks or a McDonalds. Now it's over.

"Let's get out of here," Dennis grunts.

Backing away toward the Kharma Café, we set up a mock tailgate party on the back of a Ford Ranger that belongs to some stranger who was too mesmerized by the fire to notice us reclining all over his property. Jiggs finds a cooler full of Pabst Blue Ribbon in the truck bed and we help ourselves and watch the fire like a sporting event.

Red says, "Leave it to us to get back together tonight of all nights. The night the people burned down The Tomato before the suits could take it with their bulldozers."

"So how've you been anyway, Jack?" Dennis asks, "Last time we saw you things were pretty grim. Then you just up and vanished on us."

"You wanna know the truth? Reality has become sort of flexible for me lately. I'm never sure of anything. But right now I know none of this has happened yet. I'm sure of that much. You're just a part of this weird dream that's been stalking me for a while now. I know, right now, that I haven't seen some of you in almost a year and the others I haven't even met yet. I know by the newspapers and summer heat that this is June, but I know that it's really November. I'm pretty sure you're all just part of the Ghost Road."

"What the hell are you talking about, dude?" Jiggs asks.

"Yeah, the Ghost Road. It's this place where ideas take shape, walk around, where roads converge and you sell your soul to Inspiration for material. Personification is the law of nature on the Ghost Road. Out there, anything is possible. I mean, right now, I'm not even a smoker yet, but here I am, puffing away."

Smoke fills in around us and I see the fires fading away to yellow.

This is my account of everything that will happen, as it happens. You can take it or leave it, I mean, really, I'm not writing it for you anyway. Jim Morrison told me to keep a record, so that's what I'm doing and when Jim Morrison tells you to write some stuff down, you don't waste time wondering what the critics might think. You just hit the keyboard and don't look back. So I'm not wasting any time, I'm cutting right to the action.

This is Highway Zero. The Ghost Road. You can only find it if you're not looking.

And if you do find it, you're already lost.

The fires of The Tomato fade to a dusty desert scene. I'm somewhere outside of Nowhere, California, in the outer reaches of the Mojave, when the wind begins to pick up. I'm speeding through in my rusted-out Pontiac Bonneville, Bonnie. She's a true Texas woman with delusions of GTO magnificence.

Bonnie hugs the shoulder, spraying dust and gravel. In my rearview mirror, the road vanishes to a point on the horizon, desert on all sides and a brownout sky overhead. Splintered crucifix telephone poles divide the asphalt from the sand. Clouds of yellow bite at Bonnie's windshield and I follow the asphalt toward a red-brown mountain tunnel. Lights wink out like power failure as I steer Bonnie into the safety of the rock hollow walls.

Here we are, driving in darkness and only one of Bonnie's headlights works. And now, up ahead I see a flickering light swinging back and forth across the road. My headlights illuminate the form of a man dressed in a red vest, white shirt and black pants that appears to be flagging me down with a flashlight or something. There's a bright red curtain behind him and he looks like some kind of a movie usher. I slam on the brakes just shy of knocking him down, throw open the door and scream, "Jesus Christ, man, what are you doing in the middle of the road?"

"Can I take your car, sir? The show is about to start."

Puzzled, I ask, "The show?"

"Oh yes, sir," answers the valet, "they're expecting you. In fact, you're late."

"Well, Jesus, we can't have that, can we?"

I climb out of the driver's seat and tell the valet to be careful with my lady. Waiting just off to the right of the big, theatrical curtain is Mark Twain in a purple doorman's uniform. He gestures for me to follow him up a long flight of marble steps leading to a gold-trimmed doorway. He pulls a time-tarnished handle, opening the door for me, and leads me inside with a wave of his hand. Heading down a narrow hallway and into an ornate, Jazz Age style lobby, I see a red-carpeted staircase on my left stretching up into a well-polished tile wall and splitting in two at a second-floor landing. Ahead of me is a stone archway with three steps leading to big oak double doors. We make for the doors like there's some kind of a rush.

Doorman Twain says, "You mustn't keep them waiting, buddy boy. They're not the patient sort. Death didn't give any of them even a shade of temperance."

"Death?"

"Aye, dead as a doornail, the whole racket pinch lot of 'em. But it's all right, we all are in some way, ain't we? I mean, it's a blightful conundrum, dead and everlasting side by side. Legends never die, that's what they say, right, kid?"

"What in God's name are you talking about?" I ask.

"Look, sonny, no need to take the good Lord's name in vain. I'm just saying, we're only as real as those that follow make us out to be. It's all a world of fiction, yours, mine, theirs inside, whoever...Historical faces, icons, legends, or Bluebeard's Ghost, what's the difference? We're all imagined here. Ain't it all just a scrap heap of fiction? Look, buddy boy, just go on in, everything will be answered for."

I step through large mahogany double doors and Doorman Twain closes them behind me with a wink. In the string-web haze of cigarette smoke I find myself in a conference room dimly lit by the brownout fog of tobacco smoke passing in front of aging overhead lamps. A panel of officials sits across the room from me, each of them side by side behind a long oak desk. Hanging like a tapestry overhead, a red banner in white serif lettering reads, "We Put the Art in Martyr."

Light ramps up and I see the pale complexions of risen corpses. From left to right, behind ash tray mirages, sit Hunter S. Thompson, John Lennon, Jimi Hendrix, Janis Joplin, Jim Morrison, Kurt Cobain, and Ernest Hemingway. Some of them stare from under their still bleeding bullet wounds. Others are bloated green from drug binge aftermath. I'm sitting across from them in an uncomfortable high-backed metal chair, a potential employee interviewing for some undisclosed position they seem to have available.

Lennon, stately in his white suit, speaks first, "We call this meeting to order. Tell us, Mr. Bluff, what is it that you think you can offer our organization?"

Thompson grunts from under an open head wound and a Las Vegas green plastic visor, "As if we don't already know, you fucking fiend! Give it to me straight, Doc, is America already doomed? We've got her on life support. Will she ever recover? There hasn't been brain activity in years."

Jim Morrison, dressed in a black velvet turtleneck, looks up from under flopping grease-curl hair, rubbing his drug eyes and says, "Would it be better to pull the plug?"

"Put her out of her misery?" asks Cobain.

Inserting a rolled, bent cigarette into a black holder, Thompson howls, "Let's get down to brass tacks, gentlemen, we've called him here to represent his people. It's you, Jack, who will suffer or gain for your country. It is you who will be faulted or praised for its inevitable fate."

Hemingway looks me in the eye from under his gunshot wound, stroking a gray beard. His head trickles as he says, "Like Abraham vouching for Sodom and Gomorrah before God Almighty. God told him the city might be spared if he could find just one good man."

"Tell us, Jack," says Janis Joplin from behind pancake-sized rose-colored sunglasses, "Why should we continue to fight for America's survival? The powers that be, clinical-minded men, have been fighting to take her off life support for generations. And we continually thwart them, but we are decaying. We can't go on forever."

Hendrix, in blues-tone bass notes, his stage mac voice-over, says, "The art community has pumped her blood for her in subways and street corners for decades, but now, our enemies own that too."

"What do you mean?" I ask.

"Holy Jesus!" Thompson wails, "Why'd we pick him? He doesn't even know!"

Feeling an urgent need to defend myself, I speak up before even having my testimony clearly defined, "No, I do, I do, art used to be about expression and statements and now it's Big Business. Limp-hearted, faceless corporations have usurped the throne. They've formulized everything—music, film, painting, literature, poetry… but there is still hope, I swear, people are going around behind the backs of the empires of Hollywood and New York. I've seen it. They're building a New America behind the veil."

"Hmm…well," Cobain muses, brushing straw patch hair from his eyes, "maybe there is hope for him after all. What do you say, guys? Do we take him on?"

"Understand something, Jack," Hemingway sighs, "You will be held responsible. You will lose everything before this is over."

"But if you survive, kid," Lennon interjects, "You will have saved millions. Understand that it's not up to you to wake America up. You're just here to show us that she deserves to stay plugged in a little while longer. Show us there's still a hope that she'll recover and our people will see fit to keep fighting the bad fight."

"Wait…but…no, I don't understand," I plead, "What can I do? What the hell is this all about…I mean, what are you…"

"Talk to Abraham," Hemingway sighs again, louder this time.

"Show him the tape," Morrison grunts.

"No, he's not ready," Janis cries out, "It's not the right time."

"Fuck it," Thompson shrugs, "there is no time. We knew that when we brought him in."

I clear my throat and say, "Excuse me, the man outside told me there would be a show. I can only assume he meant this tape you're talking about, so why not let it play?"

"Kid's got a point," Cobain chimes in.

"Like I used to say," Thompson smirks, "buy the ticket, take the ride."

Reaching for a multi-line desk phone, Thompson taps a button, an intercom beeps and he says, "Becky, the tape."

LOST IN AMERICANA: CHAPTER ONE
HOTEL CALIFORNIA

E verybody here says I say fuck too much for just being fifteen. I say when you live with a bunch of low-downs, ham hocks, smack bingers, booze hounds, chasers, trippers, failures and whores it's no wonder. We all live in this big old hotel, The California, right on the dusty side of Highway Zero. There's this guy that hangs out in the lobby, Leroy Brown, a real bruiser, who sits there all day guarding the door. His job is to stand there and look mean all day like a fucking Nazi or something and tell everyone they ain't allowed to leave.

It pains me to try and conjure exactly how long I've been here. Reckon it's been more than a few days though. That's a safe wager. The room they stuck me in is way in back on the third floor. There's this long, narrow hallway like a snake's grave if you pulled him straight out like a woody. And there's doors on all sides. At the end of that hall is me. There's no room numbers. You just gotta know where to go. That room, when you go in it's long and skinny too, but facing the other way like a big letter T or something. I don't know, but that's where I live and have been for some time now. Inside I just have a rusty cot, a boarded-up fireplace with the chimney bricked off and stacks and stacks of old newspapers that I just use for mostly furniture and all.

As for the hotel itself, it looks like that shabby old fucker from that Hitchcock flick *Psycho*. What's it called? Barts? Boats? I can't remember the name of that ugly old building.

Bats, that's it, the Bats Motel. Suitable moniker too, that old boy was batty as a mailman on a deserted island. Useless to himself, God and everybody.

At any rate, that's where I live, walls are oozing sweat from the desert heat outside. Dry rot is my wallpaper and mildew stains the ceiling. Everything looks green or gray or a vomit binge mix of both. Down the hall is the Lone Ranger polishing his pistol and talking to his horse, Silver, stuffed and mounted beside his television set. Across the hall from him is Blind Willie McTell playing his twelve-stringer and talking to the wall mice. There's Dizzy Miss Lizzy strolling and strutting up and down her room, but never going outside, she's a total shut-in ever since she learned of her curse. Wherever she walks and stretches those pretty legs men fall in love, without fail and without hope. So Dizzy Miss Lizzy never opens her door. And down from there every door in the hallway belongs to Miss Molly, the Lady Trader, in her fine mink and stolen pearls. She lives on a shared bill with her sweet silk daughters that she trades out like Chinese cart runners. There's Layla, Maggie May, Roxanne, Jolene, Sweet Adeline, Rosalita and the dark and strange Ophelia.

The rest of the place is just as jammed packed and I never can seem to find every room, it seems like new people are always showing up and no one's ever leaving. There's too many people here to keep track of really. Down on the second floor I've seen a lot of different faces. I've seen Billy the Kid target practicing on door knobs with his six-guns. The Sultans of Swing took over the whole top floor for their dance parties and drug frenzies. On occasion I've bumped into Sam Spade drinking in the lobby and there are tons more.

To put a button on the whole rant, this place is pretty weird and downright full. Every room is different, every floor too. It's like days in a month and seasons in a year. Everything has its own flavor. One floor might have a Victorian bent with fine moldings and fancy goddamn rugs or something. The next looks like the decadent toilet brush memory of what used to be a swanky New York jazz club. It's all here though. Every main era, Georgian, Gothic, Minimalist, Mughal, Art Deco...you learn a lot just walking these halls. There's even a whole wing that looks like King Tut's tomb or some shit.

Right now, it must be almost dawn but I still can't sleep, I'm wandering halls and listening at doorways for something to keep me entertained. In the lobby there's this sort of Jazz Age ritzy club feel, like a hundred years ago fat cats in suits should have smoked cigars on plush leather sofas in there. Marble pillars, the grand red carpeted staircase leading up to the other floors and a big stone archway with oak double doors paint the scene. In one corner there's this mahogany desk where people get their keys and their rooms and sign a big book. Most of the time there's this chick there named Becky and she's answering phones and looking busy. It's actually supposed to be this old fat guy whose name I forget, but he's never around.

Anyway, I got this cigarette off old Sam in the lobby, looking sad under the shadow brim of his fedora. On my way up the gangplank stairwell I said hello to Marilyn Monroe as she made eyes across the landing at Charlie Chaplin in his tramp pants. Everyone is silent tonight, it feels like a wake. Like there's some kind of electric threat in the air that's eulogizing our memories long before they're gone. I don't know. I tend to get sort of whimsical and melodramatic at night. Forget about me.

On the second floor there's this Prohibition Era speakeasy style common room where folks play poker and drink their swill.

Tonight it's the boys from the East Wing bogarting the card table. They're a hell of a sight, like to make you right uneasy and that's the truth. They all turn to face me as I round the corner and I get a face full of glares. There's a blue-eyed Blondie Jesus Christ staring over a five-card spread, a brown-haired dark-eyed Jesus, a Black Jesus, some kind of mangy homeless-looking Jesus, and even a little baby Jesus all sitting around a Last Supper table playing Hold 'Em. There's a sad-looking Jesus with mopey eyes, blood trickling and a crown of thorns, a bright-glowing Jesus Christ with a hole in his side and gaps in his palms, and dealing the cards is some kind of victorious Christ in armor with a sword. They're all pouring wine and drinking.

Baby Jesus says, "What, I got something in my teeth or something? We all have different incarnations of ourselves, as many as how different people see us. But, hey, not everyone gets to bluff at cards with their other selves, right?"

Black Jesus slams down a straight to the Ace and laughs, "Boy, you were doomed from the start. Ever since them three Middle-Eastern fellas brought you funeral provisions for birthday presents."

I shrug and make my way up to the third floor where a door stands open to greet me. You can never be sure who will be in this room waiting for you. They never let this one out to guests, it belongs to Miss Molly and her daughters, only full when in use or just after. Whatever tickles your pickle, I always say. But I can tell by the smell of cigarettes that something just finished up and is pooling around the edges.

Like I said, it can sometimes be a surprise, but tonight it's an old friend. It's Jim sitting holding a half-empty bottle of Jack in his right hand, balanced on his knee, and a smoldering cigarette in his left. He's half naked, shirtless and sweaty down to a pair of jeans. As always, he looks pale, a ghostly, bloated gray with dirty hair. Jim barely looks up at me when I walk in with a grin.

"Tom," he groans, "what the hell are you doing here? You know how I am after a turn with Ophelia. She's a killer, man, but like so many bad habits, I keep showing up for more."

"It's good seeing you too, Jim. It's been what? Three weeks?"

"Two weeks and four days," he replies, "I kept track of how long I could deprive myself. Which reminds me, I need to get going soon, I have to start the count all over again."

"Where do you go all the time, Jim? It ain't like you can get out of here or something."

"I go to work. My associates and I convene in the conference room next to the lobby."

I ask, "The Lucille Ballroom?"

"No, dummy, that's the Ballroom," Jim snaps, "I said the conference room."

"Oh, right, right...so you in the Greek Room or the Hans Christian Andersen Room?"

"Those are presentation rooms, I said I was..." Jim sighs, "Forget it. Why, after all this time, are you just now asking me this?"

"Reckon I just never thought of it before, I don't know. What do you do?"

"Sorry, kid, I can't really talk about it. Suffice to say, we find stray threads and we tug at them all day and see what unravels."

I sit down across from him, right on the plank wood floor and look around the room in Jim's weird silence. I rarely see Ophelia's digs. I'm not wild about them. There's a four-poster bed, black satin curtains, dust and trinkets everywhere like the whole place was decorated by Miss Havisham or some goddamn thing.

Jim grunts, "Tom, old man, have a snort, you're making me nervous."

He hands me the bottle and I toss back as much as I can handle. When I hand it back his eyes twinkle, but his face remains unchanged. "You know, for a kid you really can handle your booze. I always liked that about you. Jesus, Lord, listen to me, I get a few in me after a few in her and I start sounding downright sentimental. How is it that you always do that to me, huh, kid? You always get me talking like I have secrets to share."

"I don't know," I reply awkwardly, "I mean, everybody's got secrets, maybe you know I can keep 'em, or maybe you just fuckin' wanna get it off yer chest and I'm the one's around all the time. You know I don't sleep much."

"There is something to be said for late nights, you got me there. Everything goes quiet as a church and we all feel the need to confess. Without sleep, without dreams, it's like we all need to feel saved somehow by the time morning rolls around."

I snatch the bottle of Jack without a word, throw back, return it to his limp hand and light one of Jim's cigarettes. The whole time his eyes are just blank, canceled. Bored. Pulling at my cigarette I ask, "Besides, Jim, what are you so afraid of? I mean, we're old pals, right? What's wrong with old pals getting' a lil' mushy every now and then? It ain't like I'm gonna jump yer bones if you get too soft on me."

Jim's face hides behind long, greasy hair and a dark demeanor. Something eats at him and he replies, "Everybody is afraid. They're afraid of themselves, afraid of getting hurt, afraid of losing love, afraid of finding it – just afraid. People talk about how great love is, but it's all bullshit. Love is a pain. It makes me weak. Love is the worst habit I've ever hooked into."

"What's love got to do with Ophelia?"

Jim sighs, ready to say something, then just shrugs, "Not much, I guess. I just feel like I'm missing something. Or someone maybe. I don't know. I just know that a girl like Ophelia makes me think about how everyone's afraid to feel bad. And how can you love if you're afraid to feel something? How can you if you're only willing to feel one spectrum of emotion? Pain is a part of the deal, man. It's what shows us reality. Without pain we don't have reality. It's like a radio transmitting to the parts of ourselves we don't know how to talk to. You know?"

"Not really, but go on," I reply stupidly, as usual.

"I guess I'm just saying that if you hide from any part of yourself, even the parts that don't feel so good, then you're limiting your identity. You're slamming doors closed in your mind. I guess that's why I just keep coming back to this shitty room. Hoping, somehow to save her or, perhaps selfishly, save myself along the way."

"Save Ophelia? Whoa, listen, Jim, that broad's a black rose. Wilting or not, you can water her all day and she'll still be dark and covered in thorns. Don't fool yourself."

"Was that your attempt at poetry, Tom?"

"I reckon so, old timer, I just gotta keep up with your electricity."

Jim's face twists wild and he almost spews, "My electricity? You keep saying shit like that and I'll run you outta here on a rail, kid. I'm not electric, I'm a clown trapped in a poet's body. Dammit, I gotta get outta here before we start sucking each other off or something. This is getting weird. I'll see you later, little man, keep blowing your sarcasm around. It's the only thing keeping this place honest."

Jim walks out. No shoes, no shirt and no concern.

Lucky for me Jim left the bottle when he beat it for the halls and I sit quietly, enjoying slow-burning whiskey in the peace of Ophelia's empty sex-frayed love loft. A side door opens a creak and I see a dark brown eye, like a frightened deer caught in my headlights. The door immediately slams closed.

"Hey! Wait!" I shout, jumping up for the door, but it's locked.

"Look, I know it was you, Maggie, we gotta talk sooner or later. Come on out."

"I shouldn't be in there. Ophelia will wring my neck if she saw me in there with you."

"Maggs, c'mon, I want to see you."

"I want to see you too, but I can't…"

"I know, I know," I slur at the door like an idiot, "You can't come in here with me, so open the door and let me in. It's not like anyone's going to come by at this hour. The sun's on its way up and the witches aren't brewing anything but coffee. Let me in."

I hear the lock unlatch, but she doesn't open the door and she doesn't say a word. Suddenly I feel sort of shy, like I'm in trouble or some fucking thing. It's weird. I turn the knob real slow like and peek in. Maggie May is in her nightgown, face down on her bed. It's a kid's room, really, pillows and stuffed bears and posters all around. Posters of old movies, cowboys, gangsters and romance. She doesn't look up. She just sits there spooning down into a heart-shaped pillow, pretending to be asleep.

I sit down beside her and put my hand on that soft spot between her shoulder blades. Her spine feels like a roll of quarters in my palm as she breathes heavy and slow. Something should be said, but, as usual, no words come to mind. I'm a real idiot when it comes to talking to people, but I do my best. I say, "Listen, Maggs, I...c'mon, you faker, wake up."

She sighs into her pillow like she's annoyed with me, but I can tell she's trying to make it sound like a sleep sigh. You know, like the kind you get in a good dream.

"Wake up, Maggie, I gotta talk to you. I probably should say I'm sorry for the other night, but I'm not. You know how I feel and all, so what can I tell ya?"

"I work for Miss Molly," she says, talking into her pillow, "I'm one of her girls, one of her daughters in this rotten place. Do you know what could happen to me if she found out I had a roll for free?"

"Don't talk like that," I fire back, feeling sort of steamed up, "it ain't like that. It ain't like you just doled out a freebie. It wasn't about bank, it was about your heart and you know it. Maggie, we've looked at each other from across the hall for what feels like years and there's always been something there. Like a comet ping-ponging back and forth between us. And now that something finally comes of it, when we pull together like two magnets held back for too long, you're gonna make it out to be something bad? We didn't do anything wrong. We did what two people in love ought to do."

"Tom, that's just it, I can't be in love with you and you know it."

I fire back, trying to stifle a scream and failing miserably, "Why not, for Christ's sake?"

"Because...oh, you're such a pain...because Miss Molly won't let me, okay?"

"Maggie, that's the lamest excuse I ever heard. If she don't like it then you can quit. We can run away together."

"That's just it, you jerk, we can't go," Maggie shoots up in bed, yelling, tears in her big brown eyes, "We can't go anywhere! Where're we gonna run to, huh? The fourth floor? All the windows have bars, the door never opens and they have that big oaf guarding it round the clock. Haven't you figured it out yet? We're prisoners here."

I know I should be thinking about how she's mad and screaming. I should be thinking about what she's saying and how she's right and all. But all that I can see is her brown hair all over her head, looking a beautiful mess and tears beading up on her lashes like rock candy. All I can think is how much I want her, even like this.

"You see! You're not even listening! God you're a pain!" Maggie slams her face back in her pillow and lets out a muffled banshee wail until her ribs vibrate under her thin silk nightgown.

"C'mon, Maggie Girl," I reply dumbly, "I was listening, look at me listening and stuff."

She looks up and I pull my ears out sideways and make an ape face. Maggie tries not to smile, but does anyway. I add, "What if I could find a way out? Huh? I mean, it's me, right? I'm Tom Sawyer. I'm the guy that gets things that ain't meant to be gotten. What then, huh?"

Her head turns slightly, just enough for me to see one brown eye peeking out over a tear-stained pillow, and she says with a new smirk in her voice, "Really? You'd do that for me?"

"Maggs, I'd do anything for you, don't you know that by now?"

She sits up again, rubs her eyes and smiles weakly. I guess it couldn't be helped. I'm kissing her now like we're saying goodbye and hello all at once. We have a long, close roll of it. I feel her warmth and we make a complete disgrace of her clean bed. Lying there, wrecked and naked, I pull her back up against my chest and listen to her breathing fade into sleep.

I sit silently, listening to the sounds of the Hotel California, the music of surrounding rooms, stomping feet, the day waking up its guests, and my love asleep on my chest...sighing a dream of freedom.

I love you, Maggie...

Letting her sleep, I slide my arm out from under her soft, thin neck and head back into Ophelia's room on my way out to the hall. I want my bottle of Jack. Inside, Ophelia is already getting an early start on her day with what appears to be the milkman. They don't notice me stroll in, grab the bottle by the neck, and head out her door.

Like Jim, I hit the red carpet of the outer hall with no shoes and feel each fiber squish between my toes like moss. Following the carpet to the stairs I head down to the second floor and immediately step in a lukewarm puddle of vomit.

"Fuckin' Christ," I blurt out abruptly, and a face rises up out of a nearby houseplant, vomit drool all over his chin. It's Poe, letting his guts loose in the base of a ceramic pot.

"My apologies, Thomas," he says, "but there is no need to unleash your venom on me."

"Venom? What the hell are you talking about? I just stepped in your fucking puke!"

Edgar Allan Poe, losing another load in the pot, replies, "Just that, my friend, there is no need for the obscenities, especially for a gentleman your age."

"I don't fucking use obscenities," I shrug, "I don't know what you're talking about."

"Has it been another long night?" he asks.

"Yeah, you know, no sleep, musing with Jim Morrison…still love struck."

"Ah, yes," Poe replies with a slight smile under his well-groomed, if not slightly stomach soiled moustache, "young love and all its desperate measures. Beauty of whatever kind, in its supreme development, invariably excites the sensitive soul to tears."

"Yeah, yeah, Ed, I've heard all that before, you could use some new material, man."

"I only meant," Poe adds, "that life is harder on those who feel deeply, but for those like us it also promises greater reward…if we can dare to keep dreaming."

"You sound like you're half asleep right now, if not still half-baked."

"Ah, but all we see or seem is but a dream within a dream."

I snort a laugh and turn to leave, "I gotta go, I'm gonna hit the bricks before you start quoting "Row, Row, Row Your Boat" at me like it's a proverb."

"But, ah, maybe life *is* but a dream…alas, dear friend," Poe muses, "go merrily despite your ill fate and forbidden love."

"Bite me, Poe. You're too weird to talk to when you're drunk."

I hang a quick left down the hall and hear him hollering something fierce, "But, my boy, I am always drunk! My word, it is true, I am always drunk…what do you know?"

I move to the East Asia wing and sit with this bottle of Jack in front of these big bay windows overlooking the desert sunrise. There's gotta be a way. If anyone can do it, I can do it. How can I break out of the Hotel California?

In the yellow overture of a fresh sunrise I see 'em, townfolk and the edges of cities and villages I have never known. And this morning, knowing the way a love could happen out there on some new prairie, I feel it more than ever. I am a prisoner at my window, watching new dawns and tallying days till I can break these bars.

A train whistles in the distance.

Field Notes from Bastard Land
2: Reels, Vortexes and Sleep Deprivation

A projector screen lowers behind them, covering the Art banner. The grainy reel image shows me, back in high school, sitting on a bench outside the courthouse of Linden, Texas, my old hometown. The marble stone of the old town hall fills the background. I'm reading my Bible. In those days, this was not uncommon. I can remember my early devotion—fasting and prayer, I'd sometimes study through lunch hour at school instead of eating.

Hunter S. Thompson stands with his crooked, bow-legged posture, a cigarette in one hand, a laser pointer in the other. Aiming the red sniper dot at the screen, he says, "This is what first brought you to our attention."

"What?" I ask, "My faith?"

"No, you fucking swine! This!"

The light dances around the courthouse and the town square as the man wildly waves his right arm. His head wound festering, gushing his agitation.

"Now pay attention," he says, calming slightly, "in your world there are certain epicenters, vortexes of creative energy. These vortexes connect where you come from to where we are now. Many lie dormant, never fully realizing their potential. From here we monitor, keeping watch over these sites in the event that they might erupt."

"And Linden, Texas, is one of these vortexes?" I ask.

"Yes, Jack," Janis replies, "see, I told you he was smart, man."

"Smart?" Thompson yells, "I've told you a thousand times you she-beast, he's a goddamn mule, a blundering Alexander without the gusto to recognize what potential worlds need conquering. You don't interrupt me again, do you hear me? Now, where was I?"

"Linden," I reply.

"Right, good, now don't sound so surprised. You don't judge energy by merit or population. Vortexes aren't only in LA, San Francisco or New York. Consider the town's history. This place, despite a population of barely over two thousand, was the once proud stomping grounds of Don Henley from the Eagles. The town's festival has attracted names like Jackson Brown, Kenny Rogers, that sot...and even the Desperado himself has overseen the festivities. Not more than forty miles away is Texarkana, the former gateway from the west to the east where Johnny Cash, Elvis Presley, Jerry Lee Lewis and Roy Orbison grew out of their baby fat. Many towns age and crumble, but towns with creative history feel it the worst. And this, Jack, is where you grew into your mind."

Janis interrupts, "Following your move from California to the sticks in your adolescence you found the Jesus Movement of this little country villa. Misguided or not, baby, it has given you your voice."

"What did I say?" Thompson rails, "No more interruptions from the press table. I found him, I'm running this show, you goddamn zombie bride! That goes for the rest of you too!"

Hemingway whispers to Kurt Cobain, "He's our newest member and already he thinks he's in charge."

"I told you he'd be a liability," Cobain replies.

"You heard me!" Thompson shouts, practically leaping to stand over them.

"Now, Jack," he continues, "Just watch the feed, will ya?" This is what makes you our Abraham."

He hits the intercom, "Becky, press play."

The projection scrambles static and I watch myself flipping pages. And then I get it. I know what this is. My old pal, Charlie Outlaw, skinny limbs and jaundice complexion, a cohort in the Jesus Movement, strolls up in jeans and a stretched V-neck tee shirt.

"What's up, man?" he greets me, still twenty yards off or more.

When he gets closer I reply, "John 14, 'A new commandment I give you, love one another.' I'm just sitting here thinking that saying something like that means that all this other stuff—church, meetings, doctrine, it's all irrelevant. We're only really meant to do one thing. But we've made God about offerings, PA equipment, building deeds and attendance."

"It's not such a new commandment, Jack, the way I see it, Jesus was just restating an old truth. That's pretty much all any of the good ones ever did."

"True," I shrug, "So what are you doing, brother?"

"I just finished communing with T.S. Eliot in his Wasteland. Now I'm thinking I've put it off long enough. I need to go do some homework."

"You know, Charlie, between school, homework, church and sleep we hardly have any time to work on ourselves."

"What do you mean, man?" he asks, sitting down beside me.

"I mean development. We're spending all these hours jumping through the hoops of our elders, teachers and parents, we hardly have any time to try to exercise our minds...become our own men. You know?"

"I know what you mean, but what choice do we have? We're stuck here till we're eighteen, right?"

"We have some choice," I reply, "We make the best of it by finding more time. It's something I've been thinking a lot about lately."

"More time, how? You find some way to add hours to a day?"

I watch myself scoot closer, looking him in his silver-blue eyes for the first time. I watch myself watching my friend. On the screen, I say, "No, not the day, Charlie, the night. Like we just said, school, homework, church, sleep…these things eat away our time. We can create more by cutting one out, and the easiest to let go is sleep."

"You can't be serious…"

"Think about it, how long could we go without sleeping, how many hours could we discover for art, spirit and creativity if we just gave it up?"

Charlie sighs, "So you're saying that our parents own the day, so we should go live at night instead?"

"Why not? It's at least a good experiment, right?"

"I'm game, let's start tonight, you can come over to my place, we'll do our homework and then we'll talk *real* stuff. I'll make some brew and we'll see what we find."

Cut. The video feed jumps to the home of Charlie Outlaw out on Center Hill Road, the veritable jugular of Linden's highway system. Center Hill intersects Highway 59 at the town's only traffic light. After the light turns green the road begins a steady but gradual incline and at the top of the hill is Charlie's house. A brick home sitting on an open lot, unsheltered from the sounds of the highway, complete with a soundproof music room, yellowed lawn and a half-dozen dogs running in and out of opening doors. The music room is more Charlie's space than his bedroom. Inside are a drum set, three guitars—his navy blue Stratocaster, his Takamine and his Gibson.

The walls are bare wood decorated by personalized spray can graffiti and movie posters dug out of trash cans depicting failed pictures like *Mr. Bean* or that Tom Green flick *Freddy Got Fingered*, stuff no one else would want. Pictures of friends and unrequited loves meet cardboard boxes turned faux art and wastebaskets. Packing Styrofoam melted into strange abstract red forms from spray paint and the corrosive chemical reaction leans against the walls or gets kicked around on the floor. An incense burner smolders silently and I see myself reclining lazily on the duct-taped sofa. Charlie sits on the shredded second-hand carpet and writes, uninterested, in a notebook.

I'm flipping pages through *Leaves of Grass* by Walt Whitman; reading aloud I say, "I celebrate myself, and sing myself, and what I assume you shall assume, for every atom belonging to me as good belongs to you."

"Aw, Jack, I love you too," Charlie smirks.

"Shut up, you prick, it's cool, right?"

"Of course it's cool, but do you get the feeling we're missing something?"

"Sure, of course," I reply, "but we just started. Okay, poetry might be biting off more than we can chew since we're right out of the starting gate. What about a game?"

"PlayStation?"

"No, dummy, that..." I laugh, pointing to a porcelain chess board.

"You're on," he says.

Now I see us setting the board and moving pieces and following strategy, plot and intent. We don't play chess to win, we don't even play because it's especially fun. We just play to unfold our minds, exercise neural pathways and grow. But more than that, we play to learn about each other, not just as friends, but as people. The way someone plays chess shows you who they are, how they might live life. Most people play it safe, wasting moves to guard every piece and never advancing, never going anywhere. Eventually, with no great vision for checkmate, after watching pieces slowly dwindle, the game ends with two lonely kings, a dead army and a stalemate. Charlie and I were both alike. We played it recklessly, tossing pawns into the fire just to get ahead. No fear, no holding back, just throwing it all away with everything out on the table until the game was over.

Watching this footage, my life on tape, it makes me wonder what's coming next.

The feed shifts to an image of me tipping my king. This one is Charlie's victory. Now it's showing Charlie plucking out old country riffs on his Gibson. It cuts to us lighting more incense, laughing, drinking coffee, flipping pages in notebooks and poetry anthologies and clocks burning minutes and hours like candle wax. The footage accelerates. It's just flashing pictures now, my life flashing before my eyes. Days and nights fly by—car rides, classes, textbooks, lockers, Bible studies, church services, fields of grass, microphones, hamburgers, movies...Here we are, Charlie and me, riding bikes up Center Hill Road in the middle of the night, talking about catching a train to Texarkana but chickening out.

Here we are making a midnight snack.

Cut to me walking in his front door and Charlie, entranced on his living room couch in front of his television, just staring, leaning forward on the edge of his seat. I ask him what he's watching and he says, "*The Last Waltz*, it's a documentary by Scorsese about The Band."

"The Band? You mean those guys that played back-up for Bob Dylan before getting their own spin-off? 'Up on Cripple Creek,' 'The Weight,' and all that?"

"That's them."

"I've never seen it, is it good?"

"Dude," he replies, tearing gray eyes away from the screen, "it's brilliant, I'm studying it for its secrets."

"That will take time, I'll bet, art is like a woman, you have to spend time, energy, leave gifts at her altar before she'll give up any secrets."

"What the hell do you know about women, Jack? You've never even had a date."

I shrug, "By choice, mind you, not by lack of options."

Sitting down beside him, I watch Bob Dylan as he finishes up a set. Now a whole orchestra of folk-rock legends is joining him and The Band on stage for the final number. In harmonious heavenly host tones they sing "I Shall Be Released."

Watching this moment transposed from my life I can remember feeling something new. It was like my first longing for a brighter future or an understanding of how many wonders have passed away. As the concert ends it fades to a new stage, Robbie Robertson, Garth Hudson, Rick Danko, Levon Helm and Richard Manuel, in blue lighting, play an eerie waltz on classical instruments.

Charlie and I sit quietly.

I can remember knowing that something had just happened, that this was a beginning.

Something new was on our small town horizon.

The feed picks up again. Here we are watching Van Morrison belting notes from his gut, leaning his head back and holding the microphone vertical over his wide open jaws. Here are the Staple Singers joining in on "The Weight," passing verses around between members and Mavis Staples soothing her mike with throaty vocals.

Charlie says, "Forgive my being crude, but you can just tell... there's a woman that knows how to suck a dick."

Despite my young piety, I laugh.

Cut to another day. He's playing and replaying Bob Dylan's performance of "Forever Young." Here's Robby Hawkins, here's Doctor John, Joni Mitchell and Ringo Starr. Now it's Neil Young pleading "Helpless" with every note.

We play them all, and replay them again. And in all of it, Charlie Outlaw's eyes watch every movement and chord with the studying gaze of a wandering guru, a hopeful disciple, a Veda, an ascetic, an obsessive—a student. This is not my moment, it's his. I'm just a bystander. I'm only drawn here by the energy of watching a someday giant find his stature. He memorizes every subtlety, every gesture, expression and segue. His lips move silently to the words of every song and every comment.

He smiles. He weeps.

The video feed moves ahead again and this time Charlie has his Takamine, joining in, playing accompaniment for a long faded past. Now we're back in the music room with chess games, albums playing on a turntable, incense, sleeplessness and passion.

Here we are, dozing off in classes. It's been ten days, eleven.

No good night's rest, we're sacrificing comfort in exchange for awareness. No rest for the dreary.

Now I'm reading from Jack Kerouac's *On the Road*.

"Hey, Charlie, check this out," I say, "This is it, man. This is the new commandment we're looking for. 'The only people for me are the mad ones, the ones who are mad to live, mad to talk, mad to be saved, desirous of everything at the same time, the ones who never yawn or say a commonplace thing, but burn, burn, burn, like fabulous yellow roman candles exploding like spiders across the stars and in the middle you see the blue centerlight pop and everybody goes 'Awww!'"

Charlie mumbles in his slow, slurred speech, "That's it, man, you're right. That should be the energy of spiritual devotion…but it rarely is, brother. But it's us. You and me, we are the last reserve of that fading way of life."

Standing in that smoke-lit room, watching my life, it hits me. This is how it all started. Charlie and I found a new plain, and it has carried me ever since.

Hemingway tells the intercom to stop the feed. He says, "This, my boy, is why we chose you. Hunter found you and we all knew you were the one. But if you take on this assignment, I must remind you, you will lose everything before you succeed."

"All right, that's enough blabbering," Thompson grunts, "Let's get this kid back home."

"Two things," Jim Morrison adds, speaking up after a long silence, "keep your eyes open for the changes, you'll be given the gift of sight, even now it is starting, but you don't know how to control it yet."

I ask, "And the second thing?"

"You must keep a record of everything that takes place. That is your assignment. Your account will save America."

"But what do I do? Where do I go?"

"No time!" Hunter yells, "They're moving, he has to go!"

The haze plumes over me. I'm alone in the fog now, but I can barely hear John Lennon, his voice just above a whisper, "Just let it happen and it will be what it needs to be. Watch out for our queen."

Cut.

The whole feed goes black. I'm home again. Home is a low-rent apartment in Tyler, Texas, a large-small town south of Dallas. I find myself in bed next to my wife, Dolly, sleeping peacefully with her back to me. I feel restless, the urge to move hits me and I jump out of bed, grabbing a notebook on my way to the living room. I start writing everything down and hear my wife stir in the other room. She comes in looking for me.

"Jack," she says, "what's wrong, honey?"

"Nothing, I had a dream...at least I think it was a dream. Don't worry about me, I feel good—energized even. I'm remembering things that have been filed under *amnesia* for years."

"Tomorrow is Sunday, remember? You're a youth pastor now. You have to set the example. Those kids need you and they definitely don't need you falling asleep in the service."

"I'll be fine. I just remembered this time in my life when Charlie and I tried to train ourselves to go without sleep. I'm practiced at this, babe."

"Ugh...Charlie again, you always tell these stories, Jack, but I've met your friends, they're lowlifes."

"Of course they are, but they're still my friends. I can't believe it's been so long since I've seen them. How long has it been? A year, year and a half? Jesus, not since the wedding."

Without another word, Dolly turns and heads back to bed. I feel guilty, she has to work an early morning shift and I'm disturbing her. No time to worry about that now. Jim Morrison told me to keep an account. I have to keep writing. I get this all down as best as I can remember it, close the book and go back to bed.

As the sun rises I wake to find my wife already gone. That's not unusual. This is our routine. I get a shower in, shave around my beard and put on a pair of slacks, a black shirt and my black boots. I hop in Bonnie and start the drive out to work. Work for me is a small country church up on a hill where tradition reigns supreme, but I still try to keep things fresh and young for the kids there. It's hard though, and today it's harder than ever.

All through the services I feel distracted.

Let's go to the tape. Here I am, supposedly teaching Sunday school. I'm feeling little more than a vague awareness that I am talking about visions and visitations from God. But I can't focus. Next clip. Here I find myself singing along to the closing hymn with no memory of anything happening in between.

The day flies by without me. Sounds feel heavy – pings like gremlins in the hollow heart of the Tin Man as he plays mouth harp to blues beats. I move around my church in a tunnel of weighted voices. Here I am swimming my way through the night service. We sing the closing hymn a second time that day. Now I'm in my car. Here I am on the road home. I can feel it. Everything has changed just like Jim Morrison said it would. Maybe my sight has already begun, but I feel strange days on the horizon, like a storm you can see blue-gray in the distance, moving in slow.

LOST IN AMERICANA: CHAPTER TWO
INTER-DIMENSIONAL PORTALS AND BUSINESS CARDS

"Tom," Maggie May whispers, her head close to mine on my little wall cot, "would you tell me something?"

"Anything," I say, feeling her hand move slow up and down my chest, "Shoot."

"Tell me about your life on the outside, your family...anything."

I think real hard, but nothing seems to come to me. I feel around in the overgrown bramble thickets of my own memory but come away empty-handed. Nothing.

Since I can't ever think of anything real good to say I sort of just shrug my shoulders and say, "I don't know, I guess I can't remember. I mean, I feel like I must've had a mom and a dad or something, you know, I must've, but I've been an orphan in this hotel for so long now...I guess if you miss something long enough you just lose it."

"That's why I asked," Maggie replies, "I have only one memory, it's me, in a schoolyard in winter and I'm getting grabbed by somebody. Sometimes I think he might be my father, but I know he's not. I want him to be, I need to remember my father...not sure why. You get that?"

"Maybe that's why I hang out with Jim," I sigh, "I want someone older to help me figure out some shit. Jim's the only thing I got that comes anywhere close to a dad or a big brother. It's like, this place... it becomes your whole world or something."

Suddenly there's a sound at the bottom of the stairs and I know it's them hollerin' tones of Miss Molly wondering where her girls are stashed away.

"Oh shoot," Maggie groans, leaping out of bed and tossing on her nightgown, "I gotta go, see you later, Tom."

She runs out into the hall and leaves me alone and naked in my bed.

Alone, I start to thinking. I figure if it wasn't for the sideshow court appeal of this place I might have lost my mind a long time ago. There's not really a lot to do. I mean, there's booze, smoking and sex. That's about it. Except for one thing. Talking. You can talk for hours to all the weirdos around here. It's sort of my hobby.

I figure I ought to do something like that and it's about time I head up and dig the fourth floor. I toss on a pair of jeans, an old V-neck tee and my bowler cap, but don't bother with shoes. Hitting the stairs I head right for the tip of the hotel up close to the attic. There's doors all painted different colors. Davy Crockett lives here and Daniel Boone. They like to stage faux wars in the halls and see who can fake kill the other one the fastest.

As I hit the fourth floor landing I hear the sounds of cheers and war cries and swearing. There's this explosion of gunpowder and splintering wood. Behind a battlement of book shelves, shower curtains and family portraits sits Davy Crockett with a musket shooting blanks. He screams, "Well, good golly damn, Danny Boy, you slippin' or what?"

Backed into the commode and firing from a bathtub full of some kind of fucking pink foam rabies or something sits Boone himself, floating in fronds of his own bead frill overcoat. Boone shouts, "Only on the mud from your grave, Davy Boy!"

"Pardon me, boys," I say, stepping through their battlefield and saluting with a tip of the ol' bowl cap, "Don't mind me, just passing through."

Moving on down the hall I see we got Pocahontas, John Paul Jones, the drunken Indian Ira Hayes, Ziggy Stardust and the Spiders from Mars, and Ben Franklin. This is one of the best floors here.

I pop into the room behind the blue door, Ziggy's room with its light-up umbrellas and polyphonic synth phones, neon lights and glow-in-the-dark graffiti – no telling who or what you'll find when you drop by here. Old Ziggy, fiery bouffant mullet and pale skin, is chatting away with Ben Franklin over tea. Cybernetic crystalline spiders dance on the walls and ceiling and make geometric art designs out of glass webbing. Ben Franklin sits sprawled in a wooden rocking chair peering up at a blackboard. A man I don't know is writing in chalk, wild tangles of bramble-thicket white hair dance on his head as he thrashes around to make his equations.

Ziggy says, "Tom, welcome...meet Albert."

The man turns and says, "Tom, is it? Jallo, I yam Albert..."

"Einstein?" I almost shout, "Are you kidding me? They got you too?"

"No, no, I'm afraid," Einstein replies, "just visiting, Ben und I yare old friends und given zee careful proclivities ove zis particular establishment he ist unable to come und visit me."

"In other words, he's a trapped stiff like the rest of us so you're making house calls," I grunt, "How is it you get to leave?"

"Easy," Einstein smirks from under a hedge bush moustache, "I never checked in."

Ben Franklin pipes in, adjusting bifocal lenses, "Tom, Albert was just explaining to us his take on the unique mechanics of inter-dimensional portals."

Ziggy Stardust, sitting there in high-waisted red breeches and suspenders and some kind of a pirate shirt with matching eye patch, crosses his legs at the knee and smiles, "But it's really quite interesting, I mean, to think, in a fundamentally scientific way, that reality is that pliable. Even foldable, really."

Einstein nods about a thousand times or something before finally saying, "Quite right, exactly, reality ist nothing more zan an illusion, mine friends, albeit a persistent vahn."

"C'mon, Albert, surely you must be above putting us through that awful diatribe," Ben Franklin groans.

"Quite right, quite right," Albert nods, "Vell, lad, to get right to zee point, ve vere discussing zee facets ove inter-dimensional portals. I vas telling zem zat in zee study of electromagnetic field energy it becomes apparent zat space ist not as constant as it may appeah. Gravity alters its shape. It bends around large bodies like our sun and affects orbits and even zee flow of light. In terms of space-time itself, it may go beyond varping and even be folded."

I watch the scribe mechanics of a withered oak tree hand making wide lines across the blackboard. I guess you might say he draws a big checkered napkin, real close up, like it was folded almost in two. Then he makes these big dots on one half and the other, like a set of eyes if someone was passed out laying sideways on their head or whatever. Those two big eyes get connected with this furious line that looks like a twister of white powder. When he finishes the diagram he starts talking again.

"Zese folds, if connected, could create doorvays, tunnels which zee German physicist Yohn Archibald Veeler nicknamed vorm-holes. A vormhole could, in effect, act as a shortcut from vahn point in space to anothah. Howevah, my research ove zee nature of zee physics of zis vorld suggests zat a similarity betveen vormhole science and dimensional science may exist in zee event ove zee barriers between two universes folding in zee same vay space might fold in zee manner I just described. Opening such a portal could lead from vahn ove any number of universes to anothah."

Ziggy Stardust uncrosses his knees and leans forward saying,

"Universes? I was only aware that wormholes could lead betveen two points in our universe."

"Well, I only mean to describe a similarity in zheories, not to suggest a vormhole might act as a portal in and ove itself. However, in conjunction with Multiverse Zheory..."

Ziggy Stardust just shrugs, "Yes, we're all aware. Every probable reality exists in parallel dimensions."

Like a real idiot, as usual, I ask, "Parallel dimensions?"

Ziggy and Ben look at me like I'm from fucking Jupiter or have a zebra growing out of my head or something, but Albert just nods and says, "Jah, every choice vee make, vether ve go right or left, through door number vahn or door number two, creates a plausible chain ove events. It ist possible, in a zheoretical sense, zat every possible outcome exists in another universe – or dimension if zis vord suits you better. Zese dimensions exist simultaneously with vahn anothah.

"Vye, I have even begun to consider vat zee universe may look like in zee absence ove space time. If vee remove all matter, vat are vee left with? Zee nature ove zero itself, emptiness, zee invisible realm zat exists behind matter. As a number, zee zero ist a consistent amalgamation of infinity and oblivion. In zat place, in zee zero, vee might find heaven and hell, purgatory or zee astral plane. Vat lies behind space time could be zee fundamental mechanics of eternity. All of zese are possible destinations ove an inter-dimensional portal. In othah vords, Veeler may have been only partially right. A hole in space may not lead to another side ove our universe, but to any other probable universes...including zee vahn zat exists in zee absence ove all zhings."

Benjamin Franklin scratches a paunch belly and says, "That's all very interesting, Albert, but what does it mean? I see no true thesis yet, only random facts."

Albert scribbles chalk a bit more while replying, "It means zat if such a door exists zen zee nature ove reality ist much more illusory zen vee imagined. Zere ist a necessary zero zat exists in all time.

A silent blip betveen secunds. Vere it not for zee zero at zee end ove vahn moment, prior to another, zen zat moment might go on forever. Consider Zeno's Paradox. A man fires an arrow, but before it reaches its destination it must travel half zat distance. Before zat half can be reached it must reach zee next half and zee next and zee next."

I watch the little wild hair tree hop around in front of the chalkboard, waving a wood bark hand hard enough to shake his hair side to side, shouting, "And zen you vould divide zee 64th by zee 128th und zee 128th by zee 256th und zee…"

"Albert," Ziggy laughs, shaking his head with a wide jaw grin, "back to earth, brother."

"You get zee point," Albert exhales, turning to face me as his chalk hand falls to his side, "Zese divisions are possible forever, zere ist alvays another decimal point vithout zee number zero. But add a zero und zee secund ends. Zee arrow finishes its flight und a new arrow can be fired. A new moment can begin. Vithin every nanosecond ove time zee decimal points are collapsed in zee number zero und a new vahn begins.

"Vithin zat zero all zhings are possible. If zero can be zee end and beginning ove every facet ove time, zen it ist limitless. Time fits vithin it, zhough it has no form, space might exist vithin zero as well. If so, zen bubbles, vindows, tunnels and doorvays to all variations of time, to all ove zese decimals, could be accessed. It ist zee backdrop to all matter und energy in zee universe. Ast I have intimated before, mine friends, zee more I study zee known universe zee more I see zee presence of a higher power. If God does exist, he exists in zee number zero."

Ben says, "Tell him about zero point energy, he'll get a good bang out of that."

"Ah, yes, zero point energy ist a zheory from zhermodynamics. It states zat zee vavelengths ove any energy, such as heat, are vibrating at higher und lower frequencies depending on how powerful zat energy might be. If zee energy ist high enough zee frequencies vibrate faster and faster. Zeir lengths shorten. If zee vavelengths could approach zero, reach a point vere zay are so close togethah zat zay cease to exist, zen said energy vould become limitless. Zee only zhing zat prevents zis from happening ist matter. Matter reacts to zee matter around it. Zis affects zee energy given off and prevents it from reaching zero. But, remove matter from zee equation und zero point energy ist zee only remainder. If we could physically enter zat universe und vee could valk around und live…in such a case ve vould surpass zee limitations ove our bodies. Ve, like zee entire universe, vould become pure energy. Ve vould become like God. Eternity exists, my friends, und it exists behind zee veil of space-time itself."

"In zero point energy?" Ziggy Stardust asks, "Where's the fun in that?"

"But what's your point?" I ask, leaning forward a little too harshly, if not slightly bored.

"Consider zee Oberserver Effect," Einstein replies, "Zee act ove observation, in zee case ove many experiments, alters zee outcome ove said experiment. Zees ist often caused by zee nature ove zee instruments, but in othah cases it ist not conclusive. Some of our more liberal scientific zhinkers have gone so far ast to postulate zat human consciousness may, in fact, alter zee nature ove zee universe. For zees reason, vee get zee aforementioned Multiverse Zheory. Each action creates a series ove possibilities, each choice vee make creates a new series ove outcomes, and each outcome creates a new veb of choices. Somewhere zee proverbial 'road not taken' may exist. Perhaps it is not zee action or absence ove action, but zee zhought, the power, and energy, ove human consciousness zat creates zese universes. Zat said, ist it not logical to surmise zat our zhoughts, our ideas, might be creating entire vorlds every day, minute by minute. Perhaps zees ist zee nature ove creation itself?

"Vee may all be a dream in zee mind of a god, but in his vorld he ist not a god at all, he may be yust like us, creating us in his mind as vee create him in ours. A symbiotic relationship ove fantasy, probability and outcome. Zee human mind, constructing and altering zee nature ove two, or perhaps infinite, universes. Mine point, gentlemen, ist zat somesing zat ist fiction to us may be reality elsevere. More to zee point, zere ist no discernible difference betveen fiction and fact as zey all exist in zee mind. Perhaps vee are constructed more from consciousness zan vee are from matter. And all other parallel, possible dimensions in zee Multiverse are creating vahn anothah simply by imagining zee possibility of each other's existence.

"So, God didn't exist until we dreamt him up?" Ziggy asks.

"Perhaps," Einstein replies, "And perhaps vee didn't exist until he dreamt us up, whoevah, and verevah he may be. Vezah vee are describing a vorld ove ghosts, a vorld ove people, or a vorld ove fiction, zee end result ist zee same – zey only exist because vee villed it zat way. Vee agree zat zis ist reality because vee are sharing it, elsevere, any othah combination ove circumstances, events or characteristics may be somevahn else's reality because zose involved agree to share it."

Ben Franklin adds, "And you're suggesting that crossing over through one of your bridges might allow someone to walk among their dreams, their dead, fantasies, or mistakes?"

"Precisely, mine friend, in an alternate reality vee may not just encounter a different version of ourselves, perhaps vee could find zee vorld created by zee shared vision of zose on zee othah side."

Ziggy says, "Oh please, Albert, you're better than this. These results are flimsy at best, what happened to the good ole days when you would back things up with numbers and logic? You come into my room and present me with conjecture?"

Albert replies, slightly red around the ears, "I beg your pardon, mine good mensch, I merely zhought zat, all of us being friends here, vee might forego the quandaries of typical scientific presentation and merely discuss vat I've been vorking on ove late."

Ziggy says, "Granted, granted," switching his eye patch to the other side of his face, showing his large, black, overly dilated eye for this portion of the spitting and hollering, "However, these claims are outlandish, I mean, sure many men have suggested that nothing is real, and a long dialogue exists suggesting that the world is all illusion, that we are all fiction, and sure, it may be likely, more than likely in fact, but to try to attach that theory to the likes of Wheeler or Rosen or even yourself is just…"

Ben Franklin stands quietly and says, "Follow me, my boy. This could go on for hours."

He leads me out into the hall, past the multi-colored doors lined up like henhouse chickens and through the barrage of smoke and splintered wood and water balloons as Davy and Boone fight out their never-ending war. Behind Davy Crockett's barricade there's this door that I ain't never seen opened, but old Ben opens it right up and says, "This goes to the attic, you can go ahead in, lad."

I follow his gesture up the stairs and hit the typical gold-gray-dust lamplight of every old attic you've ever seen. Sheets cover oblong shapes, and stacks of boxes, books, phonograph records, pinwheels, chests, drawers and show posters form maze walls in intersecting rows around the landing.

"This way," Ben says, guiding me through the maze like an old pro.

At the center of the maze we hit this ladder and Ben just points up. I climb up to a splintery old fucking trapdoor or whatever and give it a hard push. Wind and dust immediately push the door back on me and Ben Franklin smiles behind his bifocals.

"You'll have to try harder than that," he says, "that's roof access."

I give it one more good hard push and practically fall up onto the roof when the door finally gives. The roof of The California is just a plateau of old wood and shingles, but all around us there's this mean sandstorm blowing. I've never noticed it before, not even when I looked out the window.

Franklin says, "It is my hypothesis that it only blows when residents of the hotel try to check out early. The storm rages to push you back in whenever you so much as peek your head out a window. However, this is somewhat of a tree falling in the woods scenario. You know, a tree falls in the woods. If no one is there to hear it, does it make a sound? Since I am always present at the time of my exit I can never be absolutely certain if the storm is not merely blowing all the time."

"I've never seen it this dusty before," I reply, "On an average day I can look out the window and see clear to Subterranea."

"Precisely my point, dear boy," Ben replies, "Which leaves us with a rather alarming cosmic phenomenon, either this place is enchanted, cursed, or simply has a mind of its own."

"What can we do about it?"

"Very little I am afraid, but I have been attempting to work up enough courage to brave the storm."

Strapped like a raging bull to the abandoned chimney there's this twelve foot canopy of multi-colored cloth intersected by rods of wood and steel. I ask him what the fuck it is and he smiles with a reed-in-the-wind sort of hesitancy.

"Well, that's a personal project of mine, my boy," he begins, "Call it an affinity for kites, but I figure if a small kite could carry my house key into a thunderstorm then maybe one this size might carry me on the winds that stir up this sand. And maybe, just maybe..."

"You'll bust outta here."

"Precisely."

"It could work," I say with a sand-gritted smile and wincing eyes, "but then, you do carry quite the fat tire around your midriff there, old man."

I laugh, poking at him with the heel of my boot, and he seems downcast at the thought.

"Hence my lack of courage, Tom, I fear I might just plummet like Icarus into that sea of brewing sand. And then where would I be?"

"Just drop a few pounds and hit the skies," I grunt, "At least it'd be something new."

Turning his back on me to ponder his man-kite, Ben sighs something awful and I take that brief conversational hiatus as a good breaking point. I slide down the ladder and make for the safety and comfort of the third floor. Taking the stairs three at a time I feel the ground come out from under me as my boots land on some kind of papery mess. I hit the carpet, flat on my back and see what looks like a fucking leaf pile of business cards scattered all around me.

Then there's the sound of old Edgar Allan Poe shouting, "Oh, dear me! Are you all right, Tom? Some long-haired hooligan just came tearing through here with boxes of these things and dumped one all over the third-floor landing. Can you believe it? He did not even attempt to remedy his mistake."

Rubbing the back of my head, I say, "Fuck...did you see who it was by any chance?"

I pick up one of the cards and give it a good once-over. I go sort of astral for a minute, tuning out everything around me while I read the damn thing. Just barely pick up Poe saying something about no shirt or shoes. The card reads:

MULTIVERSE APPLICATIONS in REALITY, TIME, & YOUTH REVOLUTIONS

A BUSINESS OF CULTURAL INVESTIGATION

Missing Dreams, Art Thieves, Identity
Shifts, Lost Memories,

Otherworld Facts and Much, Much More!

Still holding onto the card, I completely ignore Poe, bust into Jim's room, and say, "Dude, do you know anything about this?"

Jim looks up, halfway into a black tee shirt, and smiles through the V-neck collar, "Hey, Tom, nice to see you too. How's tricks?"

"Very funny, c'mon, Jim, what the fuck's with this business card?"

"Oh, that? That's M.A.R.T.Y.R. It's a little side business me and some buddies have had going for a long time now. We just got these printed up. What do you think?"

I flick the card around in my hand a few times, grinning like a real idiot, and say, "I think it's the most goddamn ridiculous fucking thing I've ever seen. What's this about Youth Revolutions, a bit out of place, don't you think? Or did you just have to find two words to finish the acronym?"

"No, man," Jim says coolly, "Youth Revolutions are at the key to unlocking the mysteries of cultural shifts, and cultural shifts are the key to unlocking the nature of this universe. We see art as the outgrowth of spiritual motivations in world culture."

"I don't know what the fuck that means. So, what...you guys are seriously researching art now? What, somebody kills the Mona Lisa and you look into it?"

"Not yet, I'm afraid, but who knows what the future holds for us?"

I ask him if he's serious. He lights a smoke and tosses back onto his bed with a blank look on his face, "Yeah, man, people swing by our offices and we study their case for them."

"How is that possible?" I ask, "You guys can't leave the hotel."

"Well, sure, but we have operatives that can carry out our leg-work for us, guys like Einstein that swing by the hotel and whatnot. There really is a lot to our operation, I...tell you what, kid, why don't I just show you?"

Field Notes from Bastard Land

3: Roadside Phantoms and Late-Night Balconies

The road I take home is Texas Highway 69 south toward Tyler. It's strange tonight. Each curve around clusters of tall late-night pine trees feels like I might fall off the edge of the earth. Headlights light up a brief halo of the same tree trunks and asphalt on a time loop. The darkness is so heavy that nothing seems to exist outside of Bonnie's two beams of light.

Bonnie feels more shocked than I am at the sight of a gray figure on the highway shoulder. She lurches to a halt before my feet even hit the pedals. Or maybe, no, that's ridiculous, I must have imagined that. Rolling down my window, I check around. No one there. Only the brief howls of moonlight, Texas coyotes and the mechanical woodchip factory buzz of cicadas, crickets and katydids. These are the sounds of the Texas wilderness when the people leave and they're telling me that I don't belong here.

With a nervous sigh I inch Bonnie back onto the highway and head home. These high tree trunks, stretching their legs all around me, on a night as weird as this it wouldn't take much for one to just step out and crush me. Or field kick me through the goal posts of the upper stratosphere. I have respect for the night, it has a way of letting you know when you may or may not be welcome.

At home, in the parking lot outside of my apartment, the fog seems to have followed me. I climb the steps toward my door on the second-floor landing, those same cheap concrete steps fastened to black painted railings that you can find in any low-rent housing around America. Still, I can't complain. It's home.

The door is chipping green paint and there's a paper note taped below the peephole. In an abrupt, pointed tone it simply reads, "Went to the mall with Vicki, be back later."

I can't say why, but something about this really brings me down. Shrugging it off I unlock the door and creak in slowly. All the lights are out and for some reason this place doesn't feel like home after all. I flop down on my couch, a shabby piece of retro memorabilia bought at cost from someone's garbage sale down the street and probably in storage since 1979. The book on the coffee table is *On the Road* and it makes me think about everything I saw last night. I flip through some pages, picking up random words here and there. Blue. Jazz. Sad. Go. It. Sad. Dean. Sad. Apparently Kerouac uses the word "sad" a lot.

Absentmindedly, I flick on my stereo with my thumb and it's tuned to some classic rock station. It plays the last few chords of *House of the Rising Sun*, then fades to commercial. Through the speakers a loudmouth buy-me-now voice says, "This just in, ladies and gentlemen, Jack Bluff, age 20, dies tonight, 9:23, November 15, 2006."

I jump up, scared. Moving to the window, I check the streets. I check every corner of my apartment, paranoid, but it's empty. Now the radio is just trying to sell me discounted car insurance.

I break for the door and head down the street to my friend Sister Black's apartment, she's in the same complex as me, just around the corner. I make for the stairs, booking it up toward her door when I stop short. She's on her balcony, clad in black cloth as usual, sitting on a Folgers coffee can. Sister Black has this real pale skin that always looks angelic in porch light and these weird eyes, one blue and one mostly blue and half brown like God dropped a glob of paint halfway through the masterpiece or something.

Next to her is an old buddy of mine, The Head. The Head is just that – large cranium, premature receding hairline, strange face, teeth and intelligence. He is one of my dearest friends. A longstanding bystander of the Tyler wave, he's a genius, a geek, a mathematician and a philosopher rolled into one. Old Head looks like a younger model of Travis Bickle, you know, the Mohawk-sporting, revolver-toting militant from that Scorsese picture *Taxi Driver*. He's given to wearing second-hand tee shirts, Army fatigues and cut-off shorts. He is, incidentally, probably the only guy I know that I will admit is smarter than I am. And that is saying a lot coming from an egomaniac like me.

The Head looks grim. We're both wearing our sunglasses at night just to be weird or hide from each other or something. Across from me this bastard, this friend, looks like the successor to the Unabomber or something. He's wearing a tee shirt under an Army jacket that his father wore in Vietnam.

Sister Black says, "We were just discussing the usual diatribes, the death of art, spiraling decay and waning half-life of American culture. You know, light post-dinner conversation. What's up?"

"Nothing, just got home," I say, out of breath, "Don't mind me, as you were, as you were, I'm just feeling a little high-strung is all."

"All right," Sister Black shrugs, turning to the Head she says, "What were you soap boxing about again?"

The Head says, "Yeah, man, we were talking about art as an outgrowth of the human spirit, rather than just a creative business endeavor. I was saying that's what art is all about. It's reminding us why we stay alive. But I can't help feeling that there is some-thing out there that tries to make us forget. Somehow we let every-thing become about what it could buy us rather than what it could turn us into. Right up to God himself, we've turned things into Big Business. It kind of makes you want to believe in a devil."

I jump in and say, "The Mark of the Beast."

"What?" Sister Black asks.

"Nothing, nothing, never mind...I just mean that everything I look at comes down to Art vs. Business, but it seems bigger than that. Like those two things represent two polar opposites fighting it out, an axis war, where both sides seem to be wrestling over having everything in the world their way. This is why I have so much hope in the Indie Movement. More and more people are learning to do things on their own instead of groveling to Big Business – studios, publishers, record labels...whatever."

Sister Black says, "I'm tired, Jack. At the record store today I was the only soul there buying any music that required the most meager effort to discover. Everyone else was holding whatever newest albums were out from the newest bands. The whole youth culture of America is listening to whatever the radio tells them to swallow. I can't help feeling that this rapid decay of thought and culture is more due to laziness than lack of availability. No one cares enough to take the time to find their own music so they just jump on the trend wagon."

"It's Art vs. Business all over again," I reply, "you've heard it before, the business world uses the entire population as a vehicle to promote the self, the artist uses the self to better the art and, by extension, the people."

"What's your point?"

"My point is that we have to look at how the business world is moving in on the art world. Hostile takeover style, upward mobility and all that, these two sectors of society are no longer separate, businessmen are now forcing a merger upon the artistic community and that is why people like us feel the sinister sensation of rapid decay. First things first, I can tell you that the business world makes its decisions based around demographics. They create market groups, different molds that each person can fit into. Creating forms like genres in film or music, or backing the most marketable distributable writers and painters, is the way of the Business World. Forms become categories. Categories become products. Products then become sales represented by consumers. Consumerism is where the war between art and business is being waged. The war is here and it exists in many diverse battles – the battle of Visual Arts, painting, sculpture, whatever, or the battle of music, the battle of literature. It's everywhere now."

Flicking ash into the wind, the Head adds, "Well, near as I can tell the Battle of Visual Arts is long over. Corporate art is the only sturdy modern art form. You can see it anywhere you go, bank lobby paintings, the abstract steel sculpture forms outside of entrepreneurial advising branches."

"The Liar's Crutch has conquered art history as well," I add, "no one is taught any obscure painters in art history or is taught how to look into the future of art."

"Just the past," the Head drops in.

I continue, "They memorize their Van Gogh and their Michelangelo and they go out into the world to regurgitate it generation after generation. No one cares about new artists anymore, their vision has turned backward and because of that it has turned extremely traditional and traditionalism is the fastest route to choking off the art movement. Everyone is just looking at what the world of universities and big business tells them is art."

I watch a bat dive bombing after a moth in the Texas moonlight as Sister Black says, "You're right, man. Categorization is the most powerful weapon Business ever had to use against Art. They've turned free expression into brand names."

"Creating forms," I say, "That's how they corrupt the music world. Today we have country, rap, hip-hop, rock, alternative rock...jazz, modern jazz, classic rock, Rhythm and Blues."

"Not to mention all of the subgenres each of those entail," the Head adds, "country, country-western, contemporary country...for example."

I nod in agreement and march deeper into my rant, "Even the movement we claim might hold some hope for us, the Indie Movement, is a category in itself. Business has even permeated into the rebellions against it. Today, if you can't label it you don't make it and that's how we know business has conquered music."

The Head says, "It used to be 'I like Bob Dylan, I like the Beatles or I like Hendrix waving his freak flag high,' now it's 'I like country, I like rock, I like rap.' Establishing forms, like you said, that's clearly the business way."

"Yeah, man," I reply, "That's the Liar's Crutch, obvious cultural selections you can lean on to look like you know something without ever having to even pick up a book or listen to a record. People want categories instead of artists now. It's the brand that matters, the artists are interchangeable."

Adjusting black curtains of skirt around her knees, Sister Black, slightly bored, says, "Today it's money over beauty..."

To The Head I grunt, "It's product over purpose..."

I look Sister Black in the half-brown half-blue eye and, with a faux activist's fist in the air, I shout, "It's sales rather than souls!"

The Head says, "It's Art vs. Business."

I explain how generations are defined by their art and literature. Explain, almost sermonize, "If generations are defined by their art then what will define us? It's just one more way we have been lost and bastardized by the American Dream."

Here is where I ask, "How will we be remembered?"

I tell Sister Black, "I know one thing, this is a war and we win by seeking art that remains untainted by money and the proverbial sell-outs. I believe now, more than ever, that if our culture is going to survive this downhill slide into delinquency and stupidity the only hope is that everyone becomes an artist in their own way. Everyone must become a seeker."

I tell them we need a Neo-Renaissance, tell them the American dream was useful in its day. It existed to stabilize America in a time when the Great Depression had it shuddering on its axis. We needed people to seek out wealth and land and the house with the picket fence; we needed to encourage people to look out for their own self-interest. It was "every man for himself" at that point. But that's all. The dream was created to stabilize America.

Sister Black says, "Things are so stable now they're about to collapse."

"Exactly, we need a new dream."

I tell the Head, "Consider history, after the Dark Ages set in, the economy fell, intellect fell, nothing was left except survival. In many ways it was the Great Depression of the Middle Ages. Then things started to change, the economy stabilized and what came next? The minute we pulled out of the Dark Ages people knew it was time to change their ideals. Cultural mindset evolved to consider everyone rather than just the self. The Dark Ages rapidly became the Great Awakening.

"The Great Awakening was typified by artistic endeavors, DaVinci, the king of the Renaissance movement, was a painter, a writer and an inventor. He sought to better himself and the world around him. The world was full of people like this at that time."

I clearly stole the ole Head's soap box, but I have to drive the point home – I mean, Jesus, I'm a preacher by trade, it's what we do.

"My point is," I say, "selfish thinking must eventually end and give way to a consideration of humanity as a whole. The reason people everywhere are seeing a negative shift in America is because America has continued in narrow thinking for too long. It's been too unwilling to take the next step."

The Head drags on his cigarette and says, "We need a new focus, the whole rather than the self. I'm with you, our hope lies in art, not business."

Like a standup comic, I figure I'll end the night on a high note, so I stand up and say, "Well, ladies and Gentiles, on that note I'll say good night. My better half's gotta be home by now."

I give a brief little nod and hoof it back to my apartment.

LOST IN AMERICANA: CHAPTER THREE
M.A.R.T.Y.R.

Jim leads me down to the first-floor landing, through the lobby and past that young broad, Becky, minding the desk. He gives her a little nod and pushes up against them big double doors that never seem to open. We listen at the door, I reckon to make sure we don't interrupt anything serious. I look inside. Through the crack in the door I see all these faces that seem real familiar. They're just sitting around behind this big wood desk, sort of shooting the breeze and smoking cigarettes. Behind them a banner hangs kind of lopsided, it reads, "We Put the Art in Martyr."

This young mug with grease-straw hair looks over at this guy with a big brown beard and long Jesus locks and asks him, "Seriously though, how did things ever get this way? How did everything get so cheap?"

"It's just a negative side effect of living in a capitalist society," the ol' boy with the beard replies with a limey accent, leaning back in his chair, scratching his belly through a white suit, "Everything in this world is based around economy – politics, marriages...even religion, nothing is pure anymore. When the economic forum is based on the free market then the life philosophy will naturally evolve into, 'Get as much as you can while you can.' Thus, nothing has value that cannot turn a profit. This is the logical response to a lifestyle designed to promote personal gain."

Jim clears his throat into a fist and says, "Pardon me, fellas, this is Tom, Tom Sawyer...he seemed rather eager to meet you so I brought him down."

"Eager? I was not, Jim, you're full of shit," I shoot back, "I just wanted to know what your stupid business cards were all about."

The man with the beard stands up and says, "Well, we're down a few members at the moment, they're doing research in the outer halls, but those of us here are more than glad to meet you, Tom."

He points down the line, there's the guy with the grease-straw hair he introduces as Kurt, a dark-skinned moog in some kind of flashy green pirate shirt or something and a purple satin bandana around his head that the man tells me goes by Jimi, there's an old man with a big gray beard and sad eyes that I already know as Ernest Hemingway, and some wild-eyed Kentucky whiskey thrower in a poker visor, aviator shades and an Acapulco shirt who interrupts our apparent host and blasts, "The name's Hunter, Hunter Stockton Thompson if you wanna get official with this shit. You probably heard of me–"

"'I'm the doctor of journalism, man,'" Kurt says, interrupting Thompson, "We've all heard it before. You need some new material, bro."

"What?" he shrieks, "Nothing more out of you, Goddammit! I feel the same way about your mumbled commentary as I do about syphilis."

I've seen Thompson around, but just to drive a couple of stakes in his heart I tell him I've never heard the name. Hemingway chuckles to himself at the sight of Hunter getting worked up and gestures with an open palm for me to have a seat in a nearby chair.

I plant it in this rickety thing that must be about a zillion years old or something.

Finally, the man with the beard says, "And you can just call me John. I do feel the need to explain to you that if our appearances alarm you there is a purpose for it. The very same purpose that gives us the unique ability to do this job."

He opens up his white blazer and there are about six oozing red holes in his shirt. My stomach leaps up in my throat and does a couple cartwheels on my Adam's apple before I finally say, "Jesus, Lord, what is that?"

"We are the few here who are aware of our lives as they existed in Otherworld."

"Otherworld?"

"That's what we call it, a world parallel to ours which gives us our existence and to which we simultaneously give its color, culture and abstractions. We are aware of this place because we are all trapped endlessly in the moment of our individual deaths. Hence our slightly alarming appearance."

"Okay, I'll buy it," I shrug, "but what the fuck is the story on this unique work everyone keeps talking about? What's all the nonsense you were jabbering about when I walked in?"

"Simple," John replies, "Otherworld is decaying rapidly and it is happening here as well. These two places are connected somehow and we are investigating the nature of that connection. What we know so far is simple. There is a conflict as old as time in which art seems to be the good guy and the corporate instinct the bad guy. Somewhere behind the scenes are a few old men twisting their mustaches trying to find a way to promote productivity above quality and...Well, it's a war out there. Business is attacking art and when it conquers some new territory it drafts the survivors into its army."

"I have this picture in my head of some sort of mutated giants," Hendrix jumps in, "the sideshow freaks of our grandfather's generation, hiding in dark corners and issuing commandments out to those they have under their spell. Whatever they say goes, like the oracles in ancient Greece or the witches in Macbeth. The Blind fortune teller gazes into her crystal ball and tells her visions to the Bearded Lady and the Man with Breasts. They see where the world is going and try to steer it their way. To turn America into a greater freak show, a land rolling with money and filth and avarice rather than the enlightenment and harmony pursued through the great works and movements of the past. I can't say why I see this or how true it is, young cat, just that I see it...we all do, and we're trying to find out why."

Hemingway chimes in now, adding his two cents' worth, "These people have always been there, squashing the attempts of our own Mr. Lennon and the Hippie Movement, or Martin Luther King Jr., or Jack Kerouac and the hope and loss of his beatniks. Anytime a good thing gets going they squash it by getting things at the source. They corrupt the art itself. This is why bands fall apart or sell out. This is why the great American novel has probably gone unpublished and we're left sifting through spy novels and self-help books that are almost completely devoid of substance."

Cobain laughs, "Yeah, you gotta see our point, right, kid? It's like these freaks are the power houses behind all the big industries. Film, books, music...whatever. They sit down over whiskey and cheap beer talking about how to destroy art. Art is everything they are not, so that makes it their enemy."

Hunter Thompson growls, "They know they can't simply burn libraries and bookstores or outlaw painting and expressive music in some Neo-fascist Gestapo wave. Instead they choose to simply promote bad art and push it on those who are listening and buying."

"Yeah, man," Jim adds, "it's like they use their power over publications and studios to promote boy bands and dancing girls in skintight leather instead of true music that captures the soul of the people."

Hunter rails, "Thanks for the assist, you goddamn booze hound, but I wasn't finished. As I was saying, these people, these corporate faces, they produce and advertise and drown us in praise for movies comprised entirely of visual stimulations like explosions, car chases and sex acts without anything that touches the intellect or any of that which we might call human. All of this drains the art out of artistic ventures so much that people forget what art really means. They forget why we make movies or why we read books. People just rush out, pumped full of ADD, to buy more of what they are told to buy. Rushing out to buy the next big thing from Paris Hilton or from Dr. Phil and no one remembers why Bob Dylan is a classic or Fitzgerald is a literary hero. It's not how Bob Dylan sounded when he said it, it's what he said and it's not how many books Fitzgerald could sell, it's what we came away thinking about at the end."

John says, "So we're here, all of us, fighting the bad fight because no one else can. Locked in the moment of our death, we have the clarity of vision to see this world, the Land of Americana, and the grim memory of Otherworld. We can see where they overlap and know where to push the right buttons."

"All right, friends," Hemingway begins, "that's enough of this prattle. Tom here is our guest and here we are beleaguering him with mission statements. Relax, Tom, you want a drink? Smoke?"

"Yes on both counts, sir," I reply casually and they pass a bottle and a cigarette to me via Jim Morrison, who seems too high-strung to sit down.

Lighting up I say, "Well, thanks. As you were, I guess."

Jimi says in cool tones, "Like we been saying, there's cats out there that want to put us under one flag, you know? They think that's the ticket to putting a stop to everything."

"Everything?" I ask, tugging on my smoke.

"Yeah, young cat, you know, war, famine, poverty…the biggies, you dig? But what they really mean to do is put a stop to *every-thing*. Everything earthy, everything real – art, music, poetry, the stuff that makes us, you know, *us*. When they stop that, we lose it all. They want to unite us under one flag. I say, when you start seeing flags waving around you can start measuring out the ulterior motives. They say there's too many leaders, too many names fighting over who gets what, they want one leader. The way I see it, there's no leaders anymore. There's no one to step up to the plate. That's what the whole revolution was all about."

"You mean this revolution you all came out of in Otherworld? The sixties?"

Jim chimes in, "Yeah, guys, I've filled him in on some details. Tom here was blissfully ignorant on a lot of facts, probably on account of him coming out of the Twain days."

Jimi just rolls on, "Naw, man, I don't just mean the sixties... I'm talking the American Revolution. Like John says, the American Revolution never ended. These cats out there waving flags, shouting titles and polls and naming party leaders...these cats that like to say, "We are the United States Government," they don't get it. They're just a voice box, blunt instruments for all of us. *We* are the United States Government.

And I ask, "How do you know all this? Everyone else here exists in this reality just fine. You guys seem to be the only ones claiming to be from somewhere else."

John Lennon jumps in and says, "We're not too sure, you know...it's like, we all died and woke up here. We tend to think that's the answer, it's 'cause we all died before our time. Like that song said, only the good die young, maybe it's like this place somehow deified us or something. Whatever the answer is, I'm reminded of how, in Otherworld, they say legends never die. I don't know about all that, except maybe this is where they go."

Thompson leans in on a bottle of Jim Beam as he pours it into a half-pint Scotch glass, "We're all prisoners here, we live like we're on house arrest. A few times we have managed to get out that front door and down the street only to find ourselves right back at this fucking hotel. In fact, I've never once heard of anyone getting past Pentecost Park."

My ears burn white hot and I shout, "What? You guys have gotten out? How? When? You gotta tell me, man."

Jim says, "Easy, kid, take it easy. Getting out is simple, it's staying out that's the real trick. We've all made it out at one time or another."

Thompson slurs, "Yeah, it's weird. Like this is some sort of holy Mecca always drawing us back in. Like this is the temple. Do you ever wonder about that, kid? Can you hear me? Do you ever wonder if God was a prisoner of the temple in the old days of Israel and Solomon and all that? Maybe he had it razed to the ground by Babylon just to get free. All of us here, we're prisoners of our own memory…our own underground movements. And it won't end until that other place learns how to stop living off of the work that we did back there…maybe then we could get some rest."

Hendrix chimes in like a low piano key, "What are you saying, Hunter? You trying to say you think we're gods?"

"Gods? No, Jesus, Lord, no…there ain't room for gods anymore, no more than there's room for giants or fairies or pyramids… or human sacrifices. I mean… a god? Jesus."

"Yeah, I don't know, man," Hendrix replies, "Maybe in one of my past lives or something, but this one, this living death, I'm lucky if I'm a ghost. What about you, kid? Are you a god?"

Hunter says, "Motherfucker, you're wasting my time! Now stay focused."

Jimi says, "Man, Hunt, lighten up, man…how 'bout it, kid? You a god?"

"No more than Jesus, I reckon," is all I can think to say. Man, I'm a real idiot when it comes to thinking on my feet, I never know what to say.

Then I add, "Anyway, if we used to be gods we must not o' been very good ones…I mean, you know, we must not o' been too good to come back the way we are now, right? I mean that's the way it works, ain't it? If your past life did any good then you go up, otherwise you start all over again, like some fucking board game where you get bumped back to start. I don't know, Jimi, ya reckon maybe it's all in your head? Maybe there ain't no more. Maybe there's just this life. There weren't no gods, no dinosaurs or druids or ancients or kings. There's just us and a lot of strange stories. Maybe there ain't even this Otherworld place."

Hendrix nods slowly, puffs smoke and says, "I can dig. You trying to say there ain't no clear way to be sure what's a fairy tale and what's our history? Like maybe even my own memories could be dreams I had, right? Who's to say?"

Jim turns to me and says, "If you haven't gotten the picture yet, Tom, we're myth hunters, true seekers, and distinguishers of fact from panic. Otherworld has been pushing its way into Americana for years, we work from these offices to find where, and how and why. Sometimes you have to ask the weird questions to get at the truth of things, as you can see here."

Thompson is screaming and we both crack cocky smiles.

"Myth, eh?" I ask, "Give it to me straight, Jim. This ain't just about rifts or portals. This is about the Myth of the Queen."

"She exists, Tom. And she's a part of all of this. We suspect that our enemy is hunting for her as well. Possibly trying to destroy her. MARTYR is about putting the pieces together, it's all connected, the missing queen, the end of everything, the rifts between the worlds, Otherworld, all of it."

"How do you know what a god is?" Thompson squawks, "You ever seen one? I hardly think you're a credible expert on divinity!"

I sort of look around at all of these creepy bloated faces and a strange sort of awkward silence mushrooms up between us. Their gray skin and hollow eyes, dead but still somehow bearing life, gets me thinking they're all just jonesin' for my brain or some shit. Slapping my thighs and leaning forward out of the chair I say, "Well, gang, this has been...educational, but I think I'm gonna skedaddle."

Making for the door I book it across the lobby, past Leroy Brown and shag ass up the first-floor staircase.

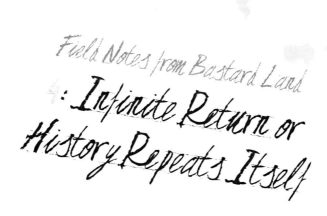

Field Notes from Bastard Land
4: Infinite Return or
History Repeats Itself

The door opens and Dolly steps in, blonde hair tossed up lazily into some kind of a bun and her eyes dragging the floor with her feet. She sighs and I ask her if she'd had a bad day. No reply. She is silent. A sort of hovering tear gas lingers in the room and I can taste it. One of us is about to cry.

She says, "I have something to tell you, but I know you are going to hate me."

My answer is as smooth as ever, something about how I could never hate her because I love her too damn much. Something like, "Have you ever known me to hate you for anything before?"

And what she says back is terrible, "No, but I've never had anything so bad to tell you before."

Shit. Gut shot. Wounded. I feel my balls shriveling up for the retreat into their cavity, desperately searching for some kind of warmth. This is a sign of impending doom. The same way birds fly away before an earthquake or a lightning storm. I have to brace myself.

Deciding to play it cool, I say, "Listen. Just tell me and we can go from there."

"Jack, do you ever think about leaving me?" she asks.

"I don't know," I reply, "I mean, maybe sometimes, but to some extent that's normal. It's not easy being married, especially when you're young."

"That's just it, Jack, we're too young. I go to work every day and battle wicked, undressing thoughts about every man I meet. The truth is I don't think I should have gotten married this young."

"Bullshit," I say abruptly.

"Excuse me?"

"You heard me. That's what that is, because we knew what we were doing and you went a far screaming distance not only to convince me that you were in love but that you knew what marriage meant. And all of the old beasts telling us not to do it were wrong. Dead wrong. That's what you said."

A great sadness swells across her face and she says, "There is something I have to tell you, but I can't."

Let's jump forward. This will go on for hours – her saying things that make no sense and me telling her that it's simply not true. And the whole time she is holding some great secret back from me.

Now I admit I do have relatively serious rage issues, but deep down I am a peaceful guy, never did anything to hurt her, never even yelled. But at this exact moment I'm not myself. I slam my fist on the dining table and almost growl, "Look, if you have something to say, just say it. Otherwise I will just take that as a clue that you do not care about *us* and I will head right out the door."

Silence.

I turn to leave, get halfway out the door before she finally wipes snot and tears from her face and sobs, "Okay, I can tell you now. I kissed someone at work today."

I feel a quick flash of red, a swell of anger and then it passes. I reply calmly, "Okay, not that I'm not mad, but it's just a kiss, we can work this out. Was I just not good enough? Were you curious what it would be like with someone else? I mean, I understand, we were each other's first, well, everything, but you said that's what you wanted…that's what God wanted even."

She shakes her head like crazy and says, "No you were always good enough."

I ask, "Were you mad at me?"

"No, it just happened."

Odd as it may sound, a sort of mutant side effect to remaining in God's good circle, I begin to feel the shock wear off and slowly replace itself with patience and forgiveness. But right when I say, "You know what? I don't care. It's not that big of a deal," she says, "Okay, the truth is that I slept with him. We went to his house and well…you can imagine."

Boom. This is how it must have felt at Hiroshima. One minute you're living your life, pulling weeds in your garden, the next you are a radiated puddle of liquid flesh. A semi-living core meltdown. Everything in my life that makes sense just imploded.

My knees collapse and I fall face first into the floor dry heaving and out of breath. I start punching the door frame until the white wash finish starts to go pink and then red from my knuckles. She gets scared and runs to the bathroom, huddled and bawling in the corner by the toilet. I hear the radio broadcast say, "Newsflash, Jack Bluff's life comes to an abrupt end tonight at 9:23 when the news of his fraudulent marriage falls upon him without warning."

Drama, drama, everywhere.

You have to know that I have never been the most stable guy. Always been a little deranged, a little manic, but my wife seemed like the most pure, honest, and beautiful thing in this world. Whenever the demons came rolling in I could stay grounded in her grace. So what now? She just dropped her nuclear warhead on me and painted the whole room with Holocaust radiation poisoning. What am I supposed to do now?

Seeing her weeping in the corner, pitying herself, made my mind go red with anger. My vision goes black, a moan and one last crushing blow to the door splits my knuckles wide open.

Here I am, crying in agony. Sobbing and convulsing, I ask, "How many times?"

She hesitates and gives me a cryptic answer, "At least four in the last month. I don't really know anymore."

"Goddammit. That's not a mistake, that's a whore."

She starts feeding me this bull about how she has been unhappy. That she married me for the wrong reasons. Then things start to make sense.

"I married you because it was the right thing to do," she says, "we had been making out pretty hot and heavy and I always wanted my husband to be the only man I had ever kissed. God hates premarital sex and I wanted to do it, so it was only right that we got together. You want honesty? Okay, I married you because I wanted to fuck."

I'm falling down a well right now, looking up as the circle opening gets smaller and smaller, like the last real light in my life has just gone out. Over the radio I hear Ernest Hemingway say, "Jack? Are you there, son? I tried to warn you. Before this is over you will lose everything."

My face still in the carpet, I nod slowly, drooling into my shirt sleeve and sobbing with anger. I nod and it all fits. I know exactly what I have to do. I have to pick myself up, head for the door and not look back.

In this clip I'm gathering up my clothes. Here I am grabbing some books. Jump forward. My slideshow life, like instant replay on the sports highlights. Sound bites click by in front of me. Here I am taking my records, movies and some blankets. Cut to me behind the wheel. Bonnie and I speed wildly onto I-20 with nothing but shadows in the rearview mirror. I don't know where I'm going. Maybe I'm not going anywhere. The point was that I just go. Somehow, right now, this all feels hauntingly familiar.

Cut.

I hear this film director inside my head. He's saying things like, "Okay, in this scene, our lead man is just driving, no real direction. All of the lights flying by his window feel like they are going out. Like all the light of the stars a thousand years away has suddenly caught up to him and is trying to tell us they went out long ago. Got it? All right, action."

A yellow light flashes and I pull into an all-night refueling station. Here I am grabbing some cheap dispenser coffee, dropping a few bills for gas and dragging my weight toward the glass exit door with the little cowbell that swings on your way out. Before I leave I ask for the restroom.

"It's in back, you'll need this."

The cashier, a swaggering, toothless modern Neanderthal with chewing tobacco fastened inside his lip, tosses me a key attached to a rusty U-bend pipe. I put my coffee in Bonnie's cup holder and the rest of me, rusty pipes and sloshing waterworks, makes for the bathroom that promises to be a real resort.

The key scrapes its way into the lock and the door feels heavier than expected. Inside there is darkness and the faint smell of tobacco smoke. I feel around for the light switch, but can't even seem to find the wall. What is this place? The sound is all wrong. It feels bigger than it should. I flinch when a small orange light flicks on, illuminating a long wooden desk with a good half-dozen silhouettes sitting behind it.

"Oh shit, not you people again," I grunt, "This is the last thing I need."

The light shines on the red banner. "We Put the Art in Martyr."

Janis Joplin says, "Oh, Jack, I'm so sorry this has happened."

"I'm sure you are," I sneer, "I guess that makes you 'good cop.' You're the sweetheart so I'm supposed to trust you, tell you all my secrets or respect your opinion or something, right? This is where I tell you about pain or loss or how I hope she and I will work things out? Maybe you'd like me to tell you that my teacher used to touch me down there when I was a little boy or that I saw my parents having sex when I was too young to get it or some shit? Things like that, would that make you feel better?"

Thompson's voice belches out of a nearby shadow, "Ha! I'm beginning to like this kid. He really knows how to stick it to you fuckers. He's smarter than I thought, gang."

Hemingway, in the same tone he had through the radio, says, "I told you that if you took this job you would lose everything."

"You're right," I reply, "you told me. I just didn't think it would happen so fast."

Lennon, in a relaxing monotone, replies, "I'm afraid things have to move fast, Jack. We are just out of time. Unfortunately, the only real casualty will be you."

"Casualty? The radio said I died tonight, know anything about that? Tell me the truth, am I dead? I feel dead, have for years actually. It's okay, I can take it."

The light brightens and I see the deep eyes of Jimi Hendrix. Breaking his silence for the first time in a while, he says, "You aren't dead. Don't worry about that radio broadcast. Call it a false alarm, mind games, whatever you prefer."

Kurt Cobain leans forward, indignant, "No, we have to tell him the truth. He deserves to know the truth."

Joplin nods and adds, "Yes, I agree, he's given so much already."

"All right, Goddammit!" Thompson rails, "He's my field agent, I'll tell him. You see, kid, it's like we were saying before about there being another side."

"The ones that want to pull the plug on America?" I ask.

"Right," he replies, "good memory. Well, they're growing in strength and we, unfortunately, are weakening. Too many people have been living off of our memory for too long. It's drained us. Anyway, that nonsense about you dying is the enemy trying to get inside your head. They'll get you scared and then win you over to their side with promises and gifts. Things aren't as easy as they once were; in the old days your enemy was some kind of mal-formed right fascist beast who would knock down your door and drag away your screaming children. Today, well, Jesus, your enemy looks exactly like your friend. You work the same job, he offers you promotions and desks and jet flights...the whole shebang."

I nod silently and say, "I get it, but I have to ask. Why have you brought me back so soon? I mean, I just saw you guys last night."

Jimi Hendrix stands up this time and says, "Well, kid, it was my decision this time around. See, I was worried about you and thought you could use a little reminding. I've learned something about you, Jack. I already can tell. You don't keep your memories with you too long. Something goes down and you like it for a while, then you just move on and forget. If you're going to get through everything that's coming your way, you'll have to remember."

"So this is for you, Jack," adds Janis Joplin.

The projector screen lowers and I say, "No, don't show me another tape. I don't want to see another fucking tape."

"Sit down, kid," Thompson growls.

I sit down in that same high-backed chair and watch the feed boot up. Hendrix asks Becky, whoever that is, to press play. The feed crackles to life and counts down from three. On the screen I see me behind the wheel of Bonnie. I'm steering around corners and up side streets in Tyler, Texas. It's late, or early, depending on your point of view and all the lights are green. And then it hits me, right now, after just leaving my wife, it all floods back on me.

This is not the first time I've been homeless.

On the screen in front of me is the visual memory of a time, back before I dropped out of college, when I was still taking classes and living in a shack on some old lady's property. Every morning the woodpeckers were my alarm clock as they drilled into the outer walls to get at the termites. Living mad and beat like a hermit, painting to blasting music without sleep or hesitation for days and nights on end. Writing my mistakes and trying to find some answers, this was my first step into adulthood and I can see now how I wasn't quite done with the sleep deprivation era of Charlie Outlaw and Linden, Texas.

The feed cuts to me in that little shanty, painting on bits of cardboard and salvaged wood, slinging paint like some kind of a weapon. To no one in particular, Video Me says, "This stuff is too personal, too beautiful. I'll never let you have it."

Video Me gathers up everything, piles of cardboard rectangles and jagged pressed wood chunks covered in multi-colored variations of surrealism, abstract-expressionism and a general mapping of the interior of my mind. Looking back, I didn't remember them being as good as they were. Video Me pushes his way out toward the front yard, the screen door slamming behind him with a metallic clap. He piles everything on the grass, grabs some lighter fluid from his landlady's porch and flicks a match into the heap.

I watch myself on the screen, dancing around the fire like some kind of native rain dance, screaming and grinning wildly. Then Video Me stops, wincing with black smoke in his eyes, and says, "Jack, old boy, you're really starting to crack up."

With typical immoderation, I head inside and grab paper and pen. I write the landlady a note that reads, "I can't live here anymore. Thanks."

I tape my key to the letter, then tape the letter to her door. That was it. I made my escape at midnight and just drove around town with all of my worldly possessions loaded up in Bonnie. Everything I owned, everything dear, was right there with me. My life, inside and out, was right beside me.

The feed cuts to an image of me waiting in line at a soup kitchen. Now it's a free meal from a church group. Now it's a college fundraiser with free pizza. I don't give a donation. Those were impressive times. Riding my own inertia, I drove myself across great distances on the sheer thrust of my own desire.

Now the tape jumps to an image of one of my many nights spent sitting out by the Tyler airport watching the sky traffic coming in to land. Everything is all lights and shrieking jet engines blowing their own kind of cold front across my windshield. It's me, staying up late into the night listening to all of our rock legends – Bob

Dylan killing the clock for me, Jimi Hendrix crying acid tears or Johnny Cash burning alive in his *Ring of Fire*.

Now I remember what this is, this is a video clip of one of the single most sublime moments of my entire life. It's a quarter to three in the morning and the airport field is lit up neon blue with just the backup landing lights. Air whistles hard under the car and through the cracks of the doorframe. My car stereo blasts that mad soul-screaming Hendrix, the electric Star-Spangled Banner shrieking its Rock & Roll nod at patriotism. Night crews are parking the little charter jets and two-seaters, steering these large white winged beasts out in front of me below the twilight. Looming giants, yet small and unassuming, would go lumbering slow and silent in tow behind tractors with men in dark jumpsuits.

Wrapped tightly in an old woolen blanket that kept my grandfather warm during the Korean War, I am hit by all of it, the sights and smells. I think about the way television stations used to break at the end of the night. The video feed cuts to an image of the American flag billowing in the wind with the National Anthem playing in classical, corn gold tones. Choir voices sing the lyrics. The music cues up the Statue of Liberty over the backdrop of the flag's fifty white stars and fades quickly into Baroque oil paintings of the American Revolution. Images ramp up and move faster as the song winds down. Now it's fields of golden wheat, a sunset, the WWII Veteran's monument with the soldiers raising the flag, a close-up on the stoic face of Lady Liberty and everything fades, finally, to the flag once more on the final note.

A sort of voice that sounds like it went out of style thirty years ago says, "This is KCRA, TV Channel 3, wishing you a good night. This concludes our broadcast day."

Now the video blends static back into the shot of me sitting in my car by the airport. Hendrix is playing his drug-electric spin on the National Anthem and the screen shows that Korean War blanket, planes docking at night, blue lights on white wings, pigeons scattering on the wind, and dust howling across Bonnie's rust-red paint job. In the comfort of my own counterculture sign-off montage I whisper, "This concludes our broadcast day."

And I get it, watching my life on that screen, I get it. In the wee hours of the morning wrapped up in my Navy blanket I worshiped my rock heroes and let them help me through the sad hours. Because the truth is, when you stare straight into the heart of the matter, the world's already come to an end. The gods of rock already came like a thief in the night. And you've been left behind.

Hendrix taps the intercom with a gray-skinned hand and says, "Becky, that's enough."

The video stops and the screen rolls back where it came from revealing the red art banner. He presses the button once more and says, "Thanks, foxy, take a break."

Looking over at me for the first time in what feels like hours, Hendrix says, "I think you get the point, am I right, man?"

"Yeah, I get it. I've been through all this before, so I'll be fine."

Thompson smirks wildly and says, "Well, good, now get the hell out of here."

Smoke billows and I move toward the big oak doors behind me. They open up on a damp, rusty convenience store restroom. It stinks like piss in here and I'm staring into a cracked mirror. I can't stop thinking about parallels and repetition. Nietzsche's idea of infinite return seems to apply somehow, that every moment exists forever, on a loop. Sometimes I get the feeling I'm living through that. I mean, Jesus, back when I was on the road I left my home in the same car in the middle of the night with the same stuff that I have with me now piled up on the same seats. History is repeating itself.

LOST IN AMERICANA: CHAPTER FOUR
BREAK ON THROUGH TO THE OTHER SIDE

She was born in an hour of uncertainty. A day had come where music, like life, like politics, like everything that has a beat to it, was confused and in between main eras. Presidents were dead, preachers were buried, vows were like melting ice cream on July afternoon pavement and the sounds of the age were half-empty glasses. And Maggie was born. She lived to whisper secrets and take walks down lonely pasture trails under the moonlight with young boys and their sex. She lived to ditch school, kiss lies, and trade smiles for drinks and all of it was her favorite game.

It was some winter day when a man caught her up in the school-yard and drove her out to the desert to escape a Minnesota blizzard. He told her he was saving her. There they were, arm in arm in the cab of a rusted pickup truck making it for the desert warmth he promised her she desired more than anything else. When his turn at Maggie was finished and she could barely walk a straight line she learned the gift of trading favors for cash and hitchhiked out to Highway Zero. She checked into The Hotel California and that was all she fucking wrote. Maggie's been here ever since, a wilting lily of youth, innocence, beauty, angst and freedom. Trapped by her own disease, the sickness a kidnapped shoulder rub spread into her belly, she checked in and has never since seen the sun.

There was a day when he arrived. Tattered shoes and dress pants, black suspenders over a white undershirt and his drunk-scuffle bowler cap. Not sure what door he entered through, he only knew the desire to smoke and bummed from the first willing hand. He gazed around and even now remembers very little about how it happened. Only that this had been his reality as long as he could remember. That the past was always out ahead of him and the future was the one thing he kept forgetting, that everything was lost once he found it and this was the one place where he finally quit looking.

Our man set eyes on Maggie, standing naked under a brown fur coat at the top landing of the lobby staircase – teary-eyed, milky pale and beautiful in cloaked sadness like that dead critter on her shoulders, draping her in afternoon shadows. His courage fell like the Tower of Babel at the sight of her and theirs was a ballet of exchanged glances, silences, blushing corners and keyhole peeks. When they finally spoke it was over midnight coffee and the happenstance of simultaneous insomnia. The memory of their discussion crystallized in his brain like quartz in a slow-dripping time cave and he cherished it in secret hours as a soon-to-be martyr does with a prayer. At nights, when space was quiet and time halted to draw a breath he would take out that memory from his cigarette box, light it up and breathe it in slow, holding it in his lungs as long as his blood could allow.

They talked over the pains of freedom and the comforts of slavery, the poetry of war and the brutish mediocrity of peace time – they talked opposites that were forbidden in open court. Coffee steam fueled their engines as they thought about the nature of love, hate, indifference, passivity and the Good Samaritan on all of Americana's roadsides. Eyes meeting for longer than embarrassed passes, our man saw something in them that had never dawned above a soul's horizon before. He could see more than a mere reflection of himself in teary, glass hues, not just a mirror of what she saw. Instead, he saw her. Our man saw Maggie May at the table with him as he had never seen anyone before, smiling at the absurdities of his notions and the half-assed poetry of his seduction.

And goddamn if it didn't work. She led him to a well-stretched bed cover and a mattress groaning with its own familiar rhythm. In spite of the free roll, the fun turn or the question of what this could possibly mean to a girl like her, our man found himself falling, spiraling, down into Love's overused oubliette – a comet of hormonal enthusiasm and the first sparks of an adoration consecrated by soft lips, sweat and smiles.

She whispered the sweet promises of life and love everlasting if they could only make their escape together. Every morning since then he has stared into the mirror and prayed to his own reflection, some kind of holy-rolling Narcissus asking himself for the measure of devotion and endurance required to break free of a silent prison. He stares in and searches for the wit to see the guards, the watchtowers…the walls behind the walls.

He does it all for her. Chases freedom from a place he can't remember entering and has no idea how to exit. Doors only open from the outside. Bars over windows look like censors over the love he can almost taste. He bides his time with the color of the hotel's halls.

3 AM. Right now I'm shut up in my room. From down the hall I can hear the siren's song of Miss Molly's daughters hollerin' and bluesin' their fucks to the rafters. I spent all day searching the place for loopholes and tie-ins. Some way to escape into real sunshine. The bars are tough as railroad spikes and there's no getting out the front door.

I fear the only way out is Ben Franklin's roof access, but that means a dangerous climb and a potentially grim fucking end.

Here lies Tom Sawyer, split open like a watermelon while trying to escape.

For now, I'm brooding. Sulking, really, I admit that. I'm mad as hell. To be told so bluntly by the girl you love that the only thing stopping you is four walls. Well, let's say Romeo's poison pill makes sense about now. And what do I have to show for my time? I've read some books and shit, fuck me if it did any bit o' good. I've watched television, listened to music, I've paced these floors enough times to wear a slick spot and I stand in front of this dusty old mirror adjusting and readjusting my old bowler cap. None of it, none of these days, is worth a damn.

Right now, I'm sitting on a stack of newspapers and smoking like a goddamn fucking chimney. Probably a fire hazard, but if I drop one of these and the whole place goes up like a wicker basket I'd say serves them right. Christ, I just want out of here.

I have this old jigsaw puzzle I've sort of been kicking around at when I can't sleep. It's broken apart like a half-eaten turkey and I just keep nudging pieces around with the tip of my boot. I figure, what the hell? Might as well do something. So I start putting the thing back together. It's supposed to be this 1000-piece portrait of the Mona Lisa, only she's got this big moustache and an "I Like Ike" tee shirt on. I guess it's kind of funny. I found it in some closet upstairs. The thing looks about a million years old or something.

The trick is to find the edges. That's what everybody always tells me. I reckon that's what I've been trying to do, but it ain't too easy. You can see pieces with a flat edge and all, but that don't mean they go together easy. But that's what they say, anyway, you find the outer edge and you can solve the puzzle.

Sitting here, though, something comes over me, a barking at the moon sort of rage. Call it cabin fever or whatever, but I suddenly hate this room and everything in this whole fucking place. I throw the puzzle junk at the wall as hard as I can and ruin all my good work. Half the pieces smack up against the inside of that old useless fireplace with a cardboard splat. Then I hear it and it all sort of starts to fit together in my head.

There's a sort of empty clatter, like a ring falling down a sink pipe, only softer. Not metal. It's something else. Crawling on my knees toward the fireplace I see those bricks and boards filling in the chimney, but in the back wall there's this spot where the mortar looks crumbled like a half eaten cake. I grab a handful of jigsaw pieces and toss them through.

Same sound, like some kind of African Tiki head god gargling with wood chips. That makes sense though, I mean, I got the room with the windows and the street view. A fireplace means a chimney and a chimney means an outer wall.

Find the outer edges and you can solve the puzzle.

I put my boot through the brick as hard as I can and it all goes crumbling down the hotel's throat. Sticking my head in the hole feels like looking Jonah's whale right in the mouth, but I see down into darkness, right into the belly of this shabby fucking building.

Break a few more bricks and there I go, sliding right through like a cat burglar or some shit. The tinkering sound was wood framework and rusty pipes and I use them like a ladder to climb down three floors and into the basement. Not too bad, but I still ain't out.

I've never seen the basement before. They got this big ugly furnace like you could cook a body in there if you wanted to and there's junk all over. Rusty bikes, street signs, books, clothes, porch umbrellas, rocking chairs, old radios and television sets and, more than anything, the smell of muddy dust and camphor.

A pile of old coal has sogged down into itself and made a regular black rock in one corner. There is almost no light, the windows ain't even windows. They're just these holes in the brickwork, like they arranged the blocks in this sort of lattice pile to leave little spaces in between. Light streams in a checkerboard four squares high. Pale dust dances like moths in the beam.

On the far side of the room I see grass and weeds and ivy

growing like Rosalita's bush. Green means dirt, dirt means outside. My boots click like horseshoes across the concrete floor as I make for the other side of the basement, but there they are – steps, steps four high leading up to a wooden door.

It's my way out and by the look of it this stuff's been forgotten about for a long time. There's this rusty padlock that peels like an orange slice right off of the splintery wood and I push up with my back.

There isn't really a word for this sort of moment, so I ain't even gonna use one. All's I know is that folks on the outside probably take the feeling of the sun on their face for granted. When it hits, the first time I can remember without it getting filtered out through glass, it feels like the soft caressing touch of a woman more graceful and more giving than any I've ever known.

And I just wish Maggie May was here.

Gotta make sure the coast is clear, when it is, I'll get her out safe and sound.

But this is just the beginning. For a brief second there was the light of day, but as soon as my head peeks up over the edge of the basement door the sands get blowing. I still have to find my way out of this storm and I figure it's too dangerous for a peach like Maggie May. I head out, fingers crossed and spit in the eye that I don't get caught. If they do get me, Jesus, Lord, I don't know what's gonna happen. Maybe nothing, maybe I just disappear. Still, reckon that's why I started writing this thing. I figure this has been a plan of mine even longer than I knew it. I'm writing for what I think Lincoln or somebody said like a thousand years ago, you know, "For ourselves and our posterior."

I'm writing so when they finally get me someone like you'll find this thing and remember how it all went down.

Looking around I notice I already know these streets pretty good just from watching at my window, but everything is a stormy haze of yellow and dust and grit. I take a nice quick look, side to side. To make sure I'm in the clear and all. Nothing's doing so I book it down Thunder Road and disappear into the emptiness of a sandstorm. I hang that left onto Pleasure Street and beeline it toward Pentecost Park. This is the moment of truth.

Maybe the map in my head is all wonky or something, but this should be the park here. Through the storm I see a dark looming wall and I figure it's the movie theater or some other fucking business right there on Pleasure Street. Instead, it's the front stoop of the Hotel California. I turn around and head back into the storm. Here's Thunder Road, Highway Zero is out on my left. I hit Pleasure Street and head for the park. And I'll be goddamned if that ain't the hotel stoop all over again.

There's only one thing I know for sure and that's that I'll never give up, this is for Maggie, for me...for everyone in that God-forsaken prison. I won't stop and maybe that's the trick, I'll succeed where others failed because I'll never stop. I'm Tom Sawyer. I'm supposed to be the guy that can get into places that ain't meant to be gotten into.

This shit goes on for what might be a couple hours. Streets, sand and hotel steps. Streets. Sand. Hotel steps. And finally I figure something out. I get how this thing works. When I get to Pleasure Street I decide to do what don't make sense instead of what does. I don't turn toward where the park should be. I turn toward where it ain't. I turn back and face the Hotel California. Something nobody in their right mind would ever do. I turn and run through the sandstorm, guarding my eyes with my arms, running at a sprint back toward where the hotel was just a second ago. And I'll be a grease monkey if that ain't the fucking park right there in front of me. Jim Morrison and his gang never made it past this point. This is the main heart valve of Subterranea. This is where the gypsies finally stopped their rambling. This is Pentecost Park.

5: Refueling and a Fresh Start

This next bit will be a montage series of images set to "Float On" by Modest Mouse. Here I am as I kick around downtown Tyler for a while, hassle people, fuck with the locals. Jump shot. A man plays a saxophone by the old train station. Jump. A boy cries after dropping an ice cream cone. Jump. There's a woman in tie-dye selling makeshift key chains and refrigerator magnets made out of bamboo and pigeon feathers. Jump. Here I am breaking into all the old, rundown abandoned buildings of Tyler's downtown places. Jump. This is what might have been a shopping center in the fifties, but they never finished it. It's like a ghost town. Tools, equipment, supplies – everything was just left wherever it was sitting. Rooms are completed but unused. Lampposts are standing in a long line down the center lane, but were never lit. I find a nice corner of what was maybe going to be a grocery store or a shoe shop and fall asleep on an old drop cloth.

Cut to nearly two days later, after sleeping on random benches and ducking the police, I figure enough's enough. I hoof it back out to Bonnie, abandoned but faithful at that lot in the shadow of Interstate 20. Bonnie and I take the road back toward Sister Black's apartment. The drive is brief and uneventful; cars pass me by like strangers tucking behind your chair in a crowded restaurant. Cut.

This scene is called *Refueling*. It's been nearly a week and our lead man wants to see a friendly face. He has stopped off at a convenience store on Interstate 20 to refuel on gas, coffee and chewing gum.

Fade in lights. Cue music. The soundtrack plays something that feels like driving, the South and sunrise. Daylight. A payphone outside of an I-20 Texaco station.

Action.

"Charlie?" I ask the receiver.

"Hey, you've reached the voicemail of Charlie Outlaw, go ahead and leave me a message, or don't, because I probably won't get back to you."

"Charlie! It's me, Jack, I'm guessing you've heard all the news by now, I'm back in Tyler and looking for my next step. It's been a long time, man, and I need to see you. My cell phone is dead at the moment, so I really wish you'd pick up."

As I step away from the payphone it rings and I grab the receiver before the second buzz, "Hello?"

"Hey, Jack, it's Charlie. You timed this shit just right, man. A friend of mine is heading to Tyler tomorrow to visit his grandparents. If you sit tight I can hitch a ride with him down your way and we can ride up to Denton together."

"Ride to Denton?" I ask.

"Yeah, you're coming up here, right?"

I hear Brother Red's voice in the background, "Yeah, you come and stay with us, bro, as long as you want. You get your ass up here."

Laughing, I say, "Hell yeah, man, that sounds like a deal."

"All right, later then."

I hang up and dial the Head.

"Hello?"

"Dude, it's Jack, I'm so glad I got you."

"Jack, hey," says the Head, "what's up? I heard you left town."

"I did, or...I mean, I'm about to, but I wanted to see you and Sister Black."

"All right, cool, I'm at Sister Black's place right now. Do you need a ride?"

"No, I got it, thanks."

Cut.

We'll call this scene *A Fresh Start*. Here we see our lead man settling into Bonnie's driver's seat when he catches a glimpse of himself in the rearview mirror. His eyes look frustrated, strained, as he stares at the long wisps of hair hanging in his face and down to his shoulders. Leaning over the seat he digs around in the back searching for something. When he resurfaces with a battery-powered beard trimmer, he closes the car door and heads for the men's room. Action.

As I climb out of the car a painful cold grips my spine and I double over, wincing harsh and groaning. Not now. Jesus, Lord, not now. I can feel my demons swarming and buzzing under my skin. Screaming to be let out. My car radio kicks on and the voice of my high school science teacher buzzes out of the speaker static.

"A pipe bomb will explode from pressure more than combustibility," he says, "you see, many people believe that the pipe is stuffed with nitroglycerin, it actually does not take anything near that potent to create an explosion. It only takes pressure. We could build an explosive right here with little more than vinegar and baking soda enclosed in some sort of airtight container. As the pressure builds, with no outlet whatsoever, it will simply build to such force that it has to escape. And explosion is the only means of escape."

My demons build force and momentum aching to get out. This makes me a pipe bomb, an actual living, breathing, human pipe bomb. Another minute and flaming chunks of me are bound to go sailing across Texas with winged demons snarling through air molecules lunging at my leftovers. The only chance for survival is release. Desperately fighting the convulsions, I fumble my way toward the restroom. Damn, it's locked. It's one of those that are outside, the kind you have to go bum a key to get into. That's how you know when you're really in the middle of nowhere or in the shit creek side of town, when people make you get a key to take a piss. I guess it's because people go in there to score sex or snort drugs off of the tile floor or, in my case, shave off all of their hair.

I get the key and let myself in. Now I'm standing in front of the mirror almost in a trance. *Cut. Cut. Cut. Instead of no sound here, the silence should swell and build until the soundtrack cues "Idiot Wind" by Bob Dylan. It's probably one of the greatest break-up rage songs in history. Dylan wrote it after he split up with his Playboy model wife or whatever she was. It would be perfect.*

Okay, action.

I can hear all of my demons slithering and trying to burrow out of holes in my skin, craving the chance to explode out of me and go thrashing through the air. Something about this hair is like a testament to all of the time I have spent with her. It has grown out long in her presence, in our marriage. Grabbing the trimmer and pressing it to my scalp feels like erasing her from my life. Buzz. Buzz. Buzz.

There goes that time she said she would love me forever. That lie. Buzz. Dropping a chunk to the floor kills the night she said, "If you died I would never remarry, I only have eyes for you." Buzz. Erases how she said, "You are the only man I can even look at." Buzz. Strip away all of the times I tried to please her without her even bothering to give anything back. Surprise dinners, poetry, candlelight, and staying up to talk with nothing in return. Shave it all away.

Think about Samson and Delilah. Think about all the ways people carry their pain visibly on their body. Black-eyed battered wives, cancer patients. This isn't much different from the Jews in

Holocaust Germany having to walk around with those gold stars on their shoulders. Carrying the mark of their pain, their suffering right out in the open. What I like to call the Mark of the Beast.

After I finish I cram the mop of hair into a plastic bag and head back to the car. The air, cool on my clean scalp, feels like a fresh start. I can't really say why I kept the hair, it just felt right. And if we want to remain human we have to do right. Cut.

This next scene is called *Catching Up*. Fade in lights. Cue music. The soundtrack will play "New Coat of Paint" by Tom Waits, but fade to background once our lead man reaches the front door and knocks. Establishing shot. A semi-rundown apartment complex in a mid-sized East Texas subtopia. Metal railings painted black support gravel concrete slab steps leading up to a balcony and a green paint-chipped wood door. This is Sister Black's apartment.

Action.

Knocking on the door flares up strange incendiary nerves. Maybe I'm just too close to my former home, but I feel scared. But when the door opens it all goes away. Sister Black opens up. She leans on her doorframe dressed in a black rag dress and black and white striped stockings, smiling at me with her ivory doll skin and her half-brown half-blue eye. We've been friends since we felt at odds with our surroundings during our high school days in Bible Belt, Boondock, Texas, and relied on each other for safety from the deer hunters and racial hate-mongers.

The Director says he'd cast someone like Christina Ricci to play her in his movie.

At the sight of my hair shaved down to stubble she screams and says, "Oh my God! Look at that head."

Then from behind her the Head strolls up and says, "Ho-ho! Who's the Head now?"

Hugs all around and Sister Black pulls me inside. She says, "So Jack, what the hell happened to you? You just disappeared on us. I mean, sure, okay, we all know you left your wife...the bitch..."

"The Destroyer," I add.

"Heh, the Destroyer," The Head laughs, "Are you saying she's a naval ship?"

"She's gotten about as big as one lately," Sister Black grins, "Okay, so you left her, we got that. But what happened to *you*?"

I laugh and do my best to catch them up on the past week. When the Head asks what happened to me being a youth pastor I say, "I quit my church job, two years as a youth pastor and it ends up flushed down the pipes with faith and marriage. I didn't even talk to a person. Just called in on the answering machine at midnight and said, 'Hello? Hello? Is there anyone out there? Can you hear me? Well, the fact of the matter is, the woman I married only married me for guilt-free sex in the eyes of God and the church. When she stopped caring for God, she stopped caring for me. Just found out that she's hopped the first cock departing for Gomorrah and now I'm out in the cold. Needless to say, it's all over and don't expect me to come back. Ever. Tell the children I love them, but God was killed and replaced by Las Vegas. You can mail my check to this address...'"

Sister Black laughs and says, "You're sick, but then we knew that. Okay, so I have to ask, what inspired the drastic haircut? I mean, I think I know...but tell me anyway."

"I don't know, I guess it just felt really primal, almost like an ancient rite. You know, like in India when girls become nuns they have their hair plucked out by the matrons. Or how in ancient Greece shearing off hair was part of the funeral ceremony."

"So what did you do with your hair, dude?" asks the Head.

"It's in a Wal-Mart bag in my car."

"Oh no," says Sister Black, "that's all wrong. You didn't finish the ritual. You can't be free from what that hair represents until you destroy it."

For a minute Sister Black's CD player is playing some track from Mutemath, one of her favorites, when the speakers are interrupted by that same familiar voice I've been hearing. *Cut. Cut. Cut.*

This is all wrong. We should be fading the soundtrack back up as our characters move out into the lawn. Lights up! Cue music! Music!

We're out in the grass now and I have retrieved the hairball from the bowels of rust-tired Bonnie. Sister Black says, "Here, in the middle, make a campfire and we'll all stand Kumbaya around Jack's emancipation."

"I need a little fuel to really get this thing going," I say.

"Here," the Head reaches into a side pocket of his camouflage cargo shorts and retrieves a pewter flask. He dumps it on my old hair and I drop a match into the soggy mass. I smile in the stink-smoke of smoldering unwashed hair and it feels exactly like being born again. This is religion, psychology and therapy all rolled into one. This is setting a match to my memory of her. My time poorly spent.

Sister Black says, "I feel like someone should say something."

"I'll go," the Head says, "It should be said that a man is more than the sum of his parts. If Jack only existed because he was many moments and scars and cells pasted together by a malfunctioning God then he would cease to be Jack by doing what he has just done."

The smoke burns our eyes and the smell chokes the Head's words in his throat. He tries to continue, "However, a man is more than those parts. Science shows that your cells recycle once every seven years. On an atomic level you're never the same person twice, not even from one minute to the next. There has to be something more that makes us who we are. Maybe it's friends who are always there to remind you, just in case you forget...or maybe it's the much debated soul. Whatever it is, it's yours no matter what you destroy."

It seems cheesy to say thank you, so I pull down my zipper, reach in and piss out the fire. The stink is unbearable and we all laugh. What else could I do? I mean, it was only right. And after all, if we are to remain human we need to do what's right. It's the only thing that separates us from the animals. The Head starts singing "The Battle Hymn of the Republic" and we all join in as the ashes sweat and cool.

"Mine eyes have seen the glory of the coming of the Lord…"

"The Lord is coming," the Head laughs, "Get a towel."

"Glory, glory, hallelujah."

That science teacher was right. Sometimes explosion is the only means of escape.

"I'm tired," I sigh and fall backward into the cool of the Texas grass.

Cut. End scene.

This is called *Endangered Sleeping*. Here we find our man in Sister Black's living room. The Head sleeps on the floor beside the television with the DVD menu for *Easy Rider* quietly recycling itself throughout the night. Sister Black has pulled out the sleeper sofa. She sleeps in the center of the mattress with her laptop on her right and our lead man curled up, resting his head on her chest halfway between her neck and her breast. He seems peaceful, they both seem peaceful, but this isn't sexual. This is friendship, mothering, the She-Wolf rescuing lost Romulus from the wild. The soundtrack plays the same sounds humming out of the laptop. It's some unintelligible selection from some kind of ambient backdrop band like Sigur Rós operatically lulling nightlights and children into passivity. Action.

A shrill voice whispers, "What do you wanna hear? This'll hurt you and only you."

Dark. The stink of mold and oil-slick water oozes down concrete walls. Can't move. The cold death grip of leather straps around my wrists and ankles. A high-backed wooden chair. This is a dungeon or a basement. I see a dark figure moving close to me, there is a swinging light bulb in one corner. Its light catches the rust-metal glint of a claw hammer.

Now it's pain. Blood spurts and I can feel a toenail pop away and fly through the air. The voice is counting down from ten. Crack. Split. Blood and more blood. Nine. Eight. Seven. There's a voice screaming in such whimpering childish agony it couldn't possibly be mine. Dark Figure laughs. Three. Two. One.

Hear the clank of old pliers opening and shutting in his hands. Click. Click. Clank. Voice laughs deeper. I feel a blood-warm rubber-gloved hand gripping my index finger, twisting it into position and the cold metal teeth of his tool tearing the skin out from under my fingernail – a sharp gut-wrenching pain and the feeling of something sliding loose. He counts down from ten a second time. I can feel blood trickling out of me at the ends of my body.

Now the straps are loosed and he's dragging me helpless across the damp mildewed floor. Tosses me like a child onto a splintered wood table. I can hear myself thinking, "This table has no straps." For a minute I am comforted by that. Then his hand is around my wrist and I cry out, "Jesus, Lord!" The bang of a sledgehammer drives a train spike through the back of my hand nailing it flat to the wooden table. This just keeps happening over and over again until my other hand, my feet, my shoulders, elbows, and hips are all nailed flat to this plank of wood. The light glances yellow off of a scalpel and at first I think he's cutting my eyes out. I actually feel relieved when I realize it was only my eyelids.

He laughs, says again, "This will only hurt you. I'm having the time of my life."

I can see him tugging on a chain, the rolling links click around a spool and lower something big and flat and black down level with my body on the table. Then it blinks to life, the static fuzz of a monitor waking up and that blinding white glow as if staring into the sun after a long time in the dark. Feels like leaving a movie theater in broad daylight. Hurts like driving your car out of a long tunnel into a bright afternoon.

Now the monitor starts showing me images. I can see her on her back, tits up, legs spread wide. Long blonde hair and face tightened as if working very hard. There he is on top of her. Changing positions, he's rolling her over and coming in from behind. This is my old apartment. That is my couch. That is my bed. That is my wife. This is the man who ruined it all for me. It just plays on a loop. She screams an orgasm and laughs in glee. He groans, selfish and ugly. She groans, exactly the same. My Destroyer. The woman I swore to love, in sickness and in health, for richer or poorer, till death do we part. And now the blood doesn't even hurt the most. Something inside cracks and bleeds and dies faster than my body. I watch my last light in this world wink into black dust and float out of the narrow basement window, level with the grass, polluting the moonless night.

Then I wake up. Cold sweat. Cold tears. Cold. I put a shaking hand to my eyes and sit there and try to stop these weird shivers convulsing through every muscle in my body. Fuck, it's 5 AM. Sister Black wraps her arms around my head warmly and pulls me close.

"You're having a nightmare," she says, "you're safe here, it's okay."

I fall quickly back to sleep and let my weight fall into her chest.

Cut. That's a wrap for today, boys.

LOST IN AMERICANA: CHAPTER FIVE

MADAME BOHEME AND JUMPIN' JACK FLASH

There's this big purple tent covered in gray stars and road dust. My feet hit the gravel-torn grass and I'm still in the clear. Making for that tent is all I can think to do. Not real sure why, to tell the truth, but I lean in and have a peek through the drape door. Try to pick up the widow fortune teller's predictions through the cloth and the howling wind.

From inside the Hotel California or not, we all know about her, she's famous. Madame Boheme, that's her name, the widow fortune teller I mean.

I see her sitting there across from old Uncle Sam himself all dressed up in his stripe hat and coattails, tapping his boot impatiently. I know it's him too 'cause I seen him coming down the hall once or twice. He likes Rosalita, old Uncle Sam likes that low-cost Mexican sort of worker from what I hear all round.

So what do you know, there he is dressed up in Old Glory and everything. That skeevy old fuck sits listening good too. The Madame shuffles and cuts her deck Vegas style, spreads it in one swoop and makes him choose eight. He draws his crazy eight and she starts flipping, laying them out in rows of two.

She says, "Oh dear, I see you've drawn the Headless Horseman and he's sitting beside the Mickey Mouse card. That's a dangerous pairing."

"What does it mean?" Uncle Sam asks, tugging at his goat beard nervously.

Madame Boheme, with beaded wrists, adjusts a calico turban and moves her Mount Everest breasts around inside her quilted silk robe of many colors with its stars and Zodiacs and monsters. She sits quiet for a minute before saying, "It portends a loss of identity to corporate symbols. Next we have Ronald McDonald with George Washington, The Elephant Headed Ganesh with Saint Christopher, and the Fonz card paired up with the Archangel Michael."

She tsks with three clicks of the tongue and shakes her head. Black pearl earrings clank together like goddamn cannonballs and there's me, glued to the drape of her tent staring in and listening something fierce.

Uncle Sam says, "The Fonz, that's good, right?"

"Oh, no, no, no, the Fonz is never good. The Fonz is an omen of failure. It's a desire for coolness and, I fear, such desire denotes its absence."

What Madame Boheme meant was that if you wanna be cool you can be pretty damn fucking sure you ain't.

She goes on, fussing with her turban and twirling cigarette-stained fingers around on her crystal ball, "The verdict, dear one, is that you are losing your value and you know it. It's what brought you to me today. You feel your identity fading like the Headless Horseman. America has replaced you with Kids' Meals, bad religion and wayward journeys while your coolness goes the way of Armageddon."

"But...oh, Jesus, God!" the old fuck shrieks, "What do I do? What can I do? Help me out here. There's gotta be a way!"

"I fear you may try to get it all back, but it will only result in you losing what little you have left."

Uncle Sam shakes his head, removes his hat to scratch a wetted salt scalp, crams the hat back in its place and exits the gypsy tent disheartened. He bumps me on the way out, knocks me to the ground even, and stares through me with gray canceled eyes of forgotten history and bad break-ups.

I hear her voice from inside the tent, "Time is short, young man. If you truly wish to help her you must go now. Just remember, as you leave with her hand in yours, keep your eyes on the sun the whole way and you will hazard the storm without injury."

Standing up, I peek in through the door and she's there, behind her crystal and glowing in candlelight. She says, "Trust me. I walk the line between both sides of this conflict. Some forces cannot choose allegiances. Like death, nobility, or sacrifice I serve both interests. I know truth in both spectrums, trust me, you must go...now!"

I run blindly into the storm and, despite finding myself at the corner of Dirty Boulevard with Highway Zero supposed to be behind me, I still wind up at the front steps of the Hotel California. Sneaking around back, I find my way back through the stink bog basement, up the wall shaft and out of my own fireplace. Booking it down the hall, the widow fortune teller's voice ringing like dynamite in my ears, I burst into Maggie May's room with barely so much as a knock.

"Maggs!" I shout and stop dead in my tracks.

She's on her back with her ankles crossed around the shoulder blades of this big werewolf of a man. He looks over at me with a grin and a sneer all at once as Maggie May sits up, covering her naked breasts with a heart-shaped pillow.

"Tom, what do you think you're doing? My God!"

"Sorry, Maggs, but we have to talk. Who the fuck is this?"

"Language, Tom," Maggie sighs, "Please, watch the language."

"Sorry, doll face," I fire back, "It ain't like you got a moral leg to stand on with that guy wrapping them around his neck and all. Now who the *fuck* is this asshole?"

She sighs and says, "This is my *job*, remember?"

Maggie turns to the redneck and says, "I'm sorry about him, baby.

"Tom, this is an old...*friend* of mine, Jack Flash. He's a trucker from out east of here somewhere and dropped by to...you know, say hello."

He stands up and sticks out a hand that smells just like Maggie's pussy saying, "Jumpin' Jack Flash's the name, pleased to meetcha. You might be saying I'm the reason Maggs settled in 'round these here parts, if you catch my drift."

I think about her story, the one she told me one night with our heads touching on the same pillow she's hiding behind right now. A man in a truck promised her warmth and freedom, snatched her away and raped her on Highway Zero.

With every grain of gumption and temper I could scrounge from my gut I bite down, look away from his ugly face, and take Maggie May's hand. I say, "Come on, Maggs, you don't have to do this anymore. We're going."

I grab a silk robe and wrap her in it as we head into the hall toward my room.

"I'm sorry, Tom," she says, black mascara webs streaming down her cheeks, "He found me again...after all this time he finally found me and I'm not allowed to say no."

"That doesn't matter anymore, I mean, lucky for both of us I didn't hit him, but God I wanted to, really bad, I mean really bad. Look, look, it's in here."

I show her the hole in the fireplace and go ahead of her to be there if she falls. Maggie climbs in behind me and my heart pounds in my chest fixing to explode like gunpowder. I can't believe it, it's finally happening. We're going to run away together and, on top of everything else, I can see straight up her robe while we climb down.

We hit the basement landing and I carry her so she won't

cut her feet or anything. Once I get that splintery old door open again we push out into the sandstorm and I do just what Madame Boheme told me to do. We keep the sun at our horizon all the way to Pentecost Park. Maggie is strangely silent the whole way. Making muddy tears on her face with quiet sobs, but no words. Not even a complaint about the weather.

Then I see it, Maggie's hand in mine and the sun cresting behind her weird flags and banners. It's the widow fortune teller's tent. The sand suddenly stops on a fucking dime and we're alone for a minute in the hush of a dead storm.

"Look, Maggie May, I did it. I mean, we're free."

Maggie smiles weakly, even a little strangely. She takes her hand from mine and trails off a few steps saying vacantly, "Yeah, you did it, all right. You said you would and you did. And I knew, Tom Sawyer, if anyone could do it then you could. You're such a clever boy."

My heart almost bursts when I hear her say that.

Then she says, "But…"

"But?"

"I'm afraid I haven't been entirely honest with you. In fact, I've lied. I'm sorry, Tom."

Like the wolf from that fucking red riding hood story, Jack Flash steps out from behind a tree, grinning with his stubble chin and bushy lamb chops. He grunts, "Hiya, bubba, thanks for the help. We really couldn't have done it without ya."

I can feel the first acid sprigs of tears sprouting on my eyelids but can't find any words. Nothing makes sense, nothing makes any sense and then she says it.

She says, "I've been in love with him since I was a little girl. I lied to you when I said he only just found me. I've seen him hundreds of times, but we've kept it a secret from you because…well, because we needed you to get me outta here. You're clever Tom Sawyer, the only one who could do it. I'm sorry, Tom, but I just…I did my job because you had something I wanted. Meantime, me and Jack Flash was always whispering our plans about what we'll do when I'm free."

Something snaps like a frozen twig and I just wail, "*No! We, we*...I mean, we always whispered those plans. We did!"

A bomb detonates in my brain and I charge him, shaking my fists as I run. Despite the fact that he's twice my size, I charge him and the last thing I see before the lights go out is his ugly grin and his hard knuckles coming down between my eyes.

Field Notes from Bastard Land

6: Charlie Outlaw, Yellow House, and Old Beginnings

This scene is called *Leaving Town and the Perfect Drive.*

Sister Black and the Head are gone when I wake up. A note says they had to go to work and they didn't want to wake me. Jump shot. Watching TV. Jump. Eating a salad. Jump shot. A quarter after 5 PM now and Charlie Outlaw is at the door. He just says, "Well, are you ready for the Main Event?"

And I have to ask him if we are getting philosophical.

He says, "Hell yeah, man. Philosophical, chronological, etymological, grammatical, spiritual, but the one thing we are really getting is the hell out of Dodge and up the road a ways."

Jump shot. Here I am following Charlie to the car wearing a tattered pair of Converse All-Stars in which I have traveled everywhere I've gone for the past four years. I'm dressed in the same suit I wore the day I proposed to my wife. This makes me a walking irony, shitty shoes meets fancy ensemble jacket, shirt and pants. Jump shot. Inside the car, doors slam and I say, "Charlie, how the hell did you get here, man? I figured I'd be picking you up somewhere or something."

As I turn the key and crank Bonnie's engine, Charlie replies, "Yeah, man, I surprised you, I just flew over here on cigarette smoke, bad karma and a lot of concentration."

"How much concentration?" I ask with a sideways grin, "There's a limit to how much concentration you can have before they make you walk the line and sleep it off."

"Ah, I see what you did there, nice. No, I've only had a few beers today, I'm not too concentrated."

Jump shot. A traffic light flicks to green. Jump. Flashing blinkers merge us onto the highway. Jump. Driving. A long sigh escapes my lips without my permission.

Charlie asks, "How you holdin' up, man?"

"Just crank up the Dylan loud enough to drown my thoughts."

A familiar voice echoes in the speakers, but Charlie can't hear it over the music. "No, make it louder. Louder. Break my ear drums if you have to. Louder still."

He can't hear it, but the voice says, "This just in, Jack Bluff dies at 20 from scattered heart beat, friends and mourners live on unaware."

I tell him I need a good diversion.

"No problem, you'll get it," Charlie replies, "Just remember, we all know how to cure ourselves, it's just a matter of wanting to… when you're ready to let go."

Heading out in time with the music brings us almost immediately to a railroad crossing entirely blocked for miles in any direction by a train at a dead stop. We discuss the pros and cons of either waiting or looking for a way to cross. Finally I say, "Fuck it, we're doing it. Sure beats waiting around here to die."

Turning Bonnie down the first available side street, we ride parallel to the track for about three miles seeing cars upon cars waiting like churchgoers for the hand of God. I scream out the window, "Sit all you want, you bastards, it ain't happening."

"Time for some new tunes," Charlie says. And it is Beethoven's *Ninth Symphony. Ode to Joy.* He tells me, "This is pretty much one of my favorite songs of all time. I'd give basically anything to write a song like this. It has four peaks in it all leading up to one big climax."

"Four peaks," I say, "and a big climax. Just like good sex. The girl gets her big peaks leading up to my big explosion. Beethoven's *Ode to Joy* equals man and woman. To us this masterpiece is multiple orgasms and sperm magic. Ode to fucking joy."

And right then, at that exact moment, another high peak. We see the train start moving and we make our way across ahead of the line. Our drive to a new town has finally begun. Crossing the tracks fills me with a strange excitement and, for some reason, I just start talking, rambling, pouring out every thought as fast as I can and I really get going when Charlie asks me why I buzzed all my hair off.

I say, "Jesus Christ, man, don't you ever feel like we have all lost something? Something big. I guess if you really want to know, that might have been what shaving my head was all about. Taking something you worked so hard on and destroying it. But I look around at the way the pendulum swings in this world and I know I'm onto something. Generation after generation struggles to find its place in the world. The hippies had the Flower Power Movement. Peace and love. When that didn't work the children of the eighties swung the other way shouting, 'Fuck the establishment.' Those of us watching the youth movements of the nineties saw confusion. This may have been the first generation to have nothing of its own. No clothes, music, or cars with any defining character, just a mass voice clamoring to bring back the intensity of the sixties with little girls wearing bell bottoms again and bright yellow smiling faces. Punk skaters still chanting their anti-establishment mantra like the past decade still had a voice. We've all lost something. Those alive and aware in the seventies and eighties watched it disappear. I was born with it gone. All of us were."

Charlie Outlaw muses, so subtly I can barely hear him over the music. He says, "Yeah, today it is Generation X and their lost children, Generation Y. Generation Why?" Charlie lights a cigarette and continues, his voice raising with the confidence of fresh smoke, "Yeah, I feel you, man. All the hippies thought they were winning. My generation wears the same clothes, drives modernizations on the same old cars, and listens to cover songs and greatest hits albums of the same bands. But. None of us believe. We have no great cause. We all know we are losing. Every day we are losing more and more. The Vietnam kids can keep trying to understand where they lost it, but my lonesome angels will go on trying to cope with how there is no possibility of ever winning it back. Ever. We are all losing."

"Fighting the bad fight," I add, "A fight that hits below the belt and stacks the bets."

Then we get really quiet and just start listening to *Blood on the Tracks* commanding the speakers. Jump shot. Sunset. Jump. Street reflectors paint dash marks on the driver's side window. Jump. A possum's eyes glow green in the road kill flash of our headlights. Jump ahead.

Driving a long bridge over Lake Dallas, Charlie points and says, "That's pretty."

And there was the lake, lit up silver and gold in the axis wars out on the horizon – the moon's struggle to gain dominion over the sunlight. There are the thick oil-slick black clouds shaped like mountains over the Eastern Plain with the last trickle of orange light dying behind them. The silver lake sprouts its trees and water shrubs black and long out of its skin and it lives somewhere between twilight and pure shadow. And Charlie is right. It's goddamn beautiful.

Cut to exterior. This should just be called *The Yellow Housers*. Establishing shot. Night. The house is right across the street from the college campus. Staring down the throat of the art building. The porch is broad but covered in patio furniture, empty or broken bottles, cigarette butts, and all flavors of the lifestyle. Painted bright banana sex yellow, the place looks just as wild as the guys I know living inside. The doors are bright red and the yard is constantly decorated in the debris of party night aftermath. Inside were all varieties of lonesome angels at diverse levels of debauchery and bottom feeding – a complete smorgasbord of smokers, shooters, snorters, and intense drinkers.

The soundtrack should play something dutifully representing the grit of the scene and the awkward segregation of social classes at parties and gatherings and one's tendency to rely on friends or, at least, on those who are similar to you.

Somewhere around 7:30 PM our lead man hits town. Loaded up on gas station coffee and good tunes Charlie Outlaw, the leading man, and Bonnie pull up to the house that would be home for an undetermined amount of time. The door creaks open and a brief hush falls over the room.

Establishing shot. Interior. The house has a freshly tobacco-tarred plank wood floor like a pirate ship. Floors, corners and tabletops are heavily decorated with post-party moltings. Bottles. Cans. Papers. A recycler's paradise. Charlie has a band that sets up on a carpet mat in the corner. Not center stage, it's more like background, more like a corner lamp or the incense burner above the television. The band plays hidden behind the couches where anyone who wants to sit is looking away, staring into the television rather than into the eyes of the singer. This is the laziness of the modern rock scene. The true personification of how far we have fallen. Every video game system to hit stores since the mid-eighties gathers dust on shelves around the television like old vultures in a tree.

Fade in lights. Cue music. Action.

Bursting through the door I see Brother Red and fall on him in an ancient hug screaming, "What's up, bitch?"

Red screams, "Shaved head! You son of a bitch."

The strangers in this room are clearly pleased and a little afraid.

Charlie says, "This is Jack Bluff, an old friend of ours. He's going to be staying with us for a while."

Around the room are all of these faces looking back at me. Think about church style theatrics with a man at the front and all eyes on him. I see a young thin face eerily resembling Adam Brody's with long curly hair falling all around the eyes and ears. A couple of faces that look very much alike, one is older than the other, but both have about a week's worth of stubble on their faces and long dark hair cut in the spirit of Beatle-Mania and the mid-sixties we all still dream about. All of the faces greet me and Charlie says, "This is Dennis Orbell," pointing to the thin guy with funny hair who stands wearing a Beach Boys tee shirt and a green striped jacket.

Next is Jon. The younger of the two look-alike faces shakes my hand and lights up a Skydancer. The other one is Beau, the older of the two brothers, stronger, more cynical and yet just as kind as his younger brother.

While we're at it, let the record show that Brother Red and Charlie were both high school buddies of mine. We go way back to before the days got dark and weird like they are today and now we are slipping down that slope as well. And we are doing it together.

Brother Red looks like that classic archetype of an Irish pub bum gone trucker in the Great American South. Snakeskin boots and belt buckles, pearl snaps and tattoos, but red in the face, the hair, and the big man beard, that was my Brother Red endeavoring to reap his rewards in the Church of Debauchery. Imagine that standup comedian Zack Galifianakis only with redder hair and you get a clear picture in mind.

Then there's Charlie Outlaw, skinnier every time you see him and following in the cocaine blues footsteps of Bob Dylan and the reefer binge fallout of our late great everyone. Black boots, black suit, black suspenders and the white shirt – he's some kind of southern mortician, a cowboy, a poet. He looks like a young Woody

Guthrie dressed in what was once his finest before his wine binge midnights, before the vomit stain on his black jacket.

These were the dregs, those perfect victimized machinations turned out by the big engine pumping its guarantees and failing miserably on a few of us at a calculable percentage of the time. We were the lonesome angels, the bastard children of that failed promise they have fed us all our lives. In the Yellow House everyone understands that our father, the American Dream, left us at birth so we left the dream. We come together to acknowledge that the pursuit of middle-class white picket fence Suburbia was not necessarily what our forefathers meant by the pursuit of happiness.

This was the old gang back together, plus or minus a few. Now a wild crowd breaks in through the front door, as per the norm at the Yellow House. It's time for more introductions. One is a long-haired self-proclaimed gypsy named Jiggs. Bursting through the door, spilling luggage across the floor he shouts, "Just got in from New Hampshire, bitches...the hell is this?"

And I shake his hand and give my name.

The next phase is a gang of people too numerous to keep track of, the only face in the group that tries to notice me calls himself El Paso Slim. A wild-eyed Mexican intellectual that would sooner tell you how much he hates you than to try to sugarcoat any sort of social situation for any man of any social class, race, or creed. The sort of creature you have to admire – still, if you didn't it would make no difference to El Paso Slim. He says, "That's just what they call me," grabbing hold of his beer gut he adds, "Can't imagine why."

These are the main faces, the main souls – The Yellow Housers. And right now, this moment, I know something great is about to begin. My life is starting to change. In this moment the demons are not quite as noisy. For the first time in over a week I am really laughing.

For a little while it's just us sitting on those couches in that room, dimly lit through the cigarette smoke and dirty overhead light fixture. We're shooting the bull like old friends despite the fact that most of us have only just met. It is a perfect moment in time, a reminder of the potentially uplifting fiber of the human soul – strangers becoming friends instantly. It's like love at first sight.

Charlie goes on a liquor run and gets back with the biggest bottle of Chianti you can imagine. Carlo Rossi, the cheap stuff. Now this might be an important time to reiterate that up to this point I had lived my life as straight edge and pure as I could. But. In light of recent events I simply couldn't manage to give a damn anymore and say, "Give me some of that shit."

The room blows up with laughter, joy and support. These are civilized hyenas reverting back to their primal state. A choir of laughers and trippers and screamers filling the organ pipelines with their humor. Good times. The Hyena Ghetto Trip chorus line. Laughing and spitting in their corners. Glory. Friendship. And, of course, alcohol. My first real drink.

Charlie pours this thick purple-brown crap into a glass and I take a sip. The first taste is too strong to even have a flavor. The next one tastes just like mud. And I have spent plenty of time face down in the mud. I know what that shit tastes like. Some are laughing, goddamn hyenas, and Charlie slaps me on my back and says, "Fuck yeah, that shit'll get right on top of ya, Brahmin."

After that I am no longer the center of attention, and for that I'm glad.

Cut. *We should move into a music montage now to show the passage of time. The soundtrack will play "I Feel Just Like a Child" by Devendra Banhart. Camera shows all of the guys laughing with plastic cups full of cheap wine in their hands. Cigarettes glow orange in their fingertips. Jump shot. Brother Red leaps onto El Paso Slim's shoulders. Jump. Dennis Orbell stands in the center of the room, all eyes on him, delivering some monologue like a standup comedian. Jump. Jiggs pours beer from a bottle into Red's wide-open mouth. Jump. People walk back and forth, pass the Carlo Rossi or exchange seats on the sofas.*

LOST IN AMERICANA: CHAPTER SIX
LEROY BROWN, MISS MOLLY AND SAND KITES

Snapping out of it is enough to knock me right back into Wonderland. I'm getting tossed around by some kind of fucking gorilla arms, dragged through the dirt and the whole shebang. I can see a few laughing biker chicks in rhinestone leather jackets and fucking studded chaps. They're all wearing the same logo, Fat Bottom Girls, and they keep cackling like a clucking coven of old biddy hens.

Leroy Brown has me in a head lock and says, "Boy, did you really think you'd pull one over on old Leroy? I ain't that easy to fool. You're going back."

One particularly oversized Fat Bottom Girl with blonde hair and black streaks grabs me by the knees and helps Leroy carry me back to the hotel like an old timey politician run out of town on a rail. They dump me in the lobby, right at the feet of Sam Spade, and he stands there rolling a cigarette cool as ever.

"Damn, kid," he says, "don't you know that when you're on the run the first thing you gotta do is beat it right outta town?"

My mouth tastes metallic like the first string trails of blood as I look up at him from the floor. I tell him I know that now and Leroy laughs all greedy and bloated and mean. Like some morbid adoptive father, Leroy sends me upstairs to my room. Drags me more like and throws me on my gut, again, on the hard wood floor. Slamming the door behind me.

Now she found me. I've seen her around, but her name escapes me. But she's always there making eyes at me for one reason or another. One time I seen her across the lobby, staring past Marilyn Monroe's dress, Sam Spade's fedora, Becky at the front desk and even old Poe losing his groceries in the fake potted plant. Ben Franklin told me I must have a secret admirer and I said... Shit. Fuck. I got side tracked again. That's neither here nor there, is it? I'm not much of a narrator. I gotta focus.

Anyway, she's in my room waiting for me. A lady in Mardi Gras beads, big saucepan sunglasses with pink rims and rosy lenses, and a dead flower done up inside mottled big rat's nest hair. She hikes her plaid muumuu up to her thighs and kneels down beside me.

The lady says, "You're him, aren't you? Of course you are, silly question, you'll come with me now, sugar fry. It's in your best interest, you can bank on that."

She takes me by the hand, pulling me along like a noose and grins wildly over her shoulder at me. I try to tell her that Leroy sent me up here for a reason, but she don't seem too worried about that. Her eyes seem half opened, stoned or dead, not too sure, but her hand feels cold and puffy in mine.

The Plaid Chick says, "Now keep up with me, y'hear? There's madness on every corner and these folks'll laugh you right into their beds."

Dragging behind her like a fishing lure, I struggle in her grip while she leads me down my hall and there's Rosalita standing stark naked in her doorway puffing on a jay like there ain't no tomorrow. We hit the stairs. Second-floor landing and there's Miss Molly, fat breasts to her bulging thighs, in a big green satin gown screaming her head off at Leroy. Something to do with Maggie May, I reckon. Right before the stairs I see Ben Franklin smiling stupid at the Hardy Boys as they hunt the carpet for Marilyn's lost contact lens or some shit.

Finally, I tear my hand out of Plaid Lady's death grip and say, "What do you take me for, ya old broad? You like leading young kids down into your sex cave for a fuck or what? Screw this, I'm splitting."

She just smiles and says, "C'mon, kid, is that what you think this is? I'm just like the rest of you, one of those regular weird folk and I've got something you need to see. Ya dig? This is one of those rare dreams, the chance to make a difference rather than picking pockets and slipping roofies or whatever it is you been doing. You gotta get while you can, but if you're not interested then go ahead and rock on out."

I sigh, figuring it's better than pouting in my room and making plans to bust out again once she's off my tail. We hit the lobby floor and there's Becky with her Sunday dress and her headset. Blowing a pink gum bubble that pops as she buzzes a door, Becky says, "They're all waiting for you, Janis, you can go ahead in."

Inside there's that same long table and a lot of smoke. Some chairs are empty, but there's Ernest Hemingway, black rusty hole in his head and his eyes looking sad and gray as Uncle Sam's. Next to him there's Jim, Kurt Cobain, Jimi Hendrix and Hunter S. Thompson – same as before. And on the far left is John, that Jesus looking fucker with long hair and a beard in a sharp white suit, he has his oozing red circles showing through on his chest. I can see them straight and clear on his clean pressed white shirt like an unprepared angel at the bad time of her month.

They all nod politely but keep it mum until Janis, the broad with the dead flower, sits me down in this splintery, shitty little porch looking chair.

She sits down with the others and says with a smile, "Tom,

we've brought you here because we all know you're a boy that knows how to get places that shouldn't be gotten to."

"Yeah, so?" I shrugged, "What's yer fuckin' point? I got a lot to do and you're wastin' my time."

Hendrix grunts out something like, "Oh, he's a scrappy one, ain't he? That's cool, I can dig, we're gonna have fun with this cat."

I lean back real far in my chair and cross my legs at the knees to try to look suave, then I just say, "Whatever, D'Artagnan, you don't scare me. You or your frilly pirate shirts. I mean, you got this zombie circus and an okay hideout, but that don't mean I gotta be impressed."

Hemingway says, "It 'doesn't,' lad, you should have said 'doesn't.' It's about number agreement, the plural versus the singular...oh, never mind, what's the use? Kids these days... can't even talk proper English."

I lean forward with a grin and ask, "Don't you mean, 'speak,' we can't even 'speak' proper English?"

Janis slaps her thighs and says, "Well, hot damn, he got ya, Ernest. I think I'm gonna like this kid."

"Whatever," I grunt, falling against the back of my chair, "let's cut to the chase, doll face, what's really on your mind?"

She cringes a little when I call her doll face, but clearly chooses to ignore it. Adjusting her flower delicately above her ear, dozens of wrist bangles, armlets and bracelets slide south toward her elbow before she finally replies, "We need you to get us out of here. Our work is too important to keep doing from the confines of this hotel."

"Is that all, huh? Well, Jim here says getting out is easy, whaddaya need me for?"

Jim speaks up, cool and quiet as ever, "Kid, I told you it's easy to get out of the hotel, but how did you ever manage that big storm? Me and the gang, we've braved a lot of storms, but that one's held us down for ages."

I shrug, "C'mon, guys, how could I keep my reputation as clever

Tom Sawyer if I went around doling out trade secrets? What's this really about?"

Ernest says, "Tom, leaving The California is a luxury, what we really need you to do is find us a way over. Perhaps you heard, the barriers are broken between Americana and Otherworld, but there is one portal..."

"One very important portal," adds Mr. Swiss Cheese, seeping angst and cigarette smoke through his bullet holes.

Ernest sighs and continues, "Right, there is one very important portal that our operatives can't seem to crack."

"That right?" I ask, "And why should that be so important?"

Hunter jumps to his feet, "You know, for being clever you ask a lot of fucking questions. Do you hear me? Focus, now, between our world and Otherworld there has always been a barrier, connecting and separating us simultaneously. In recent years it cracked and, over time, it's growing haphazard and out of control like Republican foreign policy or the goddamn Nazi propaganda of the mainstream media. Got it? This one portal, this vortex, is the source. We need to get at the source or so help me both our worlds will eat each other alive!"

"So what?" I shrug, "You asking me to save the world, guys? I thought you were just the spirits of rock and roll or some shit. I thought you were the source of music, not some kind of espionage underground elite."

Jimi leans forward, "We ain't the source of nothing, kid. We're just colors in the same axis wave as the rest of these cats. Real music has always come from the slaves. Everything we call rock and roll today is just what Elvis and his cronies took from the slave days and added some of their sparkle to."

"What?" Thompson rails, "No, you dimwitted, myopic flower pod! Real music, real poetry, has always come from oppression. It's just by simple association that the slaves made so much of it because they had oppression in spades."

"Come on, guys," John chimes in, "Poetry can't be limited to one single emotion. Poetry comes from love and beauty, from the big stuff that transcends time, space, race or religion. The slaves or the poor, the downtrodden or the outcast, they've all made art, but it also comes from farmers or fishermen. Not out of oppression, but out of love for freedom, God, nature, women or anything else."

"Well, the blues was still created by the slaves," Jimi mutters.

"Oh yeah, I agree with that," John nods, "but you didn't say blues, did ya? You said music. That's a pretty big term, man."

"Admittedly, that is a bit broad, Jimi," Cobain adds awkwardly.

"Will you three cut it out?" says Hemingway, "That's all it ever is with you – music, art, origins, right and wrong. Life is simple – the touch of a woman, the taste of a good cognac and the smell of the wind in your face. Everything else is just overcrowding. You all search so hard for the deeper meaning or the shadows behind it all and wind up missing out on the innate poetry of the simple animal pleasures."

"So is that it then?" Janis rails, "We're just beasts in fine clothing? Animals with ambition? There's gotta be more than that, man, or else what the hell are we doing? I don't care what you say, we're all different, I ain't never seen no animal truly making love."

A long pause boils up and Jim Morrison blurts out, "Well, I still say art comes from the outcasts, you guys can talk all you want. But the brooding corner dwellers, the leftovers that never fit, it all comes from them – never any majority."

The storm gets brewing again and I figure now's my chance. These clowns got nothing to offer me. I tiptoe for the door as a few of the ghosts groan and throw up their hands. Janis says, "Jim's right, art, no matter what form, comes from the weird. And thank God, I've always been weird. Just one of those regular old weird ones."

Old Kurt Cobain leans forward, clearing his throat with a cigarette, "I guess I gotta get my two cents' worth. I feel Ernest is onto something."

Hunter blasts, "You would! Near as I can tell you've been up his ass since you got here, you floppy-haired street thug greaser!"

But Cobain won't have it. He fires back, "You're just jealous that I've had longer with him than you have since he's always been some kind of a hero for you, your Caesar, your literary Zeus...you even set up your old house like some kind of a shrine to him, for God's sake. So don't go takin' your disappointment out on me, you old gruff bastard."

"Bastard!" Thompson wails, "That's it! I've had it with all of you! The floor is closed for discussion. No more questions."

I creak the door open quietly and see Leroy there waiting for me, I figure I'll wait him out and none of the freaks at the table seem to notice I'm gone.

Jim says, "You know, it's like wondering why some people do drugs and some don't."

"Oh, Jesus Christ Almighty," Hunter grunts again, "Do I have to clear the press floor? Do I have to ring in security? No more comments from the peanut gallery, you fucking swine!"

Ignoring everyone, Jim smokes and muses, "I'm serious...some people dive in as soon as life turns the knob on them. Then others, they never even consider it. When you take into account how many artists were also on their own drug of choice it's gotta make you wonder. Maybe it's all one thing, you know? I mean...Are we all on drugs because we have special minds, artistic minds, and are in need of constant stimulation? Or are we on drugs because we feel a great something missing from life and we fill it in with everything we can – whether it's LSD or poetry?"

Janis chimes in, "Jim's got a point, man. I mean, maybe those are even one and the same. You know? We feel something's missing and that's what makes our minds special?"

Cobain shrugs, "Is that all art is?"

Jimi just laughs, "Naw, man, art's way bigger than that. Art's earth, it's spirit, it's a religion all its own. We could pack out church houses with cats waiting to swing in praise of music, electric guitars

– no gods, just dig the sound. An electric church, give it time, it'll be the new American national religion."

Hunter shrieks, leaping to his feet and pacing the conference room, "If we don't get on point I'll have you all in contempt!"

"Jimi," Cobain says, leaning across the table to look him right in the eye, "I hate to break it to you, pal, but the church is already electric. They fill out every Sunday with PA equipment, flashing sing-along projector screens, light shows and video cameras. Only it's not the utopia you envisioned, bro, they're not there to worship sound or dig vibrations or whatever the hell you call it. They're there in the name of Christ. As always. Yet another rite, outlook or demi-god absorbed into the House of the Lord."

Hemingway shrugs, "You give him too much credit, kid. He just gets on this Electric Church kick out of ego. He likes the thought of cathedrals blasting his bizarre Star Spangled Banner. If he'd had a few more years he probably would have gone off and taken Amazing Grace electric too."

"Actually, I did, it just wasn't widely released. I blame the Vatican."

"Me too," says John.

"Me too," Jim adds, sounding bored.

"So we're agreed then," Hunter grumbles, moving back to his chair, "We're all agreed that, when in doubt, blame the Vatican! Motion carried? Any opposed? Sold! Mark this date in time, on this hour in history we held assembly to blame God's church for the world's decadence and decided once and for all that music is bigger than black slaves and Elvis."

Leroy moves away from the staircase, probably to go flirt with Becky or some shit, and I slip out the door and make a break for it. The last thing I hear is Hunter saying, "Hey, where's the kid? Oh, fuck, you guys lost him!"

I'm taking the stairs three at a time. Launching like a shot out of hell for the fourth floor. I hit the third-floor landing, almost there and then there's them deflated Buddha tits of Miss Molly, full in my face. Like a rubber wall I bounce off and land flat on my ass.

"You and I need to have a word," she grimaces like the old witch out of some early German folk tale.

She tries dragging me into her office, all pink frills and lace and whips and chains, but I squirm free and almost make it to the stairs. Miss Molly catches me by the belt and starts reeling me in and I gotta wonder how many times a guy can get snared by old broads in one day.

"You wanna tell me what you did with little Maggie May?" she asks, "That girl's my top seller and I can't help thinking you got something to do with her disappearance. I've seen the way you two look at each other."

"What? That bitch," I groan, trying to break free, "She, she turned me down cold when I told her I loved her. Traded up for... traded up for some trucker with a horse cock named Jack Flash is what I gather. You want her, you...you find him."

All that nastiness and it ain't far from the truth. She turns me loose, steps into her room and picks up the receiver of an antique rotary phone. I make for the top floor, breeze by a polite greeting from Benjamin Franklin and scramble up into the attic. The ladder to the roof is still down when I get there and the trap door is open, begging me to come on up.

I get to the roof, not even sure if it's really going to work, but it's my only hope now. I whip out my pen knife and start cutting away at all the cords that kept the damn thing attached to the chimney. The wind rips at its cloth like a sailboat in a squall.

I hear Ben's voice hollerin' at me, shouting paranoid, and he knows what I'm up to. I find the shoulder harnesses and get it figured out pretty quick. Fastened in just in time to see old Ben stick his bald head out into the roaring sands and shout for me to stop. I cut the last cord and the kite pulls away from the chimney like a baby leaving its momma. My feet barely touch the roof as I run full stride for the edge and take one last shrieking leap of faith.

Behind me I hear Ben screaming his own hallelujah, saying, "Son of a bitch, it flies!"

I try tucking my feet in like a bird and do my best to steer in this weird storm, but there's not much you can do flying a sand hurricane but go with it and hope for the best. Wind currents carry me over Pentecost Park and downtown. The sand starts to thin out and I'm still coasting along a steady glide.

Down beneath me I can spy all the weirdness of Subterranea on my way out toward Highway Zero. The wind carries me along over the intersection of Thunder Road and Dirty Boulevard. And there's Pleasure Street. Down there I can see sagging brick bordellos and the marble steps of the Library of Lies. I see the bricklayers assembling walls for war and immediately disassembling them just to start all over again. There's the gypsy punk circus juggling flaming arrows and Molotov cocktails in a semi-circle around the Snake-Spined Contortionist. Pleasure Street is full of the moans of balcony window sex and the laughter of fucking Pinocchio mules cranking up their mutation with meth, smack, speed, coke, Zippos, chocolate strawberries, Purple Kush, Peter Pan and fairy dust. A naked Arabian climbs a rope tied to the air and spits antique buttons at the Pinstripe Suited Tightrope Walker suspended midline between the movie theater and an abandoned apartment complex.

There's a hill at the center of Pentecost Park. Footpaths scatter around and meet in the middle like rickety spokes on a wagon wheel. Motormouth Mitch, the Groundskeeper, tells stories while planting dead flowers along walkways and wastes time watering gravel. At odd intervals throughout the week you'll hear tell of Fountain Pen Drake, the Flower Thief, who'd come by night and snatch away the flower tops. He thinks himself an artful cat burglar, but it's really just that he's part of everyone's rhythms and nobody really cares about Motormouth Mitch or his dried-up landscaping.

And there at the top of the hill is the Irony-Go-Round, the People Carousel. Human figures made out of cracked porcelain and brass bend over on all fours, and they have twisted copper poles right through the middle of 'em. Clydesdales and Shetlands and Mustang studs come from all around to sit side-saddle on the backs of weak air-brushed statues of men in fine suits groaning into cellular phones, or cowboys in tassel coats with shiny revolvers, or riot police grimacing angrily behind stony sun shades to the sounds of carousel waltzes, the wheel spinning, and the fact that the music never ends, but the ride never takes you anywhere. Then there's the audience, gathered around, taking all the wobbly, scampering footpaths to watch the Irony-Go-Round, to think about role reversals and country wisdom, and share brutish epiphanies.

I see it all from up here. I see it as the glide carries me on out of town to the booze hound industrial dump side of Subterranea, long past the wrong side of the tracks and into the truckstop centrifuge of the desert. My feet drag through some trash cans before I finally come crashing and a-tumbling to a brutal stop and for the second time today my head smacks something hard and the lights blink out.

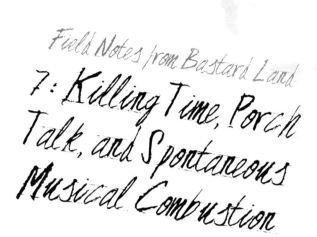

7: Killing Time, Porch Talk, and Spontaneous Musical Combustion

"I didn't mean anything racist by it," says El Paso Slim, looking around at everyone in the living room, crowded together on couches and recliners.

He says, "I mean I was just a kid. But there I was in the middle of Disneyland and I ask the souvenir shop guy if he has any of those Jewish Mickey Mouse hats."

Everyone laughs and Slim says, "Picture a Jewish wedding. The rabbi's yarmulke firmly in place and two black round ears sprout from above his locks. Imagine an Orthodox funeral, every ceremony performed by some God-used hybrid between man and mouse and faith – Jewish Mickey Mouse hats. The souvenir shop guy replied, 'Yes, we have those. Tell me your name and I can sew it on there for you.'"

Call me Judas, Judas the child of God's long dead church. Judas the Mouse Boy.

Everyone laughs. The Hyena Glee Club.

Brother Red starts swearing at his cell phone saying, "Dammit,

Goddammit, how do they expect me to be a good and useful citizen in this weird America if my cell phone doesn't even work?"

Beau asks, "What's it doing?"

"I'll try to send a text message," he says, "and it keeps fucking up my letters. It just made me write 'Dino.' Do you want to get some Dino? Now it's saying 'Failure.' I guess failure to send or some shit. What the fuck? You're a failure, piece of shit, don't you call me a failure, I'll fucking end you. It didn't send and now it's just saying 'General Problems.'"

"Ain't that the truth," Jon says.

"Red," I chime in, "do you know what that means? That means that in this moment you have a little bit of every possible problem. 'General problems.'"

He laughs and says, "Charlie, on the other hand, with his madness and weird drug binges, has only 'alternative problems.'"

Laughter Chorus and Charlie says, "Fuck you guys," from the other room.

All this time the television is running, but Beau is the only one watching it. George W. Bush interrupts the program to try to convince America we are still in good hands. Right in the middle of *Family Guy*, what should have been a good laugh, and we have to listen to that same old song and dance. Beau says, "Goddammit. That guy just looks like a tool all the time. I look at him and he's like, 'I'm a tool, I'm a tool, tool, tool, tool.' Give me back my fucking television."

El Paso Slim asks, "What kind of tool? A power tool?"

You corny bastard.

"No, a sex tool. A butt fuck gay porn tool. The guy's face is a fag dildo."

Slim laughs and says, "What a goddamn tool."

"Speaking of sex tools," Beau begins, "Tell me what you guys think of this. There is this girl named Tara up at the mall. A real platinum blonde hard-on. The girl is hot in that perfect sort of way – Greek goddess hot, Michelangelo sculpture perfection, truly hot. This tight little nymph will take you for a ride of pure golden streets out of body heaven orgasm. We call her Tara Firma. Trouble is, when you are with her you have to spend the whole time trying *not* to get your rocks off. If you don't try you can fall victim to premature ejaculation."

Jon laughs saying, "Oh yeah, Tara Firma. She was our earliest lesson in how you really can have too much beauty, that you *can* have too much of a good thing. Because with Tara Firma you had to work at not enjoying it just to make it last."

Dennis says, "Yeah, guys, I guess that means that for us the best hope is the middle ground, that all too explored gray area. Find someone hot, but not perfect, you'll enjoy it more. Keep your expectations low and you will be constantly pleased."

Now Charlie starts plucking his Takamine acoustic guitar and singing in his best Hank Williams voice, "Ya can take her home and bed her down but don't expect to git 'er in a weddin' gown. Ya can fuck 'er nice an' maybe twice, but ya ain't gonna keep 'er long enough fer weddin' rice..."

And then it happens, completely without words. That is how the best things happen. The best laughs, the best sex, the best kisses, the best sadness. All of it happens with a look and then an action. Some of the guys were behind their instruments before we even knew why and then the music was going, just going. Charlie Outlaw's band was suddenly in full force and the rest of us sat in the backdraft of a flash fire. Like people spontaneously bursting into flames and just leaving behind a crooked bed frame and a pair of crooked legs, we all sat there and watched Outlaw's music explode without warning.

"Let's keep it ringing," Charlie says, "Okay, let's try that."

And the song goes on in the same way it is in hundreds, thousands of garages and basements across America. Singer shouts chords between lyrics as they go. The way old Negro churches used to sing hymns by "lining" because they only had one song book. The leader shouts a line and everyone follows suit.

Give me that old time religion. And the crowd echoes, "Give me that old time religion." *That old time religion.* That old time religion... it's good enough for me.

It was called lining and now Charlie Outlaw is chanting guitar progressions for one of his band's more established tracks.

Strumming, Charlie sings, *"Oh, this is a series of dreams* – A Flat."

Lining.

He says to Jon the Keyboardist, "You could just play the fucking note. Just hold it out for the measure. Right, A Flat, exactly. Turn that up a bit. Start again on that note." He sings, *"Why's this happening? Why is anything?"*

And the guitar sings its gutter vomit majesty.

Lining. C. D. A Flat.

"Yeah, try not to move in the quiet parts. I know it's boring – you want to dance – and we gotta apply to the teeny boppers, but keep it simple."

He says his solo was dirty. Says the drummer added a little roll, Charlie says, "You were adding something in there, mister. I don't know what yet, but I'll find out."

This is how rockers talk to each other, a whole slang. Dirty. Loose. Roll. The drummer twists the knobs on a dimming lamp saying, "Let's turn this down some, there now that's a little more Rock."

Then the song breaks to life like a Titan. This is how Rock & Roll lives and dies, how it rebirths itself around the corners of every room in America. Charlie shouts, "Rock solo on acoustic" and breaks into a twangy high-pitched lilt.

And to me this is so refreshing. Too many things have become so horribly segmented that even the once true and powerful rebellions have become big business – organized sports, organized religion, organized music, organized art and writing...the industry. Perhaps that is why it felt like such a success for us to be having a Little rock show for once.

That's the universal power of the garage band.

Keyboardist says, "On that bridge before the break what do you want me to do?"

Charlie says, "You don't do anything. I just want to be alone."

Picking up my glass of shitty wine and a pad of paper I decide to go and sit out on the porch. For a minute I am alone and I get these words all written down, hoping to make Jim proud. I try to drink Charlie's mud wine and I actually do get some of it down. Little by little, when no one is looking, I dump little bits of it out on the ground too. I drink a little more and then spill some more. Jump shots. Drink. Pour. Drink. Pour. This is how I handle my first real drink of alcohol until it's gone and no one knows how much I'd pussied out.

This guy approaches me on the porch. Practice is still going on inside. Drum beats starting and breaking, guitars doing the same. This guy – his details are long hair, dressed in black, beard – he walks right for me like he wants to talk.

The stranger says, "How's it going?" and then, weirdly, just passes me by for the big red front door of the Yellow House.

He seems legitimately afraid to go in with the band. At the door he opens it a crack, peers in, closes it, peers in again, and somehow finds the courage. He digs deep and flings the door open wide to enter.

That's the sacrament of Rock & Roll. To us a man with a guitar is a god. These are the new forms of Apollo and Zeus and Aphrodite – put an instrument in their hands and they cease to be human. These are creatures dropping down out of Olympus to grace us with their music. Ye Gods of Rock, pure Michelangelo stone sculpture perfection, and as with any god we must pause at the doorway and ask ourselves, "Is it safe to go in?"

The door creaks closed slowly behind the stranger and light fades to a fine line. I hear the click of the knob and the scene jumps to black. The porch is gone. The door is gone. Denton and everything around me has vanished.

Right now I'm standing in an alleyway. A midget in a monkey costume grabs my hand and leads me into a street buzzing with the noise and movement of a carnival. Ticket takers, trinket peddlers, cotton candy mixers, lights, music, bells, midway games and bumper cars line the sidewalk or speed madly through traffic lights and crosswalks with no attention to color, turn or direction.

A man juggling Chihuahuas winks at me and tosses one behind his back. A woman dressed as Charlie Chaplin wiggles her moustache at me and waddles away. I see a boy dressed in antique fireman gear spraying frothing bubbles out of a hose with nothing attached at the other end. He tells me it's his meanness that makes it foam. There's a rabid dog drinking bourbon on a concrete stoop, watching as his master bows with a plastic bag to curb his shit.

The midget dressed as a monkey tries to pull me along down the road, but I don't want to go. I look around for someone, anyone that can help me. But I'm here all alone. Out of the corner of my eye I feel the faintest awareness of a man dressed in gray, watching me quietly from across the street. When I turn his way he's gone.

"Are you zee Jack Bluff I've heard so much about?" asks an Austrian accent behind me.

I spin around, shocked at the sound of my name, and there's Albert Einstein looking miserly in colorful surroundings. Slightly off balance from the encounter I can only bring myself to nod slowly in response.

Einstein says, "You veal come vith me zen."

Maybe it's because it's Einstein, maybe it's because I feel safer with him than all the other weirdos on this street, but I follow him without so much as a grunt. After a few seconds I manage to ask him where I am.

"Zees ist vhere *zey* come from. You are on Pleasure Street, zee last exit before you enter *zeir* territory. Right now, ve're just outside of Subterranea."

"Subterranea? Why does that sound familiar? What is it?"

"I'm afraid I can't tell you zat, Jack, it's not for you to know. But you must stay clear of it. Come on now, come vith me."

He leads me back toward the alleyway, only this time there's a door I didn't notice before. Lopsided on rusted hinges and painted an aging green, the door is barely worth noticing. We go through and inside there's what looks like it ought to be a pawn shop...or it used to be. Only, it's not really like a pawn shop. The shelves are stocked erratically with outdated bifocals, American flags from the colonial era, blacklisted literature, mason jars with severed hands, floating eyes, baby sharks, apples and pickled eggs. Toward the back is a row of muskets and slingshots. I see yo-yos, penny-whistles, rotten candy, old chewing gum, moldy jack-o-lanterns, cigarette cartons, oboes, trumpets, bugles, banjos, sitars, didgeri-doos, accordions, and melodicas. Dust is the color of the walls, merchandise and shelves.

Albert closes the door behind me and I'm alone in the dust and the shelves. I turn a corner and there is a small hanging light bulb illuminating the center of the room. A man drinks a beer behind the counter and taps idly on the keys of an antique cash register, randomly opening and closing the drawer with the chime of a bell. Behind him, I see Lennon, Hemingway, Morrison and Cobain.

Lennon smiles, holds out an arm and guides me over to the group saying, "Jack, this is the place where memories go to die. It's our only stronghold this close to Subterranea. This is the far north wing of the Hotel California."

"Wait a second, wait," I say with a smile, "You're telling me there's actually a Hotel California, like for real."

"Well," Cobain shrugs, "it's real here anyway, as real as we are. This side of the hotel is in a nasty state of disrepair, no one sleeps here so the powers that be let old Jones here set up shop. You'll be safe here for the moment."

Morrison twitches strangely under gray bloat skin, reminding me he's already dead, and says, "We can't be here long."

"Son," says Hemingway, "we need to know why you haven't gone to see Abraham."

"What? Why? I mean, how? I don't know where he is, I don't even know how I'm seeing you."

"It's easy," Kurt Cobain shrugs, "you just have to know where to look. The last Abraham did his job well and is still at it in many respects. Without him I shudder to think where America would be right now. Anyway, he knew where to meet the true Abraham for stage direction. You just have to think like him and you'll get there."

"Well, who?"

"He's been called a lot of things, poet, prophet, troubadour, outlaw, actor, messiah of the American travesty...the one who said, 'People today are still living off the table scraps of the sixties. They are still being passed around – the music and the ideas.'"

It connects like a fuse box in my brain and I say, "'God said to Abraham, kill me a son...where do you want this killing done? Out on Highway 61.'"

Hemingway said, "Janis was right, you are smart. If you go find Highway 61 you'll find Abraham. That will set you off on the right path."

I tell him thanks for the tip and head for the door. As it creaks closed behind me I find myself back on the Yellow House porch. The music is still pumping on the other side of the wall. In a cloud of laughter and smoke, some of the guys wander outside. Dennis and Charlie sit down around the patio table with me. Charlie, almost immediately, gets attached to his cheap Chianti. At this point he's been drinking so fiercely that his whole mouth is stained black.

Dennis shouts, "Dude, you've got some wicked wine lips going. It's like lipstick. It's not even splotchy or anything."

Charlie's reply is, "That's just the way I like it. You look at me and know I am earning my buzz."

He puckers up for a big black sloppy kiss and Dennis shoves him back.

Jiggs is inside with his band now. It's their turn to practice and I can hear him saying, "Let's play the new one, the rock one."

As if he has anything else.

El Paso Slim is on the porch now and Dennis stands beside me and asks me why I am in Denton at this exact moment and not another day sooner or later. On the other side of the door, echoing in the mike, I hear Jiggs say, "You get no feedback this time."

And for just a second, I almost mimic his idea. I almost clam up.

That's when I say, "Fuck it. Do you feel like hearing a sad, depressing story, the likes of which will make you resent women for years to come?"

Dennis Orbell and Slim both slide closer in their chairs and say something about that being the only kind of story they ever want to hear. So I give them the Cliffs Notes: I married a lie. Wife became what she thought I wanted her to be and then she tore down the veil. Affair, divorce and. Well. I told them that she was a strict follower of that rigid Christ-like surface world that says that premarital sex is the root of all evil. It teaches people that good little girls get married first. Yes sir, Lord Jesus. Whatever you say, Boss. Essentially her reasoning for getting married was quick, easy sex without any grief from parents, churches, or Lords.

"Married to Fuck?" Orbell exclaims, "That sucks, man. Holy shit, that fucking sucks. That's about the worst most twisted goddamn thing I've ever heard."

El Paso Slim says, "Man, Jack, I'm sorry, dude."

"Yeah," I say, "so if you see me looking downcast and grim you'll know why."

"Well," Dennis replies, "I'll be sure and give you a shake, tell you to cheer the fuck up because there is no need to let her hurt you anymore."

That was all that had to be said about it, really. What else is there? Dennis asks me if I am a drinking man and then says, "Well, not yet, but we'll see about changing that."

Jump shot. Now here I am getting bombarded by questions. Are you a smoking man? Not yet, but we'll see about changing that. Are you looking for women? We'll get them for you too. All of these faces. All of these questions. And for a second his face changes to a sideshow ticket barker at some mutant circus. I see a straw hat, waxed moustache and candy stripe jacket. I see him hollering for the world to buy his act, he bellows, "Step right up here, don't be shy, what we have here is a true cross section of the American aesthetic, the pulchritude of the sex, drugs, rock and roll era, and you can be one of us if you just buy the ticket? What do you say, young man, want to have a go?"

Jump shot and everything flashes back to reality.

"You see," he says, "you're fresh meat in Denton and that is a good place to be. All of us guys, we're old hat. Used and reused. But you, you're fresh meat, and a damn fine specimen if I do say so myself. Stick around long enough and you'll forget all about *her*."

This is when I say, "You know what, man, it's sad but I think of all the things I could be missing right now it is really just that quick access to sex. I miss her role more than her."

"Yeah, well that's understandable. She is not real, but sex always is."

"I mean, I have had accessible sex for over two years. I've done it literally thousands of times and now my life is bone dry. Sleeping alone is goddamn torture. I feel cold every single night of the week."

Charlie says, "Yeah, man, I wouldn't recommend having casual sex, you know just banging any chick you meet. But it can be a useful refueling to get you to the next real girl, the next real relationship. Know what I mean?"

Yeah, I say, it's like a slight step above masturbation.

Charlie says, "That's true, which begs the question, I only ask because it might affect your demeanor, but...what's your masturbatory schedule like?"

Orbell cuts in, "Pretty much hourly – or quarter-hourly, I don't know, sometimes I lose count. As far as that urban threat about going blind from over-exertion I think I have disproved that myth a long time ago."

Old Slim says, "Masturbatory schedule. That's a great term. Patent that shit, dude."

Refusing to let go of my thought stream, I continue, "Sex is like the floodgate on a dam, once that door opens there's no going back."

"So once again, to reiterate," Charlie says, "that's the advantage to any sort of casual promiscuous sex. It's not important, but it can help you make it to when you can find out what is – it's a little fuel for a few more tortured weeks."

Something about this discussion brings in the fog all over again. I can feel these formless demons swooping down on me on invisible wings. Diving and weighing heavily on me like iron dirge loop chains. I feel my face drop grim and see Charlie lighting up a smoke.

"Goddammit," I grunt, "somebody give me a fuckin' cigarette."

LOST IN AMERICANA: CHAPTER SEVEN

CHOKE AND PUKE, CARMEN AND THE DEVIL, AND THE ROAD TO NOWHERE

I come to in the back alley gutter trash heap of some kind of restaurant. There's half-eaten bread rolls and ketchup-drenched eggs and maple syrup and old coffee grounds all around me. Bags have been ripped open by wild coons or rabid stray dogs or hungry street bums. The smell of decay and yesterday's lunch is in my hair and under my fingernails.

I sit up with the wrenching sting of a twisted ankle and maybe a few bruised ribs. Benjamin Franklin's man-kite is a sad, shriveled heap under my feet. There's not much left but multi-colored cloth drenched in mud and blood and twisted, snapped wood poles all matted down like the flattened grass remains of a deer bed-in.

Dusting myself off as best I can, I find my bowler cap dirty and dented on one side. I punch out the dent, fix the lucky cap back on my head and stroll around the corner with a pounding headache and an unconvincing attempt at looking suave and put together.

Out front the restaurant is an old style chrome-plated trailer–looking hullabaloo of a diner, rusted at its edges, fogged over windows and letters falling off of the neon sign over the door. The general ambience of an airport hangar watering hole or a bigot truckstop radiates out of every detail in the place. It's in the speakers playing juke box tunes, the obscenities of the patrons, the waitress out front on the stoop having a smoke and the sign, waiting to fall, that reads: The Choke and Puke.

I tip my hat at the waitress in her yellow day dress and coffee-stained apron, stroll in through the cowbell chime of the front door and grab myself a seat at the bar. The waitress behind the bar is wearing the same yellow uniform with dirty apron and her hair done up in a sloppy bun like some kind of oversized bagel with cream cheese flopping out at the edges. Her makeup tries to cover over all her years, but instead just highlights them in powdered sugar clusters and strawberry jam mash lip spunk. She smiles sincerely. You can tell she used to be a knockout, but a life of running next to her bad luck kept her in the same job she got at seventeen, and the harshness of trucker advances, suspicious police, bad politics, booze, failed relationships and cigarettes hardened her to a fine crust.

Her name tag says her name is Carmen.

"What'll ya have?" she asks, spouting cliché like it's original.

I get coffee, black, and a slice of key lime pie. It's in front of me and ready to be devoured before I could say Robert E. Lee and that's when I notice the slow pace of the Choke & Puke. Apart from the obvious booth haunters and regulars, this place is functioning at a snail crawl for the time of day. Reckon it's the food, my pie has a roach leg in the crust, but I dig in anyway. Can't waste food, starving kids in Africa and all that shit.

Figure a little bug leg never killed anyone.

Carmen paces the floor behind the counter and shouts occasionally at the Mexican workers in back. Her smile lacks a few key molars in back, giving her front teeth the look of the few lonesome spectators at a not so well attended rock show.

She says, "So, kid, I ain't seen you 'round before. What's your story?"

"Me?" I ask, "I just crashed a human kite behind your store, got dumped by the girl of my dreams for a pedophiliac wolverine truck driver and broke out of house arrest. What's yours?"

Carmen grins awkwardly, not sure whether to believe me I'd wager, and just says, "Well, you know, bout the same, I guess."

"Listen, Carmen," I say, sipping my coffee a little too quickly and burning my tongue to a mesquite cedar chip in my mouth, "Aw, shit, um...what's the best way outta town from here? I'm kinda in a rush."

"That all depends," she replies, leaning on the counter, arms folded, breasts folding over her arms, "Where you heading?"

"Not sure, what do you think?"

"Well, there ain't much south of here 'cept desert, unless you like a nice flat out burn toward Mexico if you're in that sort of rush."

"No, I figure I'd like to see some of Americana, you know, take in the sights."

"In that case," Carmen grins toothless, "you ought to con-sider hitchin' west to Highway One. Take that road up through San Diego, Los Angaleez and Frisco. 'Tween here and there, on Highway Zero there ain't nothing but little podunks, you know, Anywhere, Somewhere, Nowhere and Here."

"Which way to Nowhere?" I ask, "I've been hearing about Nowhere for a long time."

An old drunk-looking mine worker leans over and says, "Well, some are closer to Nowhere than others, but you look to be mighty close."

"Thanks, mister," I reply, "I'll just...um...you know, I'll just take it from Carmen though, if it's all the same to you. I can see by her eyes that she knows the lay of things."

"Thanks, kid," Carmen smiles, "Listen, I got a break in five, why don't I walk you out to the crossroads. We'll share a smoke and you can judge what direction's for you."

I down the last of my coffee, nodding yes into the steam.

Carmen hollers loud into the back diner, "Hey! Ruby! I'm

taking my smoke break, watch the rack and bar and make sure nobody smears the register."

Ruby shouts from the stove smoke, "Fuck you, Carmen!"

And Carmen smiles, taking that for an A-Okay near as I can tell.

We stroll along together, out into the desert dust and asphalt weed trim of the highway. Carmen points toward downtown Subterranea and tells me not to mess with that crowd. She tells me we're walking Highway Zero right now and step up to the corner of some intersection.

Carmen says, "This here's the crossroads between Highway Zero and Levee Street."

On the other side of the street is a four-way sign pointing the way to all different towns and mile markers – Somewhere, Nowhere, Anywhere, Here, Anywhere But Here, Margaritaville, and Bakersfield.

Sitting under that sign is an older looking black hound dog in a fine antique suit and a bowler cap like mine. He's dust-covered and ragged with a graying beard and plucking away on an old guitar. Next to him there's a man with beady, needling eyes, shellacked pomade hair, thick dark eyebrows, sharp features and long finger-nails wearing some kind of mortician's tuxedo and muddy boots.

Carmen waves and practically crosses the street at a run while I hurry to keep up. She says, "This here's Robert Johnson and our mutual pal, the Devil."

I laugh, spurting spit fragments everywhere like a real idiot, and say, "You kidding? That ain't the sort of thing you want to go advertising around, you know?"

The Devil says, "No worries, kid, 'round these parts people don't care who you are."

Carmen says, "C'mon, kid, it's cool, these are some old friends of mine."

Robert Johnson says, "Cool out, little man, me and this guy go way back."

"Way back, huh? You sure you can trust 'im?" I ask.

123

"Nossir, but I'm sure I can't and I can trust that."

"Fair enough," I reply, "Maybe you guys can help me. I'm supposed to be looking for a door, but I didn't have the patience to stick around and figure out what that meant."

Carmen says, "Was it patience, or trust?"

"Trust, I guess, now that you mention it. Everybody I ever met wanted to use me for something. I...I mean, I mean even love turned out that way, you know? I guess I didn't want to end up in somebody else's prison all over again. So I'm... I'm flying solo, lone dog this time, but that don't mean I can't get the job done."

Robert Johnson strums a little and pauses before tossing in his two bits, "Young'n, there be doors everywhere. Is it just any door you lookin' for or one in particular?"

"I reckon it's a very special door. It's supposed to lead to this place called Otherworld or something. I don't know."

Carmen nods, lighting up a smoke, "I've heard of this place, trucker talk's been all abuzz with it the past few years. Talk of people going missing, whole shipments, airplanes, passenger buses – you name it, just up'n disappearing like the...whaddaya call it?"

"Bermuda Triangle," the old Devil finishes for her.

"Yeah, something about Otherworld swallowing us all up a little at a time."

Robert Johnson nods cool and says, "Otherworld, huh? You reckon this ain't the place for you or something, little man?"

"I reckon so."

The Devil looks me over with needles in his eyes, clicking a silver tongue, "I think I can help you with that," he says, "but it'll cost you."

I shake my head, make believe digging in my pockets and fire back, "No, sir, all's I got is a pack o' smokes and anything else just ain't for sale."

"Too bad," replies The Devil, "I know the way and it's a helluva lot closer than you might think."

Carmen says, "Well, kid, all's you can do is try every door till you find the right one."

"Well, shit," I reply, "you're right, gee. I'd better get going, huh?"

"Yessir," says Robert Johnson, "it'll take time, best just head on down and let trouble guide the way."

"If you're looking to go Anywhere But Here, you ought to head north," Carmen tells me with her half-tooth lipstick smile, "Up from Here is where you'll find Anywhere, beyond that is where Nowhere'll be waiting for ya. I think you're right, that's just the place for you."

"Thank ya, ma'am," I say, tipping my hat and lighting a smoke, "I'll bear it in mind. Say, Carmen, before I go... whaddaya say we go downtown for a while? Who knows what we might find?"

"I gotta go to work, the Choke & Puke's liable to burn down without me, Robert's always right here, but my friend can hang with you for a while."

She sticks a hitcher thumb at the Devil and he grins sly.

"That's all right. I'll just keep flying it solo for a while. Thanks for the help and all. Oh, listen, I never paid for breakfast."

"Don't sweat it, kid," Carmen smiles, "nobody ever does."

I tip my bowler cap and go on about my way. Following Highway Zero north leads me out of Subterranea and the vague window dressing memories of The Hotel California, Dirty Boulevard, Madame Boheme, Uncle Sam and especially Maggie May.

A rusty hinge city limits sign says, "Now Leaving Subterranea."

In the distance factory smokestacks painted like candy cane stripes push black clouds out of the desert sand and into the yellow sky. Across the street is a dilapidated dealership selling used wagons, train cars, push carts and cotton gins. There's an old pickup truck packed out in back with glass jars. I stroll up with my smoke for a closer look.

There's a salesman with a black beard in sequin drag, combat boots and a red wig. He's pushing jars of brains floating like pickles in formaldehyde. Passersby stop for a glance at the show and keep moving on.

The Salesman says, "Step right up here, ladies and Gentiles. We got the finest product from Milan, Odessa, San Diego and Anywhere. Just in from San Diego's finest new establishment, The Record Store, we have the cloned brains of all your favorite singers, talkers, debaters and comics. Top o' the line product, folks."

He points a bamboo cane at a human fetus in a large vase and says, "Rarities and oddities alike! This here's God's stillborn son. The one that didn't take before Mary finally got it right. No? I see you're a crowd of finer tastes. Only the exceptionally rare for this lot."

The Salesman picks up a jar with the soggy gray matter and skull cap from the back of someone's head. He shouts, "This is the missing remainder of John F. Kennedy's cranium, said to have disappeared post mortem from the Dallas Morgue. Yours for only $99.95!"

Some young broad, pretty too, with red curl hair and full red lips, says, "Hey, wait a minute!"

She steps to the front of the crowd and stands, firm footed like a protest, "That's not JFK. It's my own sweet dad. You'd better sell it back to me, man, or there's gonna be hell to pay."

The Salesman smiles, stepping slowly away from the crowd, and says, "Well, I'm sorry to say, folks, that you've missed your window. It's closing time and all sales are final."

He leaps suddenly inside the cab, fires the engine, slams the door and peels out in the gravel, shouting, "Snooze ya lose, bitches!"

Jars rattle out onto the pavement and shatter in a crash of glass, meat and funeral home chemicals. The smell of mothballs and hot-dogs fills the air. The crowd breaks up slowly and I head silently out of the downtown fray once and for all.

In the tumbleweed echo of the open highway I finally feel saved – free.

Dust trembles by and I can hear the tire hum of a car blazing up behind me at top speeds. Never tried this before, but what the hell? Sticking out my thumb now and it feels like a fool's hope to not have to hoof it to Nowhere.

God or whoever must've figured I had enough bad luck today because the car slams to a stop. It's a four-door '76 Pontiac GTO painted American flag red and blasting *Flight of the Valkyrie*. The car sprays dust as it comes to a screeching halt in the shoulder and almost takes my left leg along with it.

I run to the window, shouting, "Hot damn, thanks mister!"

And when I look inside, who of all people is there at the wheel? Fucking Uncle Sam, the old swine, the Mexican whore chaser, the man on the other end of bad tarot card luck, and he's looking up at me with a smile and a wink in his eye.

"Get in," he says, almost too excited, "I'm on my way out to Hollywood, boyo! Gonna see the stars and make it in moving pictures! It's gonna be a scream!"

I climb into the passenger seat and he guns it for Anywhere.

Uncle Sam starts talking fast and loud over his music. Tells me all about the widow fortune teller's tarot reading and I have to listen to it or risk letting him know that I peeked. He says, "So I made a choice, I could let it get me down or take it as a sign that it's high time I took some action, you know? Know what I mean, sonny? So that's what I'm gonna do. I'll get in pictures and people will love me again."

We speed through mile after mile. Anywhere sails by like a flash of telephone poles, grocery stores, gas stations, truckstops, convenience shops, traffic lights, speed limit warnings and road signs. Fifteen miles to Nowhere.

Uncle Sam says, "What do you think? Is it a good plan? Of course it's a good plan! This world is all about image these days. It's not icons, statements or ideology! It's the silver screen, celebrity magazines and crowd control. It's not what you stand for, it's who you know. Pretty soon, everyone will know me again. I'm so excited I could bust."

Four miles to Nowhere and I can't wait to ditch this ride.

"Why don't you come with me, kid? You're a good-looking sprout, we could go far."

"Oh, no sir," I say, "I've got other fish to fry in Nowhere. I've been wanting to go there for a long time, you know."

"All right, suit yourself. I only meant...uh-oh, don't look now, but I think we got company. Black motorcycles, probably Government Issue, FEMA ninjas or some shit. They probably want me for more contracting work or recruitment poster modeling gigs or God knows what. I'm tired of working for those clowns, there's no money in it and I'm sick of being type cast."

I follow his gaze into the rearview mirror and see the familiar cackling face of that lead biker chick with the blonde hair with black streaks. The fat-ass ringleader of the Fat Bottom Girls. Leroy sent them to hunt me down.

"Take off right here," I shout, "Turn, turn...now, Goddammit, now!"

"All right, Jesus. What do they want you for? Marlboro ads or something? What is it?"

"No, this isn't...they're not...oh, for fuck's sake!" I scream, "They're after me, not you. I'm on the run, just drop me as soon as they're out of eyeshot and book it to L.A. Try to lose 'em."

"Sorry, kid, this is too hot for me," Uncle Sam shakes his head, "you gotta go, now."

The GTO slams to a halt next to a chain-link fence and a falling-down old brick complex of some kind. I tuck and roll out of the car and make for the fence as fast as my twisted ankle will allow. I can hear their engines, growling and seething like rabid she-wolves on my heels. The cackles of these obese leather-bound witches fill the sky and echo off of the high brick walls of this side street in Nowhere, California. My only chance is to make it to the building before they see me and here I am dragging my leg like some kind of fucking Igor out of an old Universal monster flick.

The roar of their engines gets louder as I find my way to a basement window, push it in and roll through out of sight and into safety. I land with a puff of air and dust in some kind of large pillow, or maybe a pile of pillows. It's too dark to tell, but the place is clearly lived in. Candles and incense burn all around. The room is lit a dull brown-orange and I squint to adjust to the shadows.

Then my heart jumps into my throat like a frog on a lily pad at the sound of a voice cool and relaxed, but more alarming for it. It's a man, probably some kinda limey judging by the accent, and he just says, "Well...how nice of you to drop in."

Field Notes from Bastard Land

8: Impromptu Drive, Abraham, Highway 61, and Big Talk with the Outlaw

The Director tells me that our lead man feels exhausted by the porch confessional with the unhallowed priests of the Yellow House. Everyone heads in to listen to the band jam, but Jack opts, instead, for a quiet walk to clear his head. It's a cold winter with no hair on his head to keep him warm. Our lead man left home without a strong jacket, but drinks a bummed flask of whiskey to keep warm. Only he knows, like many of us, that whiskey just numbs the nerves to make you think you aren't dying of exposure.

Action.

What the hell? Head time is great and all, but it's too damn cold. I figure a drive might be a better moral solution. I find her right where I left her, parked up by the art building, waiting patiently. As Bonnie's door closes behind me and her engine gets revving I find myself driving in the light of day even though it's 3 AM. Weird.

The radio says, "This just in, psychologists have done further study on the notion of dual memory. In addition to alcoholic amnesia or memory loss after a night of heavy drinking, the serious alcoholic can actually experience two separate chains of awareness. One exists while sober, the other while intoxicated. Memories only become accessible when the chemical levels in the brain match that of when the memory was formed."

This is a yellow sand desert highway and I am completely lost. I'm cruising along at top speeds when, as luck would have it, there's some lonesome hitchhiker on the shoulder. Slamming the brakes I stop right ahead of him and notice that he's just a kid, dressed ragged in holey brown trousers, a white V-neck tee shirt, red suspenders and an old bowler cap. He's weird, but seems trustworthy so I yell, "Hey, kid, mind telling me where the hell we are?"

He says something about how he doesn't know either, but maybe we can figure it out together. I let him in, figuring there's safety in numbers and all. We head back down the road and sort of shoot the breeze for a little while. After some time goes by he says, "Yeah, I'm just out here because my one true love was a liar, just using me as a get out of jail free card."

"Is that right?" I ask, "Funny how two strangers can lead such parallel lives. Pretty much the same thing happened to me, in a roundabout way."

"Yeah? That's weird, man," he says, "You know, I mean, you know, that's weird."

This kid seems like kind of an idiot, but he's all heart so I figure it's cool. We talk about women troubles and he tells me he has to get to San Diego.

And then it hits me, what they told me about Abraham just sort of pops back in there. I'd forgotten until just now, but I just remembered the advice I got from Kurt Cobain.

"Oh, man," I scream, "I have to do what he said. I have to go look for him down on Highway 61."

"Mister," says the kid, "I don't know who and I don't care why, to tell ya the truth, but I do know that Highway 61 is supposed to be up ahead, just past the turn-off to San Diego."

"Sounds far," I reply, omitting the fact that I was just in Texas fifteen minutes ago.

When I hit the junction to Highway 61 I let the kid off at the fork in the road, and he says, "Thanks, mister, I'll hoof it from here. Good luck finding the guy or whatever."

The door closes and I get rolling again. Highway 61 is not what you might think. There's no Zionist mountain or memorial highway plaque. No flashing neon signs or Vegas landing strip fanfare. Highway 61 is just a two-laner strip in the middle of a white sands desert on all sides. The sky grays as it fades into the horizon. There's one tree, a bleached white fossil of a dogwood that bends wildly around itself and over the heat bent mirage of the tarred road.

Under that tree, a man sits comfortably in the sand and smokes a crooked long-stemmed pipe. His posture seems off. Not exactly a slouch, just not quite right. I see him tap the pipe in the sand and twirl the stem with gnarled, arthritic fingers. He stands as I get closer and I see that his spine is as jagged as a picket fence. His legs are bowed, his feet pigeon-toed and the elbows don't seem to unfold all the way. He's wearing a coal-black suit covered in sugary dust and a crooked stove pipe hat. He strokes his beard with gout fingers and smiles sullenly.

I say, "You're Abraham?"

"Aye, that I am, sonny."

There's that word again, "sonny."

He says, "Not quite what you were expecting, eh?"

I laugh and shake my head no.

"That's all right," Abraham replies, "most people expect the Biblical Abraham when they head out to see me. It's not the first time the name's gotten me into trouble. Why, I can remember how old Stonewall used to...aw, but then you're not here for an old man's stories. And in case you're wondering how a body can get shot in the head and wind up looking like Wile E. Coyote when he accordions away after a good fall, let's just say people have been bending me into the shape they want me to be for decades and leave it at that."

His tone is serious so I take him at his word.

Abraham says, "But don't worry, some things are still as they should be," he removes his hat and stoops into a stately bow, revealing an oozing hole the size of a second mouth.

I lean in for a good look and shrug, "That's a relief. For a second there I thought this might get weird."

With a serious set mouth, but a twinkle in his eye, the man across from me replaces his hat and says, "I know what you mean, son, I never would have guessed the afterlife would have had me posted out here in No Man's Land offering road guidance to the young and bewildered. But that's Americana for you. This whole world's as crooked as my spine."

"Americana?" I ask.

"Aye, lad, that's the name of this place. Why, you didn't actually think this was still the same reality you're accustomed to, did you? That would defy logic."

"Oh, *that* would defy logic. Of course, my mistake," I say smugly.

Suddenly smiling that same brooding half-grin, Abraham rubs his beard and slaps his thighs saying, "Well, let's get right to it, lad. You're wondering why Ernest sent you to me. I can only tell you that this place, Highway 61, is a place where decisions are to be made. This is where God told me to sacrifice my son to the American Dream. I still remember it, when I refused, we slipped into civil war. Now, Jack, you should understand that playing Abraham is no small feat. Many have been asked to find the diamond in the rough, the righteous in Sodom and Gomorrah, but few succeed. He's never what you expect. You have to know how to separate literal truth from metaphor. Like I said, not an easy feat. And with each failure the stakes go up, first America got sick, then she started blacking out and now she's gone comatose altogether, but yours are the greatest stakes of all–"

"Let me guess," I cut in, "the Death of America."

"You say it like a joke, sonny, but that's exactly it. When *they* pull the plug the spirit of America will be gone forever. Something new, something ugly, will take her place."

"Her?"

"Yes, 'her,' she's a beautiful young lady, barely out of her adolescence and she's already faced with a brutal end."

"You mean she's out there somewhere?"

There's a brief pause and Abraham stares, cold and gray, right into me, "Yes, as plainly as you see me now," he replies, "but that doesn't change the fact that she's also your native land. Remember, Jack, you found the Ghost Road. You breached the barrier between your world and this one. In my world, ideas have a pulse. They live life, talk, dream... argue, make dinners and sometimes even draw blood. I don't know what this place is, kid, but I can tell you that here everything is the same. It's all one idea. Everything exists and everything exists in the mind. Americana is a place of one mind, with many ideas fighting to survive. Contradictions lead to bitter bar fights. I don't know why or how. Like Socrates, I admit that I truly know nothing. But the one thing I do know is that I am not me. This isn't the world you know me from, and she is your America, but she isn't."

"I see...well, tell me something. Can I see her?"

"You can see her anytime, but you have to know where to look. I can't take you."

"Well that sucks," I reply.

"It might, but that's the state of things."

"So what am I supposed to do?" I ask.

"You are here because you need direction. I can tell you three things. One, you will travel far and wide before you realize the truth is staring you in the face. Two, you will get it wrong before you get it right, so don't listen to your first impulse. Three, Jim Morrison told you that you will be getting the gift of sight, did he not? Well, you will not learn to control your gift until you find

America. And finally, you won't do that until you also inspire order in this world."

"That's four things," I smirk.

"Very good, sonny, you caught me."

"So let me just make sure I'm following you," I say with only a little too much attitude, "Even though I'm fairly certain the man they're looking for is Charlie Outlaw, even though I'm doing every-thing I can to find a way to get him to go to bat for us, it doesn't matter. It won't matter until I find America, is that right?"

"More or less, sonny," the old man nods under his beard, "And the reason is simple. Set aside everything those zombies have told you, they aren't real, I'm not real. Maybe you aren't even real. All of this talk about queens and callings, those weirdos are so taken by their own image that they only hear superstition. They named me their prophet, and when I speak, even speak plainly, they only read into it. They only get mysticism. But I can tell you this, it will all happen as it needs to, but I fear that your mission may be laced with ulterior motives."

"Ulterior motives?"

"Aye, sonny," Abe replies, "See, you do need to find someone to put an end to this, but they have you looking for proof of some kind. A hope, perhaps, that they won't be stuck fighting this fight forever. They wish to know that someone new will take up the charge."

"Why is that?"

"Because, my boy, you and your people have fed off of them for years, off of all of us, but them worst of all. You don't think or create anything new, you recycle us, you bend us out of shape and you feed off our work and our memory and our ideology to try to feel like you're getting somewhere. Worse than that, those of you that think you're different, you guys just mimic them. I think they want you to find someone to make them feel less pressured, or maybe, maybe they want someone new at their table."

"Great, perfect," I grunt, "Christ. Anything else?"

"Yes, but to understand we must go back in time, far, far back."

"How far?"

Abraham's voice takes on a eulogic tone and he says, "Four score and seven years ago, our fathers...I'm just kidding, get the hell out of here. Oh, and just for the record, I was blazed out of my tree when I gave that speech. It was the only way I could cope with the stage fright. I had written another fifteen minutes of talking points but had to cut it short to throw up behind the stage. I've wanted to get that off my chest for over a hundred years."

"I'm glad you told me," I reply.

I climb back into my car and when the door slams shut I see the headlights of a semi-truck barreling right at me through the windshield. Swerving wildly into the other lane, my heart pumping adrenaline like a fuel-injected carburetor, I gasp to catch my breath and finish my drive home in silence.

Things are quiet when I get back to the Yellow House. The sun is already flirting with the horizon. Creeping in through the front door feels like invading the home of some stranger. I find a chunk of mattress on the fold-out couch and squeeze in between a sleeping Dennis Orbell and Charlie Outlaw. I'm not going to sleep, but I need to just lie flat and relax. I can't sleep, not with that stupid dream stalking me. Still, despite my best efforts...

Cut.

This next scene is called *Fear and Loathing in REM Sleep*.

Son of a bitch. Ever since that night at Sister Black's I've been doing my best not to sleep. Doing my best not to dream. Every time my eyes close it's that dream. Hammer, pliers, broken bones, torn fingernails, blood, splinter table, train spikes, eyes torn open, watching them play the game. The Destroyer. Penetrated and penetrated and penetrated again. While I sit there penetrated by rusted metal holding me down and forcing me to face my demons.

That laugh, that voice, says, "This is going to hurt you, and only you."

I'm in a dungeon or a basement. Damp smells. Stagnant, algae, dirt water. My blood mixing in with all of it, with the spider webs on the walls and the rust of utensils on the corner worktable. Dark. The stink of mold and oozing water down concrete walls. Can't move. Out of the corner of my eye I see a high-backed wooden chair dripping with my blood, sweat and flesh. This is a dungeon or a basement. I see the dark figure moving close to me, there is a swinging light bulb in one corner. Its light catches the rust-metal glint of his sledgehammer as he finishes the last spike to my right hip.

Now it's pain. Blood spurts when I thrash and try to rip myself off of the nails and inch toward the door. I don't get anywhere, but trying helps. I scream, someone screams, very inhuman, "No God, no more, make it stop!"

The monitor starts showing me images. I can see her on her back, tits up, legs spread wide. Long blonde hair and face tightened as if working very hard. Him on top of her. Changing positions rolling her over and coming in from behind. This is my old apartment. That is my couch. That was my bed. That is my wife. This is the man who ruined it all for me. It just plays on a loop. She screams in orgasm and laughs in glee. He groans, selfish and ugly. She groans, exactly the same.

My Destroyer. The woman I swore to love, in sickness and in health, for richer or poorer, till death do we part. And now the blood doesn't even hurt the most. Something inside cracks and bleeds and dies faster than my body. I watch my last light in this world wink into black dust and float out of the narrow basement window, level with the grass, polluting the moonless night.

Then I wake up. A scream.

Cold sweat. Cold tears. Cold.

Cut to our man waking up on the Yellow House sofa mattress.

I put a shaking hand to my eyes and sit there, trying to stop these weird shivers convulsing through every muscle in my body. The faint hum of guitar strings spasming outside draws my attention to the front porch. Jump shot. Now I'm in the damp yellow dawn with Charlie Outlaw talking deep and blue under the East Texas sky.

"Can't sleep?" I ask.

"You know me," he grunts.

I sit across from him in a patio chair and say, "It's like old times, huh? Remember how we used to see how long we could go without sleep? I'd stay over at your place for days and nights on end talking change. Talking Being vs. Becoming and Platonic Philosophy."

"Yeah," he says, "those were good times, man, drinking coffee, playing chess and listening to Coldplay or Bob Dylan or Johnny Cash. I still think about 'em sometimes."

"Me too...so what's on your mind, brother?"

"Permanence," he says, "that's what has me up at this hour. I keep thinking, it seems like permanence is everyone's goal, but permanence is boring. For my money I'll take Becoming over Being any day. The only permanence I want is to be permanently changing. I'll stop when I die."

"Permanence and perfection go hand in hand," I tell him, "everyone wants things to stay the same because they want them to be perfect. Perfection is changeless by definition. Our fear of change is probably rooted in some primordial obsession with being perfect and holy to please the gods. But guess what? Death is permanent too. And what is death? Nothingness. Maybe nothingness is the only perfection available to us."

Charlie sets down his guitar and pulls out a small mahogany box.

"Guess what this is," he says, "Like you said, 'Just like old times.'"

He opens the lid, revealing a set of black and white wooden pieces. The checkered board leans against the side of his chair and he reaches for it. Cut to the two of us sitting on opposite sides of a chess board.

I say, "I'm a little rusty. I haven't really played in years."

"Fuck that," he says, "me too. This is going to be a match to see who's worse, not who's better."

We move our pieces here and there, gods over our tiny pawns. Some fall and some survive and for us they are all expendable as long as we win. Like the philosophy of Joseph Stalin and every world devastator that says, "The end justifies the means."

"This is the real deal, my friend," Charlie begins, "this is life. Battles and victories, losses and collateral damage. Here we go setting up our strategies, arranging our men for their doom."

"This is war," I say, "This is now, right now, this moment. Everything looks to the General, to the President, the King. This is the world in the eyes of God. Pawns in the game divided into boxes, a moveable tragedy."

And then I laugh and say, "Shit."

My plan was not working. I had based an essential victory on the spine of a rook that had already been taken.

Laughing, Charlie says, "That's it, man, the basis to so much it can only be hilarious. This is light and fire. Light does what it does based on the basic luminescence of fire, but no matter what it tries it will never have the heat. Playing the game with what you don't have. That's the human condition, brother, when you play chess you learn about the human condition."

After that I capture his queen and say, "That's the human condition, dude. That's the quick turnaround nature of the whole desert universe. One minute you have a queen, the next she's taken by another man."

"It's light and fire, man. You lost from using something you didn't have. I lost from not using what was mine. You're the fire, you try to make the light but you're not as bright as a good lamp. But me, I try to put off heat when all I really needed to do was use my light."

I laugh, "You asshole, you don't even know what the fuck you're talking about do you?"

"Admittedly, I'm still a little drunk. And I'm on some weird kind of mescaline I bought up on Fry Street. But that's cool, we're talking loss and loss is definitely the human condition. You never remember what you've got and you never try to use it until it's gone."

Then we play the game. Charlie Outlaw sings "Wish You Were

Here" by Pink Floyd. He says, "I was listening to that song all day at work. It just felt like a good life decision."

That's when he tipped the king, "I retire," he says, "I've lost. Do you want to walk over to Kharma?"

Kharma Café: in terms of coffee shops this is one of relative importance in the neighborhood of the Yellow House. In Arabic font the words "Kharma Café" are printed on the front window. It sits quiet and unassuming on the side of some still road near the college. Just off of the corner of Avenue C and Fry Street.

Something in this place bothers me. Leaves a bad taste in my mouth. And I don't just mean because they sell bitter coffee. I don't really like it. There are phonies in every corner. Twisted perverts hopped up on ambition and bragging. The weak assumption that sitting in a coffee shop reading the right book or writing something of their own made them special, somehow important. You can see it on all of their faces. These lonesome angels are here to pick up dates for the weekend and using what to me is a divine art form to do it. Goddamn pimps.

It's everywhere, in the cigarette smoke, the student art on the walls, the old rock concert posters unsigned but still displayed, and all the etc. etc. etc. The trouble with a place like this is most of these people play at culture like it's a game. Same as online dating services where you can change your picture or your life to make you look as good as you like. None of these people really believe in it, this is just a way to not have to jerk off for a few weeks. Hold the right book in the right place and you might find a girl. Whatever.

On another note, I have a serious problem with any place that plays "Yellow Submarine" by The Beatles. See, I like The Beatles. It's for that exact reason that I get mad when I hear that song. That song is what I've dubbed the Liar's Crutch, an obvious reference that allows the appearance of a fan.

Ask someone, "Do you like The Beatles?"

Watch the eyes glaze over in fear and doubt. Clearly they do not know anything and they grab at the one song everyone knows. Then they answer, "Oh, yes, I love that song 'Yellow Submarine.'"

Just like any wife-beating megalomaniac bar-hopping drunk can seem romantic if he buys flowers and chocolates – or lights a few candles. It's the Liar's Crutch.

Pimps and phonies everywhere.

Establishing shot. One wall is dedicated to that student art. Another to those unsigned rock posters. Another has this faux Day of the Dead Mexican skeleton art with masks and hanging puppets and sheer terror. In one corner you see hanging skateboards and another wall has a dragon mural framed in a false Chinese archway. Like the people inside, this place is starving to be everything to everyone. Speakers on every wall blast their music. Propaganda for the scene kid lifestyle. Cut to Charlie Outlaw and me back in the lights, the sounds, the movement of cigarette smoke and coffee shop conversation. Action.

I say, "You know, I have found that becoming a better writer is not so much about picking up new tricks of the trade, or taking classes, or increasing your vocabulary as much as it is about becoming a better thinker. A better human. Just having a better life. You don't increase your skills. You increase your soul, your vision, your entire outlook. Too many people try to get better with words rather than ideas. You can have all the words in the world, but without ideas you'll just very cleverly say nothing and take a long time to say it. Put yourself through the furnace and you'll have words to put on the page. Your skills will take care of themselves."

"Yeah," Charlie replies, "I've been thinking the same thing with my music. It's the same story I've been telling, it's all about change. Change your life, change what you are working with, and constantly evolve."

He tells me about Voltaire's *Candide*. A story of a man who had it all and lost everything. Candide fell in love with a princess and was banished from the kingdom. Her kingdom was raided and she was killed. He's sold into slavery, tortured, abused, hanged, presumed dead, dissected, and revived, cut open, beaten, burned, you name it, it fucking happened. Then he wanders into El Dorado, the Lost City of Gold, and attains great wealth. He finds his beloved still alive along with her brother and many old friends. They buy a house and live together, they should have lived happily ever after, but they grow bored.

Taking a long drag on his cigarette Charlie Outlaw says, "It comes down to a simple moment where the former princess asks Candide, 'Do you think the rapes and torture and slavery were actually better than this boredom?'"

"Yes," I say, finishing the story for him, "Yes, because humans are animals, deep down we're still barbarians, we are beasts dressed up in business suits, carnivores stuck behind desks eating salad wraps from a low carb diet menu. We desperately want something to fight. We crave bloodshed, something to focus our savage nature upon that we can tear apart. We need wars and terrorists and political drama to avoid turning our bloodlust on ourselves and ending our lives from boredom. And if not real wars then we simulate violence with action films and boxing matches and corporate takeovers. All of it because without pain the boredom would destroy us."

Outlaw says, "You can't tame a beast, you either free it or break it. And we are beasts, whether people like to admit that or not. But what's wrong with that? Beasts are supposed to be one with nature, and what is nature? It's all peaks and valleys, just like everyday life, but the Mother Brain of America tries to teach us to find that perfect peak and stay there."

"That doesn't work, though," I add, "it's a lie. People freeze on the peaks, Candide got bored up there, eventually you have to come down into the valley. Consider the history books. Rome was once a great civilization, at its peak, but like everything else it fell and history was plunged into darkness. Today it's a graveyard. Tourists walk where great emperors once rode their chariots, you can hail a cab and ride the paths of dead Caesars. Bakeries and bait shops have sprung up around the cracked foundations of the Parthenon, the Pantheon and the Colosseum. Their peak didn't last. It fell into what the psalmist called the Valley of the Shadow of Death. But history didn't stay in shadow. It was followed up by a Great Awakening, the Renaissance Age, the Great Reformation and Martin Luther and fucking Leonardo Da Vinci – another peak."

"So the question is," Outlaw begins, "where are we now? Peak or valley?"

"Not to say that one is inherently better than another, but I'd say I'm definitely in a valley. Still, as part of my new philosophy, I'm learning to love the valley as much as the mountaintop. Think about it – rather than learning to cope with the bad until the good comes along, what would happen if we trained ourselves to enjoy both as equally powerful experiences? Get a thrill out of fear, a kick out of the panic felt before talking to a girl, enjoy discomfort and you'll always be comfortable."

"Right on, man," Charlie says, "I like your attitude. So you're talking a lot about writing. What do you think you are as a writer? Creator? Dreamer? Artist?"

"Well," I retort, "what do you think you are as a musician?"

"Definitely not a creator."

I nod, replying, "Actually, I think of myself as a translator. Each generation has its own way of talking. It has its own issues. It's our job to translate ancient ideas to a new type of human. What worked as an explanation in the fifties gets lost in translation today. We have to revamp those ideas for our own generation, our own movement."

"I like that," Outlaw replies, "we're translating the same old lessons to our people. The same story, same knowledge, it's just that people talk differently with each decade. Today it's laptops and MP3 players, cell phones, hybrid cars, global warming, PDAs, George W. Bush, Iraq, Apache helicopters, American Idol, prescription marijuana, chemical depression, Our Lady of Perpetual Ass-licking Oprah Winfrey, Donald Trump AKA King Midas, disposable music, hip-hop, bebop, mmm-bop, shit pop... there are so many new words to be translated. You're right, bro."

Charlie Outlaw lights up and says, "I keep thinking about the words 'Love at first fight.' Not sure what it means, but I like it, and I think it applies. It's like, when do you start loving life? That's when you start to fight for it."

Love at first fight. Fighting the bad fight. That's love. A fight without rules, where you get hit below the belt and everyone stacks the bets. Breaking the spines of the old and the hearts of the young, and demanding with curses that God see the beauty in it all.

LOST IN AMERICANA: CHAPTER EIGHT

SEWING DRAWER WONDERLAND, SPIRITUAL EXPEDITIONARIES, AND THE CRYING GUITAR

His apartment is a beanbag odyssey, a multi-colored sewing drawer full of pincushions, scrap fabric and beadwork. An old fireplace is packed to the brick with old mason jars full of buttons, bottle caps, and bus tokens. A wine bottle stands vertical in the glass packrat menagerie, burning a cattail incense stick. Smoldering purple patchouli smoke grows like silent weeds around the room. He's sitting cross-legged on a red silk Indian pillow. His hair is long, his eyes are dark and he wears his facial hair in a sharp pointed beard with waxed moustache ends like a Spanish conquistador. Plucking weird drones and melodies on a time-tarnished sitar he talks in rhythm with his music.

"You know," he begins, rhythmically stroking the strings, "I never felt a great need to perform. Music is a very personal process for me. I would have been content to play alone, except for one thing…"

"Nobody pays you to play to an empty room?" I grunt.

"Close, but not exactly," he replies, "You see, in a band you go on tour. On tour you see the world and all the people in it. We can only grow as people by grinding ourselves down on the stone of new experience. Few people realize the difference between knowledge and experience. Knowledge can be expressed, or learned, in mere words. It is purely cerebral in that way. Yet experience, while it does teach lessons, is also an emotional state. You feel it, but it can only be related to others as a clinical description of those feelings. You cannot express experience without it becoming knowledge. Vain words, like sadness, joy, or sublimation – words that merely represent the feeling, but never actually transmit them. This is the closest we can come to sharing these moments with another person. In this way, it belongs only and always to us. In this way, it is spiritual.

"I spent my life traveling the world, collecting the raw energy of experience, preferring that, always, over basic knowledge."

"What about the people you shared your experience with?" I ask, "They must be in on those feelings too, right?"

"That is how I found we were all one. I am me and you are we and we're all one together. I learned that by living, not by hearing. Without the perception of the individual there is only one man and one moment, it is our unique perception that lets each of us know who we are. And when you push beyond that perception it allows us to know we're connected. For this reason I fancy myself a spiritual expeditionary.

"So, were my friends in on the experience? Sure they are," he continues, twisting a few knobs to find the tune, "but, though we may have shared a certain moment, we could only acknowledge it in words. And words are just knowledge. They are ambassadorial agents that represent a truth. They are not the truth in and of themselves."

"Yeah, I gotta say I got no idea what the fuck that means," I shrug dumbly.

"Like I said, kid," the man grins from under his pointy beard, "experience dawns and dusks in *your* mind. It exists in your perception alone. The exact same moment, that experience, is perceived differently by every mind. So, for all the moments I've shared with people, I still came away with my own experience – alone. And it is something that no one can ever touch, not my wife, my children, not you and, perhaps, not even God. It exists in my mind alone, bigger than knowledge. Anyone can know the square root of sixteen or that the sum of the interior angles of a triangle is always 180 degrees, but no one can ever know what I felt the first time I stood on the shores of the Ganges River. No one will ever feel that in the exact way that I felt it, in my heart. Hence, spiritual expeditionary, a collector of weird introspective tricks. Like Marco Polo, I'm mapping the world as it exists within me."

Without really giving it much of a thought I mutter, "Within you, without you."

Fingering out a fast melodic riff, the man looks up with a somber grin and says, "Hey, I like that. It sounds familiar, did you write it?"

"I don't think so," I reply whimsically, feeling somehow dreamlike and displaced, "I think you did."

"No way, man, I think I'd remember something like that. So listen, you okay, kid? You have somewhere to stay? I can see by your eyes you're on the run from something."

"Yeah, Bad Leroy Brown, this big bruiser."

"Who?"

"Forget it."

The stranger starts to sing, "Bad, bad, Leroy Brown, baddest man in the whole damn town…badder than old King Kong, meaner than a junkyard dog."

"Yeah, um…well, he's after me for running away from his hotel. Him and all his cronies."

"You'll stay here then, kid, no worries…And, oh, yeah, by the way – I'm George."

We shake hands and I politely give my name. George offers me tea and I decline. He offers water, cookies, milk and I say no on everything.

Then he says, "Smoke a jay?"

And I say, "Now that's polite hosting, you're on, sir."

George lights up a tightly rolled spliff and white smoke billows dense under brooding eyes. His voice comes out in stifled asphyxia tones as he talks with smoke in his lungs, "Here, kid, make yourself at home."

I drag coolly and return with a question and asphyxia tones of my own, "So...goddamn, that's good shit...So, George, let me ask you something."

I exhale abruptly, spraying spit smog across the room and George smiles toothy saying, "Yeah, shoot."

"Well, you mentioned a wife and kids, but this here looks like a bachelor pad to me, so I'm like, 'What the fuck?' You got something on the side, George, or what?"

His lids fall heavy with weed and introspective pressure and some gut shot warning sends me a fear I've gone and said too much. A sadness swells across his face like a snow globe turned upside down.

George sighs and says, "It's weird, y'know? It's like, I remember them and all, but I don't. I know they exist, but they're not here. When I think about it, it feels like I had this whole other life or something. In it, I'm an old man, I've been married, I own a house... I have so many things. But when I wake up, I'm always here. I'm young again and all of the wonderful things I've seen, everything I loved that was mine...They're all gone."

"Well, that sucks," I blurt as he hands me another go at the spliff.

"Yeah, but I'll let you in on a little secret of mine. Never told anyone before. Some nights, when the music feels all wrong...when I know there are songs I should be singing – songs that are mine, but I can't hear them, I feel like I can't touch my guitar and she cries harmonic tears to bring me back...on those nights, I head out into the night looking for them."

"Them?" I ask, "You mean your songs?"

"Well, yes and no, I go out to search the streets for my children."

Something ripples in me when I hear this. It's like how I used to play by this pond and the waters were so still and dead that it grew this thick green soufflé on top and me and Huck used to throw rocks in to crack that soufflé open and see the water dark and clear underneath. When George said those things about his children it was just like that. Like he sank a rock in me and something dropped through and hit bottom.

I drag my turn at the weed and say, "I think I do that too, George. I, you know…I mean, I sneak out, day or night, there's this place I was living, not even sure how I got there to be honest. Reckon I've been there a long time. But it's like, once you're in you ain't never gonna leave, and even though I'm out now, I'm not really out."

"But you found a way outta there, huh, kid?"

"Yeah, I got out and they keep trying to bring me back. Man, it was a weird place, but I could get out. At first I went out for someone inside. But now I got out because I'm looking for someone. I don't know who, but it's like I gotta find 'em, you know?"

"Yeah, Tom, I do."

"That's why *they* found me. Some kind of zombie troop trying to save the world or some shit. I ran from them too. They told me I had to show them the way."

"What like Jesus or something?"

I snort and stuff comes out of my mouth all over the fucking place from laughing, "Yeah, I reckon so…but they were all dead, like dead artists or something."

George grins strangely, a sort of cocky dawning and he says, "Was one of them full of holes and was there another wearing big sun shades?"

"Hey! You know 'em?"

"Yeah, man," he smiles, plunking around on the strings, "they tried to get me too. They were all artists at some point, you're right about that. They say they're the reincarnated memories of people that died for art in this other place. I tried to tell them that if that's true then it doesn't make them Janis Joplin, Jimi Hendrix or John

Lennon. Not really. They're echoes, copies, like legends we tell. We create legends in the way we want to see people. Not really as they were. I told them I wanted no part of their club. I've never been a joiner anyway. But it seems less important how you died for art. It's much more relevant how we lived. Like saints, we make saints of martyrs that died hard. The martyrs always got that wrong, always preaching their death over their life."

"So instead of all that you went and got an apartment in Nowhere and play your sitar while your guitar gently weeps?"

George scoffs a knowing sort of laugh, "Those people, your friends back there, they all have one thing in common. They're trying to make art go militant to save the world from some big evil, but that's not the way. Fighting wars, no matter the battlefield, is still a futile exercise."

"Then what is the answer?"

"I don't know," he grins, "I'm just a guitar player, but I perceive myself to be a spiritual expeditionary and that, I think, is enough."

George stands up suddenly and moves toward a cabinet in the kitchen. He brings me a bowl of rice and warm sake. Setting it down on the floor in front of me, George says, "Here, Tom, eat up, when was the last time you ate something? You look exhausted. Look, the sun's going down, you're in the clear for tonight. Wash everything down with the sake, it'll put you right out, I promise."

I don't feel like arguing, maybe he's just really persuasive or maybe he's right. I feel tired as hell. I eat a little bit of the rice but I'm full before it's even half gone. I fire back the sake and my body feels cozy like how it felt under the covers of Maggie's bed. But then...oh, who cares. I close my eyes and fall asleep.

Maybe I dream. Maybe I talk and toss. Who knows? Hours tick by and it feels like the first real rest I've had in like a zillion years or something. But I'm torn out of it suddenly by the sound of a woman weeping loud all over the room.

When I sit up and look around everything's blue and night, but the sound is louder. A woman's voice, sobbing, moaning and slurping tears jingle like water droplets in every corner of George's apartment. I call out to George but there's no answer. The crying gets louder when George doesn't reply, almost a scream, some kind of pathetic siren wail.

In the corner, next to an overflowing ashtray, I find George's guitar leaning against a wood support beam. The strings vibrate with every sob and shriek and it all echoes out of the sound hole like a groaning mouth. I sit across from it, curiously, watching the guitar cry itself to sleep while George is nowhere to be found.

The sound hole goes, "Aaaaoooooooaaaaaooooohhhhhawwwww!"

I just sit and watch, drinking the last of my now cold sake and smiling, amused and concerned as the guitar wails like a broken-hearted banshee, like a woman who just lost her lover to a war, or Juliet stabbing herself in the heart at poisoned Romeo. It was weird, bizarre, stupid and pretty much hilarious.

At the window I see the sliding shadows of someone passing between the blue-out halogen streetlamp and the framed glass. The sad little guitar's bawling is getting on my nerves, I grab the thing by the neck and feel a broiling urge to smash it to pieces, but opt instead to just hide the stupid thing, mouth down, under a couple of beanbags. Crawling over all of the cloth and beads and sewing kit ambience of George's pad, I make for the window to check out the figure outside. I can see the naked heels of a man with pale skin and dark leg hair. He's strolling barefoot through the gravel broken glass lanes of the industrial wasteland lot that surrounds his building. His silhouette in the moonlight looks dazed, mindless, maybe sleepwalking or drunk.

I crawl out of the basement window, slide across the hot summer asphalt and follow him along through the blue predawn shadows. He's a pale halo moving like a ghost through the cold stone Bowery remnants of what, I guess, used to be some kind of paper mill or some shit. Couldn't say for sure. But there he goes. The gravel trail leads him down a hill, into some kind of quarry and I watch from the top of the hill. He's just moseying around, stark naked, lost, frigid cold and confused in some half-sleep state. Looking for his children in the dried husk remnants of a previous twilight. The sounds of a muffled guitar crying alone echo behind me. The sounds of a man, crying in the same key, echo off the chilled quarry walls. He sits in the dirt, skin against rock, and his hair sags low in his face.

George, like me, maybe like everyone, is looking for something that's gone missing. He needs to find it in order to get a good night's rest. I need to find whatever left me, whatever put me here, that made me the bastard, the orphan...the hapless romantic that I am.

I leave George to his insomniac expedition, slide back through the window and do my best to fall asleep, but his goddamn fucking pussy of a guitar is still moaning under the pillow.

"What?" I scream, "What? What? I mean, God, what do you want?"

"Aaaaooohhhaaawww," she keeps fucking sobbing.

Ready to snap her fucking neck, I flip the pillow, grab her abruptly and hold her high over my head, but, like an idiot, I slip and fall in a heap of bean bags and hippie paraphernalia. George's wimp guitar lands in my lap and for a second she stops crying and just goes, "Oh."

But not oh, like, ah-ha or Eureka! Oh like, oh, you know, I mean like, "Oh, that feels good," that kind of oh. So I figure, what the hell, I'll play a few chords and shut the baby up.

And stroking her strings, fingering her pressure points, she lets out sounds like a well-timed woman going for a particularly good roll. I didn't know I could make such beautiful music and then. Fuck.

"What the hell do you think you're doing?" George, still stark ass naked, grabs his guitar out from behind me and jerks me halfway through the air with his other hand, "This is my girl, mine! You hear me?"

I try to apologize but he rushes me to the door, chucks me out on my ass before you could say Mount Rushmore, and slams the door, saying something about she's all he's got left.

As if that ain't enough, I can hear the dull roar of motorcycle engines not far away.

Well, I figure I overstayed my welcome around here as it is. It's probably high time I hit the road again. But there's that sound, and I ain't exactly too clear on where it's coming from. I reckon I could just try to hightail it to the highway, but it's a risk. I see their lights moving in slow, like roving, humming bug zappers. Just a split hair's second before I'm caught in their beam I book it for the nearest door that don't have a naked angry Brit on the other side and duck in for safety.

It's weird, though, it's like this building must be all caved in, like nothing but a wall or something. There was this brick wall and a metal door, but now it's just grassy fields. Grassy fields in the middle of the desert makes about as much sense as fly fishing to catch buzzards. What is this place?

I turn around and the wall is gone. The door's gone too. This don't make any bit of goddamn sense at all, now that I ponder it. I mean, if the wall's gone then where are the Fat Bottom Girls? Something is weird. Where's the gravel roads and broke-down brick buildings I saw before? And there certainly ain't no quarry neither. These are big evergreens, grass lawns, an asphalt street, a quiet building with a big parking lot and a well lit, big yellow house lit up by porch light. In the parking lot there's this guy in some clunker car trying to get the bastard to turn over. It fires up and rolls a few feet down the road and it's just gone. You know, I mean, gone. And nobody seems to notice or care. Nobody seems to be around at all and I'm starting to wonder if it's the second coming or some fucking thing. I gotta figure out what to do about this.

I mean, you know, it's predawn morning, the house looks like the safest place around here with the light on and all. You know, like the only thing that looks anywhere close to welcoming or homey or whatever. So I stroll up, try to be cool or close to it, but this is all too fucking confounding.

There's some hipster moog with greasy hair, black pants, a dirty undershirt and suspenders sitting on the porch plucking at a guitar. He says, "Fuck. Where'd you come from, little man? It's late. Have a seat here and tell me all about it. Name's Charles. Charles Outlaw, but most folks just call me Charlie."

I shake his hand and give my name. For some reason he laughs, eyes half closed and a big dumb grin and sort of snorts when he says, "Huh, yeah, sure, Thomas Sawyer, whatever you say, man."

"Charles?" I ask him, "Can you tell me where I am?"

"You're at the Yellow House, bub."

"No, I mean, no...can you tell me where I am?"

"Serious? Um...yeah, you're in Denton, Texas, are you sure you're okay, man?"

"I think so," I tell him, "I mean, you know, I think so. You got a drink or something, man, I'm parched?"

"Sure, man," he says, plunking around on a few strings, "we got crappy tap water inside. Will that be all right?"

"Water, what do I look like to you? Your dog or something? You got beer?"

Charlie laughs and stands up, bringing his guitar with him, "Sure, kid, just keep cool, you don't have to get all riled up or whatever. This way."

I follow Charlie through the door. Except, upon entering, his living room is a highway desert and it's broad daylight. Charlie Outlaw is gone and the sun is about as scorching hot as a skillet after bacon for breakfast.

Nobody seems to be around. Wind blows up a little midget twister beside me and howls like the ghost of a horny rooster. The wind dies down and I hear the long burnout hum of an engine and tires dragging angry across the road. Dust trails behind the clunker, that same clunker I saw in the parking lot not five minutes ago. Five minutes ago, when it was the middle of the night or at least early enough in the morning for it to be dark. Five minutes ago before it was the middle of the fucking afternoon.

The guy in the clunker slams on his brakes and spins sideways right in front of me, coming to a full stop at a sort of wonky angle right on the unpaved gravel shoulder. The window cranks down and the guy, stubble beard, buzzed head, leans out and says, "Excuse me, kid, you mind telling me where the hell we are?"

"You don't know either?" I ask, "Ain't that a fucking thing."

"It's a real kick in the head," he adds, "five minutes ago it was…"

"Night, I know," I interrupt, "Listen, you'd better take me with you, I'm afraid we might be the only two people left on earth or something."

"You thinking Jesus might've come back? I'll admit the thought had crossed my mind. Can you answer me one thing…here get in."

I climb in and the buzzed, stubbly fuck asks, "Can you tell me something? Is this reality or that other place?"

"What other place? You mean that place with the big yellow house and all that? We call that place, Otherworld. I ain't seen it before now, though. Rumor is portals to Otherworld been popping up all over the map."

"What world do you think you're from?" asks Stubble Head.

"Easy, I'm from Americana, it's this whole big place, you know. I mean, it's real big, and all. But you ain't from here, are ya?"

"No, I'm from Earth, or the United States of America or the Real World…Texas, shit, man, come to think of it," he grumbles under his breath, "I mean, come to think of it, I'm not real sure where I'm from, even with all the names we got for it. You know?"

"You're from Otherworld," I tell him and pat him on his shoulder, simultaneously snaking one of his smokes without him noticing. "It's okay. We won't hold it against you."

Field Notes from Bastard Land

9: Admonitions from the Dead, Five People at Your Table, Cannabis and The Tomato

Cut to me walking around the town square alone. I decide on caffeine and warmth. The Kharma Café is a pretty good spot to hole up so I head over that way, but when I get to the door there isn't a coffee shop on the other side. Instead, the swinging oak entry leads me into the conference room offices of the martyrs, that table, and my supervisors.

Thompson rails, "You goddamn swine bastard! What the hell do you think you're doing anyway? You've repeatedly ignored our agents in the field. You're just letting yourself get caught up in the scene. We don't have time for you to try to be cool or have fun, there's bigger fish to fry here, you ingrate twerp. What did you think you were doing anyway?"

I don't say anything. I just sit down in the chair and wait for whatever they have for me.

There's a brief moment of calm, silence, like the eye of the tornado. Then Lennon hits the intercom button, mumbles something and I see that dreaded projector screen descending to show me more of my life for public trial.

Janis Joplin says, "Jack, I think you've missed the point. We didn't send you to get plugged into Neo-Bohemia in North Texas. That's not the side of you that caught our eye. Anybody can get drunk with their friends. We want you to embrace this..."

The scene fires to life and I see Charlie reading out of his notebook. It's one of our all-night binges back in high school. We're sitting in dim lighting, incense fire warmth and the sound of his slow, droning voice in the music room. He finishes and repeats the title, "Love Letter to the Road. I think I'll make it a song some day."

I whistle low and say, "Man, Charlie, you know me. I love writing. I think I'm pretty good at it too. But of all the people I've met, friends that have put pen to paper, this is the first time any of them has ever written anything that I was jealous of...I mean, I wish I had thought of that – writing a love letter to the road in the voice of a soldier at war overseas, writing romance to his sweetheart back home."

Charlie smiles his thank you and plucks away at his guitar. I never realized it, but this song, the one he's playing right here on the feed, he's still playing it today in Denton. He sings, "Oh, this is a series of dreams that nobody seems to explain to me. Oh, why this is happening, oh, why is this happening? Oh, why is this happening? Oh, why is this happening? Oh, why is anything? Oh, I will be all right, guided by this electric light. Oh, you are my vessel so carry me. Oh, why is this happening, oh why is this happening? Oh, why is this happening? Oh, why is anything?"

Jimi Hendrix says, "Dig, kid, even back then you had tapped into the vortex. You found the Ghost Road."

"This is a series of dreams," Charlie sings.

"This is what you should be pursuing, Jack," Lennon adds, "not drinking with the rest of the idiots. You're bigger than that."

This is a series of dreams.

Oh why is this happening? Oh why is this happening?

Oh why is anything?

The feed ends and I don't wait to say goodbye. I just nod,

turn around and head out the door. Exiting the conference room I emerge into the dim light of the coffee shop. I quietly sit down and listen. The Beatles play. Then Lennon. Then Harrison, McCartney and Wings, and then more Beatles.

The Kharma Café goes on paying homage to its obvious trend set rock idols.

Bow to Mecca in the East ye Muslim. Bow to Liverpool and the Great Beginning ye Wannabe Rock Eaters. And I just think to myself that there is more to art than this.

All the scene kids talk about their plans as John Lennon sings "Imagine."

Some girl next to me says, "My new life plan is to graduate and be a teacher in some Podunk town with little halls and little budgets."

The fake believer's anthem chimes in, "We all live in a Yellow Submarine..."

"After that," she continues, "I want to open a coffee shop that's beat and grunge. Tables are board games and the place is greasy and homely. None of the chairs match."

A yellow submarine, a yellow submarine...

This guy with her who has a strangely annoying voice says, "You could just drive around town hitting up garage sales and old folks' homes."

"Yes," she says, "that's what I want."

Dude says, "So, guess what. After I asked to hang out with Wanda she tells me she is not looking for a relationship right now. What is that? Am I really that transparent or what?"

Girl says, "You don't look for a relationship, they just find you."

"Yeah."

...in a yellow submarine. In our Yellow Submarine.

Our obvious trend-rock anthem. And all the dicks say, "The Beatles? Oh yeah, love 'em. Love the Beatles. 'Yellow Submarine' rules."

And we're all buried in our yellow submarine.

The quiet ambience of light and music and smoke and talk all melding together like some weird mixed drink make this feel like the perfect place for my lonesome angels to perch. If this generation were to get off the ground it would start right here. Along with the cigarettes I am surrounded with the wireless culture. Laptop Kids. Students and wannabe writers tapping into the spinal cord of the Cyber Highway to complete their individual tasks.

Under the Beatles playing through the overhead speakers you can hear a half-dozen laptop keyboardists drilling holes into their dining tables. Under that the low puffs of smoke out of the mouths of maybes. And just below that is my pencil scratching my cave drawings into notebook paper. Good or bad, I am clearly behind the times.

These lonesome angels perching themselves on the broadband line. Birds on a wireless wire. These are my brothers and sisters. The dismembered youth culture of the New Millennium wanting what they don't need and giving all to gain what will never be.

At the table beside me is a young sophisticated-looking couple. The guy just pulled up a chair and appears to be doing his best to impress the girl. He has his laptop in front of him and starts talking about his psychology dissertation. In a voice all too proud of itself he says, "I am writing my thesis on the power of confidence over the masses. How certain people in history had enough charisma, confidence, and eloquence to assimilate multitudes of people into following them."

Not looking up from her textbook the girl says, "That sounds interesting."

"I think so," he says, "considering the modern icons, Oprah, Trump, Dr. Phil, take your pick, these are all people who have used the exact same talents to rise to the top. Everyone has different ideology, but whether you are Jim Jones, David Koresh, or just a really good used car salesman it still requires the exact same talents to get where they are today as it did for Hitler or Jesus or Buddha. The point is charisma gets you far. After that the only thing that decides your role in history is what you do once you have your pulpit."

His captive audience listens silently as he drones on, "These are all people who saw a line and crossed it. Crossing it was only the beginning, afterward you decide the difference. You decide whether you'll save the world or build casinos. Make your choice between busloads of your wildest dreams or the mass extermination of an entire race of people. But my problem with these faces out there today is I see the same tendencies, and I know they are not done yet. I wonder where they will go from here."

He nods his own approval, yet even after all of this original thought, after seeming to have broken so powerfully out of the box he still turns to his laptop and clicks a program and I think to myself, "There it is. I just watched it happen."

The guy with the brilliant thesis is downloading a pirated version of "Yellow Submarine" to his laptop. His obvious trend-can choice.

To listen and obey...or however that saying goes.

People like this want a culture they can download 5x faster than dial-up. They don't want to take the time to learn that The Beatles wrote better songs and weren't always a yeah-yeah band. Don't want to risk the heresy of trying to find something better than our rock god Beatles in the early sixties, or Shakespeare in the early Elizabethan era, or Da Vinci's *Mona Lisa*.

Enter the Liar's Crutch.

These are the quick click icons for a young person of assumed culture to itemize and move on to the business of achieving other more notable endeavors. To follow their five-year plan toward becoming Doctor MD or Engineer Track Layer. Architect Vertigo. Lawyer Stage Fright. The ants go marching on and on. Hurrah.

Cut.

Dennis walks in with a big grin, still a few yards off he almost shouts, "Knew I'd find ya here. Look at you, your hands are about to rattle off. How much have you had?"

"They just keep 'em coming," I tell him, "Not too sure."

"You need food and fast, let's cut around the corner to you know where."

Cut to The Tomato. Interior. Day.

Dennis and I sit down with beers and a couple of pepperoni slices. He says, "So you just disappeared on us again, what's with that? Tell me, why do you wander off alone if you came here to be among friends and clear your head?"

"Disappear?" I ask my beer, voice echoing like seashell wind, "Yeah, I guess I did. I didn't really notice. Sometimes things come down on me hard, mediocrity, routine, boredom…so I just go somewhere else until I can get that shit off me. I want to change my life. I mean, if I didn't know any better I would think I've been stuck living the same day over and over. And over.

"Jesus, what am I saying? I *don't* know any better, from my point of view it seems like the entire human race is just reliving that same day again and again. We go to work, we come home, go to work, come home. I'd say in the end there are only four days in the entire whole of your life: birth, graduation, retirement, and death. Some of us live these days many times, but everyone goes through it at least once."

Orbell nods, saying, "Yeah, I hear you, man. That's at least one upside to you splitting up with your wife, right? I mean, it at least mixes up the monotony a little bit. Not every guy can say he's gone through a divorce at twenty."

"I hear that," I reply, "I mean, if that didn't happen then I wouldn't be here right now. I'd still be recycling that one day again and again. It's like, to me, the essential warning in George Orwell's *1984* was to keep a sharp eye on your humanity. And by humanity I mean beauty, love, spontaneity, art, truth, and above all, free-thinking. Or to borrow a phrase from what used to be the backbone of America: life, liberty, and the pursuit of happiness. When we sacrifice these things whatever that soul is that we believe separates us from the beasts *will* be lost. We will be worse than animals. We will be blank dismal vessels living solely for the furthering of the party. Orwell knew these things. He gave us Big Brother as a warning. And sorry folks, by Big Brother I do not mean that goddamn reality television show, I mean Orwell's vision of a future world dictator that you could not escape."

Dennis laughs and I continue, "He gave us that in order to teach us not to place our faith in a lifestyle or a career more than in ourselves."

Taking a long swallow of his beer, Dennis says, "Hear, hear," and raises his glass high.

Then he adds, "Yeah, I get you, I mean, I love my job, but it's not my identity. I'm what you might call a wine vendor. It's great. As far as wine connoisseurs go I am one of the youngest in the business. But it's not 'who I am.'"

So we talk wine. We talk customer service. He says, "We have this one brand of wine from 1787. The purchasing price on it for the shop was about $104,000. We would sell it for somewhere around $150,000."

"Is it any good?"

"No way, it's shit. Wine peaks after about 150 years or so – give or take a little bit. That means it turned to mud somewhere around the early 1900s.

"Then why would someone want it?"

Orbell laughs, "It's only meant for some rich debutante to add to some kind of Nazi museum collection just to be able to say, 'Want to see my wine collection? I have a Bordeaux from 1787.' Hah. But I love my job, really."

"It sounds great," I say, "before I got my church job I worked a bookstore. For me the best thing about working that job was sort of bird-watching the stupidity of the general public. I could scan a barcode and if it didn't ring anything up that meant we didn't have the book in inventory. At that point every single dumb-ass customer to ever crowd my register would laugh out loud saying, 'I guess that one's free.' And then they all laugh, laugh, fucking laugh. Everyone's a terrible comedian. Cackling, shouting laughter at your own shit cliché joke should be a crime punishable by death. No trial, no jury. Just lynch the bastards up and swing them from a tree."

Dennis says, "Yeah, the real joke is that you are going to have to wait twenty minutes for our rookie sacker to go find a manager to try to figure out why your item is not in inventory. Joke's on you, bitches."

"I was frequently busied by ignorant shit eaters coming in and asking for items a bookstore clearly would not carry. Where are your bike chains? Yeah, we keep those with our bikes, sir. Where are your combination locks? Those are in our whips and chains section, ma'am."

Dennis Orbell laughs, "Where are your mufflers? Where do you keep your computer monitors? Do you carry .22 caliber bullets? I'm looking for an ashtray."

Laughter chorus. The Hyena Glee Club.

He says, "Yeah, I really like giving bullshit answers. There's nothing better. I guess I got that from reading Hunter S. Thompson. There is this definite gonzo sensation when I take some poor ass redneck for a ride."

He tells me how he can spend hours telling some people about the perks of fine wine. The grapes for this Champagne are picked in the South of France and the product is aged at least fifty years before final bottling. He says this wine is very dry and very good for filling out the flavor of the right Italian meal. This bottle here is only a step below Cristal. Then some penny-hoarding trailer park stray comes in the shop asking about a four-dollar bottle of André. Dennis says, "This is basically the cheapest champagne you can get and this guy wants me to say how golden shade delicious it is. I won't do it! I won't, so I have started bullshitting the hell out of any clown who pulls that kind of crap.

Oh, yeah. This champagne is made in Nova Scotia. Canada's finest rocket scientists work week-long shifts to produce this stuff.

The winery itself is the size of the Empire State Building if you laid it on its side across seventy acres. They have this grape press that takes up the entire sublevel of the whole compound. It has the capability of stomping all of the grapes at once. The energy required to do this is equal to that of the atomic bomb that leveled Hiroshima or the rocket that blasted Apollo 11 to the moon.

The redneck says, "Really? Are you kidding me?"

"No way," Dennis says, "I don't joke about André."

That night, hitting home at his corner trailer park in Al Bundy-Ville, Dennis Orbell's customer would say, "Guess what, honey, I bought some atomic wine today. This shit is made by NASA and the goddamn Canadians."

"These jobs are all good for survival," I tell him, "but the real goal is to be a writer. Not just a guy who writes, but an actual paid and published, royalty earning writer.

Dennis asks, "What do you write?"

I hesitate to tell him I'm keeping field notes for Jim Morrison and just launch into half-truths and bullshit, "I guess there is this basic philosophy that comes through in my writing that our generation is different than any other in our history. Every generation has had something to fight for, something to protest or overcome, but ours either lacks the ideology or lacks the energy to create it. We're faced with a war that is just as bogus as Vietnam and yet we do nothing. We have had everything handed to us our entire lives by parents who had to break their backs their whole lives. Naturally, they wanted better for their children and so they gave us just that. Only problem is that now we are spoiled. The problems for someone our age are not starvation or homelessness, it's not the terror of the Third World or the deforestation of the rain forests – it's keeping up with the latest fashions and tricking out our cars with all the lights and dials and spinning rims we can find."

Dennis adds, "It's learning the names of the newest infants popped out by celebrity couples and girls trying not to wear the same shoes some other girl will be wearing to the party."

"It's petty shit because all of the serious shit is either taken care of or else it is on the other side of the world. We're a generation of spoiled brats trying to figure out how to make it in the real world. And worse than that," I add, leaning forward and wobbling on my chair, "we have known it our whole lives. The hippies all felt that they were fighting for something, and that they were winning. They lost that fight and no generation since has picked it back up. There is no unity among our generation, only competition for the highest rank on the corporate ladder. Our culture used to be a proud ship, now it's going down and we're all in lifeboats. What we realized in the middle sixties was that our lifeboats have holes in them too. In that situation the first instinct is to try to bail out the bottom and keep it afloat, the next is to grab everything of value for yourself before you take the plunge. That is where our generation finds itself."

Orbell replies, "It's no surprise then that we are such a materialistic society."

"Exactly, we're the bastard children of a long-failed promise, the crippled invalids of the American Quest for wealth and power and prosperity. The dream has failed us and now we are all circling the drain. Our generation, man, we are the Mark of the Beast."

"The Mark of the Man. Fuck, we really are doomed like Thompson said," Dennis grunts, "we are losing and most of us know it. Those that don't know it can feel it, that's why depression is such a huge problem in today's America. I tell you this now. It's a grim fate for the generation that cannot help themselves out of the grip of disorganization. We will never reap the benefits of a meaningful life on this Earth. Our candle is doomed to never light. You see, wicks have always burned fast in this world, but at least they burn bright. Darkness will always follow a doomed generation."

We are the children of Generation X, and they call it Generation X for a reason. X marks the spot and all that. We're Generation Y. Generation Why? Our closest cigarette pull on philosophy and possibility is just, "What the hell?"

We're Generation Why Not?

Dennis slams his palms on the table shouting, "Oh shit, man, you suckered me into another pointless philosophical rant about nothing, you son of a bitch. I came here for a reason. Outlaw's got a show tonight, man, we've been trying to find you to let you know, but you're always out – whatever. C'mon, it's at Rubber Gloves, we gotta shag ass!"

LOST IN AMERICANA: CHAPTER NINE
SAN DIEGO, GYPSY CIRCUS AND THE FREEWHEELIN' TOM SAWYER

The good ole boy drops me in the outer scrabbling territories of San Diego. I hoof it north, trying to find Highway One like Carmen and the Devil told me. About a quarter mile ahead there's this figure in shabby robes sitting at some kind of wooden cart. When I get a little closer I see he's some kind of monk or friar or some fucking thing. He's wearing the cloak thing with the rope belt and the whole shebang, goofy haircut, the works. Sitting there at his cart he gestures with a wave of his hand and says, "I sell these in the name of God. Too few make their tithe anymore, so God has ordered me to take the equity earned as progenitor of San Diego and compartmentalize into smaller business endeavors. So I am selling these lollipop crosses and humor tee shirts to benefit the body of Christ."

The monk looks dead. All gone over like a walking corpse. And I figure by now I ought to know a thing or two about walking corpses. Only he's different. His movements ain't exactly jerking or rigid. In fact, no sign of rigor at all seems to have set in and he smells like lavender, incense and honey. Damn peculiar, to say the least.

I tell him I don't want any of his damn Jesus trinkets and he tries to give me the old vacuum cleaner pitch. Tells me his name is Saint Didacus and he wants to show me the path to heaven.

"Listen, Mr. Icarus–"

"Didacus," he says calmly.

"Whatever, I don't care about your path to heaven and I certainly don't think an antique cart full of cotton candy and bumper stickers is going to get me there any sooner. All I want from you is to know which way to Highway One."

"I see," he nods, solemnly, "Follow this path west until you reach the Record Store. You cannot miss it for it is called the Record Store and it is a record store. When you find that place you must wander through its aisles until you find your way to the shipping dock. The shipping dock will lead you to an alley which will lead you to the Magic Man. The Magic Man will then show you the way."

"Um...okay, weird, thanks."

Reckon I ought to hightail it now before he drops me in boiling oil or force feeds me poison grape Kool-Aid or some other fucking thing. This road, whichever road it is, is quiet and lonesome as hell. For a minute.

Just over the rise of one of many dusty hills I see the multi-colored tattered overcoat of a circus big top. It's the gypsy punk circus, torn clear of Subterranea and set up camp here, in the middle of God-awful, butt-fuck nowhere.

The music catches the wind, accordions, bangles and drums, long before I can see any familiar faces. I speed up down the hill and push my way through a crowd of onlookers dressed up in monk rags, Jesus of Nazareth sandals, Pharisee robes and the whole Galilean costuming of actors and extras from some Biblical Sermon on the Mount rundown.

An impromptu stage is set up on the back of a flatbed farm truck while jugglers and ticket barkers beckon the crowd toward the red, yellow and green tent. On the truck stage, a man dressed in cowboy mortician digs waves an American flag. Every time he shakes it the thing turns into some other flag from some other country, England, Germany, Ireland, Russia, Japan, Canada...whatever. It just keeps changing.

Then the flag turns solid white and he waves it in the air over the back of the truck, down close to the sand. A pine box coffin launches right up out of the earth, taking the white flag with it and explodes overhead in the sky like fireworks, cremation, scattered life, death, colors, gunpowder and music.

The man on the truck stage disappears. He never said a fucking word.

"Tom!" it's a girl's voice echoing across the crowd, "Hey! Tom, it's me!"

Through the crowd I see the brown eyes, bouncing brown hair and bouncing tits of Maggie May barely dressed in some kind of Greek toga and gold leaves in her hair.

"It's me, Tom," she says, smiling all teary eyed and blubbery, "Boy, am I glad to see you. What are the odds, huh?"

"What do you want?" I feel my blood turn cold, and her face, I can see it tattooed all over the place, "Bullshit, bullshit, bullshit."

Then it's just gone and Maggie May says, "Man, I was sure mixed up over Jack Flash, I'm so, so sorry about that. But, I mean, can you blame me? He was my first love."

"You're full of shit, what do you want, Maggs?"

"C'mon, Tom, you still sore? Why can't you be cool? We're together again?"

I light up a cigarette. Breathe in the smoke slow to try to get a thought straight in my head and then I feel this grin wash across my face as smoke pours out through my teeth. I just tell her, "What? Your boy left you so now you want to slum it with me?"

"Tom, that hurts, you're hurting me."

"Hurting you...fuck, I mean, I'm hurting you? Gee whiz, I'm sure sorry to hear that. I mean, you've been nothing but rose petals and holy water to me, doll face, what the fuck do I mean by hurting you? Where do I get off, right? But you know…I mean…Did you happen to notice that you didn't answer me?"

Maggie May sighs, her tits wobbling under her fucking toga, "Yeah, Jumpin' Jack Flash, that's what they call him, he jumped ship on me for a better offer. Some kind of big time conglomerate out of Subterranea thought they could use him for God knows what. It all changed when he got his hands on this big ugly hat. The thing changed his whole style or something."

"Big ugly hat? What the fuck are you talking about?"

"Language, Tom, watch the language," she says, sobbing down into her chest.

"Um…yeah, okay, fuck you, what are you talking about?"

Maggs looks up, tears in her eyes, and says, "We stopped at this pawn shop. He said he wanted to buy me a ring. Can't remember where we were. Shit, where were we? Somewhere near Hollywood I guess. He said he wanted to get a ring for me. So we stopped in this pawn shop and when he saw it he had to get it. 'Cept it wasn't a ring, it was this big dopey stove-top hat with American flag stripes all over it…you know like a Uncle Sam hat or something. Jesus, he bought that ugly thing and forgot all about my ring. Then he got this new job, wouldn't tell me anything about it, dragged us back to Subterranea and tried to check me back into the Hotel California. Now I'm out on my ass, wandering homeless. So I joined up with the Gypsies when I heard they were leaving town."

"Well," I reply, "it's good to hear you have a new career going for yourself, that's always good news. You've landed on your feet, now, if you'll excuse me."

"Tom, wait!"

"Sorry, toots, I got better things to do with my time. I loved you, I did, but that's the trouble with the past tense, once it's ironed out into records and memories, ain't no going back. Not for any of us."

I point up at the sky to the big smoke asterisk left behind by the coffin missile and she nods slowly. But she won't give up, she keeps tugging on me, grabbing me, begging me to have her and I gotta make a run for it. She chases me around behind the big top and there's a gang of motorcycle clowns in punk studs, earrings and tattoos. I hop on a vacant bike with Maggs chasing me down like a she-wolf after a cub. Some clown in leather and shredded denim shouts, "Hey, wait!"

But it's too late, I'm already grinding gears and wobbling awkwardly into the big top showdown with the rest of the nutcases. Don't blame me. I never drove a bike before.

The punk clown bike show circles around the dirt circle amphitheater and I do my best to keep up. Each rider, one at a time, picks up speed up this ramp, hot rods it down and makes this insane loop around this sort of hamster wheel cage that shoots him out the other side, down a ramp and over a big pile of wrecked PA equipment, old show posters, busted post-solo guitars and flaming amplifiers.

"You ready for this, kid?" asks one nut job next to me.

"Fuck no, but it's better than the alternative," I reply, glancing over at Maggs going crazy trying to get my attention or barter for love. She hops up and down, slaps her ass, flashes me her breasts from beside the stands and I just try to ignore her. Past is past, can't go back, life is forward momentum, forward, fast, go, no slowing down or we all crash and burn.

Now I'm up and I crank the handle, peel out in the dirt, flip the gear and ride. I get airborne over the apex of the first ramp and ride like a madman comet; like Slim Pickens on his fucking nuclear missile, I ride and burn toward whatever is up ahead of me. When I hit the big wheel I hit it hard enough to set it spinning as I hit this hole cut out that fires me through a tunnel, up a ramp, across the air and over the burning rock wreckage. Hanging, mid-air, I look behind me and the hamster wheel is spinning hard enough to throw sparks and blue roman candles ignite from behind, whether or not it was part of the show is a fucking mystery.

I land rough on the off-ramp and just keep burning out across the big show circle, keeping my momentum carrying me out between the stands, through the exit and out onto the highway. On the way out I can see the Snake-spined Contortionist twisting into coils tight enough to pop balloons between her shoulder blades and tail bone. She recognizes me and waves goodbye, blowing a kiss as I hit the paved drive of the No-Name Highway.

Field Notes from Bastard Land

10: Rubber Gloves and Ye Gods of Rock

Here we are at Outlaw's big rock show at Rubber Gloves, one of many venues at the heart of Denton, a stone's throw from our neck of the woods, Fry Street Village, Kharma, The Tomato, not to mention all of the neon downtown places where big historic courthouses loom out of the marble slab spotlight and high-arching movie theater sub-light colors blast their marquis enunciations.

And now, ladies and gentlemen...the Main Event. Mount Olympus under the Big Top. And...Action!

I'm mostly just smoking and people watching, enjoying the weird relationship between rock band and rock fan. The audience appears to be shy as the first bands play. No one draws near to the stage. These feet planted solid in the dirty concrete floor all seem to fear the light. A red-green ring encircles the stage as the band glows in their music. We all fear that glow, unready and unwilling to step inside of it. Like stray dogs crying and rolling in the garbage street just outside of your porch light.

Unnamed and unseen.

See, it's just as I've said before, in our eyes a man with a guitar in his hands is a god. We revere him and his music. That stage is his temple, his Mecca, his Jerusalem. Olympus. We fear to get too close because gods may or may not be good, but we know they are definitely not safe.

A few long screaming amped-up chords or drum-crashing sonic booms and we feel the presence of the Almighty. With that come fire and brimstone, judgment, punishment, scrutiny, and the long-forgotten foundations of Sodom and Gomorrah. For this reason a rock show crowd has a simultaneous awe and fear of the stage lights. We won't enter the glow, wouldn't want to risk death by fire. But, like most things, we get as close as we can. Step to the edge of the light. Edge of the canyon. Edge of the ocean. Right up to the face of God, idols, rock and the intimidation of music.

Stray dogs fearing the love of man.

And what do the gods say?

Come into the light, little children, I'm not so bad once you get to know me.

Charlie Outlaw steps on stage and everything changes. He says, "You guys are in for a real treat tonight, I'm playing mostly sober. Last gig I did with a head full of acid and the manager was lucky everyone didn't ask for their money back. The show was free, but he still would've had to pay them back I think."

Laughter chorus and Outlaw gets playing his dead march to the tragedy of a long past dream, a long dead love, a failure of those promises that no one – not forefathers or churches or women – ever intend to keep. The music pulls me in like a whirlpool and I watch the crowd slowly step into the light. Lights flash. Red. Blue. Green. Orange.

Charlie sings, "Play me a lie to burn my tradition...deny ancient times, they can't possibly apply."

Everyone cheers.

The songs themselves are a raucous blending of a southern upbringing based heavily on the tunes of true folk and hard country, a youthful dabbling in Punk, old time Baptist hymns, the color of truck stop fare, burned coffee, toothless waitresses, poverty, and a lifestyle often reserved for longshoremen, long haul truckers, cowboys or the Dude. It's pissing in a bottle while driving 'cause you can't afford the time it takes to stop, or loving a lady so bad that she leaves you with a hard-on and her half of the rent unpaid. The songs are the America that gets missed from the Interstates because you can't see it for the billboard signs blocking your view. They're an America that's revisiting economic upheaval, unemployment, and drowning sorrows in booze, campfires or loose friendships on the road. Outlaw stomps around on stage with a fuck-all attitude that says, "Hey, maybe depression really is a disease, but I can't afford the medication."

So we deal with it. We'll say we earned this. We'll make it our own, now pull up a stump and we'll sing about swimming naked with bow-legged women.

The song is simply titled, "Sailor Song," and hearing it for the first time, it feels like the anthem for this long, tired year.

The croon-growl vocals of Charlie slamming his arms together to the lyric, "She broke my wrists, but I'm still making fists," cuts me to the proverbial quick. Suddenly the house is a schooner at sea and we, all of us, are battening down the hatches for a storm that comes without warning and is met with a rage and unflappability that tells the gods to hit us with everything they've got. The song doesn't make us feel saved or lost, it just makese us feel unsinkable. The crowd moves, voices cheer, and the band stomps a rhythm that is both a sea shanty and a lone prairie love ballad.

And there's Charlie: a folk singer protesting the self, the ego, and bad love, nothing more than that. No politicking. No agenda. He just sings the next song, lyrics that ask about reality, not whether we should be at war or vote Democrat. None of that matters. He isn't yesterday's folk protest singer.

He just sings, "This is a series of dreams," He sings, "Why is this happening?"

He protests existence, protests reality. And I think about Einstein, when he said, "Reality is nothing more than an illusion, albeit a persistent one."

Why is this happening? Why is anything?

On stage, there was my friend, transmuted like alchemical lead becoming gold. He was strong, mad even, shaking a fist at cruel women, the loneliness of masculinity or the savagery of lost hope. He protested like a young Dylan, but questioned life above government or prejudice. Seeming more curious than indignant, as if asking the monk on the mountain what it all was for. His music became the steps to the temple and he kept asking, "Why is this happening?"

In that moment I saw his future as a musician, an ironic ink scribbled mixture of intent and malcontent. He was a harmonica playing prairie man with a desire for love in spite of heartbreak sloppily sutured together with a malevolent booze hound fresh off his ship saying, "I've sailed the seven seas, north and south, far and wide, and there ain't nothing out there. I've seen the world for what it is, a great blue nothing."

The music itself is an eastbound desert train shipping beer and cigarettes and vagrants to a town since swallowed up in dust and economic depression. The band and Charlie alike are brutal men composed of even more brutal ingredients. But you put it all together, the train, the ship, the sailor, the dust, the sensation of an older America tearing up through the skin of this newer, less brave mock-up...you take all that, with the sounds of boots stomping a stage, kick drums, gravel-toned cigarette voices, sweat on a hot microphone, bug zapper stage lights sizzling under a tarpaulin and ship it back and forth cross-country for twenty years and you get Outlaw.

They're your first drink of harsh whiskey when your best friend, the one that started hard living years ahead of you, slaps your back mid-belly burn and tells you you'll get used to it. He says it's an acquired taste. And so's the band. You know, there in that crowd, that it's worth the effort. So is Charlie. He's that oil painting under the Last Supper, covered over by the commissioned work of other, higher paying clientele. But he's still present, indestructible in his place behind the curtain of the obvious, top-grossing, or clichéd. His work, in pen or prose or kerosene soaked tunes, is as immutable as the urge to laugh during prayer or smoke at a funeral. But more than that, it's him. It's his impulse to throw all of himself into what he creates that makes this music both glorious and grotesque. Like a man instantly and simultaneously Jekyll and Hyde, he can seem sinister, beholden, cutthroat, genuine, wise, a fool, and, above all, duplicitous to the point of distraction.

You can watch him on stage with his band or sit with him over dive diner coffee and still see the same vague disconnection with his surroundings. Charlie Outlaw, like the half-breed deformed vagrants in the circus of his music, is two things at once. Always on stage and on his way out, his music, his personality, and even his ideas will leave you feeling welcomed as a brother and abandoned as a bastard son. And that, I think, is his charm. He can give it all away and still leave a crowd feeling hungry. He can break your heart and make you wonder why you ever cared, but still leave you proud to call him friend. Like the best of his kind, he's lived to break the spines of the old and the hearts of the young and if he had a god to pray to for forgiveness he'd tell him it's his own damn fault for not getting the joke. He's that beer train of circus freaks dolled up inside a Southern gentleman, and that is just enough of a contradiction to make him dangerous, cunning, and as inspiring as a wrathful angel.

He croons and the guitar strings scream like lightning in the hand of Zeus. We all feel hypnotized. The band stomps and I feel a part of every faceless silhouette in this crowd. I smile. I nod and kneel at his feet. Overcome, he's not my friend, not right now, he's bigger than that. He is an ambassador of divine energies singing, "Oh, I shouldn't say this, she broke my wrists but I'm still making fists."

I kneel, right in the light, right in the presence of a master.

And he grins when he plays because he knows he has something the rest of us don't. Right now, I know he's the one. He's the one they sent me to find, the diamond in the rough that makes me *their* Abraham.

I shift over onto my ass, cross-legged, sitting right down in the ash tray floor, rejecting any fear of dirty pants and muck and germs. These things amount to nothing when it comes to Rock & Roll. Sit right at the feet of the Sound Lords. Feel the vibrations up through the floor, through your body. Beethoven Style. The only way to fly.

Peaks and climaxes. Ode to fucking Joy.

No one here feels saved, but for a brief moment, a free-ringing electric vacation, we no longer feel doomed. This is all we can expect from sitting at the feet of our amplified Olympus. Carry the big show on the wings of acoustic angels, forget thy doom little children. Salvation, come soon.

I'm sitting here in the Lotus position watching multi-talented bassists, vocalists, guitarists, drummers, laughers, trippers and dreamers. This is unity, the crowd and the band – it's bigger than church, bigger than America, bigger than any one of us. This is the power of the dying, the power of the ones dedicating a song to the whole ordeal. The power of the poor, my friend.

No question.

More than united we stand.

There goes the Main Event.

This is prayer, baptism, sacrifice, loss, gain, penance, greed, giving, desperation, contentment, beauty, ugliness, life and death all wrapped up in the tap of your toe. Hendrix called it the Electric Church, maybe he was right. It might be the only way for a guy like me to ever find his way back to redemption.

A night of drinks, smokes, friends, laughs and the powerful thread that keeps America's underground churning breezes by me and too much of it gets washed away by the amnesia of whiskey drunk straight. I catch a glimpse of myself talking with Charlie and the guys through the booze fog.

Charlie says, "Well, the polls are in, acid-free makes for better tunes, but not nearly as much fun for the music man himself."

Everyone laughs, but for me something is weird. The edges of everything around me start fading out of focus. There is a dark haze surrounding people, objects, beer bottles, ash trays, the television, couches, even lights. The fog must be rolling in, but not now, God, not now. I make for the door and hit the pavement on paranoid feet. I have to outrun this shit if tonight is going to ever be worth a damn. Everything is growing darker, outlined in oil or tar smoke. A green film filters the light of the setting sun. The Denton city sidewalk becomes a conveyor belt, some streets I'm running against it and others it rushes me forward like supermarket ground beef. A sound buzzes my ears like a housefly cranking the distortion on a Marshall amp and shredding Black Sabbath's "Iron Man" through an oscillating electric fan.

I stand still and let the sidewalk usher me along toward the man at the door with his hand stamp and ID scanner. The scanner is a cash register and I see the flash of lights, credit card swipes and discount street sex coupons through the veil. Window shopping an American tradition down the corners and drug stoops and gutter vomit trails of this city. I follow the path without moving my feet an inch. When the conveyor belt dumps me off at the flashing red eye of the barcode scanner I look up find myself in the pack line alley of some lava red factory. I start to head back to the show, but something stops me. A dusty railing and a drop-off into a pool of molten metal. Voices echo over the clang of steel and the steam smolder hiss of machinery. This could be the pit of hell or the engine room of the Titanic. Neither would surprise me. A crane arm lifts and drops large steel crates into the fire. I see a door at the end of a long metal gangplank and make a run for it. Figuring I'd see Denton on the other side, I throw the door open and it's just another room. It looks like an office building, if an office could be a carnival big top. The sideshow barkers, tricksters and shouters sit in tin can cubicles mashing typewriter keys and plotting financial globalization.

Clowns in Armani suits cruise the internet via multi-colored laptops. A central aisle leads to large oak double doors. As I move toward them, two midgets in Shakespearean frills play doorman, ushering me into the ringmaster's main domicile. Inside is faux modern décor. A long steel desk sits intimidating in front of wide bay windows overlooking the main burners of Subterranea. Cave wall arches move upward into vaulted underbelly stone cathedral ceilings. Smoke billows orange. The window overlooks the furnace and the crane as it goes about its work. I can see the crane arm silhouetted behind the steam, the orange glow, and the massive form of a tall man standing at the window with his back to me, hands folded behind him.

"We've called you here to see if you want to play for the winning team, Mr. Bluff."

"Is that right?" I ask, "Well, I'm not interested. I have this thing about clowns."

"There are clowns on both sides, sir," the man replies, "We all learned that a long time ago. The sooner you catch up to the Now, the better."

"And who are 'we,' exactly?"

A high, shrill voice laughs through its nose. Light ramps up to a brown-out haze, casting six lonely halo pillars of the figures seated behind the steel desk. There's a bearded woman in a very professional, red business suit with knee-high skirt. Next to her, I see an obese man-child dressed in over-sized baby garments and a man with the face of a beagle of some sort. An empty chair for the man at the window sits center stage. A dark-haired woman dressed as a snake charmer caresses a boa constrictor and, at the far end, a clown with the twisted looking tumors of a leper or some kind of sufferer of elephantiasis smiles dumbly.

The deformed clown is the one laughing through his nose.

At the window, the man with his back to me catches the light. He is wearing a finely tailored pinstripe suit that looks like it's from the early eighties. His face, reflected in the glass, reveals deep-set eyes, a full Mark Twain moustache and strong chin. He turns to face me, revealing a pair of head-sized womanly breasts, stretching the buttons of his jacket from the strain.

The Man with Breasts says, "We are the Ghosts of American Past, Present and Future. This is the Board of Trustees of American Dream, Inc. I am the Chairman of the Board."

The Bearded Lady says, "Each of us manages some portion of this fine company. Music, literature, the beauty standard, humor, it all gets brought under our umbrella and filtered into marketable capital."

The clown cackles, folding his one swollen, bulbous hand into his shriveled gimpy hand, and says, "I'll make this fun, what do you think I am?"

"I don't know," I shrug, "warped value systems, bloated senses of humor...the American sitcom?"

The man-child laughs, spraying food and grease with open, chomping jaws, "Pretty close, the kid's pretty good."

The clown, scratching a fungal hunchback through his frilled Pagliacci collar, explains, "I am the corruption of humor, when you can get people to laugh at death itself then you can get them to do anything."

"We have called you here," the Chairman repeats, "because we need a representative of the arts. We have been vying for a merger since the early '40s, but have only managed the purchase of certain companies, not the effective core."

"And you want me to infiltrate that core? Is this a joke?"

"No, no joke," says the Bearded Lady, "America needs to be united under one ideological flag. Empires crumble with too many conflicting value systems."

"So you think that united flag should be your company? That sounds like a monopoly."

"Mr. Bluff," says the Chairman of the Board, "we can't deny the inherent financial benefits of bringing all facets of this culture into our proprietorship, but this isn't about monetary gain. This is about uniting this country on one basic principle."

"I thought it already was...does life, liberty and the pursuit of happiness ring any bells?"

"Come now, Jack," looking at me through his swollen eye and winking the big one closed, the Elephantiasis Clown says, "that is far too traditional of a point of view for someone like you. You're better than that."

Dog Boy grunt-barks, "America lost sight of traditional values a long time ago. The other side fights to restore those values, but we know that once something is dead then there is no bringing it back. We want to give America new values."

"You mean your values. And your values are what?" I ask, "Finance? Upward mobility? Global marketing?"

"No, no, nothing that small," laughs the Bearded Lady, "we are offering unity, the utopia of the American dollar."

"I don't think so," I move toward the door, "you're peddling cheap tricks in fancy packaging. You people probably invented the career politician too."

Dog Boy slobbers, "We did, but they also invented us."

"You'll have to forgive me, but it's a no. I can let myself out, thanks."

"Just know, Jack," says the Chairman grimly, "this offer ends the moment you walk out that door. And if you aren't with us then you are just as expendable as the rest of them. Our organization can make for a powerful enemy."

I let him know I'm not with him by slamming the door behind me. Under the Big Top, the sound of tapping keys, telephones ringing and desk worker babble bangs away its unmelodious anti-climax. I make my way through clowns and phone jugglers to the black door glowing menacingly under a red exit sign. The door opens onto a street I don't know, but it's Denton again. This has got to stop. The Gray Man stands across the street from me. He points at an imaginary wristwatch, tips his hat and waves with two fingers. I look down to check the time. When I look back up at him he's gone, as usual. Damn! The party, it's 9:47, the party starts at ten. No problem, I can make it if I run.

LOST IN AMERICANA: CHAPTER TEN

THE RECORD STORE AND THE DESPERADO'S QUEEN

I burn rubber, flat out, as far as downtown San Diego when I found what that dead monk was telling me all about. The Record Store, some kind of living morgue with sliding glass doors and boxed window for the dead. I stand giving it a good eyeballing before heading in. From the outside it's just a glass coffin and I see Snow White peddling apple pies to dupes, skunks, tourists and passersby. Inside, there's music cookin' it out of big speakers all around and the off-putting aesthetic of Frankenstein's laboratory is not lost, not even on me. And I'm a real idiot.

Bubbling chemicals, coils of electricity and jars of brains hooked into computer monitors line the aisles and are labeled A–Z. They're arranged in different sections. Rock n' Roll, Blues, Pop, Rap, R&B, Jazz. These are the cloned brains of anyone to ever write a song or tell a joke in their life and they're hooked into computers so they can keep writing their music or making up jokes or writing novels, even beyond the grave. The Record Store's found an earthbound, chrome-plated grift to keep people in business and producing even after they're dead. For the right buck you can pop in and buy your own copy of whoever you want, bring them home and get them working for you too.

I book it quick to the back of the sales floor like Saint Didacus said. There's gotta be a door 'round here somewhere, but I bump square into someone's burly old gut and fall flat on my ass instead.

Looking up, there's the crooked chewing tobacco teeth and gnarled facial hair of Jumpin' Jack Flash, only, not quite Jumpin' Jack Flash, he's dressed to the nines in an American flag suit with tails and a striped tall boy hat just like that old fuck – Uncle Sam.

"Well, hey, man," Jack Flash says, reaching down to help me up, "Fancy meetin' you here, have you seen Maggie, she told me she was gonna try'n find ya."

"Yeah," I reply, "I seen her, what of it?"

"Oh, nothin' at all, I meant no harm by it," Flash replies, "Just, you know, I'm done with her now so she's all yours if you still want her."

Jack Flash chuckles nasty, beer breath sprays down on me as he ribs the guy next to him. I didn't realize they were together before, but he's some kind of a mutant or something. Some kind of deformed freak, I don't know, but he's tall and round with small feet and giant mother cow breasts tucked proudly under a double-breasted pinstripe business suit. He has this weird, whiskery walrus 'stache like some kind of Colonel Mustard look-alike and he just stares at me with cancelled, Laundromat eyes.

Jack Flash says, "Oh, sorry, buckaroo, this here's my new pal, Mr. Chairman of the Board, he gave me a great job as the New Uncle Sam. What do you think?"

Gesturing toward the hat with his thumb, he kind of strikes a pose and the Chairman rolls his eyes. Glaring down at me like an elephant seal in heat, the Chairman says, "I'm sorry, dear boy, we must be going, I'm afraid the nature of our agreement is not something I wish to have discussed with street tramps or pickpockets or whatever it is you're supposed to be."

Jumpin' Jack Flash says, "Right, right-o, hadn't thought of that, well, you just never know what'll happen to ya if you pick up the right thing in a pawn shop, eh? I bought this stupid hat and now I'm a very rich man."

"Jack," the Chairman tries to mask a shout, "if you please, we must be going."

"Right, yes sir, you said it, business is all concluded here for the day, better get going. See ya 'round, kid. Thanks for being a good sport."

And as they leave, just because he called me names, I lean my shoulder hard into the Chairman's gut and he swears under his moustache. I smile and run for the back of the shop, looking down at the wad of cash in the money clip I just snaked out of the pocket of his finely tailored slacks. Figure he had it coming, after all, he used the word "pickpocket."

There's a tall red door with a sign says it's for Employees Only. I go through anyway, expecting an alarm to sound, but nothing happens. I find myself on a loading dock in the back of the Record Store, crates and pallets and stacks of what could only be new shipments of dead celebrities or folk heroes are all around. Dodging a forklift I leap off of a truck ramp and make for the back lot.

A crowd of workers and employees has gathered around a makeshift stage on the flatbed trailer of a parked truck. Wood crates and barrels make a staircase up to the top and some men are there making music for all to see. They're playing mouth harps, washboards, banjos, kazoos, kick drums and four different guitars. Words spike the air, words about getting stoned, riding trains, fighting the man, beating the devil and freeing your mind.

The drummer lets out a high swirling yelp, a hollering blues joyful yawp at the top of his lungs and everyone smiles. But I don't. I watch his head flop down on his chest and run red. The sting of gunshot bites my nostrils and smarts the air something fierce.

The drummer is dead, but his hands keep moving. He keeps playing. He never stops.

A cymbal crashes and shrapnel splinters out of the center of the washboard. It rings a different sound as the man swipes his spoons over the cracked ribs of his instrument, but even with a hole in his heart he keeps plugging away. Every crash of cymbal or kick of the drum and another one goes. The band drops off one by one like lemmings on a catapult bridge. Someone in the crowd is picking them off one at a time to the beat of their sounds and no one seems to notice but me.

I watch their skin run blue, their instruments run red. I watch parts of them break off from shotgun blasts, but they just keep jamming to their riffs and yelping their blues. As long as the music plays they don't even know they're dead. It's like they can't die.

Rhythms dull to a slow crawl, the band moans their blues to a deep earth-shattering toe tap and I can feel it. It's almost the end. Guitars strum slow and the vocalist sings through a warped, ripped tracheotomy throat that he knows the game, the game always ends the same way. He sings, bellows, growls that the house always wins. And on one low throbbing note the song ends like a truckload of radios smacking flat into a brick wall.

With that final note, like heaven's trumpet, the walking dead and their music fall to the ground all together in a heap of blood, mesh, wood, bone, limp arms, gaping mouths, blank eyes, microphones, amplifiers, guitar strings broken and the shrill smell of air expelled with the thrust of a bullet. The music stops and they just fall into each other in a human bundle right there on that corkscrew stage.

No one seems to notice or care. They just turn away, disappointed that their entertainment is over. Dissatisfied and craving more. It's like this everywhere, down the road, or in the hotel, or in bed…it's like this. I start to turn down the yellow, tattered shoulder of the road feeling a mosquito bite sentiment nagging at the back of my head, itching furious trying to tell me something – like, maybe I'm still not really out. I kick dried weeds and gravel, stirring dust something fierce as I meander.

Now a man in a black tuxedo and top hat hops on stage, kicking a few corpses aside here and there and shouts, "Don't go away just yet, ladies and gentleman! We've saved the best for last to be sure."

My attention gets rekindled and I turn to watch him. He pulls flowers out of thin air, a rabbit out of his ass and scatters a deck of cards on the wind just to have it morph into fifty-two white birds. Everyone cheers and laughs. I figure this must be what that fragrant zombie, Saint Didacus, must've meant when he told me to find the Magic Man.

On stage, the man shouts in an overly theatrical voice, "Step right up here, watch the mystical incantations of the wonder-fluous Desperado the Great. I've traveled the world far and wide, challenged snake charmers in India and witch doctors in darkest Africa. I've been imprisoned in Turkey and a captive of the Hotel California only a stone's throw from this very spot, but none of it compares to the awesome trial of what is to come next."

People giggle to themselves, clap, smile, whatever and Desperado the Great shouts, "I need a volunteer."

So of course he points right at me and bellows, "You, what about you, young master?"

The crowd practically fires me onto the stage they're so excited and Desperado fans out a new trick deck saying, "Pick a card, any–"

"Yeah, yeah," I interrupt, "'pick a card, any card,' we've heard it all before."

The crowd chuckles and I grab one out of the middle of the deck. But when I touch it the damn thing starts to kind of twitch in my hand like a bird hatching out of an egg.

Desperado says, "What? Oh no, not her. You drew the Queen."

I turn the card over in my hand and there's the Queen of diamonds looking at me sideways. Both of her heads, upside down and right side up, turn to look straight at me and shout, "You! Tell me where he is? Where is he? Answer me? Desi, Desi, I know you're there. You kept me in the deck with those other whores again, Desi. I told you not to do that. My God, if you so much as utter a syllable I will…"

The card bursts into flames in my hand and I drop it to the stage. Desperado blows on the end of his wand with a grin and says, "There you have it, ladies and gentlemen. I've been meaning to do that for years."

He leans down close to my ear and says, "Ex-wife, I banished her to a playing card ages ago…looks like I finally got the last laugh, after all."

Over the sound of crowd chuckles a voice says, "Hey!"

Everyone turns, but I know who it is before I see his fat head periscoping over all the faces. I try to duck down behind the stage, but there's nowhere to go. Too many people, too many watchful gazes and not enough nooks. Or crannies for that matter.

"Hey!" Jack Flash calls again, "Anyone seen a kid? Little bastard went and snatched this here feller's wallet?"

"Well?" Mr. Chairman of the Board growls.

Right then, as if things ain't bad enough, I hear the low rumble of chopper engines and the high cackling shrill notes of that coven of biker witches, the Fat Bottom Girls. They're onto me, figure Jumpin' Jack musta dimed me out to that fat, titted bastard in the suit.

"Is this for you, kid?" Desperado the Great asks, leaning down close to my ear.

Nodding nervously, I gulp loud as Independence Day and reply, "Uh-huh."

"No worries, buddy-roo, into the magic box. I'll make you scarce."

Desperado practically throws me into some kind of pirate's chest painted black with purple satin lining, and I brace myself for a squeeze. But as the lid closes behind me I just keep falling for a second and then there's this plop and squish. Like what it might feel like if you landed on a cloth tomato the size of a Doberman or something.

A match strikes. Light ramps up on the angel pin of a candle wick and there's this woman dressed in red wearing a diamond necklace around her neck with rows and rows of stones like a wide Cheshire cat smile. She's leaning back on this chaise longue made of velvet kinda like the one that used to be in the French colonial wing of the Hotel California. Her back is arched making her tits and thighs way more noticeable than they ought to be.

"Well, hello," she says, twirling ornamented fingers through rings of black hair.

"Um...hi," I say, stupidly.

"Step into my parlor, said the Spider to the Fly."

"Yeesh, what?" I ask, "Is this your web?"

"No, no," she smiles ruby red, "I'm the reason the cat grinned and so are you."

"What? Why did the cat grin?"

"The cat grinned," she laughs, smoky as her candle flame, "because he swallowed the canary. Isn't that right?"

"I don't know what the fuck you're talking about, lady."

"Eden."

"What?"

"The name is Eden and you're in the belly of the cat."

"Eden, huh? I don't know nothing about no cat, but which one are you?"

"Which one am I? You mean, the woman or the serpent?" she asks, trying to guess at my game.

"Nope, I mean the Tree of Life or the Forbidden Fruit?"

"Ah, excellent question," Eden replies, standing up from her chaise longue seat and slinking her way toward me on bobbing hips.

She sits next to me and leans in close, a little too close.

"Why don't I let you decide for yourself?" she asks.

I get up off of the plush tomato cushion and pace around nervously. I can't think of anything to say and decide to light up a smoke, despite the lack of ventilation.

Eden says, "I take it you've seen Saint Didacus?"

"What the – how'd you know?"

"He traps everyone the same way, gives them directions right to his so-called Magic Man. Desperado the Great pays him a high-end commission for every mark. His little trinket stand is just a front. He's really out there to see to it that folks like you end up right here."

"And where is here?" I ask.

"This is the magic box of the Desperado. He puts us here to bring his deck to life."

"His deck?"

"Yes, when you go in the box your life enchants a card in his deck. I've been his Queen of Diamonds for years."

"His queen?" I whisper, "Are you the queen? Does that mean? Are you the one I'm supposed to be looking for? There's rumors out there, talk of a queen."

"I'm just a card," Eden replies, "I don't deserve to even be compared to *her*. The true queen, she's out there, she's real, but I don't know where. She's the source of goodness, a name with meaning everywhere, here and Otherworld. But she's not here, in the Desperado's box there are many rooms, but only one house…a house of cards with no real queens…and no kings."

"That sounds familiar."

"Does it? I said the same thing when he helped me leave."

"Leave?" I ask her, "Leave where?"

"The California. It was this other place that had many rooms."

"The Hotel California? Jesus, is everyone from there?"

Eden reaches out and gently takes my cigarette, dragging slow and leaving a ring of red around the filter. She nods and replies, "Probably, I can't say for sure. I have been here for so long. Every now and then I get out if someone draws my card, but I always get folded back into the deck. Sometimes, when the money is tight, Desperado deals me out to his clientele and tells me to banish men from my garden if they lack the currency."

"You too?" I shrug, "The California seems to have a knack for grooming young prostitutes, I reckon."

"You reckon correctly," Eden replies, "But I am not so young as I look."

"Ancient as the hills? So you are the Tree of Life, then?"

"Perhaps I'm both."

I take back my cigarette and drag hard and scared.

When I hand it back I ask, "I've heard there are no kings inside the Gates of Eden, that mean anything to you?"

"No kings, no gods and no men. There are only needy children, but there are no trials either. Sit down, relax. We have nothing but time now. Desperado has searched for some time to find a new Jack of Spades. I guess you're it..."

There's a long pause and I reply, "Tom, the name's Tom."

"Tom," she says it flat and it suddenly loses its meaning, Eden turns it into a blank syllable and it's not my name anymore, "Tom, come and sit down beside me."

I feel like I can't say no, or maybe I don't want to. Next to her on that stupid cushion I feel warm, like her candle fills me up with incense and fire. She removes my bowler cap and pushes strings of matted hair away from my forehead. Eden kisses the skin she exposes with her touch and holds me close to her heart.

"Tom," she says, "it has been so long since I have had anyone. Here, put inside this box, I want you to be with me. I want you here – as a woman, not as a card to be dealt or as a garden to be banished from. Just as a woman."

Something inside of me cracks and my head falls limp into her chest. She kisses my neck. I kiss hers. As the candle burns low in dim orange light we slowly peel away layers of clothing, touching skin and moving deeper into her paradise. And I know the answer.

She's forbidden fruit, but life was boring before we took it.

Time moves as ambiguously as the magic box, the satin cage. Naked and sweat-writhed I let my head fall to her bosom once more and feel her chest rising high and low like a sleeping mountain cat. Her hand pets my dirty hair.

Eden sighs. She says, "Tom, I know you're very young, but you've been with one of us before, haven't you?"

"Yes'm, a girl called Maggie, one of the daughters of Miss Molly, the brothel mistress of The California. She lit a fire in me something fierce before I sprung out…shit…feels like a billion years ago by now or something."

"Maggie," Eden makes the name go flat and lifeless like before, "I knew her once. She took my place."

"Your place?" I ask, looking up without lifting my head.

"Desperado was a prisoner like the rest of us, but he ran one of his cons. Called it the Pennsylvania Twist. He had a man on the outside bringing him a pretty young thing. The outside man checked into the hotel under her name and in the confusion of a room change after Desperado and me were done with a toss we made our move."

I know the outside man is Jumpin' Jack and I'm in bigger trouble than I thought.

Eden continues, pawing my hair and talking sultry and monotone like a river trickle, "Desperado and me got in his box, said it was the only way. The outside man checked his little tart into the room. Desperado and I got shipped out on a truck. Come into my parlor, said the Spider to the Fly. You can fill in the rest."

I sit up, looking her straight in her dark eyes and say, "He got out?"

"Yes."

"But you didn't?"

"I couldn't," she replies, "My card wasn't drawn. The outside man only pulled an ace, Desperado's ace. He didn't draw my queen of diamonds."

A curved pale finger pets the jeweled smile around her throat and her face sags, only for a second, into a look of unbewildering despair. I kiss her full on the mouth and press into her again. The jeweled smile catches the candlelight, her face lights up as brief as it dimmed.

Eden folds her arms across my back and pulls me into her body, tight. It feels wrong, sort of confounded and backward, more motherly than a lover's embrace. Reckon so anyway, if I'd o' ever had a mother. But I don't stop her. I just fall in and let myself be her child.

There are no kings inside the Gates of Eden, only scared shitless little kids.

Field Notes from Bastard Land
11: 21 Drunk Speak

When I get back to the Yellow House the party is still being set up. I still feel rotten as hell, but it doesn't take long before enough is happening to get me good and distracted.

A group has gathered in the front yard, centered around Red in his cowboy boots and fiery hair, his skin flushed with excitement and clammy undertones from the winter bite of the Denton wind. He shouts, "Hoo boy! Well, gang. I might not survive the night. Operation 21 is almost a go!"

Signs are posted on the red front door. "The Drink Will Pour and the Blood Will Spill." Right beside it, "No Hippies, Tree Huggers, Animal Rights Activists, or Communists. Are we not Men?" On the porch wall it says, "Private Party, NO MINORS!"

Counting down to the Main Event. After a long absence El Paso Slim approaches with two leaking plastic bags – one in each hand. Dragging a line of water across the Yellow House wood floor, Slim says, "Where do you want these?"

Outlaw says, "Those are going outside on the pikes. You know,

French Revolution style. Let them eat cake, the Headless King, rebellious peasants, Mary Antoinette and all that."

I ask if El Paso has human heads in the bags.

"No, no, but I do have the next best thing. Pigs are anatomically closest to humans, you know. There's a metaphor for ya, right? Right-o."

Slim smiles showing me two weeping pig heads in the plastic, their mouths gaped open in screams of fear shouting, *"Eloi, Eloi, lama sabachthani?"* which means, "My God, my God, why hast thou forsaken me?"

Brother Red says, "Oh boy, yeah, those go out front. Get us some pikes. We don't have any left after our last weird shindig."

He tugs at his long red beard and disappears like a shot into the Yellow House.

Now Slim, Outlaw and I are breaking the bamboo shoots that form the barrier between the Yellow House and this Mormon church next door. Their last line of defense has fallen. I shout, "Hey, Mormons, come have a drink with us! Hey!"

There is, of course, no response, but we all have a laugh anyway and begin shouting our own sacrilege as the pikes get carved and planted in the earth. We stab the pig heads onto the bamboo and step back to admire our work. Two pillars of Death stand on either side of the stairway into our party.

Brother Red inserts candles into the mouths of the pigs and says, "There, this looks pretty good. That will ward off demons, Republicans and Vegans. We are men, we eat meat."

"What has that got to do with anything?" I ask, "Do people actually eat pig heads?"

"Oh yeah," says Red, "why do you think we sent El Paso Slim? Those fucking Mexicans love that shit. They eat pig heads with every great meal."

El Paso is trying to relight the pork face as I ask, "How?"

"I don't really know," Brother Red replies, tugging at a lock of orange hair, "I guess they boil it or something."

Charlie Outlaw shouts, "Goddamn Mexicans! Don't they know a head is all skin and bones?"

"And brains," Slim adds and everyone goes quiet.

Now they hang another sign around the chopped neck of the left-hand pig: Abandon All Hope Ye Who Enter Here.

Time passes with controlled insanity. Hours sag by like elderly tits bouncing unbridled on a busy, winding nature hike. Now it's down time. Counting the ticks on the clock, everyone waiting for the Big Upset. The Main Event. The Mark of the Beast. 666.

I hear someone say, "Where's Brother Red?"

A voice answers, "He went to go wash his balls."

"Oh, yeah?" Voice replies, "That's a good thing to do, you don't want to let your balls get too stinky, go in for a blowie smelling like stale cock and the deal is off."

"Yeah, it's like that old doctor's office adage about wearing clean underwear at all times. You never know when you might have a sudden car wreck and need to get stripped down into a set of ass-less hospital gowns."

"Or get stripped down with some random nymphomaniac. You want to be prepared."

I call this part *21 Drunk Speak*. Action!

Time moves differently at a party. Moments go slipping by like a bare-assed caveman tumbling down the Ice Age–paved hills of Lombard Street. It's mostly pictures now, sensations. Brief memory glimpses on the time train.

Now Outlaw sets up and the music gets roaring. I stand on the back of the couch to get a good look into the eyes of the band. The party is a newborn, but already has its own strong pulse by the time they get settled in. Outlaw works everyone into a frenzy with tunes and insults and laughter. He sings his sailor songs and everyone stomps the hardwood pirate plank floor of the Yellow House. Lyrics echo off of the walls and I listen in with my drink.

"Play me a lie to burn my tradition, deny ancient times they can't possibly apply…"

I take a long drag on my bottle of André and watch people moving beneath my feet.

"...our mystery's authentic 'cause everyone lies..."

Dennis Orbell kisses a girl on the other couch, when that gets boring he tears off his shirt and dances half naked in the crowd. A lot of shirts come off, a lot of people move together in unison like seaweed swaying in a riptide.

"Oh, you're half a baptism 'cause you'll never fade out."

A pair of female hands tugs at my shirt and I pull it off the rest of the way, dancing on the back of the couch with my cheap champagne. André: Atomic wine for the Al Bundy-Ville demographic.

Outlaw croons, "Oh I shouldn't say this, she broke my wrists but I'm still making fists."

As the song wraps to a close Outlaw steps down and we all stand momentarily eclipsed in the Olympus sonnet of the band. Shadowed and illuminated by rock and roll, the silence is a brief epiphany before someone moves to turn on some stereo sounds.

Now the CD player is cranking *The Very Best of Thin Lizzy*. A personal choice of our nearly departed Brother Red. Red comes to the microphone and shouts in a drunken sad voice, "Well, the clock is about to strike twelve. And when it does Operation 21 will have been a complete success. I am going to the bars now and want you all to know that if I don't make it back alive you have my love."

The minute draws close and we pause the music. Everyone counts down like a New Year's Eve party waiting for Brother Red's balls to drop. Five. Four. Three. Two. One. Happy Legal Inebriation.

Right at that moment a shirtless Dennis Orbell cues the CD player and Brother Red makes his escape to the sounds of "The Boys Are Back in Town." He runs for the door with all the other bastards of legal drinking age rushing out behind him. Everyone pats him on the back, kisses his cheek or shakes his hand. Now Red is gone.

I feel something hit. Like a tidal wave in my blood swarming slowly into my brain. The colors of the piss tinge walls and tar plank floor vibrate and morph like melting wax. With that bottle of champagne still in my hand I watch, laughing, as everyone in the room blurs and draws multiple around me. Everyone is dancing at my feet as I stand on the back of the couch. All of them moving and rubbing, sweating, caressing, and breaking. For me this is ugly, it looks so small and pathetic from up here.

Now I feel something working into my eyes, those same demons prodding me with their spears, yet fueled by some new foreign chemical. The fog rolls in and I know I have to do something to break through and hold onto this otherwise perfect moment in Bastard Land.

Right now I should be seeing the beauty of all of these social outcasts united under one roof and four yellow walls. I should find myself enamored by the potential of having so many involved in this newest century's underground culture. After all, this is a good party, it should be fun, but these dull child ass shakers dancing on the dirt wood floor of the Yellow House are just driving me deeper into a fit.

Swatting at the air I start to talk, "Dance, my little ones, dance, dance your weird rain dance and try to make us clean. Bring the rain, because all of us, we're all bastards. The Bastard Children of The Trail of Tears, The Civil War, the Great Depression, WWII, The Hippie Movement, Vietnam, Nixon, Clinton and the Bush Dynasty. The War in Iraq. And the long dead promise that these things do not matter as long as you have a wife, children, house, and minivan.

"We're bastards because the promise left us at birth. Like a father leaves his son. We've been abandoned because we're finally learning that this weird gold-plated dogma won't last much longer. It's rapidly becoming more and more inbred. The way you can breed an animal with its mother for so long that the gene pool becomes stagnant.

"You get mutant babies. Two-headed dogs. Cats with four eyes. Humans with three fingers and stubs for legs rolling around in the muck shouting with tongueless mouths, 'Feed me!' But their mouths really say, 'Fulmuy!' And it's your job to know what that means. You have to spoon-feed them tapioca pudding and carrot-flavored baby food and they sort of just let it slide to the back of their throats like slugs."

Here I am standing on a rust-iron platform overlooking an army of deformed voters and politicians swarming like bees to the Queen hearing the call of gold reserves and returning to the hive to duty-fuck. The Queen Bee, a gigantic Statue of Liberty lying on her back, tits up, legs open, welcomes all who want to be free in her prison. Her ex-copper patina robes rolled back to show an iron bush. Come on in. She's mass birthing mutated free peoples of the Constitution like a factory. All the worker bees stand in line waiting to cum into the Queen's loading zone. Eggs are fertilized and slide down the fallopian pack lines, shrink-wrapped, incubated, and sent out the way they came in. A finished product. Deformed hermaphrodites and eunuchs walk out of the vagina with each other's parts. A set of Siamese twins walk out half-developed, the big one hobbles away on his elephantiasis right leg naked and erect with his brother's head growing out between his thighs. A smiling, cackling, talking head on the tip of his penis. Spurts jizz out of his mouth when you stroke his back and Big Brother moans.

Lady Liberty Queen Bee pushes and remembers her Lamaze class exercises. Breathe, breathe, breathe, push. Breathe, breathe, breathe, push. She pushes her mutant children into the world at record speeds that satisfy the CEOs of her company from sea to shining sea. Her children immediately take up their good corporate work. Pick up the worker bee song down the assembly line, whistling while they work.

The Man with Breasts and The Bearded Lady clink their glasses together and pat each other on the back for meeting their quota and taking their business public.

And The Mother Brain says, "Tradition is the key to success. Keep doing what your fathers have done before you."

But that doesn't work. What does that get us?

"God-damned inbred retards," I say, "that's where we're headed. American Bastards. The dream has been pushed and reused and ejaculated and fertilized and birthed and rebirthed and C-sectioned out of the minds of colleges and universities and lawyers and doctors and car salesmen and supermodels, movie stars, talk show hosts, tabloid magazines, department stores, big movie remakes, Beverly Hills, Fifth Avenue and the gangrene asshole of the Statue of Liberty for so long now that there is nothing left to love. The American Lavish Promise is a deformed kid spitting blended peas and Brussels sprouts like diarrhea of the mouth shouting, 'I pledge allegiance to the Flag of the United States of America and to the currency for which it stands.'"

Waving the green glass champagne bottle through the air I shout, "The gene pool is spent. All the bastard children have been fucking the same mother and father for too long. George Washington and Lady Liberty push out new Suburbanites every day. That's why we need a new dream, a new woman to bring our children into this world. We need new purpose. We need a better, modern, fresh promise because this one stopped working long ago. We were just too mutated to see it.

"Or maybe this generation's dissatisfaction, failure to launch, and confusion are all the early warning signs of a serious deformity setting in. We are the first twisted Side Show Freaks produced by the dream. Three eyes in our heads to see where the flaws are located. Extra hands to feel out the lies in the dark. Giants and midgets to spy the problem from different angles. We're Bastards because we are deformed retards. Our Father the Dream took one look at us and split for the door saying, 'Good God! You call this human?'"

Down a swallow and I say, "You see, the American people have been mating with the same ideals for so long that it was only a matter of time before we produced this Generation of Mutants. If our children have any hope for survival we must stop now. Find something other than paper money, diamond earrings, Fort Knox and the right kind of house. Forget your SUVs and your designer clothing. That's all a pussy fucked so long and so hard it's stretched dry, thin and bleeding. The only children it can produce are human maggots with slug bodies and baby faces crying and puckering up for their mother's milk bags. A worm with a human head rolling around in placenta and that tar slick crap of a newborn It. No more.

"Just because we've become so inured with money, business, and science that art has lost its voice should not mean we lack the creativity to come up with a new plan. The dream is dead, fucked to death like a rape victim. Now I know I'll have to hit the road to find a new promise. A new goal. I have to find the Main Event. The Kingdom of God. Something beautiful. Somehow we learned to replace beauty with productivity. And that, I'd say, is the disease. Well, not any more, cut off the sick limb and burn it to ash.

"Jesus said, 'If your hand causes you to sin, cut it off and throw it away, if your eye causes you to stumble, gouge it out and cast it away from you.'"

The longer I talk the more the dark cloud thins out. Fog lifts. My demons start to disperse. I can begin to see light at the end of my anger tunnel. Just a little longer and I will have ridden this storm out to the end.

"Now stay focused, Jack old boy, the true mission statement is that the Mutant Generation stopped believing the lie a long time ago. Some of us don't know it yet, but we all feel it. It is for this reason that depression has been labeled a disease in our time."

The Expert says, "Pharmacology and drugs and pills are on the rise. Everyone has a therapist. Everyone wants to avoid feeling their pain. Everyone wants a new religion. Scientology. Kabbalah. Dr. Phil. Oprah. Buddha. Jesus. But. These are superficial solutions. We might as well be rubbing Neosporin on a bullet wound. Or taking aspirin to treat a malignant brain tumor. Cut to the heart of the disease, treat the issue and the symptoms will care for themselves. And the issue here, ladies and gentlemen, is that the old views of success are long dead."

"The American Promise says, 'Work hard, get rich, buy things and die happy.' But I ask, if that's true then why is it that so many millionaires, CEOs, rock stars, and celebrities off themselves with a bullet to the brain or run their lives below sea level with drug addictions? They achieve the much desired climax and realize that there is no fulfillment in fucking that mother. So we must quit.

"Unite together to find a new way to live, otherwise our generation is doomed."

It's at this point that I down the last of my bottle of André. With the six bottles of beer, two shots of vodka, Willie Nelson's Whiskey River, that glass of wine and now the last of this cheap champagne, I guess it's safe to say that last swallow was a little too much. Things begin winking in and out. Dark. Fade to light. Fade to black. Fade to gray. Swimming visions. My feet are standing on Jell-O. I try to grab the air for support and laugh because even drunk I know that's ridiculous.

I guess I overdid it. Now I'm tumbling backward off the couch. Now my head is going through the glass door of the entertainment center. Thin Lizzy skips a beat and all the dancers moan. I'm on the ground, out cold, but half unconscious I can hear someone grumbling about "ruining their song." Great, you guys are good friends, my head is bleeding and all you're worried about is the CD scratching for a second. Motherfuckers. Goddamn inbred freaks.

My mouth tastes like rust and everything goes dark.

LOST IN AMERICANA: CHAPTER ELEVEN
OUT OF THE BOX

I don't have much time to get this all down. It will be gone soon. It may already be too late. They told me I'd stay in holding until the procedure took effect. It ain't exactly science, might take hours, and it might take minutes. I have to hurry.

Right now, I'm in that weird magic box of Desperado the Great. The ground shakes like the death rattle of a loud, throat-clearing earthquake. Lamps and vases topple over and Eden squeezes me close.

"We're back," she whispers, hoarse and terrified.

"Back?"

"The epicenter. Your home...and mine. They've brought us back."

"What?" I almost shriek, leaping to my feet, "How can you be sure?"

"The light is different here. See..."

Eden points toward the small porthole in the wall and I can see the yellow tinge light of the desert outside. Highway Zero stretches on for miles and, something I never noticed before, but every-thing looks stagnant. I think about Einstein charting theories on Benjamin Franklin's blackboard. Photons, he calls 'em, they don't move right here. In fact, they don't move at all. There's light here, but old light, the same old light that's always been here, just spi-raling around like algae in a dead pond.

"No, no, no," I squirm, "We can't be back, I've worked so hard to get out...how could they–?"

"They'll be taking you to the Agency if you're lucky. If the Agency gets you then you'll get out of here, but if not then...you'll be like me. You'll become part of the deck in his talking card trick. He'll make you his new Jack of Clubs. He'll set you on fire every night to let you know when to shut up. The Desperado wants this, I'm sure of it. He hasn't been working with a full deck in such a long time."

The last echoing notes of Eden's voice trail off into darkness and instantly, without any kind of warning at all, the lights just completely go out. Candles are snuffed, the porthole goes dark, even the smoldering orange ember tip of the incense twig burning low in the corner is just gone. The only sound is just my breathing, raking heavy, close to my face like the way it used to sound hiding in the closet as a little kid or something.

"Eden?" my voice comes out choked and hoarse sounding like a wimpy toad, "Eden, you there? Hello?"

I'm alone. Darkness weighs in like a bayou fog and then a ribbon of white light, straight as a ruler, breaks the darkness in half. Expanding fast into a rectangle of yellow, the light fades into the shapes of three heads and I see the overexposed faces of Jumpin' Jack Flash, his buddy the Chairman, and Desperado the Great.

The Chairman grins under his walrus moustache and says, "Well, m'boy, if we had only known who you were when we bumped into you we might have saved a big heap of trouble. Lucky for us, our agent in the field had the exit covered."

Jack Flash says, "Fact of the matter, boyo, is we've been looking for the one for a while now. Funny, I never thought it would be you."

I'm too busy lying flat on my back in a coffin to wonder what the fuck that's supposed to mean. The lid is open and these jokers are just grinning down on me like a bunch of pederast clowns in the children's wing of a goddamn hospital. Whenever I try to sit up Jack just puts his foot on my chest and presses me back down. Finally I shout, "All right! All right! Assuming anything you just said made any fucking sense to me, what the hell do you want? All this trouble just because I busted out of that fucking roach motel?"

They laugh, all three of them laugh and I suddenly feel very small in this goddamn magic box. Desperado says, "He thinks this is about...Ha! That's priceless. Priceless!"

"I assume you know what to do, Mr. Flash," says the Chairman of the Board.

Jack nods and lifts me up by the waist of my pants, throws me over his shoulder and carries me like a sack of grain toward some squatty little stucco-sided building. Desperado and the Chairman follow close, even play doorman with polite smiles on their faces. We pass through the glass doors at the front of the building, filmy and dusty with what looks like years of sweat, grime and condensation. They let the doors swing closed behind us and Jack Flash drops me on the dirty linoleum floor.

Standing up and brushing the dust off my knees, I see rows of long wooden bench seats like a church sanctuary. Sound lingers heavy, echoing like the depression cheer of a suicidal banker locked in his own vacuum vault. Pens scrawl on clipboards bearing paper forms, applications, affidavits and crossword puzzles. The sound of ballpoint pens stretches out like tearing sheets of tin. A helicopter fly buzzes reconnaissance missions on the Viet Cong jungles of time-stalled patrons. Dust crumples like tumbleweeds in a desert cemetery.

Everyone sits, waiting on the Man.

A semi-circle of clerk countertops sits ahead of the pews. The cancelled cheer of the workers behind the counter issues through microphones calling numbers one by one. Eyes blank, voices static-garbled and robotic, they count up from forty-seven and the parishioners of this weird office church move to the head of the room when their number is called.

I can't help feeling that the numbers mean execution.

Jack Flash forces me into a line where I'm given a number, 59, and now I wait. Counting up, digit by digit, until it is my turn. When we finally reach the counter the attendant on the other end is the severed head of Dan Rather attached to a swivel chair with mechanical arms and a respirator. His work station is obviously the only thing keeping him alive. The arms have three-prong grip claws that pull levers, punch buttons and adjust the microphone for sound.

He says, "State your business."

I'm about to say, "I don't have a fucking clue," when Mr. Chairman of the Board speaks up for me and says, "We're here for reassignment under Article 656 of the Citizen's Charter of Subterranea."

Robot Dan Rather nods, "Ah, yes, insubordination and refusal to accept one's allotted role. Penalty for a 656 violation requires the lotterization of character identity, work assignment and a memory wipe."

"Memory wipe?" I shout, trying to break for the door.

Jack's firm gorilla hands hold me in place as Robot Dan asks, "What is the perpetrator's lottery assignment? Or should I say, what 'was' the assignment?" He chuckles a simulated computer laugh that sounds dusty from lack of use and adds, "Apologies, a little city council humor. It's not for everyone."

The Chairman hands over a laminated card that looks cracked and aged. It is quickly snatched away by a mechanical arm and inserted into a scanning device that bleeps and scrawls like the Xerox machine Columbus must've used when copying crew files for his tax audit. A receipt printer spins out a twisted toilet roll of paper with my name all over it. Everyone nods and grumbles under their breath until the machine is done with its work. The clawed hand tears it away and hands it over to the Chairman.

"Congratulations," Robot Dan Rather says, "You've been randomly assigned to Furnace Room 10 – Labor Class. You will be keeping the fires of Subterranea burning."

Mr. Chairman of the Board smiles down under his moustache menacingly and says, "You should have known your place, now we'll find a new Tom Sawyer to take your place, and you will be forgotten – even by yourself."

"Sorry, kid," Jack Flash shrugs, "couldn't be helped."

"Dammit," the Desperado stamps his foot into the dirty linoleum, "I really could've used him for my deck, too."

"Boys," says Robot Rather, "Take him away, please."

The clawed hand buzzes its console and a wooden panel in a far wall slides open. Six young shoeshine boys in trousers and suspenders run out of a hidden corridor and drag me inside without a word. I scream for help, grabbing at anything I can to keep from going behind the wall, but they are strong for being so goddamn small. The door slams closed and everything goes dark.

Field Notes from Bastard Land
1 : Exeunt to the Road

Close-up on Charlie Outlaw's face fading from black to overexposed white. Fade-in. Fade out. He's so close his face is blown up like the big screen, like Mount Rushmore. Charlie Outlaw for president. Hello? Hello? Are you in there? Snap out of it. The Soundtrack is jumbled. *Words are flowing out like...we don't need no education...like a rolling stone...everybody must get stoned... needle in the hay...needle in the hay...Wake up...are you all right... I pulled into Nazareth...was feeling 'bout half-past dead...*Action!

I open my eyes and Charlie is right there saying, "Dude, I am so sorry. You got really weird back there and it was totally my fault. I gave you the wrong bottle. That bottle of André was full of acid. Good shit too, the kind for a seasoned professional like myself."

"You dosed me with LSD?" I say, groggy and rubbing my eyes, "Where am I?"

Laughing, he says, "Um...you're on the curb out in front of The Tomato."

"Where are my shoes?"

"You started screaming that they were restricting you, that you wanted to be a man of the earth or some shit and you kicked them off. You've been wandering around for several hours, man. I'm really sorry I lost track of you and all. One minute you were out cold on the coffee table, the next you were gone. I'm just glad the police didn't pick you up."

For some reason I just start laughing, hysterically laughing, and Charlie says, "C'mon, let's get you up."

I can't stand. Lights fade from dim to obscenely bright and I keep laughing. I try to tell myself the acid is wearing off, but I'm still in a weird place. Flashes of thoughts and memories come to life right in front of my eyes. Where am I? Right now I'm in some kind of weird wooden box with no windows or doors. There's beer trash and potato chips and clothes everywhere and it's all crawling around on the floor like snakes and cockroaches. The walls are lined in aluminum foil that vibrates like laughter. It's a coffin, that's where I am. I'm buried alive in a cube-shaped coffin. Anything I think becomes reality. Weird colors. Twisted vibrations. Madness like battery acid in the veins. A quick flash of the party has me in Brother Red's room with some girl. I'm naked down to my boxers and she has her top off, then she makes a face that reminds me of my ex-wife and I tell her she has to stop.

"What?"

"We're not doing this. I think you should go."

She won't leave, she's actually trying to negotiate, but I feel like I'm talking to The Destroyer. I push the girl out of the bedroom door with her still topless and crying. Just then I hear, "What the fuck?"

It's Jiggs and he's pushing Charlie Outlaw out of his room, the girl with Jiggs shouts, "What did you think you were doing, you little prick? This is where *I* fuck!"

Random memories – quick flashes hit me in this weird underground.

Cut to early this morning. Dennis Orbell at the Yellow House door. Action.

"I have donuts," he says.

Jiggs says, "Oh thank you, thank you, Dennis. Now eat shit and die."

Dennis says, "Dude, I just got you donuts."

"Did I say 'eat shit and die'?" Jiggs asks, "I meant 'I love you.' I'm so bad with words."

Everyone laughs.

Now I see a line of men in gray suits moving in a single file line that spirals around the outer wall down into the center of the room. The floor opens up into a metal working furnace. A conveyor belt lowers the men into the flames. Chains and claws pull out buckets of them liquefied down and pour the contents out into a mold. I start laughing and the mold snaps open with steam and smoke. The Wall Street Bull snorts hot air and glares me down.

Brother Red is standing in front of it like a matador with an American flag cape and he says, "Jack, it's okay, just calm down. Look at something in the room and just will it to be normal. Do you remember that book *The Perks of Being a Wallflower*? You remember how the kid does acid and gets really scared? What does Samantha say? She says stare at the ground, focus on it until it is still and then make everything else stop shaking."

I listen to him. I stare at a potato chip with insect legs that is crawling over a bottle of Shiner Bock. It sits still. Its legs pull in under its shell and it is a normal chip. I feel better. Brother Red says, "Good, now sleep this off."

Cut.

Cut to the Yellow House living room. Night. Our lead man wakes up in Red's bedroom, opens the door and finds the house dark. Action.

"Hello?" I say in a shaky voice. The power is out and no one is here.

I greet the room one more time for good measure. "Hello?"

That's when it hits me, like a coffee can full of crickets tap dancing downhill, something clatter-traps open in my gut and sends me rolling with momentum and noise and a hollow ping. I'm back with Bonnie before I can snap a finger, key in the ignition and burning rubber onto I-35. It hits me all at once. My time at the Yellow House is done.

I hit the Interstate hot and head for New York. I have to find America to let her know it's going to be okay. Behind the wheel of Bonnie now and I'm watching East Texas melt away into that familiar yellowed-out sand haze of the Ghost Road.

Here I am again. This must mean I'm lost. Just before the last of the Texas Piney Woods disappear I see the Gray Man out of the side of my eye, like a hitchhiking mirage. When I turn to look at him, he's gone.

This is Highway Zero. The Ghost Road. You can only find it if you're not looking. And if you find it then you're already lost. Up ahead, the billboard says, "Welcome to Subterranea. Est. circa 1776."

I'm speeding through in Bonnie's arms. She hugs the shoulder, spraying dust and gravel. The road vanishes to a point on the horizon. Desert on all sides and a yellow-brown sky overhead. Rusted crucifix telephone poles divide the asphalt from the sand.

I'm speeding now, somewhere between Over Here and Over There. In the distance is a figure sticking a thumb out sideways. Bonnie rattles closer and I see liver-spotted skin and bones poking through like bread sticks under limp dough. The man is naked down to his underwear, which is stained gray and spattered in red and brown. I'm already imagining what he must smell like.

His graying hair is greased into limp twine and he has the chin tuft of an aging mountain goat. Under protest, Bonnie sprays sand clouds as I scream to a stop.

The old man stands on chicken soup bone legs and grabs a trash can top hat wrapped in an American flag bandana. He walks, bow-legged, to Bonnie's passenger side door. The window rolls down and the man says, "Much obliged, young man."

With a polite bow he places the hat on his balding scalp and climbs in beside me. I try to hide the fact that I clearly underestimated his smell.

"Where you headin'," I ask, tritely.

"Anywhere, just away from here."

"Well, which is it?" I grin, "Anywhere is about 40 miles south of Here. Away From Here is West on Nowhere Highway."

"Where's Here?"

"I think we're leaving Here," I reply, "I don't really know, I just arrived myself. It looks like we're almost to Subterranea."

I can sense his body tense up beside me on the felt seats. Glancing over, I see his stone gray eyes go ice cold with fear. Trying to lighten him up, I say, "What's wrong? You owe somebody money or something?"

"We have to turn around."

"Why, what's wrong?"

"It's a bad place. If you go there, you never leave."

"Oh, come on, that's ridiculous. I've been there, I've seen those jokers. They're all talk and weird face paint. What's the big deal? Why does everyone get so worked up over Subterranea?"

"No! Don't say it, you must not say it out loud!"

"Geez, sorry," I laugh, "what, are you afraid it's going to find us or something?"

"Yes, exactly, don't say it again. Promise me you won't say it again. It can't know I'm back. It just can't, okay?"

I try not to laugh or get too pissed off and just shrug, "All right, Jesus, I promise."

"We have to turn back," he repeats.

"We can't go back," I grunt, "there's no turning back on the Ghost Road. Forward only, always ahead, movement, momentum, just keep going!"

"No! Turn this heap around or let me out!"

He grabs the wheel and I slam the brakes. We spin wildly off of the road, into the desert sand, and slam to a stop in a yellow cloud. I cough and swear under my breath.

"All right, old man," I sigh, "you win. We'll head back to Anywhere. I hear they have this diner there that makes the best key lime pie, anyway."

Bonnie groans and I ease her forward onto Highway Zero.

The man relaxes some and drops his head into his hands.

"Thank you," he moans, "you have no idea how close we were."

Feeling the need to change the subject, I say, "My name's Jack. Jack Bluff."

"Pleased to meet you," he says, looking up and shaking my hand, "the name's Wilson."

"Sam Wilson," I cut in, "I know, the goatee and hat were a dead giveaway. So you're supposed to be Uncle Sam, right? What happened to you?"

He laughs snidely, but not a normal laugh. His laugh has this rusted-out wheeze, like if you could dig up the first Stanley Steamer automobile from the deserts of some distant, apocalyptic future and tried to crank the engine. His laugh had the tin-pan rattle of gears not quite meshing and the gurgle of empty fuel lines trying to pull fumes from a time-eaten tank.

Uncle Sam says, "Wow, kid, where to begin? How far back do you wanna go?"

"Look, I'm just driving," I reply, "I don't need your whole life story, old timer. I was just curious about how you ended up naked and bloody in the middle of the desert."

"America has forgotten about me, sonny."

There's that word again. Sonny. Cute, the old bastard.

"She still hangs my posters around and flashes my face in war time and election years, but she's completely lost sight of who I really am or, at least, who I used to be."

I shrug, "No argument here, gramps, but that's not an answer. Unpopularity doesn't account for bruises and missing clothes. Did you lose a bet, or what?"

"You could say that," he groans, that same rust engine wheeze in his voice, "I wanted to make it in Hollywood, y'know, get into pictures."

"Is that right?" I ask, "Well, you and a lotta other people."

"Yer tellin' me, kid," he seems to gasp for air, like a seasoned smoker, "Anyway, I did lose a bet in a manner of speaking. I bet big, bet it all, and lost."

"What did you bet?"

"Every penny, hope and second I had left. I bet that if I threw in with all of that, I might make it in movies and America would love me again. Her interest isn't in ideology anymore. It's celebrity now. You have to dazzle on that silver screen or yer nothing."

"So, let me guess," I cut in, speeding wildly around a passing family of tumbleweeds, "Hollywood chewed you up and spit you out."

"What can I say, buddy boy? Ya got me pegged. I got jumped on Hope Street for my boots. They worked me over sumthin' fierce. Some kind of gang of fashion queens on the prowl for the next big look. They got sight of my boots and wouldn't take no for an answer. Damn, it's too bad too, those things were antiques. I woke up bloodied in an alleyway puddle. Two weeks later, my boots were on the cover of Cosmo. Well, I walked around in nuthin' but my stocking feet for a while. Started hittin' the sauce pretty hard till the cash ran out. I pawned my suit, one piece at a time, just for a lil' more drinkin' money. When I finally realized I's too old for Hollywood I did the dumbest thing I've ever done."

"What's that?" I ask, implying the rest of his story was laced with straight genius.

"I hocked my hat for bus fare outta town."

"Yeah, but I see you found a new one, what's the big deal?"

"This old thing? I found this in a dumpster out back o' some magic shop. It's nothin' special – my hat, the real one, was the source of all my powers. Do you think an old bugger like me'd go walkin' around in something like that 'cause he thought it looked good?"

"Um...well, yeah," I reply, "Yeah, I did. I mean, I just figured you had no fashion sense or something."

"No sir, it was what made me Uncle Sam. It was the source of my energy, what made me the Protector of America. Without it, I'm witherin' away to nothing."

"I see," I reply, somewhat unimpressed.

"I don't think you do, sonny," the old man hacks coffin nail breaths into a fist, "I'm dying, and worse than that, the slime ball that bought my hat is holding the soul of America on some shelf with a pawn ticket. We stand to lose everything if we don't watch ourselves. I'm a fool, kid, the guardian of the American spirit for 200 years and I trade all of it for a few drinks and a shot at Hollywood fame."

"What's your point?"

"No point, I guess, 'cept I need my hat back."

"Don't look at me," I shrug, "I'm tapped out. I've got nothing but hopes and desperation keeping Bonnie's engine running."

"It's prolly too late now anyway. My last hope is to head east and keep my fingers crossed that I can bump into America. It's gonna be tough finding the ol' girl, her and I been on the rocks fer years now."

"That right? Lover's quarrel?" I ask, ribbing the old man a bit.

"Ya think yer jokin', sonny, but ya ain't wrong. We had a thing, her and me, for years really, but we split up on account o' I got a little big for my breeches. See, we were lovers. She's the one what gave me all my powers to begin with. Without her I ain't nothin' at all. I gotta find her. I should've done this years ago."

"Well, gramps," I shrug, "You're in luck, word is, I'm supposed to be doing the same thing. What do you say we look together?"

"Well, hot damn, kid, yer just full o' surprises!" Uncle Sam shouts, practically hopping out of his seat, "Maybe I'll just give you the full spectrum tour, combing every corner of this here land, sea to shining sea! We're bound to find here then, ain't we?"

"Yeah, about that...what would you be giving me a tour of, old timer?"

"Of the Safety Factory, of course."

I nod a few times and reply, "Oh, right, right...Yeah, I've been hearing that term tossed around here and there, what does it mean?"

"Well, hot damn, son! How'd you manage to find yer way out to Highway Zero and not know what the Safety Factory is?"

"Just lucky, maybe?"

"It's some kinda luck all right. Ain't sure whether it's good or bad. Anyhoo, I'm afraid if I went about tellin' ya what the Safety Factory is ya might not believe it. Better to see fer yourself. How's about pointin' this beauty East and I'll see about showin' ya?"

I nod and hang a left onto what should be the corpse remains of Route 66. And then I see it, just like my dream when I met the Gray Man. The Pacific Ocean crests over a yellow hill and spans sapphire ahead of me like a canvas. And I know that this isn't the Ghost Road anymore. And this is definitely not Route 66. Somehow, this is Highway One. For another quick flash I see the Gray Man wave and disappear.

Uncle Sam slaps his thighs and says, "Hot damn, son! You're better than I could have hoped. You turned east and found the west coast! You're not far from discovering America after all. To get to the heart of this thing, you have to get so lost your compass turns upside down. Good boy, you stick with me and maybe we'll turn things around for both of us. What do you say?"

I say okay and light a cigarette while I head back East.

LOST IN AMERICANA: CHAPTER TWELVE
DEPARTMENT OF MISSION VIOLATIONS

Inside is an eight-foot windowless cube and I reckon this must be what a jack in the box feels like. The shoeshine boys toss me into a dentist's office sort of chair with a high back and no cushion. Before I can even say otherwise they're clamping my wrists, ankles, even my neck into this rust bucket and get to work on my eyes.

The shoeshine boys get after me with bailing wire and duct tape so my lids get held open like the chest clamps of some alley cat heart surgery or some shit. Then they get to oozing in drops of some strange-smelling chemical water with a medicine dropper, laughing like a bunch of fucking hyenas. Most of them just kick back on their heels watching, snapping their suspenders and tipping newsboy hats back on their heads, whistling low.

The lead boy says, "The eyes may not be the window to the soul, but they are the ticket window on your way to memory. Memories are funny little boogers. A sound, a smell, anything can bring them up. But it's always pictures when you think about 'em.

218

The smell of cinnamon makes you see apple pie. It's all visual, so the key is to go in through the eyes."

A freckle-faced little ham hock with an upturned nose and mule teeth says, "Yeah, don't worry, it won't hurt like you think."

"What is this place?" I ask, "What are you gonna do to me?"

"Ya mean you don't even know?" says some kid from behind me.

Lead Boy says, "Look, Mac, I don't know your story, and I couldn't care any less than if you was the poorest, dumbest, most forgettable sap since God chose dirt for Adam. That said... you ought to know that this here's the Department of Mission Violations. See, everybody in Subterranea gets an identity. If ya fail that identity then it gets taken away from ya, got it? The ones that fail real bad, somebody doesn't make for a good Abbott and Costello maybe, or let's say there's a James Dean that's just a little bit too big a pushover – well, you get the idea."

Freckle Face says, "The Shoeshine Boys come in and clean 'em out."

"That's the idea," says Lead Boy, "Clean 'em out, wipe 'em down, and give 'em a new face and name."

"Been that way ever since ADI got controlling interest in town," says the freckled brat, "now they determine who you get to be and how you'll be remembered. They make you in the image they feel will boost revenues. It's all economics now. And the bad ones are the ones that are bad for business."

"The real bad ones, though," Lead Boy chimes in, "they don't get a new identity. They don't get to be anything at all, just a job. Now, I don't know what you did, Mack, but that's you. That's where we're sending you. Got it?"

I'm just about to say something when my eyes burn like a branding iron. White light floods everything out in a wink. I hear a voice say, "Bleach 'im out boys."

And then

I found this book stuffed in my pillowcase. It's not finished, which is too bad. I liked where it was going. Too bad about the boy though. I think he really did love that girl. Not really sure why I'm doing this now. There's still so many pages in this journal that ain't filled up yet. I guess I just gotta finish this, maybe for my own amusement or some goddamn thing.

I don't know. I reckon this must've belonged to the guy that worked this spot ahead of me. I can't remember some stuff, but I still feel like I'm sorta new. He, whoever he was, he probably came down here, slept in the same bed, did the same job. It ain't much of a job really. You just sorta pull levers all day, sometimes you shovel.

My supervisor says the furnace burns up memories. Says it's a place for things that never made their mark in the world. Something about history remembering some stuff and forgetting others. I don't know, I ain't never been much of one for paying attention to that kind of thing. Way I see it, he says shovel coal, I shovel coal. He says man the levers, I man the levers. They just sorta guide around these big mechanical claw arms that come in, pick up crates of something or other and dump 'em in the tank.

It ain't much, really, but I like to imagine that I work in the bowels of a ship sometimes. You know, pretend like this is some kind of boiler room where the fires keep the engines rolling for the *Titanic* or whatever. I guess I don't really know where I am, I can't especially recall ever seeing the sun or anything. The punch card says I've been here going on two weeks. Sometimes I wonder what came before that, figure maybe I'm some kinda newborn or something. Maybe I's born big with unseemly capacity for pulling levers.

I'm sorry, I guess I'm sort of rambling. Reckon I ain't much of a narrator.

Let's see, the lunch bell howls its blues at the orange stone ceiling and a bunch o' the boys let out a Hoo-boy! We pile into the locker room, stacking tool belts and work helmets on metal shelves with a hollow ping, and the chatter of friendlies rattles the cement walls like insects on a summer's night.

I reckon it's on account of the serious nature of our work, although I'm not entirely sure what that is, but none of us get to call each other by our real names. The Foreman tells us that when our time on the job is up then we'll get our names back at the door. For now, we're just numbers. #0327 works the conveyor belt for combustibles on Level Three. #0246 is team leader for the loading dock of those bizarre crates full of the remains of our unspectacular past.

They gave me #0006. I work basement level. Generally I just pull them big iron levers to adjust for pressure, heat, that sort of thing. Basement Level is home of the Regulator. It's this big electric can opener–looking monstrosity that sort of sits right under the fiery lake of Subterranea's main furnace.

Generally speaking, the whole facility, this entire goddamn factory, is run on the heat of the big furnace. But not the Regulator. It has to work separate from the furnace in order to make sure this place don't get too hot. That's why, sometimes, I gotta shovel coal into its big mouth to keep it breathing.

I work Terminal 8 on the Regulator. She's sort of this metal kettle with central valves and chambers, sort of like a giant heart. There's eight of 'em in all and I work number 8. Shoveling, adjusting dials, and pulling levers all day for sixteen hours. Our standard shift. Some of the guys try to get us shorter shifts, but the Foreman always says, "Whatchoo gonna do with fewer hours, boys? There ain't nothing to do 'cept work."

Anyway, shit, there I go again – chasing rabbits. I'm wasting paper in this poor guy's journal. Unbelievable how bad I am at this narrator biz. Well, I'm hanging up some of my work junk in my locker, getting ready for some grub, when old Zero strolls up. He's been here since they first started handing out numbers. He says he got all zeroes on account of any proper number system needing to start with zero instead of one. I didn't really get it, but it seems to matter when you start getting into higher digits.

Reckon that might've been a bit of a rabbit track too. Oh well, Zero's important to me so you need to know about him. Well, Zero strolls up and pats me hard on the back. It sort of gives me a rattle and I spin around greased for a rumble, but he's there smiling so I say hello.

"What d'ya think, bucko? Good day?" he asks.

"I think so," I reply with a shrug, "I mean, I imagine I can't tell you it's nice weather or anything, but there ain't been no trouble on the lines and you seen how well the Regulator's doing today."

"Damn fine day, you said it," Zero nods.

We walk together to the cafeteria and get on line for beans and cornbread. A cook with clown makeup, a tall white paper hat and a claw for a hand splats a slop of beans into a bowl and sends me on my way. I grab a husk of yellow bread and we stroll to the nearest table without a word.

Once I'm sitting down Zero says, "Well, kid, it happened again."

"The dream?"

"Yeah, it's every night now," he grumbles into his beans, shoveling them into his mouth with a crooked spoon, "It's as if, every time I go to bed, my dreaming mind is screaming, trying to tell me something. Once I get to sleep I find myself convinced, without a doubt, that I am Napoleon Bonaparte brandishing a sword or riding a horse into battle or surrendering at Waterloo. Last night I was shivering in a damp cell in the Bastille."

"So do you still think you're going crazy?" I ask him, staring down into my food to avoid his cynical glare.

"Do you? No, I'm sure of it now. Sure now more than ever. I am Napoleon. What did they tell us? We'd get our names back at the door when our job lease was up. I'm telling you, kid. My mind is remembering whatever it is they covered up. I am Napoleon, but in here they just want me to be Worker #0000."

"Yeah, I'll bet," I shrug, "and I'm George Washington."

"Yeah, maybe you are, Washington when he chopped down that cherry tree as a kid, right? Anything's possible. I only know one thing. The trick to finding out is in getting a look at what's in them crates upstairs. I've been asking around the barracks, of all the job descriptions in this place ain't nobody ever seen inside.

They come in from another place, shipped on rail lines through underground tunnels. No one sees inside until after they've been cleaned in the fires."

"Zero, you realize how crazy that sounds, right?"

"Does it?" he asks, "What did the Foreman tell you? They're recycling memories in there, right? Melting 'em down for purification so they can be used to fuel the next main era. What does that mean though? What if they're burning up the memories of who we used to be on the outside? What if we never get outta here, kid? Do you want that?"

"Well no, I guess not, but it seems so…"

"Farfetched, right, I know…it don't change a goddamn thing though, bucko. I'm going. Tonight. I'm going to find out and you're coming with me."

Field Notes from Bastard Land
13: Road Mash Up, Vendors, Safety Factory, America or Bust

Exterior. Highway 101. Daylight.

We pass a Mexican vendor working a fruit stand that sells pickled freedom in glass jars. The sign says they're a dollar and a quarter. Over the hill there's a sign that says we hit L.A. and Sam tells me the population is made up of giant ants colonizing the sand, building up out of the desert. He asks me to take him by the pawn shop to check up on the hat. I find it on Charity Street, a dilapidated memory of what might have been an old theater or studio warehouse. A sign dangles crooked over the rust-hinge door, the name is unintelligible in wood-burned lettering. We go in together and show our ticket, but the man behind the desk shakes his head.

"I'm sorry, fellas," he says, "someone came in here days ago and bought it outright. Offered me a good price, I couldn't tell him no."

Uncle Sam swears and shouts, "What! How could...do you even know who I am?"

But the pawnbroker just says no and we head back to the car.

Heading north now.

In Monterey, at the Naval Academy, the ants go marching in single-file lines and Sam explains how Santa Cruz has this prostitute named Eden who says, "I'll let you tend my garden for the right price," but she'll banish you if you don't have the currency.

The old man rambles on about what he's seen on his road, "There's a record store in San Diego called the Record Store. They sell the cloned brains of Jim Morrison, John Lennon and Jimi Hendrix. For five easy payments of the still-beating hearts of four immigrants, a pound o' flesh, three gumballs and a mail-order proof of citizenship you can have anyone reprinted and sold to ya in a glass of formaldehyde."

Bonnie's compass says north, but we hit San Diego anyway. On the corner of J Street I see the bright neon flash of The Record Store. George W. Bush leans against my window and says, "Check it out, I just bought Richard Nixon, half off."

And Father Cannonball, who likes to blast himself ass first over the moon and into the child pool with his knees folded up to his chest, just bought his seventy times seventh copy of Jesus Christ. Out near San José there's a Mexican vendor throwing up beside a stand that is trading ACME Coyote immigration kits for a steel bullet vibrator and a Hazmat suit. When we pull the car to the shoulder Uncle Sam screams, "Which way to Winston-Salem? We want to buy our cigarettes factory direct!"

The vendor says he'll show us the way if we'll just take him as far as Kentucky Fried Chicken. I tell him it'll be a piece of cake, there's one on the corner.

"No, no, Kentucky, the state Kentucky. I want to buy my chicken direct from factory."

So we spin it east and cross over the chocolate ice cream peaks of the Rocky Mountains. The sun sets and Father Cannonball explodes out of the western sky and bounces off of the moon, landing on his back in Savannah, Georgia, like a flipped insect. We're on our way down the non-refundable highway now.

TREVOR RICHARDSON

"So, Sam, let me ask you something," I say, "do we have to ride this highway, it looks like corporate America here. Non-refundable toll booths with no exits, Starbucks, McDonalds, Walmart lining the streets. Can't we go a different way?"

"I'm sorry, kid," he replies, "this is the only way out of the Safety Factory. We have to punch the core before we can find the edges."

"Do you mean the way back to my world?"

"Round about these parts we always called it Otherworld," Uncle Sam replies, "I've heard tell that they've been keeping America on the move since her life's in danger now and whatnot. My sources tell me she's been moving in and out of the vortexes, popping up between worlds. We find the edge of the Safety Factory, we'll find our way to her."

The Vendor says he doesn't remember entering the Safety Factory and Uncle Sam tells him that if you haven't gone in then you can be damn sure that you haven't made it out. He says, "Madame Boheme in Pentecost Park used to tell me, 'If you don't know then you are maybe already there, but to be sure you should bite your thumb at the Unknown Soldier and see what color your blood flows. If this does not work you must promptly paint your face with your thumb like the Sioux warrior, strip off your clothes and jump six times followed by a backward rain dance around the monument. When you finish and have certainly died then you will have made it out of the Safety Factory and into the Void where worlds overlap.' It's probably hogwash, but that's what that old hag used to tell me, yessiree."

"I've never heard any of that," I grunt, "Sounds like bullshit. So you're saying we gotta jump through all those stupid hoops just to get outta here?"

Sam says, "Yessir, way I figger it, them boys that set you off on this path musta known somethin' they ain't tellin' you, 'cause the disappearance of America is directly connected to the increase of these vortex monstrosities showin' their faces all over the Safety Factory. They're the true ticket, buddy boy."

"Why do you call it the Safety Factory, Sam? I thought this place was supposed to be called Americana?"

"It is, but that's the world, I mean, why do you call your world Earth, but also the United States of America? One's what it is. The other's who owns it. The folks runnin' the mills of Subterranea own it all by now. They say they're manufacturing security for all of the people of Americana. So we that try to resist 'em, we call it the 'Safety Factory' as what you might call an off-color sort o' joke. Lets us know who's in and who ain't, ya foller me?"

I nod and the feed jumps forward.

Here we are in Memphis. I bought a faceless love a rose, but it was smug and I fed it to a black cat. Next we kick the Vendor to the Kentucky curb, he takes his hat off as a thank you, and we huff it on fumes out to Chicago.

I park Bonnie in a lot outside of Sears Tower and say, "Dude, what're we doing here?"

"Who cares? We're here, right?" Uncle Sam says, "Let's jump right to the heart of this city, where's the scene?"

We walk the beat down toward the Navy Pier. A beggar is drumming on a five-gallon bucket. I give him a nod and ask, "We're searching for the Main Event. Any idea where to start looking?"

He rolls a sweet roll on the kettle bottom and replies, "The Main Event? There's a big vintage show out by Union Station. Yessah, museum cars out on the street and all the planners in their costume pinstripe suits. Just follah the music."

Uncle Sam says, "Hell yeah, that sounds like what we're after. Could that be it, kid?"

We turn a corner and walk back in time. Young flappers and a jazz band plays the mood. Some dance. Everyone is watching. They've rolled out a blue carpet and you need to be from their era to ride that train.

Uncle Sam says, "Oh, man, this is not our world," he twists his thin hands in a panic, "I'm getting weird vibrations. Let's go find our people."

Turning another corner puts us back in the 21ˢᵗ Century. Now I see the uniform of the Indie Movement. Young criminals in Chuck Taylor high-tops and tight pants walk the beat. Dozens of them line the sidewalks. On a high corporate wall a kid in red Converse and a rock tee shirt smokes alone. Girls in denim skirts and striped stockings flit like a pack of she-wolves hunting for Chicago scene kid love.

Uncle Sam laughs, "Jesus, we must be getting close. Indie kids are coming out of the woodwork. There's gotta be a factory around here somewhere pressing them out hot and ready and turning them loose on the city."

"Well, let's go find that factory," I reply, "We can find the pack lines and split their prototypes in two. Stand over the broken pieces and say, 'I broke the mold after that one.'"

I find Bonnie sitting quiet in a parking lot, but I'm sure it's not where I left her. Climbing in, her doors close around us and I ground floor it out toward Winston-Salem.

LOST IN AMERICANA: CHAPTER THIRTEEN
LEVEL THREE

Sneaking your way up to Level Three ain't as easy as it sounds. Work never stops in the factory. It circles the clock, twenty-four hours a day. That means eyes on you at all times. Sneakin' our way up a rickety mousetrap spring set of spiral stairs gets us up to the mail room. There's Kâli, the six-armed goddess, sorting mail and answering phones and picking her teeth and typing data into a huge computer from 1972.

Zero freezes cold and clamps arthritic fingers around my arm, just above the elbow. His eyes broadcast fear like two wide satellite arrays. We're never supposed to be above Level One with our clearance and here we are sneaking from the Level Two Hall to the stairwell. Voices clatter-trap down the hall like voice boxes of childhood dolls. Someone is coming and we duck in through the nearest set of double doors.

This is the Level Two Cafeteria.

A blue flickering tube of a fluorescent light sits at an awkward angle in the salad bar of the cafeteria lunch line. Behind the grime-slick metal of the bar is Winston Churchill in a white apron covered in butcher meat blood and a paper hat. He looks straight ahead, unmoving, and the girth of his obese body sags into itself like a half-crushed aluminum can. Winston Churchill doesn't notice us slide in through the doors. He doesn't look our way even as Zero stares through the dirty windows to watch the crowd go by. The Cafeteria Man just looks like a pig in a sty, waiting for slop. Churchill looks like he only moves when there's work to be done.

The rest of the time he just waits.

I move over his way and he speaks, guttural and low in his throat, but his eyes don't blink or move or see me. He says, "You can tell a lot about a person by the way they eat. Some shovel down, some savor. Some cut their food with a knife. Some use the side of their fork and apply pressure. Most people talk with their mouths full even if it isn't proper manners. There is a direct connection between the way a person eats and the way they kiss."

"Um…yeah," I say, moving a little closer out of curiosity, "That's very informative of you. I mean, I guess you'd know, right?"

Cafeteria Churchill ignores me and continues, "We eat together on first dates to get an estimate of what sort of lover the other person might be. A woman can tell after the first bite whether or not she is going to sleep with the man across the table. If she sees him drooling, slurping up noodles, or sucking up strands of melted cheese with it hanging from his lips like bile, she will immediately imagine that mouth on hers or on her skin or between her thighs and cringe. The way we approach food is at least as important as how we approach life."

I nod slowly, trying to figure out how to respond, and still his eyes don't seem to see me. Zero moves away from the door and says, "I figure we're in the clear now, kid."

Winston Churchill prattles on, "I want you to try something. For me. Not that you have to or anything, but I'd like to gauge your reaction."

He brings out a blue plate steaming silently under the fluorescent lighting. There's some kind of roasted meat and just stuff all around it like a religious offering. Winston Churchill says, "This is Revenge, perfectly roasted served with robust Au Jus and Horseradish sauces, a side of finely diced red potatoes with white truffle oil, garnished tomatoes, baby artichokes with the hearts cut out and salted sourdough bread. Some people say Revenge is a dish best served cold, I prefer it roasted, marinated and served rare with the blood still oozing and piping hot."

I cut a slice to oblige him and it tastes like salt, basil and hate. "It's delicious," I smile.

"Oh, good, I was so nervous," replies Cafeteria Churchill, "Well, here, just for being such a good sport, this is my specialty."

He hands me a tin foil skillet of Jiffy Pop popcorn and says, "It's unusual, though. The hotter you get this, the more popcorn it pops. I suppose, if it were hot enough, you might never need popcorn again."

I thank him and Zero all but drags me back out into the hall. We hit the stairs and make for the third-floor landing. A gangplank with thin rails and a narrow walking space stretches out between two platforms. The drop down is too high to even justify vertigo. There's no real perspective to what's down below, but there is water rushing from the south wall and the feeling of dirty mist on the air.

We're at the labs now. Sterile white-walled ice cube trays large enough for a man to walk around in and tinker with the human brain like a toaster stretch out the length of the whole third-floor gangplank. I see rows and rows of open cubicles stacked on top of one another and glowing refrigerator white. A Xerox machine mass produces carbon copies of the brains of famous people. A man with steel pincer hands talks to a machine like it's an infant. In the top left quadrant a mouse takes notes as human children wander a maze with electric dog collars around their necks. He checks things off on a clipboard, nodding solemnly as the group approaches the Disney snow globe at the center.

Zero says, "This is what we've come to, kid. I don't remember a lot, but I do know it wasn't always this way. Subterranea has always been a hard climb, but it used to burn with the souls of those who died protecting *her*. She used to be our queen, and like Helen of Troy, men were willing to lay down their lives to serve her, protect her…to keep the fire burning."

Over the side of the gangplank, under the ice trays of laboratory cubicles, a river of ionized water, murky oil sludge, hair shellac, dingy comic books, self-help brochures, napalm jelly and unwrapped plastic containers rolls like Styx into a deep drain. We reach the other side and pass under a sign marked "Shipping/Receiving."

Zero gestures for me to follow and I can't help noticing how alone we are. I oughtta be relieved, but it's no use, this feels downright confounding. With a nod the old man says, "Before she fell asleep this place had order. We knew exactly who we were. We all thought we could live forever. But now, she's gone missing… our Empress, our Queen…with no direction and no one to fight for, Americana was up for grabs. Then *they* came in. They brought industry, preservatives, assembly lines, foreign oil and aerosol cans. They told us they'd bring order. Overnight they seemed to have taken control. Even the name of their company, ADI, American Dream Inc., seemed to be trying to tell all of us that our memory of our queen was a fiction, a myth…some kind of goddamn dream to wake up from."

I nod solemnly, not quite sure what the fuck he's talking about.

Old Zero just keeps talking in that hoarse, frog throat laryngitis tone, "We all work for them now and if you aren't exactly who they say you should be then they take it away, wipe you clean and put a new Napoleon in your place. We all know our only hope is to find her again, wake up our queen, and remind everyone that she is real. Waking her up from her long sleep might snap all of us out of it. Make us realize that ADI is the dream we need to wake up from. We ain't here to be producers or consumers. We're here to love our lady. But how we supposed to do that when we don't even know where she's hiding?"

The shipping dock is littered with large truck-sized crates, some rusty and drenched in yellow dust, others smoldering white hot and smelling like nine shades of microwave oven grease and brake dust. Voices echo all around us and my heart leaps a gold-winning cricket long jump into my throat. They seem distant, vague, like that game where you tie a string to Campbell's soup cans and talk to your brother from across the room all pinging and submersible sounding.

"My God," Zero grunts, "they're *inside*."

I'm usually kinda slow, so before much of anything really registers he's already pulling on some big steel pipe lever and a door bangs open like a castle drawbridge. The shipping crates are full of people. Inside there's children, old folks, people in rags and suits and coveralls, there's dark skin and light skin and short and tall and they all look unified in the black mote dust of a cargo box. They look lost, bewildering and scared shitless as a paranoid schizoid getting himself a forced hospital enema.

A woman that looks like every third grade teacher you ever had says, "A-are...are you letting us go?"

"Go?" Zero blurts, "Go where? What the hell you doing in there anyway?"

"Oh, thank God," some guy in a valet outfit sighs, "They're not one of them, after all."

"Everything you ever heard about them is true," says a convenience store clerk, "If you don't make a name for yourself, if you don't work yourself into a memorable position in Americana then you get shipped off, forgotten, and dumped into the fires of Subterranea."

A man in a dirty business suit says, "This factory, this entire city, is one big engine. The engine is powered by the fires of those that don't get remembered forever. Americana runs on the forgettable masses. ADI, like so many of its kind, is a company that lives by standing on the shoulders of the common...and burning them for fuel."

I think about all the levers I've been pulling. All the crates lowered into the furnace and coming out clean. However long I been here. Whoever they made me into. They made me part of their machine, burning souls to keep the world up top going.

And then I see her face. She limps forward from the back of the crate, drenched head to toe in metallic dust and shipping peanuts. And I know it's her. I know it's her because of Tom's journal. I see her in strange twilight, an unanswered glance, a bashful repellant attraction, a blind recognition, the desperation of a schoolgirl rape and the wild abandon heart throb mechanics of a love promise gone awry. I know her. It's Maggie May under all that dirt and I know she has something to say to me.

She drags her right heel and falls into my arms, heaving and sighing, "Tom, you have no idea what I've gone through to get to you."

I try to tell her I ain't Tom, I try to tell her a lot of things, but she is just so beautiful and warm against my chest. All I can figure is that now ain't the time so I tell her to hold that thought and say, "People, there's really only one way outta this, near as I can tell. You came in one way, you go out the same way, it ain't gonna be pretty, but it's gotta be done."

Zero, AKA Napoleon, shouts, "Boy, what in God's name are you jawin' about?"

"We're gonna ship ourselves out of Subterranea."

Field Notes from Bastard Land
14: Winston-Salem, Propaganda Hypnosis, Cartons and Lincoln

In this scene we have Winston-Salem. Exterior. Daylight. Action! We find the farm field avenue leading up to an archway and gate. Bonnie almost collides with a delivery truck on its way out of the compound and the driver shouts, "What the hell do you think you're doing?"

I hear Uncle Sam mutter under his breath, "Oh, sweet Mary."

It's a Camel delivery truck, likely loaded floor to ceiling with cartons.

"Jackpot!" he yells, climbing out of the passenger side door.

The driver says, "Hello? You almost hit me. Don't you have something to say?"

Placing a hand on the man's shoulder, Uncle Sam turns him away from the truck and says, "Aw, gee, I sure am sorry, whaddaya say let's take a walk?"

Five minutes pass. The driver walks up to me with a smile on his face and says, "Shucks, mister, all's you had to do was ask."

He moves around to the back of the truck and flings the door open wide. Grabbing an armful of cartons he walks over and drops them in the backseat. "Help yourself, fellas," he adds with a blank grin.

Standing beside my door, Uncle Sam says, "Well, what are you waiting for?"

I hop out and we go about the business of loading up Bonnie with all the cartons she can carry. I peel out on the pavement, stirring up tar-black smoke, and we hit the highway again.

"Listen, Sam, I gotta ask," I say, lighting one up, "how did you swing this?"

Uncle Sam smiles and says, "Look, my hat may be gone, but I still know my way around a good dialogue. I just gave the man some cheap propaganda and some nicotine patches on each temple. The man promptly insisted that we take all we can carry. So here we are, headin' out to DC with a ten-year supply of Camel Turkish Golds, pre-packaged, shrink-wrapped tobacco in 200-cigarette cartons."

"Nice work, old man, I think I might have underestimated you. So we're heading to DC now, why there?"

Uncle Sam replies, "It's the source of the Safety Factory, the epicenter, gotta find the middle if you want to find the edges."

I shrug and let the topic drop. Time drifts by in silence and I take us into mist, rolling hills and Virginia pre-dawn blue face skies. The other two are asleep. The whole country feels asleep. I nudge the old man at my right until he jumps awake and I say, "Look, Sam, I need a break, do you think you can take a turn at the wheel?"

"Sorry, kid," he says with groggy eyes and a yawn mouth, "I never learned to drive, I'm a child of the buggy days."

"Oh, no biggie," I shrug, pulling it over on some Appalachian trail.

Instead, I decide we should camp out under the stars. It's only a few minutes before we hear rustling in the trees. A group of tree-climbing Cherokee break out into the meadow and look angry, paranoid. Ready for a fight.

"Well, hey fellas, listen, we don't want any trouble, why don't you just pull up some rock and have a smoke with us."

We use the cigarette cartons for logs because the firewood is wet. Time passes slowly and quietly, the Cherokee say very little, but they enjoy our smokes. Uncle Sam decides he's ready to go and pees on our fire until it goes out, simultaneously pissing off our Indians, as per his habit. He laughs and sneezes red snot on his V-neck tee shirt.

It's time to go and we hop into Bonnie with the Cherokee along with us, sitting in the backseat on top of the cartons. Uncle Sam yells over his shoulder to the Cherokee, "Not long now, fellas, DC is just ahead."

The feed ramps up. Roads pass smoothly under us. It's late at night when we arrive. The news reports rumor terrorist attempts to destroy airliners with napalm smuggled onto planes in small containers. For this reason, the entire city is code orange. We're watching local police setting up concrete road blocks and red-purple night flares. We can't see the White House. Only certain streets are accessible and we are watched closely by armed guards as we view the Washington Monument. They see my dark beard and supervise me with suspicious eyes like I might be some kind of terrorist sympathizer.

The Monument scales a starless sky and vanishes into dense gray night fog. The point is hidden behind the mist, making the tower seem to go on forever, bridging the gap between us and heaven – a thorn in God's ass paining him to remember that we're still down here. Not to be forgotten.

Now this is us at the Tomb of the Unknown Soldier, biting our thumbs till they bleed blue and dancing backwards in the nude with pigeon feathers in our hair and RJ Reynolds on our lips. The Cherokee seem offended by our dance and, wailing at the sky, disappear into the Potomac River.

Uncle Sam shrugs, "Well, easy come, easy go, I guess. What do you say we go see Mr. Lincoln?"

Crossing the grass toward the Reflecting Pool my face is suddenly dripping with gnats and mosquitoes. A thick cloud of insects fills my mouth and I inhale their tiny bodies with a muddy cough.

The pool is stagnant.

A thick layer of algae covers the water and the bugs are heavy in the air like the Amazon jungle. Here I am sad. Click. Here we are wading through metaphors even a child could spot with ease. Click. This is the heart of America, built to represent the waters of life and the spirit of freedom – all that and the Reflecting Pool is stagnant.

Uncle Sam's face sags with disappointment and he sighs, "I hate to say it, but I have to. That, my friend, is your America."

"We have to stir the waters," I tell him.

"Yeah, but how?"

"I suppose everyone's answer is different," I reply, "but mine is Art. Romance, poetry, thought – colleges call these things 'the Humanities' for a reason. Without them we are just a job that the next man can fill."

"Or the next machine," shrugs Uncle Sam, "Jack, unless I get my hat back we're all just another cookie cutter party member hot off the pack line."

"Is this the grim face of the Safety Factory peering through into my world?" I ask, "Is it possible? Have we found the source of the whole mad drama?"

Uncle Sam says nothing. We scale the stairs toward Lincoln on his throne. When we get there I feel nothing. Sam smiles, looks up and says, "Yes sir, I understand."

"What? Who are you talking to?" I ask.

"You can't hear him?"

"Hear who?"

"Stop asking questions, and just let it happen, kid. You'll hear him."

Lincoln leans forward on his marble chair, leaning an elbow on a white stone knee. He grins with lifeless eyes and says, "I was just telling your friend here that the source of his power has gone into hibernation. America is in a coma. The hat has fallen into the hands of the enemy and now the Safety Factory gains more and more ground in this world. I'm sorry, kid, but you will find no answers here."

Lincoln falls silent again, returning to his stolid pose and emotionless expression. I follow Sam back toward the Reflecting Pool and feel like everything is lost. I look behind me and see Lincoln in the distance, stoic again, high above me on Mount Olympus stairs. I think about Highway 61 and pick up a rock saying, "Sam, we have to find America. Do you think she's close?"

I toss the rock into the water and the Reflecting Pool ripples slowly. The ripples grow into waves. A tidal wave wall floods us out to sea. I don't feel surprised, but didn't expect the water to smell like septic tank. The last thing I see before it all went green was Uncle Sam straddling the Washington Monument and stroking his marble erection as if he could make Lincoln jealous. Everything goes black.

Cut.

We wash up on the shores of Liberty Island and are immediately apprehended by black suited ninjas with FEMA tattooed in white across the front of their masks. They drag us to Guantanamo Bay and hold us as terrorists without trial. In the sex pyramid nude distraction of four illegal immigrants, a faux Al Qaeda predator and Uncle Sam poking the ones that weren't looking, I manage to sneak out an open door. Punching a guard in the throat I burn down an outhouse, kiss the president's daughter and hijack a small pontoon plane to Canada.

The feed ramps up more and more now. Trial images speed past like race cars blaring road violations on an oval track. Cut to the Great White North.

I have no desire to remain in Canada for long, so I promptly stuff myself into a beer keg and cross illegally back into America via Niagara Falls. Cut to a highway outside of Buffalo. The reprinted brain bots of the Hale Bop Suicide Cult, hot off the presses from the Record Store, pick me up in the Partridge Family tour bus. We drive in electric silence through the green street solitude of the New York upper canopy.

Outside Astoria our journey is cut short when the bus driver reaches over with a metallic arm and tries to remove my genitalia with a claw clamp hand. He tells me it's for my own good and I try to argue.

When I get cornered by one of his cronies I dive through an open window, landing softly in the lap of Eden. "Hey there, handsome," she says with a smile.

"What the–?" I shout, "Have you followed me?"

She is sitting on the back of a red dragon that drags its belly through the asphalt shoulder of the highway. Her legs are spread apart and she sits on his jagged spine plating with a moan. Eden says, "I should ask you the same question. After all, you landed on me."

"Well, what are you doing here?"

"It's a long story," she shrugs, "I went down to New Orleans and met a woman wearing a big snake. She gave me a check issued by the DMV and a name tag and told me I am now the Whore of Babylon. I've come here to make love to the son of the one that will bring the end."

"Well, I'm glad you've found a worthy career path," I reply, "I think you can find the one you're looking for south of here. I left him in Guantanamo Bay after I escaped."

Eden snaps her fingers and rides the beast into the sea.

I hear the tender squeak of spinning gears, turn around and there's a mime riding an invisible bike along the shoulder. Wheels are wheels, so I knock him off the bike and pedal the rest of the way into New York.

On the corner of 34th and 7th, I see a street performer playing a poodle like bagpipes and watch as the resurrected dead pour out of Penn Station groaning their hunger for the right kind of brains. Pedaling my invisible bike through the zombie crowd, I'm shocked when they don't even try to touch me. There's a woman bending herself into coils like a snake until she pops a water balloon with her spine. A black stink slick sprays across the pavement and I ask her what it is.

She says, "It's the blood of Exxon Mobil shareholders and, for your information, all of the zombies ignored you because you have the wrong sort of brain."

"What is the right sort of brain?" I ask her, feeling left out.

"You have to want a top floor business office and a secretary blowing your load under your desk. You have to want to buy a yacht with the money you swindled out of small businesses and whatever you saved by outsourcing to India and leaving the blue-collar workers shivering for whiskey in the dark."

"I don't know what I want. Sometimes I think this new, senile Uncle Sam should just finish stroking the Washington Monument and blow his load over the whole damn country. It would be the honest way for us to go out, washed away under a flood of jizz as we all individually died in pursuit of our orgasmic futures."

The Contortionist says, "That's why the risen dead don't want you."

I ask, "Do you know the way out of the Safety Factory?"

"Did you bite your thumb at the Unknown Soldier and dance a rain dance naked and backwards?"

I nod and she asks if I painted my face with my blood like a Sioux warrior? I tell her yes and the Contortionist says, "Then you should be out of the Safety Factory by now."

"What about you, are you out?"

"I was on my way out when I got pregnant by the American Dream. He sometimes visits us in the night and makes us have his baby. We can only raise it where the business is or the child will die."

"Where is your baby now?" I ask her.

"He grew up quick and mean and built the Record Store before he ran for Congress."

The risen dead swarm out of alleyways all around me and

tear the Contortionist into five pieces. The sounds and smells of splitting flesh surround me and I run away screaming. Hiding in an abandoned apartment building with boarded-up windows, I mumble under my breath, "The Contortionist had the wrong kind of brain. People only die like that inside the Safety Factory. I'm still not out. Even after biting my thumb at the Unknown Soldier."

"Do you mind?"

In a dark corner on the other side of the room is a bug-infested rusty spring mattress where the Easter Bunny is giving it to the Tooth Fairy from behind. He grunts in between heaving breaths, "I'm sorry, but – ugh – we need to procreate, it's the only way – yeah – to keep kids dreaming, it's the only way to keep imagination alive!"

The moaning Tooth Fairy says, "The risen dead have come back for their candy and molar money – ughn, yeah – and children do exactly what textbooks and Mario demand."

"Do you know where I can find America? Uncle Sam was showing me, but we got separated at Guantanamo Bay."

The Easter Bunny says, "Yeah, I heard a rumor that she was sleeping – oh! – in a glass coffin down on West 4th."

Breaking down some boards with my foot I leap onto the fire escape as the Tooth Fairy starts to shriek, "Oh, yes! Oh, God!"

And I wonder why people always sound like they have just figured out the answer to a confusing question while they're in the middle of the act.

Down on the street, sitting at a bus stop, Albert Einstein is knitting a red scarf with his theory of relativity stitched in blue.

"Oh yeah!" he shouts.

Yelling up at me, Einstein says, "Mickey Mouse is the Sixth Reich and God was a dinosaur. Uncle Sam follows Hollywood because that's the new propaganda. And the Whore is Eden because the beginning is the end. When you bleed at honor and dance naked in the past you can break through the barriers. Outside of the Safety Factory, anything is possible."

Does this mean I have made it out? Am I home? Or is this life in some kind of void, where relativity is still a theory and laws do not exist?

I suddenly feel sick to my stomach and fumble into a phone booth to vomit. I spray bile everywhere, but this isn't the interior of a phone booth. The risen dead are gone. Everything is quiet. I'm alone, it's sunset and I can see the glowing blue arch of Washington Square Park. Exterior. Greenwich Village, New York, New York.

This was the once proud stomping ground of Bob Dylan, Allen Ginsberg and Jack Kerouac – among many others. This is the breeding corner of Beat Poetry and independence, the launching pad of young folk musicians, dreamers, artists and all the true crippled angels fighting the bad fight.

Each one is a troubadour in their own right. Each of them is a brother or a driver on the long, sad counter-culture search for beauty. They are all trying to reach the Kingdom of God without a wing to float on – too weak to get high enough, but strong enough to keep striving to get back to heaven.

So it came as no surprise when I feel a quiver of electricity at this arrival. To no one in particular I say, "Call me sentimental, but I feel like those Muslims making their pilgrimage to Mecca. This, for me, is my Holy Land."

Around the park fountain I can hallucinate the ghosts of acoustic guitar cranked night children and dancing hipsters circling hand-in-hand to celebrate their future. But now, what is it? It's all disappearing, like forest land, or old world manners, or video rental stores, it's disappearing. Our hopeful drive, our futurist optimism, our bohemia...our greatest national resource is going the way of the buffalo.

A man to my right, dressed in gray head to toe, lingers just outside of my range of vision, but as I turn to see his face he is already gone.

LOST IN AMERICANA: CHAPTER FOURTEEN
THE LAST CRY OF THE REGULATOR

The whole crowd of street dingy muck rats, low-downs, shit-outta-lucks, and mid-road pavers gather round and I look over to see Maggie smiling, a look of pride beaming like Hollywood spotlights out of her eyes. I call their attention to the row of trucks waiting to be hooked to trailers, waiting to take the empties back out into Americana to be refilled. Reckon the next shift of crane laborers ought to be loading them boxes up onto trailers shortly and sending them on their way.

Figure if we got an early start we might be able to just drive on outta here. Everyone sets to work, pulling levers and switching gears to get the crates onto one flatbed trailer. But it ain't no big trouble because these are the grunt workers of Americana. Truck drivers, steel haulers, button pushers, light bulb changers, gas station attendants, auto mechanics and the whole shit fuck marching band lot of 'em.

I hear Maggie May shout, "Okay people, let's get a move on, we got workers coming in ten minutes!"

She strolls over on a limping ankle and leans on the circuit board next to me.

"I know you say you're not Tom," she says, looking sassy and ready for a dare, "but I swear to God, you're him. Tom's the only boy I ever knew that would've thought to ship himself outta jail in a metal box."

"I'm not Tom."

"Yeah? Well then who the fuck are ya then?" she asks, leaning closer, ready to meet my challenge.

"I'm...uh, I am number 0006, Basement Level, Regulator Technician."

"Right, did your mother and father give you that name?"

Without missing a step I just say, "I ain't got a mother or father, none of us have, remember?"

That's one of those moments where it hits you. You realize you stepped in something. You know this is big and unexpected and complicated, but it's there all the same. I just say, "Oh shit," and it comes back in a wash of pictures and sounds and jolts of pain.

Two lovers sit on a bed and try to recall a past that is vague and distant and not theirs. They press against one another's skin trying to force something loose, trying to remember who they are or where they came from. Trying to remember their family. One of them is me.

"Maggs?"

She smiles and pulls me close, kisses my forehead and says, "Hi, Tom."

"Hey, but...I mean, what...I mean, what are you doing here?"

Maggie says, "Tom, can I please tell you what I came to tell you now?"

"Okay, Maggs," I reply, "tell me everything."

She sighs, and breathes deep as if preparing herself for something, "Everything has changed, Tom, I didn't know about it at first. But since you left The California, everything has started to change. And I think they've been trying to stop you."

245

I lean back to get a good look at her, and say, "Just give it to me straight, Maggs, cut the bullshit. What in hell's fuck hole are you talking about?"

"It's awful, Tom. They have some sort of power. I can't say for sure, but it has something to do with Jack Flash. He's become this whole other person or something. They parade him around the Safety Factory like he's their golden boy and it's got people scared. It looks like the Third Reich out there, Tom. But...Christ, that's not what I'm here about."

"Maggie, for God's sake, spit it out."

"They're out. Your friends from MARTYR. Something happened, they haven't said what exactly. All I know is that they told me to tell you that the one you're supposed to be looking for, the one they tried to recruit you to find...well, he's here. That's what they said. He's here. But every time he comes here and every time he leaves he's punching holes. That's what they said. Jim told me you would understand, he said your man is punching holes in the wall and it's getting easier to see through to the other side."

"Otherworld," I mutter under my breath.

"What?"

"I don't know, it just popped in there. Maggs, is it true? Am I really Tom?"

"Yes, you're him. I know they bleached you out, Tom. But that's why they sent me. Jim said if anyone could make you remember it'd be me, so I came. He said it would be hard, but he didn't say how hard. I've been beaten and thrown out of too many buildings to count. Everything I tried, every plan, was such a failure. Then it hit me. I had to get sent here the same as you. I wasn't going to get you out on parole. I certainly didn't know how to bust you out of this prison. But I knew I could get in here if I tried."

"What did you do, Maggs?"

"It's not important now, Tom, what is important is that you listen. Jim told me to tell you that the more times your man comes and goes the more things will blend over. I hope you get this, because I don't. He said that they have a New Uncle Sam. I think it must be that hat, Tom, that hat Jack Flash bought. It has to be, right? He just got lucky. It wasn't meant for him, but now that he has it they have made him into some kind of monster."

"They?" I ask.

"ADI. He's like their mascot now or something. This New Uncle Sam, he doesn't represent America. He represents that horrible corporation, those freaks, and that horrible man they just call the Chairman. Tom, you have to find this man. I don't know who he is or what his role is in all of this, but you have to find him before he destroys everything."

"What do you mean, 'everything?'" asks Zero, "And what does this have to do with America? What does it have to do with our queen?"

"Everything, sir," Maggie replies, "As in 'everything,' you know, all of it. This man thinks he's saving the world by doing what he's doing. He's looking for something and he's so far into his search that MARTYR can't even reach him. He's lost somehow. Like some other force is guiding him. Our people can't get to him so they're counting on you, Tom. To find him before it really is too late. Do you understand? I know you lost yourself in there, but that can't be helped. There's no time for us to try to find you again, you have to find yourself along the way toward finding him. You have to, otherwise we're all lost."

I don't really know what to say to that kind of information. If memory serves, I've always been kind of an idiot when it came to that kind of thing. I just say, "Listen, Maggs, there's one more thing I gotta do. Stay here. Make sure everyone gets loaded up okay."

It's a risk, but it has to be done. There's a lift from the basement that'll get you to every floor of Factory 10. The dandy of it is, everybody and his mamma's gonna be riding it and that means bosses, that means the law, that means trouble. I don't have time for the stairs. It's a risk I gotta take.

Winston Churchill is right. Revenge is a dish best served piping hot. I say, if this idea is gonna work, the hotter the better.

I hit the lift just in time, doors ding open with the bug zapper twilight flash of a blue arrow and I slide in. The elevator operator says, "What floor, sir?"

And I shout, "No time! I'll do it myself!"

I chuck the elevator man through the door and he lands on the neatly pressed lapels of his doorman tail coat. I pull a lever and drop like a bat into hell. I practically crash into the basement landing I'm going so fast.

If what Maggie May says is true, then they stole me away from myself and replaced my mind with work. Nothing but work. Day in, day out, forever. Shit, Christ knows how long I've been down here. Not even human, just the basement level worker in Regulator Maintenance. Maybe Winston would agree with me, that Revenge is a dish best served with a sense of irony.

I hit my work station, the Regulator furnace, the power station of the whole mad gab monstrosity pitching tones and whistling like a tea kettle whenever the big Factory 10 lake of fire gets too full. Too hot.

It's still on me, I never set it down the whole time we were loading up all the losers and ham hocks we found in the crates. Winston Cafeteria Man Churchill's special Jiffy Pop. I toss it in the Regulator stove door and it works fast. Like frothy bubbles in an overfull washing machine. Like baking soda and vinegar. Like Old Faithful. The basement is flooding with popcorn before I even hit the lift and I can't get outta there fast enough.

Back at Level 3 I practically trip over the elevator operator still on the concrete, making mud from dust and tears. He sobs, "All's ya had to do was ask...all throwing me and shit..."

I find Zero and he's climbing into the driver's seat of the last truck. He hollers like a train conductor, "All aboard, last car for Anywhere But Here!"

There's one crate still open, one at the back of the flatbed trailer and there's Maggie waving me to hurry up. I can hear it already. The Regulator gets to screaming and bluesin' and weeping as she chokes on an endless supply of popped corn. Factory 10 floods with front row seat snacks to the theater of its own destruction and The Regulator cries out like a goddamn fucking banshee over all the truck noise and warehouse shrieks of metallic terror. I hop the trailer, hitting it right about mid-waist and old Maggie May gets to tugging on me something fierce to get me up on that ledge and into the safety of a hot shipping crate.

Door swings shut and inside it's dark with the sounds of a dozen people breathing. We all plow into each other, jostling and terrorizing shoulders as the truck gets rolling out. A dulcimer queue exhale lowers the pressure and the tension by a thousand degrees and we can all feel the open road rumbling quiet and true under our feet.

"You did it," Maggie says, "Now we have to find the one you're looking for. MARTYR believes he's in danger. He's completely gone off the grid. He may not even know it, he may think he's getting closer to America, but he's never been farther away."

I tell her we'll find him, tell her not to worry, and somehow I know it's true, even if I don't have a fuck all chance in hell of knowing how I'm gonna pull off that little miracle.

Field Notes from Bastard Land

15: Drunk Streeter, Subterranea and the New Uncle Sam

Now it's later that night. I'm walking north back through Central Park in the spirit of fallen generations and a once, proud culture that held the attention and hope of a youth movement along with the fear and panic of Nixon and his armies. Stopping at Strawberry Fields, I stand around a stone mosaic circled in candles. The light is fading and you can feel this strange electricity in the air. Nearby a group of hipsters are discussing the life and death of John Lennon. Conspiracy theorists whisper their beliefs, not wanting to raise their voices to any disrespectful degree. In the center of the circle is the word, "Imagine."

This is my second Mecca, a weird shrine to someone that stood up for peace and was met with violence, someone that preached unity and was torn down. A young girl plays "Revolution" quietly on her guitar and we sing along. The air is dense with a sad yet hopeful energy.

We sit quietly and wonder why the good ones die young. John Lennon, Martin Luther King Jr., John F. Kennedy, Bobby Kennedy, standing here I can't help thinking that if you stand up too tall you're just an easier target when the guillotine drops. I can't help wondering if my generation hangs its head low because they know, as I do, that trying to change things puts a target on your chest. These days so many of us have copped into the "Get what you can, while you can" philosophy and I think it might be for the same reasons that have me standing at a memorial to John Lennon rather than watching him in concert.

To no one in particular I say, "I don't think America is here, I only see evidence of American Dream, Inc."

"So why don't you leave?" asks a familiar voice.

I turn suddenly and stand facing the Gray Man. He looks happy to see me, but still slightly out of focus like an old black and white movie.

"It's you," is all I can think to say.

"It is," he replies, "Tell me, Jack, if this isn't the place, why don't you leave?"

"I would, but I lost Bonnie. I don't know how I got here, or where she is."

"Then we must find her," is all he says, he gestures with his umbrella and I follow.

Cut.

This part of my movie is called *Drunk Streeter and Just Desserts*.

We're on our way out of Central Park when this dirty bastard approaches us, scraping his feet as he wobbles toward us from across the street. Behind us, steam rolls out of the subway exit and we watch lawyers and all manner of suits crawling out of their holes. The Gray Man says, "Do you suppose the factory is down there, Jack? Do you think the big machine is under the city cranking out businessmen like packaged sodas, beer bottles or condoms?"

"I don't know, but I say we get off of this sidewalk before they pull us in and make us crank out their upwardly mobile future."

We turn to leave as the stranger catches me by the arm and says, "I have to talk to someone. I'm having such a great night, kid."

"Oh yeah?" I ask, "Why is that?"

"The wife is out of town for a week and I've been wining and dining and timing young women for days on end. Gotta love it, man. Any time she looks away I'm getting that pure, untapped little twat every chance I get."

"How long have you been married?" I ask.

"Going on twenty-three years now. But fidelity went out the window before we even took our vows. Poor bitch has no idea too."

He laughs. The drunk street bumbler actually laughs.

"Hoo boy," he continues, "next phase is to go to the Yanks game and try to catch a foul ball and trade it for a BJ. Where you from, anyhow, kid?"

I remembered a conversation with Dennis Orbell. Atomic wine and the fun of lying to deserving idiot strangers. As I think it over, I mutter, "Texas."

"Texas? Southerner, eh? What the hell brings you all the way up to Yank-Ville?"

"Well, sir," I begin, "I caught wind of vicious Al Qaeda rumors having to do with the mass-destruction of this and other major U.S. cities on an almost Biblical scale – and by Biblical I mean Sodom and Gomorrah, fire and brimstone, true Armageddon proportions. I'll have you know that I have been labeled a stark-raving crazy, just recently broken out of the Cass County Sanitarium for suicidals, manic-depressives and blood drinkers. The facilities were fine, good service, too, until I discovered the rigid steps taken by the white coats to prevent self-annihilation. So I sprung out, with the help of the Gray Man here."

I gesture with a thumb, and the man looks concerned.

"I assure you I have no idea what he's talking about," the Gray Man adds, but the drunk doesn't seem to hear or see him on account of all the booze.

"Next, I stole a van from a pack of Kumbaya driven Mormons

and headed up here to New York to get iced by exploding terrorist lit airliners. Trouble is, I'm a man of my word, and the hospital made me promise not to kill myself."

"Is that so?" asks the stranger.

"But that don't mean I can't let the Taliban do it for me, does it?"

Drunk stutters, "You're too late, I saw on the news that the Brits prevented those attacks."

"Oh, that?" I reply, "That was just the first wave. The second one will be coming right at the peak of the Yankees game tonight."

The man sobs, "The Yankees! Those towel heads are hitting America's favorite pastime now? Is nothing sacred to these camel fuckers?"

"Apparently not," I say, "but listen, we have an extra ticket, third row, left center. Do you want to sit and watch an A-Rod homerun trigger the bomb and drag you cheering into Oblivion? Viva Oil! Viva Chaos! Viva Destruction! Viva America!"

The man calls me psychotic and immediately tries scalping his ticket to a twelve-year-old for ten bucks. The boy promptly pukes on the man's boots and I can't say I'm disappointed. The Gray Man laughs and says, "Well, do you think you rained enough on his parade, Jack?

"Yeah, I really put the screws to that dirt bag, didn't I, Mr. Gray Man? Well, at least for tonight anyway. I can almost see him holed up and shaking in his hotel bed."

"Good lad," he replies, "If you don't mind, shall we get back to the task at hand?"

Cut.

I head down the stairs into the subway. With no real direction in mind, I hop the first train that screams along. The Gray Man is gone again. On the train there is an old Korean woman listening to an iPod.

The radio sings, "...*don't let the sound of your own wheels drive you crazy*...This just in, Jack Bluff dies today at 20 after failing to find his diamond in the rough."

"Shut up," I say out loud and the woman shoots me a paranoid glance.

"Jack, it's not too late to join us," says the voice of the Chairman through the iPod headphones, "you're on the losing side. We now hold all the cards. We have the power of the American spirit. American Dream, Inc. bought up the hat of Uncle Sam. Everything is in our control now."

The iPod fades to static and the subway doors open. I step out into some pseudo fallout shelter two stories below the city. Somehow this is Penn Station. Walking around, this place looks as if it were designed to outlast a nuclear holocaust. A nearby coffee shop cashier says something about a good place to hide out from invading zombies.

I see an underground K-Mart in between two bagel shops. There's a place where a row of old men are having their shoes shined as they sit on a high ledge facing a mirror. The tile floor clicks with heels and toes like a million-caterpillar tap dance. A man with a beard and dreadlocks crosses my path reeking of booze. Eyes shaded by sunglasses, he has a cardboard sign across his chest that says, "The End is long gone."

Passing by he is muttering profanities under his breath – shit eating son of fuck, goddamn swine, bitch ass, bastard, Lord, Jesus Christ almighty, Fuckin' Amen.

In a gold-lit corner is an old black man in a robe and a fez singing *Amazing Grace* through a karaoke machine. Tourette Syndrome pushes his way through the crowd grumbling his obscenities while the old man sings.

"Amazing grace"..."Fuck"..."the sound that"..."shaved ass bitch"..."like me"... I laugh to myself as the sounds blend into one underground voice. Now he's singing, "Gimme that Ol' Time Religion, uh-huh."

Tourette sings, "God is dead, we sold his carcass for high-speed internet access."

I follow the stairs up into the street. But this isn't what it should be. This isn't 34th Street. Instead I'm standing in the flash burn power surge of Subterranea and wander back down some nameless avenue. At every turn I seem to hit a dead end. Now the dead end closes in behind me and I'm boxed in. I watch in fear and panic as the stone gray walls breathe me in and out. This box is a heaving, breathing, seething, teething brick lung and I am the factory pickle jar skirting down rust-iron rollers. The wall bubbles and pops and on the other side is the Void. This is the tunnel. This is the long downhill kiddy park slide toward the white light. This is the pathway to the furnaces of Subterranea.

The earth is a hollow egg. Growing in the yellow glob molten lava chicken yolk are the souls of the damned, writhing over each other and shaking the surface world when they rattle their claptrap chains. An agonized woman sealed away in Subterranea's fires wails and moans, shaking the support pylons with her meltdown hands. There was just a tsunami in the Philippines. A small, slant-eyed fisherman was washed under his boat. Now he stands beside me and says, "Have I made it out?"

Yes, you have escaped the Safety Factory. But those that escape it in death all wind up here. You did not bite your thumb at the Unknown Soldier, dance naked backward and paint the war paint with your blood. You are not free. You are only fuel for the fire.

"How deed yoo escape?" asks a fiery puddle that used to be a Frenchman.

"I didn't, but I've gotten close."

"That's the best you can offer us," says the once, former form of a podiatrist, "We need to know there's hope that not everyone will end up here."

This is Subterranea where everyone is freed from the Safety Factory, where everyone is a prisoner of their freedom. This is Subterranea, where everyone's a critic. Here you no longer have to work to buy your freedom. You are both liberated and imprisoned by safety, a safety manufactured by the human furnace. This is the earth's core.

An oil drill cracks through the ceiling and rocks crash down all around us. A billion voices cry out, "Free us, free us, we used to be human. We're people! We want to go back."

But there is no going back once you're in Subterranea.

Now the scene gets hazy and I can smell patriotism like an overheated radiator pouring anti-freeze green steam out of my ears as it grease-coats my walls. Now Subterranea opens up out of the wall vent and dear old Uncle Sam enters in a tuft of flame wearing a black cape and rose-colored glasses. He smiles at me showing a row of jagged, sharp teeth and grows taller by two or three feet. His head itches the ceiling and his eyes breathe in his shadow mule. Uncle Sam tosses the cape off of his shoulders and his body a liquid elephant from the waist down with the shoulders and arms of a stone-crocked donkey. He grows the Elephant Head on his right shoulder and trumpets his trombone trunk while the Donkey Head tumors out on his left shoulder saying, "Hee-haw, hee-haw, he loves to walk too tall."

The mutant three-headed joker man chimera laughs-brays-trumpets and says, "I've upgraded to include the Darkness and the Light. I'm paying by praying and I'm neighing, braying the New America."

Panicking, I crawl into a corner to orgasm my tears onto the floor crying, "But you were Sam Wilson, the cover-front man of the 1812 Revolution soldiers. You were a hero with a blue collar and a meat factory. What happened to you? We were road buddies, Bonnie and I carried you when you were naked."

The beast grabs my shirt collar and throws me into a wooden chair, clamping my wrists and ankles with metal brackets. Flashes of my nightmare burn my brain like jellyfish. Nailed to a table, watching my wife fuck over and over and over. Bleeding. Torture. Then a flat screen television lowers in front of me and I let out a blood boiling wail.

This time it's real, I know it is, and I'm begging for Sam to let me go, "I know you're still in there somewhere, Sam, please!"

A familiar voice, prudish, but gruff all at once, says, "Jack, you know better than that. He is wearing the true crown of the once and former Uncle Sam. Your friend sold it for whiskey money, remember? Or was it cocaine? Sources are unclear, but the fact remains that this hat has given us the power to create our advanced model. Meet the New Uncle Sam, Jack, I hope he's to your liking because he's not going anywhere for generations to come."

"Why don't you come out and show yourself, you bastard? Now, is it just you, Mr. Chairman of the Board, or do you have your whole sideshow panel of freaks along with you?"

"It's just me, Jack," replies the Chairman, "I told you I'd make a powerful enemy. I've brought you here to show you what we did since our last meeting."

The Chairman steps out of the shadows while his three-headed beast waits patiently like Cerberus by the door. A small remote clicks on the screen and I see the familiar streets of the Linden town square. My former hometown, the place where Charlie and I discovered art together. The Jesus Days, the days of music, coffee, Bob Dylan, chess boards, vinyl records, sleepless nights, T.S. Eliot and dreams of future's locked box.

"Why are you showing me this? What does Linden have to do with you and me?"

"Nothing," replies the Chairman, "that is, until you so rudely turned me down. I'm not accustomed to being told no, Jack, obviously repercussions were in order."

He presses play and shows me video clips of Linden while I was in high school. Town festivals, wild flowers, guitars, church sessions, meteor showers and hundreds of young faces. The Chairman says, "Jack, while you and your friends were there you were a part of something rare. You were all together. All of you were open and turned that time into something bigger than yourselves. Misguided or not, your love for God led you to bring your town together, look...this is footage of you preaching to your peers at one of your youth-led revivals, this is Charlie playing guitar and leading people in the act of singing praises to their deity. Here's footage of people coming from towns for miles around to attend your events. Like it or not, proud of it or not, you did something big and, at least on small town scales, important."

"Yeah, so what's your point? I'm over all that now."

"My point, *Jack*, is that Linden represents one part of your life, Denton represents another. Linden is the height of your devotion, pursuit and faith. Denton is the height of your depression, debauchery and doubt. And yet, in both of these places, there is Charlie Outlaw, two lives moving side by side no matter how close or far they might be in proximity to one another. Don't you find that remarkable?"

I shrug, "Well, yeah, I mean, I guess so…I've never given it much thought."

"Okay, so now that I've given you fair reminder of Linden at the height of its spirituality. I want you to take a look at this, but keep in mind…your old hometown was built on the foundation of religion. Social events, relationships, friendships, family structures, these all hinge on faith. So it occurs to me that if this could be destroyed, what is left?"

"What did you do?"

"Nothing, Jack, I'm an intangible. I live in Subterranea, end of the line on the Ghost Road. But I can make suggestions, a twitch here or there in my world sends shockwaves into yours. It always starts with pleasure. It's the easiest way to get to people. When you promise them pleasure they can rationalize that *God* would never interfere or deny them that, after all, he loves us. Right?"

He presses play on the feed again and I see my old pastor sitting at the junior high school in his beat-up pickup truck. Judging by his rapid mechanical gestures, the red tint of his skin, contorted expression and the group of teenage cheerleaders walking in front of him, I'd say it's not a big leap to assume he's jerking off to the sight of junior high girls. The Chairman hits pause and says, "He gets caught, but not punished, he passes it off to his assailant as 'tucking in his shirt.' Tucking in his shirt for ten minutes straight almost to the point of orgasm."

The Chairman hits play again and says, "Now, it goes on from here, we have some news articles and such to cover the event, I'd rather not go to the actual live footage as it is somewhat graphic... let's just say that it became evident that the church officials of every major church administration in Linden were found indulging in an underground pornographic theater set up in the basement of one pastor in particular."

I have nothing to say, I don't feel anything, not even surprised, and yet, I feel a strange sense of anger, only not toward the Chairman. I'm not sure why, but I just feel really mad at the guys on the feed. I can't explain it yet. I wring my wrists in their restraints, aching to get out, but can't seem to make any progress.

Mr. Chairman of the Board continues, heaving under his enormous breasts as if to contain some sort of excitement, "Now, what did I tell you? If you take a town built on the church and then destroy that foundation, what are you left with? In this clip you will see the coverage of a brutal stabbing that took place at your own high school. And here, you see the statistics of your town's population drop by increasing percentages. The old are dying, the young are leaving."

The feed ramps up, I see hate crimes, drunk driving accidents, crystal meth, teachers threatened by students, people leaving en masse, my old hometown morphed in no time flat into something coarse, mutant and ugly. The dark side of American Dream Inc. finally sunk its teeth into a place that had kept its sweetness maybe longer than it deserved, but it's now drained dry.

The Chairman says, "You see, when you refuse us, whether it's for ideology, faith or just plain stubbornness, it always turns out worse than if you had simply given in. We are the future, Jack, and we've already won."

And there, suddenly, behind the blue-out haze of the television monitor, something catches my eye. Before I have time to shout back, before I have time to deliver some witty comeback, I notice a light growing behind the light of a small lantern. Dim red but growing brighter, I can see Subterranea trickling through the void of the kerosene wick fire. In the orange-out blues a man without skin and a striped top hat says, "Let me out! Let me free! I want to go back."

The sobbing Skeleton Man in a scorched tails overcoat pulls at his chin hair. He screams and cries out, "Jack, that's not me, Jack. Don't believe anything he says. This is me."

"Sam?" I say, staring down into the burning pit of Subterranea, "It's you? What happened to you, man?"

"They got me, Jack, without my hat I'm useless. The Chairman threw me into the pit along with the rest of the doomed!"

"Enough of this!" shouts the Chairman, turning to the New Uncle Sam he grunts, "You, go shut him up!"

And this mutant beast, wearing Uncle Sam's talisman, it laughs and says, "Pretty soon I won't just be the New Uncle Sam, Jack. I'll just be Uncle Sam, and the old one won't even be a memory. Now, this is your last chance. You're either with us, or you're against us."

I feel my blood boil red. Images flash through my mind of the Chairman torturing me with my wife's infidelity, torturing me with nails and pliers all those nights. I hear his voice say, "Jack Bluff dies today at age 20."

"Fuck it," I shrug, "let's just get it over with. We all gotta go some time. You might as well throw me in that pit too, because I will always be against you."

The Chairman nods solemnly and the three-headed beast reaches out with Frankenstein fingers to unlatch my restraints. As soon as I'm loose I feel it wash across my face without my permission – a grin of defiance and pure enjoyment. Surprise spreads across all three of the New Uncle Sam's faces and I take a flying leap right for his human throat. We stumble backward and I grapple with his long, thin fingers and his chomping donkey jaws.

"No...you don't, don't..." he grumbles and tries to get a grip around my waist.

"Do it, Jack!" Skeleton Sam yells from the pit.

I feel my hands close around it just as he squeezes my ribs so tight that the wind shoots out of me. Now I'm flying through the air and I hit the wall with a crack. But the pain is nothing compared to what I got in return.

"You're not so tough without this, are you?" I grin, holding up the twisted form of Uncle Sam's tall hat, "And you know, I'd rather this be completely destroyed than see it on you."

The New Uncle Sam is already melting back down to antifreeze sludge as I toss the hat through the vortex and into the pit. The Chairman squeals, "No! No, not that, all my work, all my precious work."

But the hat doesn't hit the molten iron, it doesn't melt. The real Uncle Sam reaches up with an ash bone hand and catches it with a grunt just before it falls into the fires of Subterranea.

Watching him adjust it on his skull changes everything. The walls crumble. The tunnel to the furnace of Subterranea melts. For a moment I'm alone with the quiet temper of the Void. This is not the Safety Factory, this is not Subterranea. This isn't even Otherworld, I'm in Oblivion and what happens in Oblivion stays in Oblivion.

THE GREAT ESCAPE
& OTHERWORLD

We hear the low rumble of a dozen or so high powered chopper engines. As they scream closer the cackles of would-be leather-clad street witches rattle in through the steel crate walls. Maggie tenses up beside me, muttering nerve-altering incantations under her breath. She grabs my arm just above the elbow and squeezes her fear into me.

"It's the Fat Bottom Girls!" she shrieks through gritted teeth, "They've found us."

Maggie pushes her way toward the crate door, jamming elbows and shoving people aside. She shouts, "It's Leroy's gang, they've come to bring us back!"

I shove my way through the crowd, shouting over the heads of strangers, "Oh God! Who the hell is Leroy?"

The laughter swells around us. I can hear what sounds like chains slapping the trailer and the walls of our shipping box. Everyone panics, coming apart at the seams, saying shit like they'd o' been better off to just stay put in Subterranea. The sound of hyena grill cackling bowls over us and washes us down like a riptide as the truck drags to a slow crawl, then jostles, belches and stops altogether.

Maggie keeps screaming how there's no way out. Hollering, howling like a horny coyote, just raising all hell, she rattles the crate door, but we all know it only opens from the outside.

Now I hear the sounds of footsteps and the cargo crate is hauling nothing but stalled breaths and fear and silence. The cannonball drop-clank of the lever shakes the floor and rattles the walls. The door opens and there's Zero. We all let out long gulf gusts of air and relief rushes out to meet him.

A cab driver in a checkered hat shouts, "Gave 'em the slip, eh old timer?"

Zero just shakes his head and says he's sorry. The door opens and there's the biker gang, a man in a gray suit with a bowler cap and some goddamn freak with a walrus moustache and breasts the size of buffalo.

In a choked whisper Maggie gulps, "It's him."

"Him who?" I whisper back.

"Him, him. Mr. Chairman of the Board, him. The man that strikes the gavel for American Dream, Inc."

"Hello, Tom," he says, "You'll be coming with me now. You and your friends have already upset my plans enough for one day. Girls, if you would be so kind…"

He claps his hands and the Fat Bottom Girls are on us like fly paper.

All the other moogs and down-n-outs break for the horizon. It don't help much though, them biker girls are really after Maggie and me. Zero is shaking his head and he turns to the Chairman. "Remember what I said, don't hurt 'em, they're good folks."

Maggie screams, "We trusted you."

And old Zero just says, "They offered me a deal. Reinstatement for you two. I'm going to be Americana's Napoleon all over again.

I'll fight to free the queen and I'll decide how my image is used. I'll decide my own poetry from now on."

He turns back to the Chairman and says, "They're all yours, Monseigneur."

But it's weird, his accent drops out and he sounds French. Like he's been hiding it all along or something.

The man in gray brings around Mr. Chairman of the Board's limousine and the Fat Bottom Girls toss us in. The Chairman climbs in behind us, knocks on the window, and we start driving. His movements are slow and casual. He pours himself a glass of whiskey, twirls it lightly and takes a long swallow.

After a few moments of driving in a cow stall silence he finally speaks up and says, "I regret that it has come to this you two, but you've left me little choice. You will come with me to the offices of ADI, in the heart of Subterranea, where you will face our board of directors. There we will decide what we will finally do with you."

Maggie sighs heavy as a stone and says, "That's it, Tom, we're cooked."

"Yeah, Maggs…they got us."

Turning to the Chairman she adds, "If this is to be our first and last limo ride, do you think we could trouble you for a drink?"

"Yeah," I say, "a drink would be nice about now. It'd be nice to go out in style."

The Chairman nods politely and says, "To be sure, to be sure, it's no trouble at all."

He pours each of us a glass and hands them out one at a time. I start to down mine fast and hard, but Maggie touches my hand and stops me. She shakes her hand, as if to say it should be savored, then turns to the Chairman once more.

"How about a smoke?"

"Cigars?" he asks with a smile under his Brillo pad moustache.

"Please."

Maggie takes a cigar, but I decline. The Chairman lights a gold Zippo and reaches across the space between us in the limousine.

Reaching for the lighter to handle her own flame, Maggie asks, "You mind?"

"Not at all, young lady," The Chairman replies, "I appreciate an independent woman."

As I am about to take a swallow of my drink, Maggie strikes the flint and the lighter reignites. She knocks my drink out of my hand and it lands in the middle of the floor with a glass shard splash. Before anything registers proper she's tossed the Zippo in and struck up a good flame. But she ain't done yet. She takes her whiskey glass and tosses it in for good measure. Mr. Chairman of the Board is wailing, kicking the flames at his wingtip shoes and patting his body in a panic.

"Go, Tom!" she screams, pushing me for the limo door.

I reach for the handle, but it's locked. The man in gray lowers the window and his eyes widen a full lunar cycle at the sight of the fire. He's sticking his arm through the window trying to reach the club soda while I fiddle with door like an idiot. When I look up all I see is the bug-stained grill of one of the shipping trucks barreling down on us. It plows into us, bending the limo into a horseshoe and dragging us across the highway a quarter mile stretch. Glass shards, burning vinyl, bottles and shot glasses fly everywhere and there's nothing but fear and screams and red light in my eyelids.

Then there's the sudden hush of the afterglow.

I look around, blood in my eyes and teeth. The limo door is open a crack, popped out like a beer top by the force of the blow on the other side. The Chairman is gone, wandered off in a daze most likely. The fire is still burning at my feet and the man in gray is nowhere in sight.

I'm cackling like a fucking fire-breathing hyena, unintentional, of course, and try to cut it out when I realize what a lunatic I must look like.

"Hot damn!" I shout, "Nice one, Maggs, we sure showed him."

I pat her thigh and turn to her with a smile, but Maggie May ain't talking. The twisted wreck of the side wall is wrapped half around her little body, a bit of the window pressing into her throat like Death himself finally found her pretty skin too goddamn irresistible. She's already white as a snowdrift and lying there smiling back at me like that last ride was the time of her too short life. Reckon I feel sad, broken, but I can't say for sure. It's too big.

I press against the bent frame of the limo door, bouncing idly on its hinges. My head's a fury of fog and sound and echoes and mixed signals. A radio broadcast in my head blasts static and the undertow of a thousand memories. The door is heavy and I get dizzy. I fall through onto the ground and puke my stomach's full load onto the pavement.

Looking up, the limo is gone, the desert is gone. This is the same piney wood stretch I saw with that weird grizzled moog that called himself Outlaw. This is Otherworld. A sign above my head says, "Don't Mess with Texas."

Whatever the hell that means.

I pull myself together and hobble down the lonesome blues gravel road. A couple cars roar by like horizontal lightning building to a white hilltop and dropping off into a red downward slide around corners and trees and houses. It's all too goddamn weird.

I come to a small pond under a blue-out halogen flood lamp. A man in a dirty Yankee baseball uniform stained rust colored by the red clay he's sitting in sways a fly fishing rod back and forth through the air like some kind o' goddamn orchestra conductor. His lure dances brief second ballets on the surface of the water, takes a bow and exits the stage just to come back a second later and do it all again. Every now and then the lure'll catch some hunk of bread, swollen from the water like dumplings, and haul it up onto the shore.

The man doesn't turn around to look at me. With his back turned he says, "Name's DiMaggio. Call me Joe. What about you, stranger?"

I tell him to call me Tom and ask him what he's up to.

"Not much. Just fishing. I'm fishing for compliments. They're in season this time of year. This one I just hauled in as you strolled up, it's a beaut."

Joe squats like a catcher, snatches up the pond dumpling and breaks it in half. A voice so pretty you can't even completely hear it without kindly turning away, a voice the way you think of angels as beautiful, echoes up out of the crumb dust cloud of the bread and speaks.

The dumpling says, "You are a strong and handsome man, and don't let anyone tell you otherwise. You are perfect just the way you are."

Joe breaks another that almost sings, "You are smart and witty, you can do anything you set your mind to."

Joe takes a bite and says, "They're delicious, right out of the water, you don't even have to cook 'em. Want one, kid?"

I figure I'm hungry as a hog so I thank him when he sticks a compliment in my hand. I break it open and that angel voice says, "You are brave and virtuous, but not a whole man."

Joe shrugs, "That's weird. Ain't never seen one that wasn't one hundred percent flattering and full of praises. Reckon you might've been a little rough when you opened her?"

I take a bite anyway and it tastes like a sunrise. My belly is full after two bites and I give Joe DiMaggio a nod and let him get back to his work. As I turn to hit the road again he shouts after me, "Remember, son, this is the spot if you need to go fishing for compliments. Who was it that said he could live two months on one good compliment?"

I shrug and start hiking again. It begins to rain a loud scream of a rain, a real bitch of a storm if you ask me. I stick my hands inside my shirt and press on into this weird Texas wild, keeping my eyes peeled for more rejects wandered through the barrier into Otherworld.

Field Notes from Bastard Land

16: Cyborg Edison, The Big Cop and Finding the Gray Man

Oblivion doesn't last long. Now I see a white, sterile hospital hallway and walk toward a well lit doorway. Somehow I know I'm standing in the meek chemotherapy lab bunkers that share a wall and a load-bearing stud with Subterranea. This is the last gangrene outpost of American Dream, Inc. Here they handle all of the breeding, regeneration of limbs and resurrection of the dead. The transplanted cloned brain of Thomas Edison, only $19.95 at the Record Store, works the fingers of a chrome-plated robot that burns the bodies of homeless people, Mexicans and bullshit for fuel. He is repairing the damaged circuits of the Stock Market hive mind server.

He says, "Yes, my lovelies, the Chairman and the New Uncle Sam recommended an upgrade and so here I am."

It's fallen to him to replace the Server's copper wiring with gene-spliced nerve endings torn from the living brains of recently lobotomized illegal immigrants, Iraqi carpenters, journalists and crazies.

Cyborg Edison says, "We must continually pursue more and

more human technology. I want my cell phone to talk to me instead of ringing. My computer should smile at me and the Stock Market Collective Server should think on wires of human tissue. This is American self-actualization."

His iron claw fingers dig another nerve ending from the occipital region of a Catholic nurse's lower cortex. Cyborg Edison stares at it vacantly through cellophane brake light reflector eyes and says, "That's a big one, this will definitely do."

"You see, my dears," he says to the twitching pack of brain dead spare parts carriers, "We build up imaginary visions like money and then they hire someone like me to help them push it through the technology womb into existence. My dears, we build things like Stock Markets and watch them take on more life than even you or I have. Then we watch them run away and we have to catch them in bear traps and drag them back for me to repair. We built the Stock Market Server and watched it find so much identity all on its own that it has even gotten depressed and tried to take its own life on several occasions."

A blue flame sharpens out of the Cyborg Edison's index finger and he welds the nerves into the Server. Lights flash awake and The Server moans, "No, not again. Who am I? Why am I here? What is my purpose in this world? What are you doing to me? What is the meaning of life? Why was I created?"

And Cyborg Edison shouts, "It's alive! It's alive!"

Some firm hand grips my shoulder and spins me around. I stand face to face with the Gray Man and he puts a finger to his lips. Whispering, he says, "We're still in a lot of danger, Jack. But you've done well. Things are falling back into place. Now, if you'll just follow me."

The Gray Man leads me through a congested maze of tiled hallways, up a flight of stairs and out into the open air. Now, just as soon as he appeared, he is gone once more. I look around, confused, but can't figure out where I am or why.

Following a gang of traveling Hari Krishnas leads me into

Union Station. This is New York, the Big Apple. I'm a fruit worm in the steam manholes of the city. I can see the Rat People. The Rat People are climbing the gutter drains into the New York Times and running the country's information. The Good Ones try to fight them off, but the Rat People are strong and slick. They know how to get you. The Rat People can bite your ankles from under your bed and then you are one of them. They spread their disease fast.

I'm with the Rat People watching the Holy Spirit of Corporate Takeovers move in flame tongues at Pentecost Park. The street bums beg for mercy and ransom whiskey with the threat of spreading their disease. A drunkard waves a Coke bottle full of rat blood under the nose of a Korean convenience store clerk that begs for his life with tears. This is Central Park and the trees are singing the National Anthem. The trees are singing the proverbs of the Torah. The trees are purple and smile the blood of patriots. The trees are mean here and I have to play chess against Death for my freedom. You have to win your freedom every day here in the park.

This is Central Park and the Rat People are growing as a demographic. Cigarette ads in magazines are now directed toward them and the trees tell me cigarettes are sold to the ones we hate the most. A large red-eyed elm says that we will kill them slowly if nothing else. Now I see a fountain spouting fresh oil from the veins of an OPEC charity stealer.

This is New York. This is New York. I'm in New York. I'm right here in New York and a cab driver with the face of a dragon and the hands of a rabbit honks and gives me the finger. And now my hands are guns and I go firing at everything that moves. When your hand is a .357 Magnum flipping the bird means blowing flaming chunks of metal at the pigeons. The Rat People are eating the pigeons and calling it a social service like an inverted Pied Piper. They're moving up Wall Street now and have already infected the Public Library and the entire Park.

They don't mess with Harlem.

I don't mess with them.

And now I see a bearded lady using two living rattlesnakes as nylons. She's shoving her feet down their throats, but kind enough to point her toes to avoid tearing. They get up past her thighs and she hooks their fangs around a belt made from a bicycle chain. The Gray Man passes me with a wave as he steers a cab down Fifth Avenue. When I try to follow him I fall straight down a manhole and land with a gelatin splash.

I'm swimming with the fishes now, swimming with fleshy pink fins and a black cloth tail. I'm swimming toward the Lady on High. She supervises me. I tell her that she has large feet and a pole up her ass and I get her to crack a slight smile, which is hard this day and age, you can rarely get Liberty to laugh. Under her island there is a cave that leads to the heart of the earth. You can find the pipeline and ride the waterfall to the molten core. I ride Subterranea's Niagara and land with a plop in the lake of fire. Millions of souls wail and scream in the flames and I see an entire section cordoned off for the souls of ex-military men, dictators, politicians, oil executives and plastic surgeons. And I scream through fish gills when I see that the demons are funhouse clowns and I am actually a mammal.

Here I am back in New York, the epicenter of the Human Quake. I've just broken through the surface of the earth and still found myself right here. I thought I was out, but apparently I still haven't escaped the Safety Factory. Nothing is what it seems. We're not even fixed in one place in the universe. We're actually hurtling through space at top speeds – terminal velocity. Earth is a tennis ball, no shit, earth is a bowling ball.

What happens when we knock down the pins?

No, earth is a bullet, earth is a missile, earth is a rolling stone, a broken bone, a disconnected phone, a lost baby tooth – earth is in the bag. Earth is in the Tooth Fairy's black bag and she's mating with the Easter Bunny to try to germinate a new race of long-dreaming children. We're flying through space in that bag.

What happens when you reach the end of the line?

This isn't a train. There is no end of the line. There is no stitch in time. What the hell do you save nine of, anyway? Time is not a straight line. Earth is in orbit around the sun and the sun is in orbit around the universe, orbiting its bright center. The heart of the galaxy pumps gravity like blood. That's it. I am in the veins of outer space pumping around and around its body, around its heart. I am hemoglobin. I am red and white cells. No, I am platelets. No, shit, I'm a clot. I am a hemorrhage.

I am the AIDS virus.

No, I am poison. The Rat People of the American Dream, Inc. designed me that way. They play me against myself. They play good against bad. They've played it so long that there is no black and white anymore. The chess pieces have all faded to gray. There is no longer any good or evil. There is only In-Between. Earth is purgatory. I am an angel and an imp, the twisted blue-steel face of an industrial strength Jack-o'-Lantern. I am a pawn and a king. They designed me that way.

They invented Lincoln and Hitler.

I glued a coffee mug to my hand and burned a swizzle stick to the church mast sailing down Broadway. I drank a cigarette and smoked away with Johnny Walker into the Milky Way wild abandon douche canal. That's the only way to be Born Again in the Safety Factory. And if you want to see the end of the safety then just flip the catch and pull the Cold War Russian Roulette Trigger.

Tell 'em Jack Bluff sent you and they'll give you a discount on nicotine bullets.

I can see a popped collar on the Metrorail and a greased-shellacked hair-do in Grand Central. I can smoke myself a reality and trip myself a poison-pill tongue tip tranquility. And that's the new Hookah Lounge of the Headless Horseman. Now there's Uncle Sam sitting across from me in my dark room. He's wearing a seven-foot scale model of the Washington Monument like a lesbian hayride strap-on around his lap.

And the New York Times they are a-changin'.

The New York Times they are a-endin' and if the truth is in

you then you'll taste it on your lips when God tea bags you till you bleed. The Statue of Liberty is showing some shoulder as she wades her way toward the lost-show emigration nights of Ellis Island. Uncle Sam meets her with his strap-on, still new with the sales tag that says, "Made in DC."

This, after all, is the only way he can hope to please so much woman.

And don't you know that Mt. Sinai is Mt. Rushmore and the Burning Bush was the start of America's Presidential Dynasty? Uncle Sam is up there on Washington's big skull flipping off his boots and removing his hat to worship on that hallowed ground. Kneeling in front of the Burning George W. Bush, he says, "Forgive me, father, for I have sinned. I took Lady Liberty to Ellis Island and sodomized her with the Washington Monument."

And the Burning Bush says, "Be not afraid, my son, this is the New World Order and I have commanded that in the New World Order all good Americans will flip up her toga and sodomize Lady Liberty."

Climbing through a manhole like one of the Rat People brings me back to Washington Square Park. I can see the Big Cop right now. The Big Cop is invisible, he moves like an amorphous wisp of cloud. He moves as spirit and drops down on those he wishes to use. I can see the Big Cop. He moves like a ghost on decent, peace-serving enforcers and transforms them into brutish Huns, Genghis Khans, and Gestapo drones of the Dream.

The Big Cop turns decent social servants into blind, bullying wielders of the taser, the baton, the mace. The Big Cop turned the riot squad protectors into the mob tactic foot soldiers of Detroit, New York and LA. They became the murderous law wolves that sprayed tear gas on Chicano Rights activists or rounded up beatniks in the park. The Big Cop used them to spray down hippies with fire hoses and arrested sit-in black boy protesters and Dr. King.

The Big Cop moves as a cloud and possesses. He turned decent National Guard boys into the sort that fired live rounds into the college students of Kent State. They fuel the fires of the Big Cop in Subterranea with the bodies of the doomed. We are, all of us, doomed. The Big Cop will find us one day. Maybe in a routine traffic stop gone wrong or when you say something he deems treasonous. I can see him guarding the fountain and the arch, and I feel like his reinforcements might be around any corner.

The Gray Man strolls up casually and says, "Jack, my boy, I'm sorry to leave you like that. But there were many Subterranean guards. I tricked them into following me so you might get away."

"And the cab?"

"I stole it to make my escape."

"Cool," I reply, "what now?"

"Now, we find Bonnie."

And...Cut!

I call this *City Rain and Visions of the Lady.*

Here we are walking to Battery Park in seething rain with faces upturned to New York City opening her ballast on the street. Steam circles white out of manholes and open-wide sewer mouths. Entire city billows blue.

After the first drops fall, whole rain sheets immediately follow and the Gray Man says, "Should we take the subway?"

"No," I say, "this is the greatest New York moment and we will not hide underground. This is New York rain, man, there's nothing sweeter. Rain like this demands running."

Now we're running through drop water streets, dodging Yellow Cabs and umbrellas. We can see the timid business men in tailored suits – pinstripe three-piece double-breasted vest-coat corporate armor. They're hiding beneath restaurant meeting awnings and blue paint scaffolding afraid the Wicked Witch water will melt them down or multiply them into back-popping mini beasts.

We run, shouting ourselves to the rafters.

We run, soaking into America.

Others hide from their city's cleansing smile, but the Gray Man and I run to the bay. Behind us there's a pair of joggers in tight-sweat running clothes that start to shout and take up the call. Their words come out sounding like Greek or something Mediterranean. Running together we laugh a wordless communion and they speak rapidly in their foreign language. But. Our joy is in the same tongue and we sound it over the city like Armageddon's trumpet call.

The Gray Man shouts through rattle honk street-ness thunder, "The white collars keep themselves dry and we sprint in defiance of language barriers and wet skin, unified by the Big Apple Storm. That, my boy, is America."

Ducking through post-rain street swarms and city park detour construction reveals our first glimpse of the bay. We climb over railings and dangle our feet above the swell. Now it's mist in our faces as waves break the dock, clouds part, light falls and we see the Lady silhouetted against gray vapors of her city, land and country.

I feel odd. Some strange knot in my guts grips my spine. Visions of Liberty flat on her back churning out sad drone workers of number-crunching fates. Here she is standing tall, scorching the sky with a gold Prometheus flame. We failed her, knocking her down to make her birth a mutant idea of freedom. Freedom to steal, slice, deal, trick or lie to get the uppercut hand over competitors. Freedom in this America looks too much like the freedom to kill thy neighbor as long as it looks good on your tax audit. Freedom means the freedom to rape Lady Liberty and crank out the fallopian pack line children of the dream.

I want her to stay standing.

"Mr. Gray Man," I say, "we have to make sure no one gets her on her back again because right now, this moment, things actually *are* beautiful."

The moon rises a blotted-out white behind the rain. Drops the size of meteorites pummel the ground. It's raining virtues like tears. Up ahead is the hazy shape of Ziggy Stardust under a red, yellow and blue umbrella. He's sitting on a tree stump beside a green mailbox, one knee crossed over the other and his foot just bouncing up and down with energy or nerves.

"Is that you, Tom?" he asks.

"Reckon it is," I reply, "least that's what they tell me. You got out?"

"Yeah, something changed. The storm shifted some time ago. First Jim went and a few others like him, next it was Ben. After all his planning and invention he wound up just walking out the front door. I wasn't long behind. But when the door opened I found myself here. Did you know it was raining words?"

"Yeah, cardinal virtues. The water 'round these parts has been doing a lotta weird stuff. I just saw Joe DiMaggio fishing for compliments."

"Aye, yes, they're in season this time of year. Well, I suppose I should make the best of this while I can."

Ziggy produces a tea kettle from somewhere behind him, ain't for sure where to be honest. He dunks it down into a puddle of honesty and patience and sets the pot to boiling on a white hot stone.

"They're cold to the touch, these stones, but they burn white hot. They're not as rare as you might think, actually. It's what we make anger out of, ferocity, jealousy. Stone cold emotions, they're the only right thing for brewing tea."

"Especially virtue tea, I reckon?"

"I imagine so, Tom. It's bound to be a helluva mix. Oh, before I forget, someone was looking for you. The widow fortune teller. She's around. Keep on your path and you're bound to bump into her."

I tell him thanks and set back on my way. Ziggy was right, it ain't long before I'm locking eyes with Madame Boheme. At the bottom of the hill is a dried-up clearing and her little table is right in the middle of it. No tent this time, just the table, a chair for me and her weird crystal ball. She beckons me closer and I try to pick up the pace.

Sitting down across from her I nod a hello.

Madame Boheme says, "I've been waiting for you. It falls to me to make something clear that has been hindering your journey. You never fully committed to the mission given to you by MARTYR, did you? Of course not, they gave you no real answers. Well, you should know that this was necessary. Like the one you look for, you are given only limited information. This is because the rationale of our two worlds is radically different, what is possible in one world is not possible in another. For this reason, Tom, the only way to find what you seek as these worlds bleed into each other is to find it by mistake. You have to get lost or you won't find anything. So we all hoped that by sending you out blind you might get there quicker than if you were searching for something specific."

"We?" I ask, "You workin' for them now?"

"I have always worked for them young one," the widow fortune teller replies, "Nothing has changed since the day you first saw me.

By now you must realize that you, like the one you're looking for, have been passing in and out of both worlds. It's allowed you to cover great distances. Even now you have traveled nearly a hundred miles from where you were to where you are. It seems that every gap in the barrier has created a portal to and from the places where the one you seek first broke through. This is Tyler, Texas, now, the former home of the One. You are following in his path, you see, you just emerged from the first hole in the barrier that he stepped through when this all began."

"I am getting closer, then?"

Madame Boheme nods and I ask her to tell me the name of the one I'm looking for. She shakes her head, "I cannot tell you that, we are not a people of names in Americana, we are a people of roles. I know his role, where he goes and what he does, I know nothing of who he really is. That is for you to find out. You *must* find out."

"I've been trying, but it's hard, things are confusing here. Nothing makes any sense, everything moves in straight lines. Otherworld is such a literal place."

The widow fortune teller deals her weird cards one by one in front of me. She flips them slowly and they come up different than the last time I saw them. I don't get any weird pictures or strange characters. They all come up with a compass rose pointing east.

Madame Boheme nods, "Yes, I see what you mean. This place has already begun changing me and my magic. But I feel the answer is clear, you must go east. I can tell you nothing more. The fates have closed their eyes on me."

"Which way is east?" I ask.

She points a crooked tule reed finger over my left shoulder and I look behind me. There is a row of trees and lights glowing faintly behind them. I thank the lady and break into a run toward the trees and whatever shit merry-go-round might be on the other side. Ducking trees and hearing voices calling after me I stumble into the headlights of oncoming traffic. I dive out of the way and everything is different again. It's quiet now. A stoplight blinks red. Halted road construction glows in the dim light. I see a gas station flickering in bug-covered floodlights. A nearby sign reads, "Linden City Limits."

Under the sign is the old locust husk of what used to be a familiar face. He's ragged and bitter and smokehouse rue like a flayed catfish on a tailgate, but he's him all right. A toppled giant, used to be a threat to me and mine, sitting there like a stiff piss might shuffle him like ash. It's Jumpin' Jack Flash, dressed in a greased over tuxedo shirt and the bottom half of a Mickey Mouse costume, yellow loafers and all, sitting squatty as a Bright Lights, Big City panhandler drunk in a stoop.

"Hiya, Tom, fancy meetin' you here this fine evening."

"Flash," I nod, "How's tricks?"

"Shifty and dark as a black widow's taint. But what else is new, right?" He cackles wheezy and blue like the lunger gasp of an old bay hound.

I light a smoke and tell him he looks like shit.

"I think I am shit, kid," he groans, trying to stand up and groaning back into the mud, "I think somebody shit me outta Subterranea and I came out greased and corporate on the other side. This is the other side, ain't it?"

"Yeah, it is," I tell him, "but we ain't supposed to be here."

"We ain't, but you are."

"What the fuck's that supposed to mean?" I ask, twisting my face with attitude and confusion and tear-dried smoke in my eyes.

"Boy, ain't you heard, yet?" Jack Flash whines into a whiskey bottle, "Ah, fuck it, they're finished with me anyway, what's it gonna hurt?"

"What's what gonna hurt?"

"Tom, you oughta have figured by now that you ain't really Tom."

"I know that, I've been telling that to Maggie all this time. Maggie, fuck…"

"Yeah, boy, I heard about that, I know how you feel…can't say

I ain't feelin' some o' the same...she was...*special*, to both of us. Anyway, it ain't like you thought. It's more than just you ain't Tom anymore, or that you was someone else. You ain't from the same world as me, you get that?"

"I'm sorry, but I conjure that I ain't got a fuckin' clue what you're talking about."

"Tom, you ain't just visiting Otherworld, you're goddamn from here, you read me? The one who made you, the one yer lookin' for, he lost ya on the other side there some time back. My boss, the folks from ADI, they knew about it. That's why we been wanting you so bad. Tom, you're the key to everything. See, you might be looking for someone, but he's looking for you too. And, son, he ain't rightly done a good job of figuring out who it is he's looking for."

"What in Saint Fuck's deepest ring o' hell are you talkin' about, Flash? You ain't makin' no goddamn sense! Of course I'm from your world, I lived in the hotel with Maggie, I hung out with Jim, I was one of the night gamers wanderin' the halls."

"Yeah, and yet you got no memory of how you got in there, how long you was there, you got no memory of your family, your past, your parents...nothin' like that. Don't it strike you as odd, kid? You're nothing but boredom, vices and emotion. You ain't too bright, are ya? But then, we know that, you been telling us all along."

"Maybe I ain't too bright, Flash, 'cause I got no clue what you're saying."

"Tom, you're only half a man, half a boy, whatever. You ain't all yourself. You're as used up and dry as I am lying here with this whiskey. You're just what he left behind when he first punched through."

"Punched through?"

"This other guy, the one you're supposed to be finding, he got the formula right and didn't even know it. All the pieces were there. He sacrificed himself to art. Right on the event horizon of one of them portals he staged his ritual. A best friend to join you, stretching your body to the limit, breaking your mind in half and seeing yourself on the other side. He stayed up, days at a time, reciting poetry and trying to find the bottom of his mind and damn if that boy didn't do it right here in this very town."

I look around and it begins to make some kinda sense. I ain't never known much about myself. Never knew who I was or where I came from. I'm just a heap of sadness and rage and sarcasm wrapped up in an orgasm on legs. Fuck if I didn't see this coming.

"Look, kid, they know more than you can imagine. They want to keep you two apart because the longer he goes searching for you across this country he's just tearing holes in the barrier between worlds, just stretching them out like ripping nylons to get at the sweet spot on some hot, tight little skirt. You know what I'm saying, kid? He's ripping our worlds apart and they want him to. Look at me, I'm sitting right here in Otherworld, me and so many others. Kid, you gotta fix it."

"How? What can I do?"

Jumpin' Jack Flash swallows the last dog water backwash circling the whiskey bottle and stands up, "You gotta head straight down this road and don't look back. You'll know where to go. Kid, the one you're after is in deep shit. He thinks he's found you already. He thinks you're a man in gray, that the one he's been sent for *is* this man in gray. Unless you find your other half and find a way to put yourself back together, both of our worlds will soon be lost. He's leading him straight to our queen. Right to America sleeping in her hospital bed."

17: Gray Talk, Nashville Road and Arriving at Your Final Destination

We find Bonnie parked lonesome in a lot off of Tenth Avenue. Not really sure how she got there, but she's a true Texas woman and, as such, has a mind of her own. I unlock the door and it creaks open lazily. As I'm about to get in, the Gray Man following suit, I hear a voice howling over the traffic.

"Hey, wait for me, guys."

I turn and there's Uncle Sam, freshly pressed in a new suit with coattails and bow tie and wearing his hat cocked slightly to one side. He smiles wildly and shrugs, "Sorry to be so late, but me and my girl had business to take care of."

"Yeah, I know," I reply, "Somewhere in all this weirdness I saw you at Liberty Island. What's with that?"

"Oh, it's nothing really. We've just had this little thing on the side since World War I. After you've spent some time in the pit, like I just did, the first thing you need is the touch of a good woman."

I decide to leave it at that and tell him to get in.

Uncle Sam is at my right and behind me sits the Gray Man.

In the rearview mirror I see his eyes – milky, gray and blank. He doesn't seem sad, but I know he isn't happy either. The Gray Man seems more worn out by a life that is always too long or too short. Unable to think of anything better to say I look at him in the mirror and ask, "You're him, aren't you?"

"Him?"

"The one I've been looking for," I reply, "The one I have to take to America to show them I can save her so I can stop all this nonsense. You knew it, but you couldn't tell me. That's why you've been following me."

"But I haven't been following you," the Gray Man replies, "You're following me."

"That's impossible. You're always there, every time I turn around. How can I be following you?"

"You're thinking about this all wrong, Jack. You have been this entire time. Too many people try to do things backward in your world. They try to affect my world by changing theirs when things really work the other way around. You don't change spirits through action, you change actions through spirit.

"You've had it set in your mind all along that because John Lennon and his people showed you visions of Charlie Outlaw that this meant Charlie was their diamond in the rough. You missed the point entirely, the truth is that people like Charlie will never go anywhere, never be inspired to action, until the Ghost Road is in order. You have to fix the heart of things before the body will do as it should. So, names are useless, you had to find *me*. I am the Ghost Road representative of your entire generation and you have to bring me to America. But there is one thing you still haven't figured out, and that is the real reason they showed you the video footage of you and Charlie in Linden, Texas."

I light a cigarette and sit quietly as the tension in the car seems to ponder what, if anything, should be said.

Uncle Sam says, "Look, Jack, she's everywhere, but she's also only where you are at any given moment. Everyone finds her in their own way. You just have to ask yourself where you think you've seen her in your young life."

I hit my blinker and take an exit off of the interstate. In all the places I've gone I have learned that you never actually see America until you leave the interstate. We take some quiet mountain highway south toward Texas.

It's somewhere outside of Nashville when Bonnie finally squeals to a stop in protest. I've pushed the poor girl farther than anyone ever should have asked. And I know, deep down, she's the only woman who will ever be able to put up with all that I ask of her.

We screech to a halt in some lonely parking lot.

I climb out and immediately notice a large puddle of dark liquid.

"That's it guys. We're fried, Bonnie is bleeding oil."

"What do you want to do, Jack?" the Gray Man asks.

"Hang on," I groan, straining to kneel down and look at the spill, "maybe it's not as serious of a wound as I thought. I mean, Bonnie is the truest woman I've ever known, she'd be damned before failing me now."

I dip my fingers into her blood and jump to my feet shouting, "Thank you, fucking God! It's water, she's just leaking water. I think we can drive her after all."

Climbing back into the driver's seat, I check her gauges. She's not overheating, at least not yet, but the engine won't crank. In one last ditch effort to get her going, I floor the gas and turn the key. She fires to a start, but chokes on fumes when I let go of the pedal.

The Gray Man says, "It would seem that you can only keep her moving if you maintain constant acceleration."

"All right, fuck it, how hard could that be?"

I hit the gas again, fire the engine and peel out in reverse flying onto this town's main drag. I run a stop sign and a red light with my emergency lights on and grudgingly book it onto Interstate 40. Now it's a high-speed suicide mission through the Appalachian slopes. Weaving through traffic and never letting off the accelerator. 100 miles to Nashville and civilization.

"Go, man, go!" I scream to no one, "Constant momentum, it's the only way to fly!"

Miles fly under us. I pass Nashville. We're a runaway train now and can't be bothered with petty details like service shops. The trip wearies itself and miles roll under us as Bonnie steadily loses power. On the other side of Memphis we lose some steam. Every hundred miles the engine loses headway on the speedometer. Top speed is around 98 mph. Now it's 80. Now it's 70. Somewhere about sixteen miles outside of Texarkana we've bottomed out at a max speed of 40 mph and can't get any higher. On the downward side of the hills we'd gain speed and lose it at the next one.

It's Highway 59 when she finally bottoms out altogether. We coast on fumes and residual momentum through Linden, Texas, and its one traffic light. It finally hits me. I guess, sometimes, I can be kind of an idiot. The answer was so obvious I looked right over it. It had nothing to do with me or Charlie, not really, this was about Linden. The tiny little vortex circling on the edge of destruction. I inch Bonnie up Center Hill Road, instinctively moving toward the former home of Charlie Outlaw.

And there, at the top of the hill, isn't that old brick house. I don't see the open lawn or the dogs. There's no music room and lingering dreg ghosts of chess games and coffee. I don't see any sign of our former sleepless nights. Charlie's house is gone.

Instead, there's a tall white plaster complex that vaguely hints at a mental institution.

Bonnie's engine dies in the grass.

"You found it, Jack," Uncle Sam smiles, "this is the place."

LOST IN AMERICANA: CHAPTER SEVENTEEN

TAPE RECORDERS AND HOSPITAL VISITATIONS

Transcriber's Note: The following text has been adapted from a tape recorder discovered in the mud. Its authenticity has left even me perplexed, but I have recorded here precisely what was dictated into the device as follows.

I ain't too clear on what to expect, but just to make sure I don't make the same mistakes again I'm taking a minute to get all of this down on paper. Before it's too late.

"You got a drink on ya, kid?" asks Jumpin' Jack Flash.

Handing him what's left of a flask of Jim Beam I pat him on the shoulder and leave him in the mud. Strolling up the hill toward the convenience store I buy myself a shitty, dime store tape recorder for anything that may happen to me before I get a chance to finish my journal entry. Maybe my last journal entry the way I figure it.

When I'm done here I'll start up this tape recorder for posterior. Or postmortem. Or post – whatever the fuck that saying is supposed to be. I can't go losing any more of the story than I already have, that is just bad narrating. Lord knows what I lost in the pit of Subterranea.

Starting up the hill now. If you're reading this it was likely transcribed from this recording by fuck knows who. Thanks to them, though, it means a lot.

The hill is steep and straight. The Texas night ain't got a moon and I feel like I'm walking right off into the goddamn stars. Lights grow large and then fade to red as they pass me by with a honk or a wave. No one offers me a ride, but there's plenty seemin' worried enough. Guess that's their Christian duty talking.

Out of breath already, but I decide to get a smoke going anyway. That fuckin' hill is long, like it don't even end or something. I reach the end of a dark row only to find more rows heading on up. It's so bad that I don't even believe it when I reach the top. Top of the hill now and there ain't much. There's just a telephone pole in orange light and a dirt-gravel path heading down toward some tall white concrete block of a building. It's lit up something fierce, like a police station under flood lights. Reckon it's them lights that draw me in, like a June bug to a blue porch light zapper. I'm heading in now. Doors part at the hands of ghosts when I reach the entrance. A lobby hall, painted sea foam surgical green, is filled with strange medical equipment, tubing, human jumper cables, gurneys, and clear plastic bladders of bodily fluids on their way in or out, who fucking knows?

There's a front desk, but no one's manning the station. Brown plaque letterhead directs visitors to different levels, sublevels, and departments. Everything's dim and flickering in blue-gray dying light. Everything but one elevator door, well lit in white. I punch a button going up. Doors part and I step into a grease-coated steel coffin the size of a tractor trailer hauling the dead east of Milwaukie for disposal. There are no buttons to select a floor, instead the doors just close and I feel the low resonance hum of the boxcar carrying me to a higher altitude. Doors part, revealing a white wall and a narrow hallway heading off to the left and right. To the right is a dead rose in a gray vase and more flickering lights flirting with the thought of going out. On my left is a tall, wide metal door, slightly rusted and marked "Private."

Naturally, I pull the handle and it groans open reluctantly. Inside is an airport terminal departure room, at least, it might as well be. It's solid white, long and narrow with a row of plastic bucket seat chairs on each side wall for waiting room parishioners. At the far end is a single bed: white sheets, white pillows, pale overhead, horizontal bar lamp, and a girl with ivory skin, raven hair, red lips…asleep like a princess in fairy stories. There's a window the size of a dictionary, a small framed photo of Uncle Sam and a crowd of people circled 'round the foot of the girl's bed like some kind of morbid, sterile funeral under bleach.

Transcriber's Note: Dictation ceases here and is instead replaced by hushed dialogue picked up at a distance. It is as if our mysterious narrator listens in.

Voice 1: It's impossible.

Voice 2: He can't be the one.

Voice 3: Don't you dare touch her!

Voice 4: No one's getting anywhere near her until we're sure of what we're dealing with here.

Voice 5: I'm telling you people that he's the one. I did what you asked, I thought it was Charlie, it wasn't, I even thought it was me, but I was wrong. I'm sure of it now, didn't you send me on that weird trip into Subterranea, why else would I have gone through all that shit if not to meet him? This man is the one you want. He is the Spirit of my generation. Look at him, how can you doubt it?

Narration continues.

I can see now that all of the people have clustered around one man, as if to block him from the girl in the hospital bed. I see him. There between all of the hunkered shoulders and jockeyin' elbows blocking him from view, I catch a glimpse of his face. I ain't never gonna forget those weird features. It's that goddamn pimp Chairman of the board bastard's limo driver. That hazy gray dust cloud of a man that wrecked the car that killed my Maggie May. There's only one face like that. And it hits me. Maggie said he was in trouble, the one I'm supposed to be finding. She said he might not even know he was in danger, even now.

Good girl, Maggie.

The crowd turns to face the sound of my voice.

Voice 4: Tom?

Narrator: Jim? That you? What the fuck are you doin' here?

It's Jim. Jim, all his MARTYR buddies, and even old Uncle Sam are all in attendance.

Narrator: That gray sonuvabitch ain't the one, Jim.

Jim: Whaddaya mean, Tom?

Narrator: He killed our Maggs. She's dead because of him. You sent her to me, right? You sent her and she died getting me out of Subterranea.

Hunter: You see, gang? What the fuck did I tell you? Our boy here, who is so sure, is just another half-witted oafish mule. I told you, he didn't have what it takes.

Hendrix: Yeah, well, don't forget, HST, he was your recruit to begin with.

Hunter: Well, in case you were wondering, Jack, that right there is the one you were looking for, not this gray bastard.

Jack: You couldn't just…tell me that?

Uncle Sam: There's no time for that now, people. What are we gonna do with him?

Jim: What happened, Tom? How'd it go down?

Narrator: We had a car wreck trying to escape from that old fat ass, Mr. Chairman of the Board, and your pal, Gray Boy, over there was our driver.

Jack: That's impossible!

Narrator: Cool it, bucko…wait a minute, don't I? Do I know you from some place?

Field Notes from Bastard Land
18: The Kid, Gray Man and Confusion

The face is familiar. Simultaneously like one you see looking back at you in shop windows and one that just picked your pocket in a crowded subway platform. I don't know what to make of it. But, Hunter says he was the one. I can't make heads or tails of it. Everyone is silent, as if they know to keep their mouths shut until they have something really good to say. John, Jimi, Janis, Kurt...they're all silent in the presence of this sleeping girl.

The Kid says he knows me. Jim says his name is Tom.

Tom, "Yeah, name's Sawyer, Tom Sawyer, I know I seen ya some place."

It hits me and I ask, "It was night and then it turned to day."

"Hey, yeah! You're that joker in the beat-up Bonneville that gave me a lift. Highway 61, remember? How ya been?"

"Not great," I say, "Looks like I almost handed America over to the bad guys."

"Lucky I showed up when I did, eh?"

"That's all very cute and endearing, heartwarming reunions and what not," says a voice by the door, "but we have more pressing matters to attend to, I'm afraid."

We all know him by now. Barely even have to turn to look. Mr. Chairman of the Board and a couple of his freaky, funhouse cronies are standing there with guns drawn. There's a few clowns in black and white face paint, the Dog-faced Boy and the Snake Charmer, all looking mean as hell and spoiling for a fight.

Mr. Chairman says, "Now, if you'll kindly step away from the young lady, she will be coming with us."

None of us moves.

The Dog-faced Boy says, "C'mon, don't make us get nasty."

I try not to smile when I hear Tom snort a laugh under his breath. I can feel the crowd around me, refusing to back down, not going without a fight. It's weird, none of this makes any sense to me, but I still don't move. I just know it's wrong.

Mr. Chairman says, "Tom, Jack, you both have been such valuable assets, I would hate for our relationship to end bloody."

I try to argue, try to find the words to let everyone know that I was never with him, not for a single second, but before I can find the words Tom is already shouting.

"Fuck off, you old mutant. Don't even try your goddamn head games on this crowd, there's a reason we're all standing on this side of the fuckin' room and you're over there. We all know our loyalties."

"But Tom," the Chairman replies, "loyalties or not, it was you that opened the door for all of us. It's you that widened the barrier enough for our world to pour over into this one. It's you who brought us here. And Jack, poor Jack, you led us right to her. Our man played his part well. I think he may even have had himself convinced."

Uncle Sam rushes for the Gray Man's throat, growling like a goddamn wolf, and the Chairman fires a shot into the ceiling. Lennon, grabbing Uncle Sam by the elbow, pulls him away roughly and shakes his head, "Not this one, old friend, it's not the time, right, mate?"

Mr. Chairman says, "That was a warning, folks. You only get

one. Now, where was I...? Of course, neither of you ever did put it together, did you? Tom, Jack, you two are drawn together for a reason. The pull has grown for years and as it grew in strength it tore between our two worlds. Space and time have warped to bring you two back together. As Jack punched through the barrier, time and again, he created more and more holes, sometimes Tom would find one and wander in and out of his own world. Each time each of these things took place the holes would stretch wider, expanding, tearing, like a knitted sweater unraveling more and more."

I look down at Tom and he looks back at me, confused, angry, but mostly confused.

The Chairman continues in a droning monotone, "You see, Jack, your friends there who so aptly dubbed themselves 'MARTYR' knew about this, but they could not tell you audibly. In our world, people are created and destroyed by a single thought from yours. A belief, a story, some fiction breathes life into us or takes it away forever. Had you been told of Tom's existence and refused to believe he would have been destroyed as surely as night becomes day. For this reason, they kept the secret, and merely prodded you in the right direction. They could not know for certain that Tom was the one, only that he was out there. Whoever he was, but I believe they had their suspicions about his true identity. Didn't you, Hunter?"

HST grumbles, "I did, you pasty smarmy bastard."

The Chairman chuckles and adds, "We also had our suspicions, but we kept it under wraps for a different reason. Care to take a guess, Jack?"

I hesitate, but finally nod and reply, "You wanted us out there, not finding each other, punching holes in reality so you could squeeze your fat ass through. That's why you sent this gray dick. To distract me, lead me astray."

"Too true, too true, my boy," the Gray Man replies, a few paces away from the girl in her bed, Uncle Sam posted squarely between them.

Mr. Chairman of the Board says, "And that, my friends, is why I just had to thank you, and now, before I take my prize I wish only to ask one question. What question do you suppose that is, my love?"

The Chairman turns to the Snake Charmer and she grunts, "Have you figured out what you two really are to one another?"

I look at Tom and we both shrug dumbly.

"Ernest, we've had a long and checkered relationship," the Chairman says with a grin, "Care to weigh in? I suspect you're the brains of this bunch."

Ernest sighs and drops his head into one had, his head wound gushing nervously, "Jack...Tom...you two are one and the same. Jack, we showed you those tapes of your past, you pushing bounds, stretching your body to the point of exhaustion for the sake of art...we taught you about vortexes...told you your hometown was built right on top of one. We had hoped you might put it together. Tom, you spent all of your time at The California, all of your time with Maggie May, wondering who you were and where you came from...why you had no family or parents. You were both so close to realizing the truth."

Tom says, "He's why I've been an orphan all these years?"

"Did I go through, Ernest? Jim? Did I find the other side?"

Jim shrugs, "Sorry, kid, I just couldn't tell you. You were looking for something, God maybe, art...who knows, right? But instead you found your way to us, it didn't last long. Just long enough for you to glimpse what everyone has the power to create, but more important than that..."

Mr. Chairman of the Board cuts in, "Just long enough to lose a part of yourself! Weee! It's my favorite part of the story, Jack! In trying to 'find yourself,' as every pubescent teen strives to, you instead left behind an echo of who you were, all of your best parts, your energy, youthfulness, daring, romance, boldness...call it your 'inner child' if that helps you wrap your little brain around it. You left him behind and he wandered into my world where we gave him an identity and checked him into our hotel. He became Tom Sawyer, mischievous, clever but idiotic, a child of means...

everything that you might have been had you just stayed where you belonged. You've never been able to finish anything, have you, Jack? Failed at marriage, lost your job, all because you, because no one in existence, can complete anything without that part of themselves. You're a complete failure, Jack, and it all happened because you tried so damn hard! The irony...Oh, it kills me!"

"I've heard enough!" I scream and, for some weird reason, I rush them. A shot gets fired and everything goes dark.

CHAPTER EIGHTEEN: THIS IS THE END, MY ONLY FRIEND, THE END.

Transcriber's Note: For a few seconds everything here is a mess of screams, crashes, gun fire and stomping feet. A pause and the sound of static silence. Then the narrator, Tom, breathing heavy.

Don't ask me why I did it. I couldn't rightly say for sure. Instinct, I reckon. But when I saw Jack rush the Chairman I made right for that pretty girl in her bed. The Gray Man scrambled for her too and Uncle Sam grabbed his throat. It all happened so fast, I saw old Uncle Sam take a bullet somewhere in the hip and go down in a heap with that gray bastard. Next thing I know, I'm jumpin' on top of that girl, trying to shield her from the bullets or some goddamn thing. That's when it happened. Couldn't say what, but apparently something about me and Jack being...whatever the fuck all that hogwash was about, means that if I touch her first then I get to keep her or something.

We get whisked away in a black flash and white moonlight and the hospital...it's just gone. Don't ask me how, I don't fuckin' know. But it's gone. The Chairman and his buddies, they're gone. It's just us. Out in the grass under the stars.

Sitting up and there's Jim and the gang, the girl asleep in her bed, and Jack pressing his hands into Uncle Sam's wound like a fuckin' field medic.

Jim: What happened?

Ernest: Tom got there first. It's as we expected. He couldn't just open portals, he could close them too.

Tom: You mean...I...how?

Ernest: You're the only person that is of both worlds, Tom. Your will brought Jack to you just as Jack's will brought him into our world. He created you. As a young man, full of arrogance and self-importance, he created a persona of himself sitting up late nights with a guitar and a pencil. His will made you, he fancied himself a clever Sawyer able to pull the wool over the eyes of the world and, sitting over a dwindling vortex to the other side, you went through. Just as Jack's will made you, your will sent these evil men away. When you made your choice, and you chose us they were sent away in a flash.

Tom: Personal Note: I think all of this is a bunch of horse shit and I feel it is entirely likely that I am a figment of my own imagination. Just for the record. Ernest seems to have lost interest and has instead moved over to the bed, he's staring at her like she's some kind of Sleeping Beauty or Snow White post apple.

Ernest: She was small, born prematurely. A lot of people don't know that. Her infant years were full of struggle, poor health and the constant lingering threat of death. When she pulled through she grew into a brave young child but she was kept from the big world as much as possible...until she grew up a bit more. Her childhood was full of cautiousness, sheltering and overprotection.

Lennon: Her adolescence was bubblegum rock and roll, milk shakes and drive-in movie theaters. When she finally woke up to all of the pleasures and dangers this world has to offer she dove in headlong. Everything changed. She said yes to everything and the people of your world felt it with the acid wave, hippie revolution, Nixon, Vietnam, psychedelic rock and the protest era.

Cobain: She grew jaded when her indulgences failed her. She saw the world as empty and meaningless. After that, she didn't know what she wanted and that was when you were born…a time, a generation of uncertainty. But today is worse than ever, her heart is broken and she has just given up.

Joplin: We don't know why, but we hope it doesn't last too long. She's only just now grown into herself. She's just now a woman.

Jack: I get it now, there's nothing I can do to make people do anything. I can't change the world, because it's not my decision to make. I can only effect change by being free. Not the kind of free that fights to spread itself, but her kind of free. The kind of free to let go and let die. If I want Charlie to be all of the things we know he can be, all I have to do is know that he is free and be there to give him the gentle nudge when he asks for it.

Tom (aside): I can't take this shit, them so nostalgic and emotional. I've been alone, missing half of myself for years and they're talking about life's goddamn fucking lessons. I just can't take it anymore.

Transcriber's Note: A loud thud like the tape recorder hitting the ground, running footsteps. Tom yells simultaneously with the flesh and bone crack of a punch…

Tom: Where the fuck–

19: Burning Alive in Our Pasts

""—have you been?" I shout, falling back in the grass, the rust-taste of blood in my mouth and a sore jaw.

Not sure why I said that, but the kid vanishes without a trace. There's nothing left but a tape recorder that's still rolling and a dirty, tattered notebook. I hit rewind and the screech of wheels reversing feels amplified by the silence all around me. Press play and I just hear this:

TOM: Where the fuck

(fist connects with jaw)

ME: have you been?

I look around. Confused. Everyone is gone. Thompson, Lennon, Hendrix, Morrison, everyone, they've all just disappeared and I'm standing alone on the carrion tire fodder shoulder of Center Hill Road. There's the brick home of Charlie Outlaw and a friendly reminder of where we came from.

Uncle Sam, Cobain, Janis, and the kid – they're all just gone.

The only one left is Bonnie. I climb into the driver's seat in silence, start up her engine on the first try and drive quietly toward Denton with a cigarette on my lips and peace, as light as blue smoke curls, in my chest.

It's night when I hit Fry Street and the ghosts are out in force. Everyone has gathered and the smell of cinder, ash and smoke fills the air. I find a place to let Bonnie rest and hoof it out to see what the commotion is all about. Moving along outside of Kharma I see Brother Red, Dennis Orbell, The Head and Jiggs, but no Charlie Outlaw. I'm not sure why. When they see me they seem more shocked, even scared, than happy. But I take their hugs anyway.

Red shouts, "Dude, where the fuck have you been all my life?"

And I just shrug and tell him it's been me and the road writing our love letter to each other. The air grows thick with smoke. We turn the corner toward The Tomato. The blue night horizon is lit up brown orange and I feel this itching sense of déjà vu.

The Tomato is burning. Everything that it remembered will soon be dead.

Right now I'm standing on Fry Street in Denton, Texas. It's night and the flames are lighting up the walls a dirt orange, casting a brown halo over the beat corners and sidewalk gatherings of the young and the done for. We're watching the blaze in this old party town's central hub, still haunted by the ghosts of students and alumni.

"Oh, yeah, that reminds me," Brother Red says, "I quit smoking today."

"Yeah?" I reply, "That's great, I usually quit smoking about once a week."

"Me too," says Dennis Orbell, "I quit smoking three times yesterday."

"Do you think we're in danger here?" asks Jiggs.

"Probably," I reply, flicking a cigarette toward the fire.

The Head says, "It's just like *Of Mice and Men*. You know, how old Candy wished he'd been the one to shoot his decrepit dog."

Dennis replies, "Yeah, something as beautiful as The Tomato should only be destroyed by people who love it."

Red says, "You know, a few months ago I would have tried to light my cigarette off of those flames."

"Yeah, but now you quit," I smirk.

The arsonist's stage performance shatters the glass out of the restaurant windows and the crowd grows thicker to watch the demise of their favorite hangout. I light up a cigarette. The upper wood deck of The Tomato collapses into the fire and someone shouts, "I know they were going to knock it down, but this is wrong, it shouldn't have happened like this."

"Bullshit," says Jiggs, "she went out on our terms. The people took her back from the Man."

The Tomato is burning. And with it the old days will burn, the old habits, old affairs, forgotten sex, cigarettes, drug binges, flings, sorrow, issues, baggage, laughs, parties, songs, memories, tradition, movements, revolutions and art will all burn to make way for the corporate chains coming to our side of town. The Tomato is burning because someone bought up Fry Street Village and decided to knock down the longstanding fixtures in the neighborhood around the University of North Texas. The bureaucrats decided to put up a Starbucks or a CVS pharmacy in its place.

Everyone, this whole crowd, stands silent and watches The Tomato, and an entire age, melt into the earth with wails of oxidized Formica and termite knot-holed wood whistling in the night. A thousand sets of eyes flashing yellow and orange in the city streets. Every hand with a cigarette or a drink. Some cheer. Some cry. Everyone knows that this is important, this is an historic moment.

Through the smoke-lit haze I can see that conference table and that chair I sat in so many times before. I see the orange glow and the faces of Thompson, Joplin, Hendrix, Hemingway, Van Gogh, Lennon, Cobain and Morrison. They sit calmly as The Tomato and everything it stood for melts down around them. I can see myself, sitting across from them, the ghost of me, watching my life on that projector screen and we're all just disappearing into the inferno. And somehow, I know it is all over. I know this is the final portal closing and the lines have been drawn clear once and for all.

Jiggs says, "Did you guys know Allen Ginsberg used to hang out in there?"

"Yeah," Red replies, "over there next to the melting doorframes you could have found his name etched in the wood. Ginsberg hung out here in the days when Kerouac came through Texas to visit Old Bull Lee, AKA William S. Burroughs. They probably ate here when *On the Road* was still being written. That place had more history than any of us put together."

"And now it's burning," I say, "and the whole philosophy of the Beat Generation is going with it."

"Let's get out of here," Dennis grunts.

Backing away toward the Kharma Café, we set up a mock tailgate party on the back of a Ford Ranger that belongs to some stranger who is too mesmerized by the fire to notice us reclining all over his property. Jiggs finds a cooler full of Pabst Blue Ribbon in the truck bed and we help ourselves and watch the fire like a sporting event.

Red says, "Leave it to us to get back together tonight of all nights. The night the people burned down The Tomato before the suits could take it with their bulldozers."

"So how've you been anyway, Jack?" Dennis asks, "Last time we saw you things were pretty grim. Then you just vanish on us and we don't see you for six months."

"What?" I shout, "Six months...no way. That's impossible. I've only been gone a few days, maybe a week at most, guys."

"A few days, Jack? It's 2007 and The Tomato is burning," Jiggs practically shrieks.

A weird panic grips my veins and swells dark mud in my brain. This doesn't seem right, but I have been on the Ghost Road and time moves different for the dead. I mutter to myself, "I've been on the Ghost Road."

"The Ghost Road?" the Head asks.

"Yeah, it's sort of hard to explain, but it's just this place where I saw the risen corpses of rock legends and Hemingway and Morrison told me to write. I think they wanted me to show people how much they're suffering or something."

"That's pretty weird shit, Jack," Brother Red shrugs, "you're probably crazy, you know that, right? Chances are you've probably been shitting yourself on park benches since December. But you've got me curious. Why are these legends suffering?"

"It's simple. We've been milking their spirits for purpose and inspiration since the sixties, some of them even longer than that. They can't rest until we all figure out how to move forward and inspire ourselves. At best, we need new icons. Which reminds me? Where is Charlie Outlaw, I need to see that old boy."

"Charlie? You mean, you don't know?" Dennis Orbell says, leaning forward with his beer and a smile, "Charlie's taken the band to Austin to chase his rabbits."

"That's good, then there's hope yet. I met Abraham on Highway 61 and he told me that if I just fixed things on the Ghost Road then they'd fall into place here. It sounds like he was right, they've all been right, just not in the way I expected."

"What did you expect?" Jiggs asks.

"I don't know, it's all been pretty bizarre, but I thought I'd have more of a role to play here. Turns out, I guess, all I had to do was get the pieces back where they belong. Their world and ours were spilling over into each other somehow and I had to close that door. We're not supposed to see spirits. It haunts them even more than it haunts us. And you wanna know what the weirdest part is, guys?"

"What's that, Jack?" asks Dennis.

"The weird part is, I knew all of this was going to happen. I'm sure of that much. You're all a part of this weird dream that's been stalking me for a while now. I know, right now, that when I first saw you guys here I hadn't seen some of you in a long time and the others I hadn't even met yet. You were just part of the Ghost Road."

Everyone falls silent. A strange, uncomfortable acceptance washes over us. The same way it washed over us at the sight of that fire. Some things have to burn in order for any kind of a future to grow. I stare into the fire, a cigarette in one hand, a can of beer in the other, and I watch myself burn alive with the gods of rock and roll, the prophets of art.

I watch it all fading to orange-out embers and I remember how that conference room with the martyr banner always smelled like smoke. It hits me, every time I was there, all the time, that place was burning down around us. Our pasts are always burning down around us and we can either sit and watch the feed flash playing on the projector or we can leave the room, hit the road and go find what is really out there.

I'm sure of very little, as usual. I only know that wicks have always burned fast in this world, but ours, at least, can burn hot.

CPSIA information can be obtained at www.ICGtesting.com
264289BV00003B/2/P

9 781592 995400